CHASING DARKNESS

DANIELLE GIRARD

Your Free Rookie Club Short Story is Waiting

San Francisco Crime Scene Analyst and aspiring Rookie Club member Naomi Muir is passionate about her work, especially the cases where she works alongside seasoned inspectors, like Jamie Vail. But this latest case has her unnerved. A serial sex offender is growing more aggressive. He attacks in the dirty underbelly of the San Francisco streets… and eerily close to Naomi's inexpensive apartment. Each crime is more violent than the last and also nearer to where Naomi herself lives.

To solve the case, Naomi will have to rely on her own wit and an unexpected new partner as the attacker gets too close to home...

Go to
www.daniellegirard.com/newsletter to claim your copy now!

For Mom and Dad, who raised four smart,
independent kids and taught us each
to carve the path best for us. You've done good.
And yes, I have included myself with the "smart" ones.

PROLOGUE

June 26, 1993
Walnut Creek, California

SAM CHASE LEFT the house at 6:50 A.M. for her three-mile loop. The run was the single part of her day that remained consistent, five days a week. Twenty-four minutes later she would be home again. Twenty-four long, torturous minutes that she would spend cursing the fact that she could never find a rhythm. She'd met runners, people who loved to run and talked about the high they got from it like it was a drug. Sam had never understood that. For her, it was all pain from start to finish. She did it because she had to and that was it. Five days a week, three miles each time. Then she could settle into bed at night with a bowl of ice cream and a book and not feel guilty.

One mile in, she passed John Muir Elementary School and waved hello to another runner she often saw on her loop. He wore yellow nylon shorts, the kind with the slits up the sides that, in his case, exposed sinewy legs.

As he moved forward, his legs created tall, staccato arches, the motion graceful and smooth, unlike the shuffling, flat shape of her own strides.

Through the row of sycamore trees that lined the schoolyard, Sam could make out a few summer school kids just starting to sprinkle onto the playground. Their brightly colored outfits contrasted with the dull gray pavement of the yard. On the far side, a pack of them stood beside the fence. Their parents dropped them off as early as seven o'clock and could pick them up as late as six whenever school was in session. It was a great service for the parents, but it had to be hard on the kids to be at school for so long. Still, they were shouting and playing kickball and hanging upside down from the jungle gym with the energy that only children could have at such an early hour—and without the help of caffeine.

Sam ran by, noting the slow progression of cars heading toward the freeways. She thought about the upcoming day and her meetings. Anything to avoid thinking about the ache in her side and the numbing pain in her thighs. She reached the halfway mark and picked up the pace on her way back, eager to be home. As she did every morning, she'd set the timer on the coffee machine before she left, and she looked forward to the smell of freshly brewed Mocha Java as she walked in the front door.

The wind picked up, and she could smell eucalyptus and lemon verbena, their scents intensifying as the temperature rose. June in Walnut Creek was hot, this June hotter than usual. September and October, the months of Indian summer in Northern California, would be scorching. Hot was fine by Sam. The heat cleared her head. And the arid heat cleared memories of the damp, miserable South of her youth.

Rounding the corner by the school, Sam caught sight of an adult standing on the edge of the playground where the kids were gathered. The prickle of adrenaline spiked in her neck and shoulders. She took two steps forward and changed her course. Something about the khaki coat and the hunched form of the shoulders was suspicious. Silent alarms rang in her head as she pushed herself further, faster. She heard a child's high-pitched scream and shot forward.

She could see the kids staring at the man with looks of horror. What had he done?

"You!" she screamed when she was within thirty feet.

The man spun around and Sam could see his pale nakedness beneath the coat. He quickly shut his coat and ran. He was six-two, maybe six-three, Caucasian with scraggly black curly hair that hung just over the collar of his coat. The shadow on his face suggested he hadn't shaved in a while, and she cursed herself for not spotting him sooner.

He wore clunky work boots and between the shoes and holding himself through his coat, she was on him before he reached the other side of the street. She grasped his shoulders and swung him around, tripping him and landing him on the ground, face up. Before he could move, she rolled him onto his face, brought his right hand behind his back, and jerked it up toward his head.

He yelped.

He smelled like chocolate and cologne and she

knew he'd had candy to offer the kids. All the good perverts kept treats. "Don't move, you sick bastard. What's your name?"

"I don't—I don't know—"

She jerked his arm harder. "What's your goddamn name?"

"Gerry. Gerry Hecht."

"You been arrested before, Gerry?"

"Uh, no. No, I—"

Trapping his arm under her knee, she grabbed his hair and pulled his head back. "I'm a fucking cop. Don't lie to me. Have you been arrested before?"

"Yeah, yeah," he grunted. "A couple of times."

Sam let his hair go and smiled. "Then this time makes three."

*

After an hour of waiting for the proper authorities to show up and answering questions and completing paperwork, Sam walked in her front door just as the phone started to ring.

The woman said, "Samantha Jean Everett?"

The sound of that name, her old name, rose like thick tar in her throat. She hadn't used the name since she'd left the South. It had been almost twelve years. "Who is this?" she asked, hearing terror behind the harshness in her own voice.

"My name is Francis Mason. I'm with Child Protection Services in Jackson, Mississippi."

Sam stared at the phone, trying to remember a case— any case—that had involved someone in Mississippi.

There hadn't been one. She would have remembered. Just the word "Mississippi" burned like flaming crosses in her mind. "What do you want?"

The woman cleared her throat. "I'm calling on behalf of Polly Ann Austin."

Sam gripped the phone in terror. "What's happened?"

*

The constant buzz and whir of planes overhead, mixed with the booming loudspeaker calling out passengers and flights, made it difficult for Sam to think. Behind her she could hear a voice welcoming passengers to San Francisco International Airport and directing them to baggage claim and ground transportation. Families swarmed around her, reuniting in a dance as foreign to her as the apprehension knotted in her gut. College students returning home for the summer, siblings and cousins, aunts and uncles visiting. Even after all these years, the low drawl of Southern accents in the crowd made her slightly nauseated.

Only yesterday everything had been normal. Curled in the navy flannel sheets that covered her bed year-round to fight off a constant chill, Sam had cut herself off from reality with a book, the way she loved to do when she could find an evening away from work. Last night she had been in the middle of Joyce Carol Oates' *Black Water*, a modern re-creation of the Chappaquiddick incident with a Kelly instead of Mary Jo.

Sam read, feeling her grip on the book tense as the senator pressed Kelly down, killing her to free himself. Sam knew what that felt like. She'd felt Kelly's fear. The only difference was, it hadn't killed her.

Her focus back in the present, Sam found Gate 31 and waited as the people moved off the plane. She stood off to one side, the squeals of families barely audible over the pounding of her heart in her ears.

She imagined the familiar support of her gun under her arm and wished she was on a case, wished she was knee-deep in anything but this.

A woman stepped out of the jetway and raised a rectangular placard with the words "Samantha Chase" written in thick black ink. Sam forced herself into the throng of people. She barely glanced at the woman, instead studying the eight-year-old twin blond boys who stood on either side of her.

They were so much like Polly Ann that Sam reeled back, but not before the woman had caught her eye. The boys were tiny images of Sam's sister and, she knew, of herself. Sam saw Polly's bright blue eyes and oval face, her blondish-brown hair, wavy like the pattern the ocean left on the Southern shore.

The woman pushed the boys in her direction. One was walking with crutches. The woman had told her about that on the phone. The surgeons had put a pin in his hip after the car accident. The conversation swept past her again, flitting only long enough for her to feel her own confusion. She was inheriting her nephews, she reminded herself. Polly was dead and Sam had been appointed guardian. For some reason she couldn't get the idea to stick.

"Are you Samantha Jean?" the woman asked.

Sam continued to stare at the boys, unable to speak.

"Ma'am?" she repeated. "You are Samantha Jean Everett—I mean, Chase?"

Sam cringed. "Yes, that's me—that was me. I'm Sam Chase."

"May I see some I.D., please?" the woman asked, as though Sam were going to write a bad check for the boys. Sam presented her driver's license and the woman presented the boys. A neat exchange.

"Mrs. Chase, then," she said. "As we discussed on the phone, Polly Ann Austin was killed in a car accident. In her will, you are named guardian of the children."

Sam blinked hard. "Polly Ann."

"Austin," the woman repeated, glancing at a piece of paper she held in her fist. "Relationship says sister. This should have all been discussed on the phone."

Sam nodded.

The woman pushed the children forward, and Sam focused in on their wide blue eyes—Polly's eyes. How in the world could she ever protect them from people like Gerry Hecht?

CHAPTER 1

June 25, 2001
Walnut Creek, California

"CHASE," THE VOICE said when Sam mumbled "Hello" into the receiver. "It's Thomas. I'm in the Diablo foothills. You'd better come."

Sam sat up straight and fumbled for the clock on the bedside table, tilting it until the red numbers came into focus: 2:15 a.m. Blinking, she surveyed the room for a sign of something wrong. "What is it? Has something happened to Rob?" Her throat had the gritty texture of sandpaper as she spoke.

"I sure as hell hope not. Rob's supposed to be with you. It's the middle of the night. You want to check his room?"

"I'll look when we're done. Why are you calling?"

"We found Walters."

The tone of Detective Thomas' voice let Sam know this was business, and the business was that a child was dead. Not a fun business to be in. A victim of child abuse,

Molly Walters had been removed from her mother's home more than once in her seven years. Sam wished she had been able to keep her away for good. She sighed, rubbing the back of her hand over her eyes to clear the fog of sleep from her brain. "Damn."

"Uh, it's not the one you're thinking."

"What do you mean?"

"It's not Molly."

"Nick, for God's sake, say it in English. What the hell are you talking about?"

"You need to come up here."

"The boys are still asleep. I'll come to the station house later."

"No," Thomas insisted. "The boys are sixteen years old, Sam. They'll be fine. You need to come to the scene now."

At the tone of his voice, Sam set her feet on the floor and focused on the far walls of her dark room. Her head swam, sleep pulling her eyelids closed like a wet cloth. "Why? What's going on?"

"There's something you should see."

Sam swallowed hard. She'd dealt with abuse and death since she left homicide, but rarely face-to-face. She handled perpetrators. It was mostly bullshit with them—trying to push their buttons and act tough. She could do that. She could be tougher than any gang of criminals, but the victims she left to someone else. It was a routine she wanted to maintain. She hesitated. "I don't know, Thomas."

"Get your ass out of bed," he said, his tone urgent but not angry.

"Watch it." If Molly wasn't dead, though, what was going on? "You picked up the mother?" she asked.

"The mother's not going anywhere—ever. You coming or what?"

Sam pushed the warm covers off her legs and was instantly cold. Unmoving, she tried to sort it out, unclear why she needed to see the dead Walters woman unless the police suspected that seven-year-old Molly was the killer. Doubtful. "I'll be there."

"Good. And come with an empty stomach."

Despite the ache in her gut, Sam tried to joke it off. "Doesn't sound pretty."

"It's not. Take 680 to El Cerro. Head east until El Cerro becomes Diablo Boulevard. A mile later, take a left at the sign for Diablo Country Club. We're about a mile and a half up on the left in the wooded lot across from the pasture. You'll see the cars." As he rattled off his location, Sam committed it to memory. "You write that down?" he asked.

"Never. See you in a few." Switching on her bedside light, Sam blinked yellow flashes until her vision cleared. She crossed the room, and found a pair of jeans and a cotton turtleneck and sweater from the night before and dressed quickly, thankful for the no-nonsense ease of her short hair and her taste for no makeup. It defied everything she'd ever known for the first eighteen years of her life. Even twenty years later, it still felt great.

Pulling the holster from its post at the back of her closet, she strapped on her gun and hurried down the hall, pushing open the door to the first bedroom. Posters of Cal Ripken, hands raised to the crowd, at his record-breaking 2,131st game and Barry Bonds hitting his 73rd homer covered the two walls above the single bed. Several days' worth of clothes were scattered across the floor, creating patterns of gray that played in the shadows of the room. Despite the mess, she exhaled at the, sight of sheets pulled loose and strewn across Rob's body. He'd missed curfew again last night. At least he'd made it home. She watched the steady rise and fall of his chest as he slept. She would deal with him later.

Closing his door, she moved to the next one and opened it. "Derek," she whispered.

The sleepy boy shifted slightly, his blond hair covering his eyes. "Huh," he grumbled, his arm falling out of the covers and dangling toward the floor. Above his head hung a poster of the constellations, beside it a Bruce Springsteen poster from *Darkness on the Edge of Town*, an album that had come out while Sam was in college. His books were carefully stacked on the desk, clothes put in their place, only the most recent Grisham novel spread-eagled on the floor.

"I've got to go to a scene. I'll be back before you're up. If you need me, page me."

"Uh-huh," the sixteen-year-old mumbled back.

She moved into the room. "Derek," she whispered a little louder.

He opened his eyes and blinked hard, squinting as he pushed the hair from his face. "I heard you—you're out, page you if Rob sets the house on fire."

She smiled and winked. "If you're up before I'm back, remind him he needs to clean that sty. And tell him not to go anywhere until we've talked. He missed curfew again. You know what time he got home?"

Derek shook his head, turning away from her and tucking the covers under his chin.

Sam had a feeling Derek knew exactly when his brother had come home, but she respected him for not ratting. She would talk to Rob herself. Something had to be done before it got out of hand. "Remind him about the room."

"I'll tell him, but he won't do it."

She waved him off. "I'll bug him later."

"Won't help," Derek said, his face deep in his pillow again.

Sam looked around the neat room and shook her head. She definitely needed to have a talk with Rob.

"Shut the door," Derek groaned as she left.

✳

Sam fought off chills as she stepped from her car and walked toward the group up ahead. Thick fog drifted over the tops of the half-dozen parked cars. The cool night air in Diablo seeped under the collar of her parka and through the cotton of her turtleneck and sweater like long, icy fingers. The headlights of police cars reflected off the fog, casting muted shadows across the trees. The smell of damp eucalyptus hung in her nose, a single comforting sensation among the foreign ones.

It had been eight years since she'd been at the scene of a murder. When the boys came, she had left the sheriffs department to go to the Department of Justice to get away from the death. The immunity she'd built up in her days as a homicide detective had eroded since she'd been with the Department of Justice, leaving more than one chink in her armor.

She still had no idea what she was doing at the scene, but she was determined to stay calm and handle whatever was thrown her way. She'd spent enough time in male-dominated situations to know what it required to keep her reputation as one of the boys. Throwing up at the sight of blood was grounds for permanent weenie status.

"I'm glad you could make it," Nick Thomas said as he approached. He was tall, six-three to Sam's five-six, and lean. "It's been a long time, eh?" His voice was low and raspy, and she realized he'd been awakened from sleep too. The tone of his voice was like an old record, scratchy and deep, and she caught the gold flecks in his brown eyes and forced her gaze away.

She looked around the darkness and nodded. "Not long enough. Why am I here?"

He turned her toward the scene with an arm over her shoulder.

She stared at the arm and gave Nick a sideways glance.

He looked at his arm as though it didn't belong to him and dropped it back to his side. "We still on for my birthday dinner?"

"You didn't call me up here to discuss your birthday, I hope."

Nick shook his head without comment.

She motioned to the police, still hovering in a small circle around the body. Their voices mixed with the low rustle of the wind in the trees, and she wished they were louder, closer. She wanted to talk about the job. Shoptalk would be a huge relief. That she could handle. Everything else was the problem. "Walters?"

Nick studied her a moment longer than he needed to, then turned away to face the scene. "Yep—Sandi."

Sam let the breath she'd been holding out through her teeth as she started to relax. At least it wasn't the girl. "She O.D.?"

Nick didn't answer, his eyes evasive.

Sam looked over his shoulder. A flashbulb shot off in the distance, and Sam caught a glimpse of skin against the dark ground. Not healthy, glowing skin but skin infused with the whitish-blue tint that came with death. She looked back at Nick. "Why call me up here?"

"Remember the serial killer you had as your last case in homicide—the one they got a conviction on right about the time when I finally got the balls to ask you out?"

"Nick," she started to protest. "If this is some sort of sick fantasy, calling me out here with cases that remind you of how we—"

"Slow down and listen," he retorted. "What do you remember about the victimology?"

She shook her head and reviewed her mental notes. "Six victims—all Caucasian females from the Berkeley Hills, all between the ages of thirty-five and forty-seven with blond or light brown hair and light eyes. Two were prostitutes, three were all-night-diner employees, and one was a convenience store clerk.

"Killed by manual ligature, a eucalyptus branch with six leaves tucked over each ear. Charlie Sloan, a San Francisco stockbroker and local swim coach, was arrested and charged; convicted almost three years ago and went to the chair for the murder of the six women."

"And all that without your notes," Nick added.

"So what's the point?"

"He's dead, right?"

She ground her teeth. "Killed on death row, Nick— February 5 of last year."

"You're sure?"

Sam turned to get back in the car. She was too tired for this shit.

"I'm not joking around," Nick said.

She glanced back and the look in his eyes confirmed that there was nothing humorous about what was going on.

He nodded toward the scene and started walking back.

Sam zipped up her coat beneath her chin and shoved her hands in her pockets, heading after him. Nick carved a path through the police officers. As she stepped closer, the flash of cameras glared in her eyes and she blinked hard to clear the black spots from her vision.

When her eyesight sharpened again, she took two steps forward and gazed into the vacant stare of a stick-thin woman in her forties. In life Sandi Walters had never looked so calm. Simple white briefs were all she wore. Her straight bottle-blond hair hung limply over her shoulders, the twig of a eucalyptus tree tucked behind each ear. She was propped against a tree, one knee up and her salon-tanned arms flung to her sides. Her legs were parted slightly, like she'd passed out. Sam could see why Nick had called her. It was familiar.

Cheap bracelets lined her right wrist. A thin silver ring with a knot, the kind sold at street fairs, circled her thumb. Track marks still showed blue in the creases of her elbow.

Sam blinked hard and forced back the pictures that entered her head. Death always brought a litany of snapshots of her own youth. She saw her father with a cigarette hanging off his lip, her mother nursing a third G&T that was mostly G, her sister cowering in a corner, trying to stay out of the way.

Sam stepped forward and inspected the twig tucked behind Walters' left ear.

"Maybe Molly's father killed her in a moment of rage and made it look like a copycat."

"How could it be copycat? No one ever had the information on the eucalyptus. It was never released to the media."

"It was during the trial."

"Not the detail about how many leaves."

She shook her head. "That we know of. It's probably in some new serial killer book by now. That stuff just leaks. I say you look at the dad."

"Dad's got an airtight alibi."

Sam shook her head. "They always have an airtight alibi."

"He's been in county on a DUI for the past twenty-four hours. According to our guy's estimate, Sandi here's been dead around five."

"Who else is in the household? Just Molly, Sandi, and Sandi's mother, right?"

"Molly's grandma uses a walker. No way she got the body up here by herself."

Sam nodded, remembering.

"Plus, look at those twigs. Recognize them?" Nick asked.

Without looking away from the body, Sam nodded noncommittally. "I agree it's familiar."

"It's more than that."

She raised an eyebrow at Nick. "It's a couple of twigs, Nick, not a tattoo. It could be a coincidence."

He raised an eyebrow back at her. He had an angular jaw and large brown eyes with flecks of green and gold. His mother was black and his father was white, and Nick had the warmest color skin Sam had ever seen. It contrasted with his broad shoulders and lean frame to keep him from looking too hard.

She knew cops weren't supposed to believe in coincidences, but Sloan was dead. She looked at the twig again. Six leaves, just like the others.

Sam shook her head. "It's got to be a coincidence. Sloan's dead. This is something else. Maybe the eucalyptus symbolizes something else."

Nick nodded. "There's the c-word again. It worries me."

Fighting off the chill, Sam turned and peered over at the other twig. "Damn. You're saying Sloan wasn't our killer? The wrong guy was executed?"

Nick shrugged. "Maybe he had a partner."

Sam surveyed the area. It wasn't possible. Sloan had been alone. They'd worked eighteen months to nail him and almost six years to get him convicted and sentenced to death row. He'd never confessed, but he'd done it. The evidence had proved it. She could not accept that the system had killed the wrong man. "What else have you got?"

"Signs of sexual intercourse," Nick added.

Sam frowned. "Semen?"

"Oh, yeah. First guess is postmortem."

"Charlie Sloan never had sex with his victims."

Nick met her gaze. "Okay, not identical."

Sam found herself coming back to someone Sandi knew. "What about other relatives in the area? A new boyfriend?"

"The girl was staying with her grandmother. Dad and Grandma are it."

Sam noticed an odd pattern in the dirt by Sandi's foot. It was the faintest rectangular shape, and Sam wondered what had caused it. On her knees, she searched for evidence. She found it on the instep of Sandi's left foot. "You see this?"

Nick knelt beside her. Using his pen, he pushed on the woman's toes, shining his light on the bottom of her foot.

A gum wrapper was stuck to the arch of Sandi's foot. It was silver and Sam recognized it as Extra. She put her nose to it. Spearmint. Her favorite.

Sam studied the wrapper. "Someone left you a clue." She stood up and brushed off her jeans. "Looks like you've got a new killer on your hands—one with some inside info on our old cases."

Nick shook his head. "Not me, Sam. *We.* You're working this one, too."

CHAPTER 2

PULLING DOWN THE street where Sandi's mother lived, Nick Thomas cringed. He wanted to be at home already. Turn up the Miles Davis, pull out his bass, and maybe tinker for a while. Probably be too late when he got home after the baseball game. The upstairs neighbor threw a fit when he played after ten, threatened to call the cops on him. Even though she knew he *was* the cops. Hell, his bass skills weren't great but they weren't bad either. Or maybe they were.

His sister, Gina, had invited him to dinner at her house. But he'd probably have to miss that, too. What with two sisters and a married brother all within a ten-mile radius, Nick ate at home only one night a week as it was. And that one night was takeout. He had even less talent for cooking than for playing bass.

He looked up at the Walters house. The houses on the block were cookie-cutter styles built in the fifties: aluminum siding with chipping paint in white, yellow, and gray. Each had two windows in its ranch front. A set of shutters on the outside would have broken the monotony had someone taken the time. Even he, with no decorating sense, could have suggested that. The dandelion-pocked grass formed perfect rectangles in front, only the shades of brown differed. Each house seemed to come with three cars. Garage doors open, cars set up on blocks in each driveway. The town of Danville had very affluent pockets, but this wasn't one of them. His beat-up Honda would certainly go unnoticed.

He would've preferred company for his visit to the family, but Sam was spending her day pulling records from the Charlie Sloan murders and following up on every person who had been involved, even peripherally, in the case. It was a task he didn't envy. Paperwork had never been his forte. In comparison, interviewing Sandi's mother ought to be quick, at least.

Other than the endless paperwork, interviewing a victim's family was the worst part of any investigation. A grieving family—and he had to give them the third degree. But he knew it was a necessary step. Eighty percent of the time, families knew the killer, even if they didn't realize it. The family was a solid place to start an investigation. Still, he hated the response he always got. Guilty or not, the family inevitably stared at him like he was a cockroach.

Shaking off the thought, Nick tucked his car keys under the mat, as he always did. Otherwise he had a tendency to lose them. With a deep breath, he pulled himself out of the car and straightened his tie. He felt the comforting weight of the gun resting beneath his left arm as he approached the house. At least he wasn't there to break the news of Sandi's death. Her family had already been informed. Pulling back the screen door, he knocked firmly on the door's surface.

"Who is it?" called a haggard voice from inside.

"Detective Thomas from the Contra Costa County Sheriff's Department," he called back.

Murmured words were exchanged, and Nick heard the sliding of locks before the door creaked open. The little girl who opened the door had to be Molly. Nick knew Sandi and her husband had only one child. But beyond deduction, Nick could see the resemblance. Molly had her mother's tiny, straight nose and thin lips. Molly's hair was brown, probably her mother's natural color.

"I'm Detective Thomas. Is your grandma or dad home?"

Big, sad eyes stared at him without a response. Then someone called from the background, "Let them in, Molly."

Molly stepped back quickly and let the door swing open.

"In here," the voice called, and Nick walked inside to see the woman he assumed was Molly's grandmother sitting in a worn olive-green La-Z-Boy. The room was a blue-gray haze of cigarette smoke. He took a last deep breath of clean air and approached her. She had the look of a basset hound, a droopy face with heavy jowls. Large, wary brown eyes studied him.

"I'm afraid I can't get up," the woman apologized.

"No need." Nick stepped forward and shook her hand. "I'm Detective Nick Thomas of the Contra Costa County Sheriffs Department. I'm very sorry for your loss, but I need to ask you a few questions."

The woman pointed to Molly. "Get to your room, child. And shut the door."

Molly stared at him and then back at her grandmother.

"Now," the woman bellowed.

Molly jumped slightly and ran, her bare feet slapping against the stairs.

The grandmother shifted her considerable weight in the chair and pointed to the couch. "Feel free to sit."

"Thank you." The couch looked deep and worn, and Nick picked a stiff chair instead. The ability to move from a spot quickly had saved him on more than one occasion. A deep couch made that nearly impossible. He pulled out his pad, watching with his peripheral vision for someone else to appear. With his pen poised, he said, "I'd like to ask some questions about your daughter if I may, Ms.—"

"Wendy. Wendy Mayes. Ask away," she said, as though he were taking a poll on her choice of gasoline.

"Can you tell me about when you last saw your daughter?"

The woman cast a look over her shoulder. Nick followed her gaze but saw nothing. Only a nail in the center of a wall papered in dingy blue stripes. The paper was yellowed around an area of about a square foot where a picture must have been hung. He wondered briefly when the picture had been removed and what it was.

"I was looking after Molly," Wendy Mayes told him. "Sandi was off, and I told her I'd stay with the child."

He studied her face, the thick wrinkles in her skin coming as much from extra weight as from age. "Did your daughter tell you where she was going?"

"Never. And I didn't ask," she said without raising an eyebrow. "Sometimes it's work, sometimes it ain't."

He glanced at her hands crossed on her lap, remembering Sandi's resting pose. The two women had the same hands—long fingers with thick blue veins and large, square nails. "Where did Mrs. Walters work?"

"Weren't never married, those two."

"Excuse me?"

"Sandi and Mick weren't never married."

Nick glanced at his notes. "Sandi's last name on her driver's license was Walters."

The woman harrumphed. "They weren't married. Changed her name at the drop of a hat, she did—like there was something wrong with Mayes." She shook her head.

Nick made a note to check for priors under other names. "Where did your daughter work, Ms. Mayes?"

"Denny's in Antioch." She shot the response out like a bullet.

He nodded. "How long had she been working there?"

The woman shrugged. "Five, six months, maybe."

"And before that?"

The woman sighed. "Detective, my daughter held a lot of jobs. You really expect me to keep track of 'em all?"

Nick looked at the woman, wondering how hard it could have been. "What about friends that your daughter spent time with?"

"Didn't have no female friends. None that I know of, anyway."

"Male friends?" Nick asked.

The woman laughed. "Detective, I couldn't even

keep up with her jobs. I don't have a clue who she went around with."

"What about men living in the house?"

"Been a few," she said.

"Do you know their names?"

"Mick's one. They've been off and on since Molly. He moved out about four months ago, I think. There might have been someone else. I don't know."

"Mick's last name is Walters?"

"Same as Molly's," she said without answering his question.

Nick kept his temper under his vest. "Mick is Molly's father?"

The woman nodded like he was a moron.

"Is Mick here now?"

She shook her head.

"When was the last time you saw him?"

"Been a couple days," she said.

"He hasn't been here in a couple of days?" Nick repeated.

The woman raised an eyebrow. "That's what I just said."

"You know anyone who would want to hurt your daughter?" he asked.

"No."

"Did she ever talk about any fights or threats?"

"We didn't talk, Detective."

Nick pushed himself to his feet. Opening his jacket, he pulled out a business card and laid it on the table. "You think of anything, you give me a call, would you?"

The woman didn't answer.

Nick started toward the door and turned back, glancing again at her unstained fingertips. Patting his jacket, he asked, "You wouldn't happen to have a cigarette, would you, Ms. Mayes? I'm fresh out."

"Not a one, Detective."

Taking a last look at the blue haze of the room, Nick nodded. "Are you a smoker, Ms. Mayes?"

"I wouldn't say either way."

Nick let it go for the time being. "Thank you for your time." As he opened the door, Nick noticed Molly sitting at the top of the stairs staring down at him.

*

Nick tossed the ball to the umpire and returned to his post beside first. It was the bottom of the ninth, two outs, and the score was tied one to one. Rob Austin, Sam's nephew, was at bat.

Rob selected a bat from the pile and swung it lightly in a small semicircle as he approached the plate. Austin was a natural ballplayer. Nick had known him and his brother, Derek, since they joined one of the Little League teams coached by local police officers almost seven years ago.

Unfortunately, with a pin in his left hip and a growing disparity in the lengths of his legs, Derek hadn't lasted long. Despite their identical genes, Nick thought, the two boys were as different as night and day. Where Rob was open and loud, Derek was shy and quiet. Rob loved sports, Derek music. Rob was active and had a solid swing and a strong arm. Derek could name every rock song recorded between 1960 and 2000, and he knew the artist and album on more of them than Nick could believe.

Even their appearances were far from identical. Though both were almost six feet tall, Rob was stocky, with broad shoulders and skin bronzed to match the scatter of freckles across his cheeks, while Derek was thin and slightly hunched over, his freckles a sharp contrast with his light skin tone.

Sam was on the sidelines with Derek, and Nick forced himself to greet her casually and then walk away. Every time he saw her, he pictured her that night. It was the first time he'd seen her as more than just a colleague, and maybe a friend. It had been one flash of what was underneath the hard exterior—one fleeting glimpse. Keeping it all business while working the case side by side with her would be hard enough. Even now, after he should be used to it, he was surprised how much of Sam he saw in the boys. The short blond curls. The bright blue eyes, slightly rounder than their aunt's green ones.

The coach was talking to the other team's pitcher, and Nick paced along the edge of the field, wishing the man would hurry up and get off the mound. The smoke in Wendy Mayes' home kept sweeping across his mind, making him wonder why she would have lied to him—if she had lied. Maybe she simply hadn't wanted to offer him a cigarette. But her creamy white fingertips and unstained teeth suggested otherwise. If she wasn't a smoker, then who had been puffing away in that room? Not little Molly, he hoped.

Nick thought about Molly Walters. She had been one of Sam's cases. Sam had prosecuted Sandi on charges of child abuse but had failed to get them to stick. He'd heard her voice her frustration about the judge more than once during the case. Despite X-rays showing multiple fractures in Molly's right arm, despite the girl's own tearful testimony, the judge had sent Molly back to live with her mother. Sam's insistent appeals to the judge had gotten her kicked out of court.

It wasn't strange that Sam had been involved with the case against Sandi Walters. As a special agent with the Department of Justice, Sam's workload was mostly abuse cases. So what was it about this case that was bothering him so much?

Nick stopped pacing as the other coach left the field. Rob approached the plate and raised his arm to the ump to signal time out while he scraped the dirt in the batter's box with his cleats and planted his back foot comfortably. After settling into his stance, he swung his bat in slow motions, finishing each swing with the bat pointed at the pitcher in an attempt at intimidation.

The other team's pitcher had the best arm in the league. With a full windup, the first pitch came fast and straight. Rob swung and connected for a hard line drive down the left field line, but the ball hooked left and landed in foul territory.

"Strike one."

"Come on. They're coming straight and hard," Nick said under his breath. "Consistent pitch. Just straighten it out, Austin."

The next throw was a high fastball, and Rob swung a moment too late. Nick heard the ball smack the catcher's mitt.

"Strike two."

"Come on," Nick whispered again.

Rob steadied his arm and furrowed his brow as he set his eyes on the pitcher's hand. He had to make contact and keep the ball in play.

The ball came, again straight and hard. Rob swung, making clean contact. The hit was a long fly ball that sent the left fielder backpedaling. Then, realizing the ball was going too far, the player spun around and ran. Both benches jumped up screaming. Rob was running the bases, legs pumping as he watched over his shoulder for the ball to come back.

Nick screamed at Rob to make the turn and run for home. The shortstop threw hard and fast to the catcher, who was poised at home for the play, his mask thrown off to the side.

Nick cringed as the ball neared home plate. "Come on!"

Rob instinctively dropped into a hook slide, his left leg extended, and scraped the surface of home plate just as the catcher fielded the ball and swept his mitt home, missing him by inches. With a horizontal wave of his arms, the umpire called Rob safe.

"Yes!" Nick screamed, jumping up.

The kids piled off the bench and ran for the players crossing home plate. Nick leaned back and watched them hoist Rob victoriously onto their shoulders. He laughed.

"Nice game, coach."

Nick turned to see Sam smiling at him. He touched her shoulder, relieved when she didn't flinch. "Glad you're here."

"Any progress on the case?"

He shook his head. "Sandi's mother wasn't much help."

Sam nodded. "I remember her from the pretrial hearing in Molly's case. Not a real easy woman."

"Are any women easy?"

With a warning look, half play, half serious, Sam gave him a little shove. "Watch it."

"How about you? Find anything from the old case?" he asked.

Sam shook her head. "I got a complete list of involved parties to the sheriff's department by about noon today. The clerk I talked to recognized a few of the names from the list who are still in the area, a couple in the department and one working local security. He's running the other names through the computer. Once we locate everyone, we can pick out the people we need to talk to. I've also got someone following up on anyone Charlie Sloan knew in prison who was recently released."

Nick watched the boys celebrate as a thought circled his brain like a stallion gaining speed. "Sloan could probably have paid someone pretty generously to get him off by making it look like he wasn't the killer. Be hard to prove he committed another murder from death row. Maybe he was hoping to get a stay of execution."

"It'd be a little late for that now."

Nick shrugged. "Maybe he had it planned earlier."

"But why go through with it now? Why bother if Sloan's been dead more than a year?" She shook her head. It didn't make sense. "Maybe the family would want to try to clear his name, but I checked around to locate members of Sloan's family still in the area and didn't find any. His wife declared bankruptcy, leaving upwards of a hundred and fifty thou in unpaid legal fees, and then left the country. She's originally from France."

Nick pictured Charlie Sloan's smiling face, his starched white shirts with his initials on the left cuff, a Hermes tie and a dark suit. He looked more like Michael Milken than Charles Manson. "I can't make sense of it."

Derek reached the group and they cut the shoptalk.

"I found the *Exile on Main Street* album at Adobe Records," Nick told him.

Derek's eyes widened. "That's the only Stones one I'm missing."

Nick shook his head. "Not anymore."

"Really?"

Nick nodded.

"Wow. That's so cool!"

Rob came running up and threw an arm around Nick. Nick returned the embrace. "Nice playing, kid."

"Yeah. Good game," Sam added.

Rob was panting. "Man, I thought I was going to strike out and lose the game."

"So did the kid in left field. You sure showed him. Nice going."

Rob gave him a grin.

"Good game," Derek agreed.

"Thanks, Der," Rob said.

Trying not to stare, Nick watched the boy move as they all headed to the car. Despite the weekly physical therapy and the shoes to correct the two-inch disparity in his legs, Derek seemed to be limping worse than ever.

They crossed the street and headed up the small hill to the parking lot. Nick waved to several of the parents.

Rob turned to Sam. "What'd you think?"

Sam nodded. "Thought it was great."

Nick watched Rob search her face. He could tell Rob was disappointed with her reaction. He sensed the tension between them and knew immediately that they hadn't addressed the previous night's missed curfew. Sam was angry. And rightly so. He just would have handled it a little more openly.

He made a fist to gain control. It wasn't his to deal with. This was between them. Sam's family, not his.

"She's right, Rob. It was great," he added, hoping to distract Rob from Sam's less than boisterous reaction.

"Thanks." He turned back to Sam. "Can we go to Chevy's to celebrate? I'm starved."

"I don't think—" she started to say.

"My treat," Nick suggested.

Sam shot him a look, but Nick winked in response. "Give me a chance to bug your aunt here about some business," he added.

Sam looked at Nick and then at Rob. "I don't know. Maybe we should just head home. It's pretty late and after last night, Rob, I'm not sure you deserve—"

Rob stopped and spun around, his eyes narrow. "I was half an hour late."

Sam watched him with a sour face. "Curfew is curfew. It means home by midnight. That's plenty late, Rob. You're only sixteen."

"It's summer."

"It doesn't matter. Midnight is the rule."

Rob looked to Nick for backup.

Nick shook his head and turned away. He couldn't intervene. It wasn't his place. Still, every bit of teenage friction around him made him wish he'd had a chance at parenthood.

"That's ridiculous," Rob snapped.

Sam grabbed Rob's shoulder as he started to turn away from her. Her voice low, her face inches from his, she was nothing if not intimidating. "It's not ridiculous. It's a rule. You've got to be home by curfew. You hear me?"

Rob pulled away.

"She's right, Rob," Nick added. "It's important to obey your aunt."

Sam didn't even look at him. Her eyes were set on Rob, waiting for his agreement. He didn't give it. She straightened her spine and turned toward the car. "I think we should go home."

"I was half an hour late," Rob repeated. "Jesus Christ, I'm not one of your damn prisoners."

Several people passed them and Sam remained silent.

Nick felt his cheeks burn as he awaited her reaction.

Sam lowered her voice and aimed her glare at Rob. "I don't care if it's a minute or an hour. I set a curfew and you're home. Don't you dare make a scene about it, Rob. This isn't my fault. It's yours."

"Bullshit. It's always about you! You and your god-damn rules."

Sam's jaw set at the tone of his voice. "That's it, Rob. For the next week, you go to work and practice and that's all. You're grounded. Any more of that language and it'll be longer. Another slipup and I'll sell that damn bike. Are we clear?"

Rob waved her off. "That's not fair. I don't have to live by your rules."

Derek slumped back. If Nick didn't know better, he would have thought Derek was afraid.

"Rob," Nick warned.

"No, it's true," Rob insisted. "She runs the place like it's the military."

Sam stared at Rob as though he had turned into an alien. "Why are you so angry?"

He shrugged in a hard motion. "You don't know crap."

"Watch it," Sam warned.

"Crap is not a swear word."

"It's getting close."

"Jesus, it's like I'm in jail. You don't know anything about me, you don't care."

"I do care and I'd like to understand, Rob," Sam said, clearly frustrated.

"You don't give a damn."

She snapped back. "That's not true, Rob. I do care—I care a lot. I'm here busting my butt trying to help you, so don't try to twist this around. You're at fault here, not me."

"Of course your aunt cares," Nick interjected.

Sam threw him a look that told him to stay out of it. Then turning to the boys, she said, "That's it. We're going home. We've got leftovers."

"I'm not going with you," Rob screamed. "You're a bitch!"

Nick grabbed the boy's arm. "Rob!"

Rob pulled away. "She doesn't give a shit about me."

"That's not true."

Rob pointed to his aunt, who had turned her back and was walking to the car. "Look at her."

"Sam," Nick called after her. "Let's talk about this."

"You're out of line, Rob," she called back. "We're going home now. And you're grounded for a month. One more tirade and the bike is gone. I'm done with this acting out."

Rob didn't move.

"You shouldn't have said that to your aunt," Nick chastised. "It wasn't fair and you didn't mean it."

"Yes, I did. I hate her."

Nick shook his head, wishing he could do more. "You don't hate her. You'd better go on, Rob."

Rob started to stomp toward the car.

"And apologize," Nick called after him.

Derek followed them in silence, and Nick could tell all three were miserable.

He watched as they moved toward Sam's Caprice, trying to think of a way to make amends. He knew it would do no good, though. Sam didn't want his advice on parenting, and Rob didn't have control over his own emotions. They needed to work things out on their own. And as much as he had started to care more than he should, it wasn't his business. He watched the few stragglers head to their cars, then sat on the curb under the darkening sky and rubbed his hands over his face.

He should concentrate on things he *could* fix, things he had control over. Concentrate on work, he told himself. It's a lot less exhausting. He thought back to Sandi

Walters' death and how little he had learned from her mother. He knew his captain would want better answers than he could provide. Captain Cintrello was reporting directly to the undersheriff. A screw up on this case could put a hitch in both of their careers.

The undersheriff hadn't hesitated to call in the Department of Justice. With departments usually battling to keep others out of cases, the undersheriff's quick decision to open the case to another department let Nick know exactly how concerned he was about Sandi Walters' murder. The fact that someone had strangled this victim and left her with eucalyptus leaves behind each ear had made them all uneasy.

If Charlie Sloan didn't have a partner, it meant someone with inside information was the killer—D.A., the M.E.'s office, or a cop. If that wasn't the case, then someone sure as hell wanted it to look like it was an inside job.

CHAPTER 3

SAM HOVERED OVER the chocolate cake, smoothing the last bits of chocolate and peanut butter frosting over the spots of dark cake still visible. She could hear the thump of feet coming toward the kitchen. "Not quite yet," she yelled back, shaking her head.

"Ah, Sam. Come on. It smells so good."

She shook her head. "Two minutes. And get Derek, too." When she heard the steps retreating, she pulled the candles out of the drawer and carefully made a circle of eight candles. Eight years since the boys had come to live with her, she thought, remembering how stressful that first day had been. Her sister's instructions in her will giving Sam custody had been clear—keep them away from the South and their families. Their father's as well as hers.

Sam had never questioned that request. Nor had the boys. It was as though leaving it all behind was as much a relief to them as it was to her. Polly had told Sam that she'd been given custody because she was the one who had gotten away. Or that's what Polly had thought. But the idea of having no one to turn to, not even her estranged family, was more than a little overwhelming to Sam on that first day.

What do you boys like to eat? she'd asked them.

"Chocolate," Derek had answered.

"And peanut butter," Rob had added.

Then they'd exchanged a glance and simultaneously said, "Together."

Sam had baked her first cake that night after she'd put the boys down. Chocolate cake with chocolate frosting mixed with peanut butter. As a special treat, she'd let the boys each have a piece for breakfast that first Sunday morning. Those had been the first smiles she'd seen from them. Now, eight years later, she still repeated the ritual every June 26.

With the candles lit, she turned back to the hall. "Okay."

The boys who had been half her size that first time now towered over her as they huddled around the cake and blew out the candles. Sam cut them each a piece of cake and then watched them eat and laugh.

"I think maybe you two are getting too big for this tradition," Sam said, sitting down with a sliver of cake for herself.

"No!" Rob said.

"Really, Sam. It's fun," Derek agreed.

She winked and took a bite herself. "Just kidding." Sam smiled at the memory of bringing the boys home that first day. Her tiny house had almost no furniture. It was the way she'd lived since her divorce. They had been stiff-lipped and sullen as she put their stuff down on her worn beige carpet.

The boys seemed to finish their cake in three bites. Sam tried to eat hers slowly, knowing her body wouldn't burn it off like a sixteen-year-old's would.

"One more piece?" Rob begged.

Sam shook her head. "No way."

"Come on," Derek added. "It's summer."

She looked at them and shook her head in defeat. "One more—but small."

She cut two more slices, and the boys managed to wolf those down as well, Derek only slightly slower than his larger counterpart.

Three minutes later, the cake was half gone and the boys had fled the kitchen to go back to bed. Sam cleared the dishes and thought about the morning, savoring the few minutes of fun more than the cake.

*

Sam cupped her steaming coffee and hurried to the entrance of the Department of Justice building in the heart of Fisherman's Wharf. People on the streets were dressed in white shorts and floral shirts, looking ready for Disneyland rather than downtown San Francisco, with its brisk Pacific breeze and professional dress. Cameras around their necks, maps held open in two hands, they searched for the right street for the next activity. Cable car one block to your left, water two blocks to your right, Sam thought, Fisherman's Wharf half a block straight ahead. But no matter how easy it seemed to her, there were always tourists with maps open pointing in all different directions.

The front door of the D.O.J, building was well camouflaged by a liquor store on one side and a camera store on the other.

She was due to meet one of the assistant D.A.'s to talk prosecution on a third-time offender. She was already late. She tucked the coupon section from the paper under her arm to clip later and stuffed the rest of the paper in the closest trash can before entering her building.

In the elevator, she pushed the button for three and stood impatiently while the machine moved upward at a snail's pace. When the doors opened, she rushed out, using her key card to enter the bulletproof doors at the reception area.

"They're waiting in the conference room," the receptionist called after her.

"They?" Sam had expected the assistant D.A. to come alone.

"Two of them."

"I'm on my way."

As she passed his desk, her assistant, Aaron, wheeled toward her.

She looked down at the wheelchair. The wide, bright yellow tubing made it look like it was constructed to take on mountain terrain. "Cool new chair."

Aaron grinned and spun around in a full circle. "You like?"

She nodded and touched the yellow bars. "Looks like you're going off-roading."

"This baby's the Hammer—made with aerospace

tubing." He patted the heavy metal underside. "It's for the race."

She remembered his wheelchair marathon was coming up. "July eleventh."

"You're coming, right?"

"Wouldn't miss it."

"Awesome." Aaron spun back to his desk and snatched a spiral notebook off the surface before turning back.

Sam had to smile at the antics. She wished Rob had a little of Aaron's disposition. She shook her head.

"Williams called four times this morning," Aaron said, rolling his eyes. "And he's been by twice. He says he needs your notes on the case you worked together before you present to Corona. I could pull the file for you."

She shook her head. "Williams wants my notes because he can't read his own damn handwriting. When are we set to meet with Corona?"

Gary Williams was one of the sixteen special agents Sam worked with. But for some reason Williams was the one she'd been paired with the most, and they did not see eye to eye. Williams had been a special agent for more than twenty years and therefore considered himself more senior than his other colleagues. But he wasn't the strongest agent, and lately Corona had been giving Sam the higher-profile cases. Then, last week, Williams had made a blunder with the D.A.'s office that she couldn't fix and she'd had to get Corona's help. She knew she deserved the bigger cases, but Williams became more difficult to deal with each time something was passed to her over him. And after last week's fiasco, he'd been all but belligerent toward her in the staff meeting.

Sam suspected Corona knew she could handle it without his help. And she could. Complaining wasn't her style. But Gary Williams sure as hell wasn't getting anything extra from her.

"The meeting's Wednesday morning."

Sam nodded as she dropped her bag and searched for the file on Curt Hofstadt, who had been paroled after his conviction on charges of child molestation back in January and had since been living with a woman who had three small daughters. The mother reported him when the youngest girl, age four, was found to have developed vaginal warts, a condition the mother too suffered from after relations with Hofstadt.

Not only had Hofstadt violated probation, but this was his third offense and was likely to be his third conviction. And according to the new three-strikes law, his last.

"What do you want to do about Williams?" Aaron repeated.

"Set up a meeting to discuss it tomorrow morning. Let him know to come prepared with his findings. I'm not doing any more handholding." She glanced up at Aaron as he wrote.

"Don't worry. I won't quote you."

She nodded. "You're a good man. Where the hell is the Hofstadt file?" She dug through the stacks on her desk.

"First one on top."

She shook her head, flipping through the files. "It's not here."

Aaron double-checked, then glanced around the room. "Did you take it home?"

"I didn't need to. I was prepared for this meeting." Sam looked around in confusion.

Aaron sifted through the files. "I'll be damned. It's not here." He looked up at her as she glanced at her watch.

She was late already, and this meeting was not a good one to be late for. Josh Steiner was one of the assistant D.A.'s assigned to the case, and he always acted like his minutes were measured in gold and Sam's in plastic.

"I can easily print another copy of the argument," Aaron offered. "You won't have your notes, but I think we put almost all of it into the computer."

Sam nodded, more than slightly disturbed at the file's disappearance. She had an excellent memory and never misplaced things, especially something this important. "Do that, would you, Aaron?"

Aaron wrote something down and Sam stood perplexed for another second.

"It'll be ready in a minute," Aaron said.

"Thanks. Also, will you call Quentin and talk to the prison warden? Find out who Charlie Sloan had been hanging around with in prison before his death—any recent releases, any outside contact."

Aaron made notes. "Will do." He pointed to the pink slips on her desk. "You've got a stack of messages."

Sam flipped through the stack while she waited for the file to print. A police officer wanted to talk to her about possible suspects for a child slaying in Concord, one town over from where she lived. Two other police officers had left messages. Nick had called. Someone from Utah was calling to see if the D.O.J. had any records on a Dwayne Swift, who was picked up for sex with a minor.

The last message was blank. Dropping it in the trash, she picked up her date book and left her office.

"All ready," Aaron said, handing her a stack of papers. "In triplicate," he added.

"Thanks." Sam rushed down the hall, rounding the corner in time to catch Josh Steiner emerging from the conference room wearing an evil scowl. His thinning dark hair was combed over his head, and a piece of it dangled across his forehead like an exclamation point over one eye.

"About time," he mumbled under his breath.

Sam took a deep breath and brushed past him to enter the room. Turning to him, she said, "Do you want coffee or anything?"

"Much longer and we'll need dinner," he muttered.

Sam nodded and sat down. "I apologize for the delay," she said without details on the file.

"It's no trouble. Josh just hasn't had his morning coffee, is all."

Sam turned to introduce herself to Josh's colleague.

"Neil Wallace," he said, extending his hand.

The name wasn't the least bit familiar, but there was something about his face. "Have you been with the D.A.'s office long?"

He shook his head. "Brand-new."

"Why don't we just get started?" Josh interrupted. "You can exchange resumes later. I've got a ten o'clock."

Sam knew Josh was lying by the way he refused to look at her, but she didn't press him. Handing the men copies of the file that Aaron had just printed, Sam walked them through each aspect of the case. Josh asked a few questions, which she answered easily even without her personalized notes.

"You have a tape of the interview with the girl?" Josh asked.

Sam's copy of the tape had been with the file. Where the hell had that gone? There was always the original, safe in the evidence vault, but she would need to make another copy. "I can get a copy over to you this afternoon."

Josh raised an eyebrow. "You don't have a copy with you?"

Sam didn't blink. "I've got the original, but I can't give you that. I'll have to make an extra for you."

The corners of Josh's mouth sank into a frown. "We're in a bit of a hurry with this." He motioned to his companion, who gave a nod of agreement.

The case didn't go to court for at least another three weeks. Sam smiled patiently and leaned forward on the table, keeping her voice and eyes steady despite the lies. "If you'd like, I can make you a copy while you wait. Or I can just courier one over later."

Josh shook his head. "We can't wait. Just send it over soon." He stood and headed for the door.

Wallace followed, but paused at the edge of the room. Turning back, he raised an eyebrow. "I heard you've got another murder that looks like Sloan. You have any leads?"

Sam knew how rumors spread in a police station. It was like an airborne disease on an airplane. "We're working on it," she answered. "Nice to meet you," she added before he could ask any more questions. Then she excused herself and pushed past them.

It was almost ten when Sam finally got back to her

office. Aaron confirmed that the Hofstadt file still hadn't shown up, and the file's disappearance pawed uncomfortably at the back of her mind. Where could it have gone? She hadn't worked on the case with anyone other than the detective team and her team members at the D.O.J., who had helped with surveillance. No one in the building would have any use for it. And she didn't lose things. She asked Aaron to get a copy of the tape to Josh and told him not to let the original out of his sight for a second. Then she sent an urgent E-mail to everyone in her department, asking whoever might have accidentally taken the file from her desk to please return it immediately.

Pulling her file on Karen Jacobs—Charlie Sloan's first victim—Sam sat down behind her desk and leaned over to turn on the small heater next to her , feet. With the warm air blowing on her feet, she opened her notebook.

The first thing she did was get in touch with the warden at San Quentin who had had responsibility for Sloan. Aaron had spoken to him that morning, and he had reported that Sloan was as much a loner in prison as he had always been on the outside. Sam wasn't sure she believed it. It only made sense that the new killer was someone linked to Sloan. She dialed the number Aaron had left her and requested that she be transferred to Warden David Brighton.

"Brighton here."

Sam introduced herself and asked him about any friendships Sloan might have developed at the prison, any visitors or outside contact of any kind before his death.

"I hadn't noticed any changes in his behavior at all toward the end. He was usually in solitary because of the way he baited the other prisoners. He had been beat up a bunch of times, the last time almost to death. For a smart guy, he wasn't real bright that way, but he considered himself above the other prisoners, and you can imagine how they liked that."

"What did he do? Any letters? Anything?"

"Mostly he read. I've pulled the latest list of what he took from the library in those last months. A few more of the classics—mostly ones he had read before—Dickens, O. Henry, some Faulkner. He also checked out a trigonometry text, a physics book, and a life sciences text during his last few months. That's all in line with what he had been doing since he got here. He did receive a package from his attorney—it was a text of appeal cases. You know how they're all looking for a way out."

Sam rubbed her temples and nodded. "What about visitors?"

"None. He didn't even see his wife. She came about a month before he was executed, and he sent her away. He had also gotten a few letters, all from the same address, but they showed up unopened in his trash."

There had to be a connection between this murder and Sloan. Who else would've copied the M.O. so exactly? "No outside contact at all? Phone calls? Anything?"

"I wish I had more for you, but no. He didn't use telephone privileges except once to his attorney in the two months before his death."

Sam tried to think of another way that Charlie Sloan could have found someone to do his killing. "Anyone from his cellblock released over the past couple months?"

"Uh, only one that I can think of, but not someone who had any interaction with Sloan."

Sam was perplexed. She thanked the warden and hung up the phone, wondering if Nick was right. Maybe this wasn't Sloan. Maybe it was someone else. But only a few people would have had access to the detail about the six-leafed eucalyptus, and she hated to entertain the possibility that a cop was involved. Of course, maybe she had to face that possibility. If the theory was right and a cop was the killer, then the most likely suspect was someone who had been directly involved in Sloan's case.

Starting with her own name, she copied the list she had faxed to the sheriff's department of the people involved in Charlie Sloan's case. After so long, anybody could have found out the details. What she was counting on was that not just anybody had.

She started the list with herself as detective. Corona had known about the case because she had testified after she started working at the D.O.J. Sam wrote "Director Andy Corona." Gary Williams had attended her testimony and seen the evidence docket. Her gaze paused on Gary Williams' name. His interest in the case had seemed peculiar, but he always wanted to know what everyone else was up to. He was insistently nosy.

She tapped her pen and moved past Williams. She added the two officers who had arrived on the scene, Amanda Nakahara and Bob Haber. Her detective sergeant was Garrett Bouton. There were six cops who were involved peripherally in interviewing witnesses and following up on leads. She added their names to her list:

Monterra, Sansome, Wyatt, Bradley, and Cole. Was that all?

The crime scene team would have seen the eucalyptus. She tried to remember who they were but couldn't. It wasn't in her file, either. She wrote a note to check her journal for the names. Sam kept a binder at home with her personal notes on every case she had ever worked. It included everything from the evidence to the smell of a room and her own thoughts and opinions on a case and the suspects. If the names weren't there, the Antioch P.D. would have a record of them.

Assuming there were three or four of them, that made approximately fifteen people who had seen one of Charlie Sloan's scenes. As she compiled the list in her own handwriting, Sam considered each person. No one on the list made a good suspect. She put a call in to the clerk at the sheriff's department, but had to settle for leaving a message on his voice mail.

Standing, she stretched her arms and decided to go get lunch. When she picked up her purse she noticed writing on the back of a pink message slip sitting on the top of her garbage. Leaning over, she snatched it and turned the message right side up.

You're not invincible.

CHAPTER 4

SAM STARED AT the message and blinked hard, wishing she hadn't touched it. The handwriting wasn't familiar, but there might've been prints on it.

Aaron's chair was stopped in the doorway. "You okay? Look like you've seen a ghost."

Careful not to touch the note further, Sam tucked it into her blazer pocket. It seemed impossible that an ex-con working on Sloan's behalf could have gotten into her office. It would be one thing if Sloan could have paid someone, but he was dead. Nick's theory that the killer was a cop was seeming increasingly possible. The idea gave her the chills. "I'm fine."

Aaron shrugged, though the look on his face suggested he didn't quite believe her. "This just came off the fax, and Derek's on line one."

Sam put a finger up to indicate that Derek should hold for a second while she skimmed the faxed toxicology report on Sandi Walters. According to the autopsy, she was pumped full of heroin when she died. Not an overdose, but getting close.

"Derek sounds urgent," Aaron said.

Sam nodded and reached for the phone. "How come you're home early?"

"I just am," Derek snapped.

"I thought you had physical therapy," Sam continued.

"I did. I'm done."

"I—"

"Aunt Sam," Derek interrupted. "I'm trying to tell you that the police just called," Derek said, sounding out of breath. "Rob's been drinking at his job."

"Drinking?"

"He's drunk, Aunt Sam."

Sam clenched her teeth and nodded. "Where is he?"

"At the Contra Costa County Sheriff's Department."

"I know where it is." Sam hung up and grabbed her purse.

"Nick's on the line," Aaron said from the doorway. "Wants to talk about Rob."

Sam shook her head. "Tell him I'll call him later. I've got to go, Aaron. What do I have this afternoon?"

Aaron ran his finger down her calendar. "Nothing I can't reschedule."

"Thanks." She handed him her note about the crime scene team and asked him to call the Antioch P.D. for the information. She handed him the fax. "Fax this over to Nick. He's probably got it, but I want to be sure. And I'll try to get back later this afternoon."

"Don't bother," Aaron said. "I'll call you at home if anything comes up, and I can always fax you there."

"Thanks, Aaron. I mean it."

"No problem."

As she rode across the Bay Bridge, anger rose like a hard pulse in her chest, bringing with it a question she'd often pondered over the past eight years. Why had Polly done this to her? Leaving her children to Sam without even consulting her. Sam reprimanded herself for those thoughts. Still, she wasn't fit to be a mother. She hadn't made the choice to have children—it had been taken from her. And now she had two of them—teens, no less. She rubbed her eyes. But it wasn't anger she felt. It was frustration. She would never ask to be rid of the boys. She loved Rob and Derek.

Sam thought about the hate she'd seen in Rob's eyes at the baseball game the night before. She'd been unable to look at him. His anger was always right there at the surface—all his emotions were. She just didn't know how to handle them.

She'd spent so long burying emotions that Rob's nature seemed completely foreign. Had she done something to deserve such incredible anger? Or was Rob simply angry at the world because of his parents' deaths?

She'd been over it a million times but was never able to come up with a solution. Had Rob been that pampered by his mother? Sam hadn't really known Polly in the last twelve years of her life, but she couldn't imagine that Rob could have been so spoiled that the life Sam was providing was unacceptable. And Derek was completely mellow. How could two identical brothers be so different? There was no one who could answer that question for her.

Sam remembered the first time she'd taken the boys to the emergency room. Only six months after they'd come to live with her, Derek had come down with a fever that had persisted for three days. He'd been barely nine years old. Sam had been frantic. At the emergency room, she had struggled to fill out the forms. Did the family have a history of heart disease? Mental illness? Allergies? She didn't know.

It turned out he had tonsillitis. "I don't want to treat him without knowing what he might be allergic to," the doctor had explained. "Is there a family physician we can contact?"

Sam had shaken her head. No doctor information had come with the boys. No set of instructions.

"Is there a family member you could call for that information?" the doctor had asked.

Sam could see Polly's face in her memory—her wide blue eyes and long blond hair, as it had been when she was fifteen. Her brother's face flashed through her memory and then her mother's. Her father's face came next, and she squeezed the image away. "No, there's no one," she answered quickly.

The doctor had prescribed erythromycin rather than penicillin in hopes of avoiding an allergic reaction, and Derek had recovered without trouble. Sam hadn't prayed that much since she'd escaped the South. To this day, she hoped the boys would never be so sick that she had to call anyone in Mississippi. Just the thought made her shudder.

*

Sam walked out of the sheriff's department with Rob trailing a few steps behind. Knowing the details of Rob's arrest didn't make her feel any better.

He had gotten a job working for a landscaping

company for the summer. He and another kid were supposed to work the afternoon at Milton Peters' house in Lafayette. When they arrived, an hour late, Mr. Peters noticed that the boys smelled of alcohol and promptly called the police. Sam was glad he had.

"You've been fired from your job," she told Rob.

"So what," he mumbled, looking miserably hung over. Sam felt a twinge. She remembered that feeling. It had been a decade since she'd had a drink, but before that, hangovers had been quite regular.

"No job, no bike."

Rob shot a look at her. "You can't sell the bike."

"Like hell I can't. My name's on the title."

"But I paid for it."

"We had conditions when you got it, Rob. Do you remember them?"

"I'll still pay the insurance on it. I'll get another job," he argued.

"I'm not worried about the money." She turned and looked at him. "I don't like what's happening here. I'm not going to sell the bike yet, but you can't drive it, not until I see your behavior improve. In the meantime, you and I are going to work out what's going on, okay?"

Rob started to respond when a man cursed behind them.

Sam turned around to see what looked like a father and son standing on the sidewalk. The man was just about six feet and thick. He wore an ill-fitting pinstriped suit and cheap shoes. His suit jacket was gripped in one hand, and a gaudy red tie was pulled loose at his neck. "You idiot! What the fuck were you thinking?" The man raised his hand, and the boy moved quickly backward away from his fist, stumbling and landing on the ground.

Sam took a step toward them.

"Don't, Aunt Sam."

She looked back at Rob. "You know them?"

"It's Billy Jenkins and his dad."

"The one you were working with?"

Rob nodded.

Sam studied the lines of fear in Rob's face. She couldn't tell exactly what he was afraid of. Had Mr. Jenkins threatened Rob?

"Let's go," he said. "I want to go home."

Sam put her hand on Rob's shoulder and watched the father and son. The father had pulled the son up off the ground and was cursing him in more hushed tones. They still hadn't noticed that Sam and Rob were watching.

Mr. Jenkins raised his fist again, shaking it in the air.

Sam started toward them.

"Please, Aunt Sam. Don't."

This time Sam didn't listen. Anger was rising inside her like bubbling oil. She was ready to spit. "Excuse me," she said to Jenkins.

He looked at her and made a noise like a low growl.

"I'm Sam Chase, Rob's aunt."

"I'm fucking busy here," Jenkins sneered in response.

"Maybe you could take a moment out from abusing your son so we could talk," she continued, folding her arms and feeling her right hand on the butt of her gun.

Jenkins took a step toward her, but Sam didn't move. He was fat and smelled of sweat and stale booze. "I ain't got time for your shit, lady."

Sam felt Rob come up behind her. "Come on, Aunt Sam. Let's go."

She could sense the fear in his quick breaths. She didn't risk turning her back on Jenkins. "Wait for me at the curb."

"That's who you been hanging out with?" The man spoke to Billy and motioned to Rob, eyeing him head to toe. "That pussy? Jesus Christ, boy. He don't look like he could hold a six-pack."

Billy didn't answer.

Jenkins grabbed his son by the ear and shoved him. "You answer me when I talk to you, boy. You been hanging out with that pussy?"

Billy nodded.

Sam took another step forward until she was next to the boy. "You okay, Billy?"

Wide-eyed, Billy looked at her and then at his father and nodded quickly. "I'm fine."

The man took her arm and pulled her around. "Get the fuck away from him."

Sam twisted her arm free. "Don't lay a hand on me."

The man laughed and pushed at her shoulder. "What you going to do?"

He was like an ox. She knew that when he went down, he'd go down hard. But she knew she had to warn him first. "You ever heard of assault, Mr. Jenkins? That's what you're doing to your son. And if you touch me again, that's called assault, too."

The man let go. "How about I take out my dick and we can call it assault with a deadly weapon?" he said with a slur. He groped at his pants and took a step closer to her.

She shook her head. "I've seen pinky wrestling. Don't think it would be considered deadly."

"Bitch!" he spat after a moment of silence. He lumbered forward, raising his right fist to swing.

Sam ducked out of the way and then kicked her right foot behind his left, giving him a shove that sent him flailing backward. He landed with a hard thud and let out a groan.

She pulled out her badge and a business card and dropped the card on his gut, showing her badge. "I'm going to watch your son, Mr. Jenkins. If I see so much as a nick on that boy, I'm going to have you picked up for child abuse. Once you're inside, I'm sure you'll find some people who'd just love to see that pinky of yours at work."

The man picked her card up off his gut and stared at it. Shock had settled into his eyes.

Sam handed another card to Billy. "Memorize my phone number. You need me, you call." As she walked away, she added Billy to her mental list of kids to be watched. She spotted Rob watching her with a mixture of fear and interest.

It was a look she'd never seen on his face before.

CHAPTER 5

NICK SHIFTED IN the car, the morning paper curved over the door as he worked on the crossword. It was hotter than hell and the sun beating down through the windshield was baking him. He'd read in the paper that they were now officially calling it a heat wave, but he could have told them that two weeks ago.

Sam sat beside him not seeming to mind the fact that they were like two chickens in a Pyrex dish. In fact, she seemed to bask in the warmth. As though the hotter it was, the more comfortable she felt. He, on the other hand, was just plain roasting.

On the street where Sandi Walters had last lived with her mother, there was no shade on the block—no trees, not even much lawn, just one house on top of another.

Scanning the street, Nick didn't see any adults, but the Walters' neighborhood was alive with the sounds of children. Some rode old rusted or too small bikes up and down the street. Another group played in a sprinkler across the street, trying to find some relief from the heat, until a fat man with no shirt came out and yelled at them to stop.

Nick focused on the crossword, trying to ignore the heat. They were following normal procedure with Sandi Walters' murder, starting by investigating people known to the victim. And they had to tread carefully, and keep a low profile on their suspicion of possible police involvement. Sam was coordinating a team to delve into the whereabouts of officers who had been involved in the Sloan case. Most of them were still on the force. Many were still in the area. There didn't seem to be many good leads in either direction.

Nick felt the car shift beneath him and looked up from his crossword. Sam moved and frowned out the window. When she didn't look over, he returned his attention to the puzzle. "Papal scarf," second letter was "r." He looked past it. "Court" was the next clue—three letters. "Woo," he wrote. He glanced back at Sandi Walters' house and then down again. "Tantalum symbol." He wrote "totem." The car bounced again. This time when he looked up, Sam was staring at him.

"What?"

"How do you stand it?"

Nick looked around. "The heat?"

She exhaled. "No. The waiting. Just sitting here is driving me crazy."

He shrugged, looking back at the crossword. He kind of liked the solitude of surveillance. Of course, now he wasn't alone. Sam's constant motion made it hard to relax.

She moved again and he put the puzzle down. "You want to talk?"

Her eyes widened. "No," she snapped as though he'd asked her to strip right there. He turned back to the crossword. "I can't believe I'm on a stakeout," she said a minute later.

He set the paper down. So she did want to talk.

She caught his look. "What?"

"Do you miss homicide?"

She frowned and shook her head. "No." She stared out the windshield. "I'm doing good where I am."

"Damn straight you are."

"And it's better for the boys. Detective hours were so unpredictable. I need to be there for them. More even than I am, I think."

"You're doing a great job with them, Sam."

She smiled at him, and he turned away. He didn't remember her smile being like that last time they'd done a stakeout together. He shifted in his seat, ready to leave.

Sam leaned her head back and closed her eyes.

He picked up the crossword again, thinking it was an easy solve compared to the puzzle sitting next to him. And a hell of a lot easier than fighting his own reactions when he watched her.

"I'm terrible at crosswords," she said, sitting up and glancing over his shoulder.

He didn't answer her. He was sure he'd already used all his good answers and there wasn't another damn thing he could possibly say without evoking a negative reaction. Forty-seven down was "billiard shot"—five letters beginning "m-a." He smiled and wrote "masse," thinking about when he used to play pool with the guys from his uncle's band. Now, when he saw a billiard table, it was usually because he was in the local pool hall hauling someone off to jail.

Sam sighed and rubbed her temples. "How long have we been waiting?"

Nick shrugged. "About two hours."

"I should've brought something to do."

He looked up, unable to keep from smiling. "You want to help with the puzzle?"

She shook her head. "I can't do those things, I swear." But she pulled the paper toward her.

He smelled her cucumber soap and the citrus scent of her shampoo. Alarms squealed through his head.

Moving back a safe distance, he dropped the page and pointed to a clue. "How about 'Tennyson heroine'? Second letter is 'I'."

He watched as she concentrated, remembering when he'd first asked her what perfume she wore. She had waved her hand and sworn, "Nothing. I can't stand the stuff." And yet she was surrounded by beautiful smells, each of them reminding him that she didn't want him—hadn't wanted him since that one time. And it had not been enough.

It had been two and a half years, but he could still remember it clear as day. He had brought Rob and Derek home late one night after a ball game. They were the last of six or seven kids he'd taken home, and they had insisted that he come in to see the latest video game. Sam had tried to get them to bed, but they'd insisted. "Just one more game." They'd played for over an hour, until Sam finally put her foot down and got them into bed.

Nick had been on his way out. He had never felt

awkward with Sam. They had similar jobs, saw the same things. They'd worked together on cases before Nick had started coaching Rob's team. They had the job in common, and they both cared about Rob and Derek. Maybe Nick cared too much. He had wanted kids of his own, had thought his wife, Sheila, wanted them too. It hadn't worked out that way. Sheila found a man with more money, and she had his kids. Nick always felt welcome with Derek and Rob, though, like he was helping, but Sam had never acknowledged it before.

As he passed through the kitchen, she had stopped him. She had actually touched his arm and then pulled her hand back as though he'd been on fire.

"Thank you for being so good with them," she said.

He'd never seen anyone look so beautiful. And then she invited him to stay for a cup of coffee. Just a thank-you, he knew, but he felt the promise of so much more.

She was making coffee when the phone rang. He never found out who had called. All he knew was that her face went ashen when she answered it. She dropped the coffeepot, and the glass shattered on the floor, the hot liquid burning her legs. But she didn't move.

The phone still pressed to one cheek, she stood there, shaking her head and whispering in the smallest voice he'd ever heard from a grown woman, "No, no, no." When he finally rose from the table, the phone was dead.

"What happened? What's wrong?"

But Sam didn't speak.

She'd just shaken her head and shivered like a child.

Nick forgot about getting answers from her. Instead,

he cleaned up the broken glass and took her to her room to change her clothes.

But instead of changing, she simply sat on the edge of her bed and cried. The creamy skin of her neck, the scattered freckles that he imagined covered her breasts and stomach were all vivid in his mind. He tried to get her to talk about it, to tell him what was wrong, but she refused.

"Just hold me," she said.

And he did. He wrapped his arms around her and she accepted his embrace. He would have stayed all night—would have stayed a week, if she'd let him. But after less than ten minutes, she composed herself and showed him to the door. Ten lousy minutes, and the next time he saw her, it was as though it had never happened. The wall was back up, and he'd never been able to bring it down again.

Not that there hadn't been other women. He had dated off and on, but he hadn't found anyone that he wanted the way he wanted Sam Chase.

And now they saw even more of each other. They went to the movies, took the boys out to dinner. Friends, she told him. He wondered if there was a more depressing word in the English language.

He moved his head further out the window, wishing for any sort of breeze. Damn, it was hot.

Sam grinned. "Elaine."

He frowned. "What?"

"Tennyson heroine—Elaine." She snatched the pen from his hand and wrote it in. Then, moving toward him on the seat, she shared the page. "What else?"

Nick pointed to another one, watching her from the corner of his eye. Her eyes were a warm sea green, like the Gulf off the coast of Texas. He watched her frown in concentration as she focused on a problem, then the grin of excitement when she got it right.

Beneath the hard, independent exterior, Sam hid the excitement of a child. He watched her reactions with people. Her eyes wide when people were kind, narrow and stubborn when the odds were stacked against her. What attracted him most was her passion for the job. He had seen her go after a scumbag and not let up. And yet another side of her was soft.

Sometimes when she looked at him, he would swear that her eyes were scared, maybe even of him. But before he could understand her, the curtain would fall and he'd be staring at the strong, hard Sam again.

Surveillance made him think about the damnedest things. He frowned, trying to push Sam out of his mind. With her sitting beside him, it was almost impossible. Suddenly he wished he were alone on the job.

He rubbed his eyes under the bridge of his sunglasses, pulling them off to massage the ache he got behind his left eye whenever Sam started to take over his brain.

He glanced at the house and wished this stint was over. Maybe he was wrong. Maybe Sandi Walters wasn't killed by anyone she knew. Damn if he wasn't ready to give up. Sitting in this car with Sam beside him much longer was going to make him nuts.

He shifted in his seat and took a drink from the warm Coke on the dash. Just then, a beat-up brown Toyota Camry passed, followed by a white Buick Skylark. Nick watched the Skylark pull into Sandi's driveway.

"Company."

Sam dropped the puzzle and they both watched the car.

The driver, a heavyset man with a beard almost as big as his gut, pulled himself out of the car and dropped a smoking butt onto Sandi's brown lawn.

With a glance over his shoulder, he opened the front door and let himself in.

Nick snatched up the two-way radio. "Three-eleven, this is Thomas. Can you confirm I.D.?"

"This is Three-eleven. That is a negative."

"It's not Mick Walters," Nick repeated to confirm.

"That's correct."

He and Sam exchanged a look.

"He knows them well enough to have a key," Sam said.

"Not someone we knew about."

Sam raised an eyebrow. "Sounds like someone we ought to talk to."

"I agree." Nick picked up his wireless radio and pressed the black button on the side to speak. "Check registry on the vehicle." He repeated the plate number and said, "Three-six, please stand by to enter the premises."

He and Sam waited in silence for a response.

Nick pulled the search warrant from his pocket. He hoped he wouldn't need it, especially since it was still blank. How could he have a judge sign it when he didn't know what or who the hell he'd want to search?

"Thomas, this is dispatch."

Nick activated the radio, keeping one eye on the empty car across the street. "I read you."

"The car is registered to a James Lugino, address is listed in the city of Martinez."

Nick made note of the suspect's name. "Any priors?"

There was a brief pause. "Charged with possession during a routine traffic stop. He served ninety hours community service."

Ninety hours of community service meant pot. "Mary Jane?"

"Affirmative," came the response.

"Big step from smoking dope to shooting someone up with heroin and then raping and killing her," Sam said, pulling her Kevlar vest down over her head and strapping the heavy Velcro on her left side. She put her holster on over it and a blazer over the whole ensemble, looking in all her layers like she was about to head out onto the ski slopes.

Nick pulled on his own vest. He slid the magazine out of his Glock and checked it. "Let's hope for some answers and some damn air conditioning."

"Wimp."

He threw her a scathing look and spoke into the radio again. "Three-eleven, this is Thomas."

"Three-eleven responding."

"Please move your vehicle to block the suspect's and remain in the car for backup. We will wait for you to be in place before moving in."

"Yes, sir," came the response.

Nick waited, watching as the unmarked cruiser approached and stopped behind James Lugino's car. He saw no movement from within.

Tucking the extra magazine in his pocket, Nick holstered his gun, put on his windbreaker, and zipped it to cover the vest. He could already feel the sweat trickling down his back. The vest made it hotter, but he was better off hot than dead.

He'd learned a hard lesson in his first hours working for the detective division as a patrol officer. His partner, on a routine set of interviews, had decided not to don a vest. He'd been shot through a solid oak door as he approached a suspect's house. Though the shot hadn't killed him, he'd taken the round in his intestines. He'd been eating baby food since. And he was considered lucky.

Nick stepped out of the car and crossed over to the house, giving a half nod to the backup. Sam walked beside him, the two of them like normal people coming for a visit. Reaching the front door, he paused and looked at Sam. When she nodded, he knocked three times. After a moment, the door squeaked open and little Molly stood half hidden behind it.

Nick bent down a little as he spoke. "Molly, I'm looking for the man who's here. Do you know him?"

Molly looked up and then behind her.

Nick stepped into the house. "Ms. Mayes. Mr. Lugino," he called out.

No one answered.

"Where's your grandma?" Sam asked.

Molly looked around as though someone might help her with the answer.

"I'm the detective helping with your mommy's case. Can you tell me where your grandma is?"

Molly shook her head, strands of light brown hair falling across her cheeks. "She's not here."

"Is there a man here, Molly?" Sam asked.

Molly shook her head.

He didn't get angry with her. These kids had been trained to lie. The abused ones had been doing it since they could talk. Nick stooped lower so his gaze was level with Molly's. "Molly, it's very important that I talk to him. Where is he?"

Molly looked puzzled, then put a hand on one hip like a miniature grown-up. "He went out when you got here."

Nick stood. "Went out where?"

She pointed behind her. "The back door."

"You're sure?"

She nodded seriously and pointed to the door. "See, it's still open."

Nick cursed inwardly. "Did he know who I was?"

She smiled proudly. "I told him you were Mommy's 'tective."

Sam laughed at her antics, and Molly's grin widened.

Giving her a smile, Nick scanned the room. He didn't think she was lying. "Good girl. Now lock the doors," he said, as he raced back outside and scanned the street for Lugino. Sam was on his heels. The officers were still sitting in the car. McCafferty got out.

"He bolted," Nick said. "McCafferty, call for backup and then stay posted on this car." He pointed to Lugino's Skylark. "Lewis, head around the block from this side. He's got to be on foot."

"They would've seen him if he'd come this way," Sam said. "We should check the next block down."

Drawing his gun, Nick nodded and made his way around the side of the house. There was nowhere to hide in the Walters' small backyard, so Nick assumed Lugino had taken off. Despite his frustration, he couldn't help but smile when he remembered the sound of Molly's little voice talking about her mommy's 'tective.

Nick ran to the street behind the Walters'. Sam held back ten feet or so, covering in case Lugino appeared. Like Molly's house, the houses on this street were small, mostly ranch-style single-family homes.

Nick looked in both directions. The streets were clear. He hadn't expected to find Lugino on the street, though. If Nick were the one on the run, he would want to find a place where the cops couldn't find him. He looked back at Sam, and she pointed to the right. "Further from the main street."

Nodding, Nick followed her lead. Moving down the middle of the street, he surveyed each house. He was looking for deep bush, a hidden stairwell, a visible back-yard, an empty-looking house—anything big enough for a human body. He got halfway down the block when something stirred behind him. He whipped around to see a little black girl coming out of a house, cradling a baby doll in her arms and whispering to it. She walked down the three steps to the sidewalk and started to climb onto a tricycle.

"Back inside," he urged her.

The girl froze and looked up, her eyes wide.

"Please go inside," he repeated, motioning to her. He didn't want to scare her, but he didn't want her on the street at the moment, either.

She looked around, clearly frightened. Then, squeezing the doll tight to her, she raced up the steps and inside the house, screaming.

Sam stopped at the curb. Nick could see her checking the street for signs of their suspect.

"Anything?"

"Nada," she said.

Nick exhaled. He had started to turn around when he noticed a crawl space beneath the deck of the girl's house. Walking slowly, he pulled out his flashlight and turned the light toward the deck.

Silently, he crossed the grass and started to kneel.

"What the hell are you doing?" someone hollered.

Nick jumped back.

A woman, holding a bat, stood above him, leaning over the deck. "Get the hell off my lawn. Where do you get off scaring my girl that way?"

Nick raised his hand. "I'm a police officer, ma'am. I didn't want your daughter out here because I'm looking for a suspect in a murder case."

The woman didn't lower her bat. Instead, she took a couple of steps backward and scanned the area. "Let me see some I.D."

"Ma'am."

She waved the bat around in a small circle like she was winding up to hit one home. "I'll go back in that house and call the police 'less you show me your god-damn badge."

Sam came forward, her badge drawn. "Special agent for the Department of Justice."

The woman frowned, and the dark lines of her face suddenly looked painted on. "Not you," she said to Sam and then pointed to Nick. "Him."

He took a careful look around for Lugino. By now, he was probably on a bus for the next county.

"I D., mister," the woman repeated.

Sam was right behind him now. "You're clear," she said.

"Okay," Nick agreed. Still holding his gun, he found his badge with his left hand and brought it out, handing it to the woman.

He looked around again and slowly holstered his gun.

The woman studied his badge, then looked at him.

Nick sensed movement in the crawl space under the porch behind him.

The woman screamed.

"Freeze!" Sam commanded.

Nick spun around, reaching for his gun.

Lugino stood behind him, swinging the tricycle.

Nick ducked, unable to reach his gun in time. The tricycle missed his head but hit him hard against his right shoulder. He moaned, falling forward.

"Drop it and freeze," Sam repeated.

Lugino didn't listen. He took off down the street.

The woman ran back into the house.

"Fuck," Sam cursed, taking off after Lugino.

Nick forced himself up and cupped his right arm to his chest. He shook it loose slowly, the pain already starting to pulse in his muscles.

Lugino was moving, but not fast, and Sam reached him easily. When Sam was within arm's reach, Lugino dove right, but Sam caught his arm and whipped him around. Without giving him a chance to pause, she kneed him in the balls and watched him drop to the ground. He moaned and rolled to his side, bringing his legs up in the fetal position. She put her hand in his hair and pressed his face into the ground, her gun at his back.

"Nice cover," Nick said when he reached Sam. "I thought you were watching my back."

She didn't answer him but instead got on her knees and straddled Lugino. Her gun holstered, she pulled out a pair of cuffs and slapped them on Lugino. Nick wished again that he was alone out here. Watching her work was too much.

When she was done, she stood up and turned toward him. "You okay?"

He nodded.

Lugino moaned as Nick pulled him to his feet. "My nuts, man. That bitch crushed my nuts."

"You shouldn't have tried to crush my head," Nick muttered, leading him toward the car.

CHAPTER 6

NICK RAN A hand over his face and took a long drink of his cold coffee. It was after ten and they had been talking to Lugino for more than three hours. Sam had left early on, promising to come back later. Lugino hadn't been responsive with a woman in the room. And since she'd kneed him in the balls, he seemed to be particularly against talking to her. She'd gone to make some phone calls, and Lugino had relaxed a bit after she left. Nick knew how he felt.

Through a small one-way window in the viewing room, he watched Officer Polaski wear down Lugino. The idea was to tire the witness, exhaust him, until he was ready to spill everything—or everything you were going to get. Then you recorded the interview.

Nick had had interviews that lasted five minutes and others that had gone six or seven hours. Only one had pushed into the twenty-third hour, leaving Nick almost as desperate for a confession as the perp was for release. Twenty-four hours was the cutoff. Hold them that long, they had to be charged with something. Twenty-three hours and twenty minutes into it, Nick had gotten a full confession and detailed instructions on where to find the murder weapon. In interviewing, patience was an officer's best friend. He'd ask a question and wait—sometimes ten minutes—for an answer. If he didn't like the answer, he'd ask it another way or ask a different one and come back to it.

Over a hundred or so interviews, Nick had developed a sort of sixth sense about who was guilty and who was innocent. He didn't have the guilty feeling about Lugino. He'd missed it in others who had killed, but Lugino lacked a baseness in his gaze and the fake confidence that came with being able to carry off a lie of that magnitude.

Lugino was being held on assaulting an officer, but if they were going to charge him, Nick wanted it to be something more substantial than that. He'd left the interview room to give the other officer a chance to intimidate Lugino before they continued.

He paced the small viewing room, watching while Polaski glared at Lugino. Polaski was the ultimate bad cop. A nice enough guy, he had a rugged, pockmarked face and a scar from the corner of his mouth to above his ear. The scar was from a dog attack when he was a kid. His thick, dark hair divided at the line of his scar like a second part on the side of his head. When he was smiling, the scar dimpled, like a huge lopsided grin. But when he wasn't smiling, you'd swear it was a gash from a recent knife fight, and you'd wonder how bad the other guy looked.

Polaski's tactics certainly seemed to be working on Lugino. He had sweated a thick streak down the front of his gray Raiders T-shirt, and his curly dark hair was plastered to his brow.

"Is he talking?"

Nick turned to meet Sam's gaze. "Polaski's working him a bit."

"I got some good news," she announced, smiling. She was dangling a piece of paper in her fingers.

Nick tried to snatch it but missed. "Good news I could use."

She handed it to him. "We got a print on the body."

Nick read the evidence report. "Any matches?"

"Not yet, but maybe we'll have one soon."

"I hope you're right."

Sam moved up beside Nick to look through the window. He felt her closeness like an electrical current, but he kept his distance. He didn't let them touch and neither did she. "Any priors besides the possession?"

"That's it. I can't figure it. No history of violence."

"Maybe Sandi drove him to it," Sam suggested.

It didn't feel right. "According to the guys he works with, he doesn't have a temper to speak of. Came to work one day with three broken fingers. Guys razzed him about getting in a fight. Turned out Sandi broke them and he didn't even get mad—just said it was her fire that made her fun."

"A real tough guy."

Nick nodded. "Exactly. Not the type to strangle someone."

"Maybe not."

Nick rubbed the stiffness in his right shoulder where the trike had hit.

"How's that arm?"

He dropped his hand. "It's fine."

"Must be getting old if it still hurts."

He didn't look at her, but he could tell she was kidding. "It's fine, I said."

She was quiet a moment. Through the speaker wired to the interview room, they heard Polaski ask Lugino what he thought his chances were of not getting nailed for Sandi's murder if he didn't answer the questions. Lugino didn't respond.

"Plans have changed a bit for your birthday," Sam said, frowning.

Nick didn't blink. "That's fine," he said, though he was disappointed.

"It's just that with Rob grounded, I don't really want to take him to Chevy's. I want him to learn from this and taking him out will feel like a reward."

Nick nodded. "That's fine. I'm going to dinner at my sister's on Saturday."

"But tomorrow's your actual birthday," she said, still watching Polaski and Lugino.

"No biggie."

She watched through the two-way mirror, and he could see her thinking. "Why don't you come to dinner anyway?"

"Why don't I take you out?"

Her gaze shot to his. "Take me out on *your* birthday?"

He nodded. "Or you can take me."

She opened her mouth.

"Or we can go Dutch."

"Just the two of us?" She looked like she was holding her breath.

He laughed. "Okay, it was a bad idea."

"No," she said quickly. "It's a good idea."

He watched her, the nervousness in the way her eyes flitted across the room and she played with her blazer button. He pretended to watch Polaski, wondering what she would say.

"Where did you want to go?"

He shrugged. "I'll think of something."

She paused and tried to look nonchalant. "Okay. Tell me where and I'll meet you there."

Nick grinned. "Okay. I'll leave you a message tomorrow."

Polaski waved for Nick to return.

"Got to go." He paused and looked at her. "See you tomorrow?"

She nodded. "Tomorrow." She motioned to the room. "Give Lugino my regards."

"You gonna watch?"

She smiled without meeting his gaze. "Wouldn't miss it."

He thought briefly about the prospect of a dinner alone with Sam. Apart from work, they hadn't been alone since that night. She'd always kept at least one boy around as a barrier. Or maybe there was just always a boy around. He reminded himself that tomorrow would just be two friends having dinner. With a quick breath, Nick entered the interview room and sat down next to Polaski.

They had already agreed that Nick would take the

regular questions and Polaski would butt in when they didn't like Lugino's answers. A classic good cop, bad cop.

Nick cracked his knuckles to relieve some of the tension that had built up in his body and forced his mind back to the case.

"You ready to talk to us, Lugino?" Nick asked.

The man nodded, looking exhausted.

Nick flipped on the handheld recorder and placed it in front of the suspect. "Please state your full name for the record."

"James Lee Lugino."

"Date of birth," Nick continued.

"March twenty-four, nineteen fifty-three."

"What was the nature of your relationship with Sandi Walters?"

Lugino furrowed his brow.

"How did you know Sandi Walters, Mr. Lugino?"

Lugino nodded. "She was my girlfriend."

"But she was with someone else, maybe even married to him. Sandi was with Mick Walters, wasn't she?"

He shook his head. "They weren't together, and they never got married. He's Molly's dad, is all."

"And that doesn't bother you?"

Lugino shook his head. "He's basically a good guy. Sandi and I were good together. They weren't."

"You sure Sandi wasn't planning to get back with Mick? Maybe that made you jealous? Maybe you lost your temper?"

Lugino shook his head. "Ask Sandi's mom, ask Mick. Hell, you can even ask Molly. Sandi and I were together,

Mick's around for Molly's sake, but Sandi wasn't interested in him."

Nick continued to question Lugino on his relationship with Sandi Walters, when they met, where they went. He'd already heard it three times, but this time it was official. This time it was being recorded. It wasn't going anywhere. Even as he spoke, he wondered if the lab would get any more information on the case—some other lead to follow, a match to the print.

"Do you use alcohol?"

He nodded.

"Out loud, please, Mr. Lugino."

"Yes, I drink sometimes."

"How about drugs?"

"No."

"Did you ever take drugs with Sandi Walters?"

"No," he answered again.

Nick didn't need to see Polaski's reaction to know Lugino was lying. He was a bad liar.

"Have you ever taken drugs, Mr. Lugino?" Polaski interrupted, leaning over the table and pushing his scarred face toward Lugino.

The suspect looked around the room and then closed his eyes before answering. "Yeah, a long time ago I did."

"Don't lie to us again," Polaski warned.

Lugino looked at Nick for help.

"What sort of drugs?" Nick asked.

Lugino shifted in his seat, the plastic chair making a cracking sound. "It was a long time ago. What difference does it make?"

"Answer the question," Polaski ordered tightly.

Lugino wiped a hand across his forehead. "Yeah, I used to do drugs."

"What sort of drugs?"

The man shrugged, though he appeared anything but relaxed. "I don't know—pot mostly. Some acid, 'shrooms."

"What about heroin?"

Lugino nodded.

Polaski made a low sound like a growl.

"Yeah, some smack once or twice maybe."

"Methamphetamine?" Nick continued like he was reading off a laundry list.

Lugino gave him a blank look.

"Crank," Polaski added. "You ever do crank?"

Lugino looked down at the floor. "Yeah, probably, but a long time ago."

"Cocaine?"

Lugino looked relieved. "No. I never did coke."

Nick knew it was too expensive. "What about the night of July twelfth? Were you taking drugs then?"

He shook his head.

"Please answer out loud," Nick said.

"I don't think so."

"You don't think so?" Polaski asked.

Lugino ran a hand through his hair, which he had pulled straight and it was now standing on end in some places. The gray showed under the harsh halogen lights, and Nick noticed his skin looked gray too. "I don't remember—maybe."

"What sort of drugs would you have taken?"

"Pot, maybe some downers."

"No heroin?"

Lugino squinted, turning his head to the side, perplexed, the way dogs did. "What?"

"Heroin," Polaski repeated. "Smack, H, horse, scag. I thought you said you'd done heroin before?"

Lugino looked straight at Nick without blinking. "I didn't. Not that night."

"Did Sandi Walters take heroin that night?"

"I don't know. I wasn't with her until later."

"But you didn't take heroin that night?"

He shook his head fiercely. "No."

"Did you kill Sandi Walters?" Polaski asked.

Lugino shook his head, his eyes wide with the look of a man truly shocked. "No."

"But you do admit having sex with her that night?" Nick continued.

Lugino nodded, his shoulders sagging. His hands in his lap, he dropped his head. "She told me to meet her at that field. She loved that place. There were a couple horses across from there. Hell, she'd even named the damn horses—Cupcake and Butterscotch." He blinked hard, and his voice was rougher when he spoke again. "That night, I was late—almost a half hour, I think. She was just leaning up against the tree, almost naked."

"Tell us what happened then," Nick prodded.

"I came to talk to her. I'd been drinking some. I remember she seemed out of it."

"Out of it, meaning what?"

"Passed out."

"Not moving?" Nick continued.

Lugino winced at the implication. "Yeah, not moving."

"But you didn't think she might be dead?" Polaski pushed.

"God, no. No. I never thought that. I thought she'd passed out. She does that from time to time."

"She was naked when you found her?" Nick added.

"Wearing her underwear." He touched his neck. "With these little branches in her hair."

"And that didn't strike you as unusual?" Polaski asked, clearly not buying the story.

Lugino seemed to crumple. "No. To be honest, Sandi always loved to be naked. She'd been doing heroin lately." He looked up. "I haven't, but she had. And it made her do some crazy stuff. It made her feel hot and she loved the feel of the air on her skin. So she was taking her clothes off all the time. It didn't seem so weird. I thought it was kind of sexy." The last word seemed to leave him small and deflated.

"And you had sex with her despite her lack of movement?" Polaski continued without missing a beat.

Lugino looked up at Nick, his eyes begging someone to stop the questions.

"Is that right, Mr. Lugino?" Polaski continued.

Nick sat back and listened. Nothing about Lugino's reaction seemed off. Nick found it hard to buy the story about having sex with a dead woman without knowing it, but stranger things had happened.

"Yes. I had sex with her." His head down, Lugino's shoulders shook, and Nick was fairly certain he was crying. His voice quivering, he told the story again. When she hadn't moved after sex, he tried to rouse her.

That was when he figured out she was dead. In a moment of panic, he'd bolted.

"You didn't take her underwear off?"

He shook his head.

"Please answer the question."

"No. I didn't take them off."

"How did you have sex with her without removing her underwear?"

He motioned to the side with his hand. "I just sort of, moved them to the side," he said without looking up.

"You didn't make any markings on the body?"

Lugino looked up at Polaski. "No."

"You didn't put anything on her foot?"

"No."

"Do you chew gum, Mr. Lugino?"

He frowned. "Gum?"

"Right. Do you chew gum?"

He shook his head. "Nah. Gets stuck in some crowns I've got."

"How about Ms. Walters?"

"You mean about gum?"

"Right."

Lugino nodded. "Yeah, Sandi likes—liked gum."

"What kind?"

"Big Red."

"Any others?"

"No. Mostly just that one, I think."

Nick stopped and watched Lugino, starting to feel sorry for the guy. Nick pictured him realizing Sandi Walters was dead after having sex with her and rushing off. How long would it be until Lugino could close his eyes without thinking about having sex with a corpse? Would he ever?

"Do you know a woman named Karen Jacobs?" Nick asked.

Lugino sniffled and looked up, the cheeks above his beard red and splotchy. "Who?"

"Karen Jacobs?"

Lugino stared at the far wall and then shook his head. "No. I never heard of her."

"How about Charlie Sloan?"

Lugino frowned. "That name's familiar. He work at Denny's with Sandi?"

Nick glanced at Polaski, who shook his head. He lifted the recorder off the table and pressed the stop button. Then he followed Polaski out of the room.

"I don't buy that sex thing. He's got to be lying," Polaski said when they'd shut the door on Lugino. "Who the hell could have sex with someone and not realize they're dead? It's too sick."

Nick rubbed his eyes. Damn, he was tired. "I agree it sounds hard to believe. But he didn't even blink at the sound of Karen Jacobs' name or Charlie Sloan's."

"Maybe he didn't know their names," Polaski continued. "Doesn't mean someone didn't tell him about the case. It'll be easy to check if his blood type matches the semen at the scene. He's admitted he was there. It's got to be him."

Nick nodded, not sure what he thought anymore. His mind kept coming back to the evidence. The evidence pointed at Lugino. His fingerprints, the semen, it was enough to close the case. "See if he'll agree to toxicology.

Maybe we can find something that proves he's lying. And we've got a print on the body. We're running him against that."

Polaski nodded and headed back into the interview room.

But he knew what the D.A.'s office would want—and it was the one thing he couldn't give them. What was the damn motive?

CHAPTER 7

IN RESTLESS SLEEP, Gerry shifted against the hard, cold surface that felt like the floor of his cell. He was out of jail. He was free. What was the cold? It should be warm here. Opening his eyes, he turned his shoulders and touched the rounded porcelain of the bathtub. He was in his bathroom—the bathroom of his apartment. It should've been a relief. He should have been thrilled to realize he was no longer trapped, no longer behind bars.

But in the distance he could still hear them chanting. "Pervert. Pervert. Pervert." It was like a steady drum against his skull. He was surprised he'd slept at all. Exhaustion and fear had driven him from his bedroom. The bathroom was the only room without a window. They had broken the glass the first night.

Finally, after midnight, they had been forced by the police to leave him alone long enough to get the window boarded up. But the board didn't keep out the chill or the noise, and the small apartment had left no alternative but that bathroom.

Even worse, there would be no relief from the tiny

apartment. He had applied for a dozen jobs in the area, but everyone had turned him down flat. They knew who he was. They weren't going to have anything to do with a pedophile. They didn't call him that, though. No one did. They said things like "sicko" and "freak." He supposed they were right. He was, wasn't he? He could change, but not if they didn't leave him alone.

Without sleep, his mind did crazy things. He no longer had control. It was like being on drugs. He just needed a chance—an opportunity to prove himself again. If they would just leave him alone.

But no one would give him that chance. There was no good transportation here, and without a car he couldn't look for jobs further than a couple of miles from his apartment.

The last time he left the apartment to pick up groceries, he had called his brother in Fairfield. Bobby hadn't even heard three words before he'd hung up. Gerry guessed he couldn't blame Bobby much. It was probably hard for a normal guy to have a brother like him. Gerry didn't dare call his parents. And his sister's husband hated him. Gerry knew Stan would keep her from helping him.

His mother would have helped him if she could. But his father kept too close an eye on her for her to do much. The one time she'd come to visit him in prison, his father had found out about it and threatened to kick her out of the house. She'd written him a very nice letter explaining how sorry she was that she wouldn't be visiting anymore, or probably writing either. She had always been passive, and he knew she wouldn't ever stand up to his father. He hadn't written her back. He had enough on his conscience without worrying that she'd get kicked out of the house on his account.

Pulling himself out of the bathtub, Gerry wiped at a wet spot on his sweats caused by a leak in the old faucet. He'd tried the floor the first night, but there was a worse leak from the wall pipe that had soaked his blankets. At least the tub's leak was a slow, steady drip instead of the small fountain that sprang from the back of the toilet.

He looked around the apartment. A hot plate, an ancient refrigerator, and a rust-coated sink were his kitchen. A single bed now covered with broken glass was his bed. He had sixty-seven dollars to his name.

At least in jail he had a warm meal and a clean bed—most of the time. And he had learned to cope there.

"What're you in for?" one of them would ask.

Gerry would turn around and look the man in the eyes. It was always the big men, too. Big, meaty men with red hair and necks and goatees, tattoos, and buck teeth and ten-gallon bellies who pumped iron to pass the time because they'd never learned to read.

"Tax fraud," he'd said the first time.

The meaty man had eyed him top to bottom. "IRS?"

He had nodded quickly—too quickly, it turned out.

"That's federal. You in a state pen." The convict leaned over and shoved out his chest and a tattoo with the words "dead meat" in uneven blue writing.

"Gerry beat the rap on that one," Wally, the librarian, cut in. "Ended up in here for assault in the process."

The man looked at Wally and then back to him for confirmation.

He nodded—less quickly this time.

"What weapon?"

A 1040? "A bat. I had a bat."

"You beat someone up with a bat?" the beefy man continued.

Wally nodded him along.

"Yep. My lady. I beat her with a bat." His mind started to roll. "Was her who turned me in."

The beefy man nodded and gave him a smile that looked more like a shark about to attack. "Me, too. 'Course I killed my old lady." He looked around and added with a smile, "I still say not guilty, though. She had it coming, know what I mean?"

Gerry nodded without comment.

The beefy man left, and Wally closed the space between them. "I'm going to tell you a story a guy told me when I got here."

He focused his attention and nodded.

"Was a guy here from N.A.M.B.L.A.," Wally began. "You know them?"

He shook his head.

Wally lowered his voice. "The Northern American Man Boy Love Association. Their slogan is 'sex by eight.'
"

He furrowed his brow. "Eight?"

"Years old."

Gerry frowned. "Oh."

"Not an especially popular group. They don't get caught, most of them. They've got the most extensive underground system of any of the associations. But this guy, he got caught."

He nodded, waiting.

"They brought him here," Wally continued. "He refused to lie about the group he belonged to."

There was a short silence. "And?"

"Guards found him two days later sitting on a broom handle."

"Sitting on it?" Gerry asked.

"It was shoved so far up, it was coming out his mouth." He grimaced.

Wally looked around. "Don't you tell them what you did—ever. They'll kill you. You look guilty, too. Best learn how to lie. Make it violent. Little guy like you—make 'em think you're crazy. Keeps them away."

"Crazy?"

Turning his back, Wally started shaking and howling as he headed out of the room. He got strange looks, true—but they all stayed away from him.

Every day he'd pictured that broom handle and worried about someone finding him out, learning about all the bad things he had done. Eight years he'd lived with the fear, submitting to guard cruelty and politics, even kissing up, spit-shining shoes and pressing shirts to keep it quiet. Did the guards even know? He wasn't sure. They'd always acted like they had inside information, but really they seemed no more informed than most of the inmates—only crueler and more violent.

He couldn't forget the lady cop who had arrested him that last time, the time he finally got sent to jail—Sam Chase. The invincible Sam Chase. She'd been small and beautiful for an adult. Freckles sprinkled across her cheeks and nose, she almost looked like a kid to him. A perfect little kid name, too. He wished they'd had guards like her in prison. Of course she'd been real mad at him when she caught him in the playground with the kids, but he liked her anyway. She was his only friend out here. And now at least he could see her. He was going to get her attention now. He had the perfect plan.

And maybe she would help him get back to prison. He could convince her to send him back.

Gerry made his way into the main room and opened the refrigerator. There was almost nothing left to eat. He found a Pop-Tart and sat down on the floor, out of view of the window, to eat it. Leaning back against the far wall, he put on his headphones and closed his eyes. But even with his headphones on, he could hear them outside. There was no peace.

Three days ago, he'd passed through this same room and a bullet missed his head by inches. He'd called the cops. Citizens were supposed to report these things. They came, of course. But he knew they didn't care. No one cared. Sure, he'd had problems. And urges. But he wasn't doing anything wrong now. He was just trying to live.

The police had come and told him that they'd arrested the man who'd fired the shot. He knew that guy would be out of jail in no time. And the police hadn't been able to do anything about the picketers.

"They got rights, too," the redneck officer had told him. The look in his eyes said he might just as well have fired the shot. Gerry knew that with Megan's law, people had the right to know who lived in their neighborhood and to picket if they didn't like it.

At least Gerry had learned to stay clear of the

windows. They wanted to lynch him. He could still hear them in his head.

Get out of our town, sicko.

Stay away from our children, pervert.

You should be dead. You don't deserve to live. Die. Die.

He thought about Sam Chase again. She'd never told him that he deserved to die. She'd sent him to prison and he'd been safe there. He felt sad, but he took another bite of the Pop-Tart and thought about getting back to prison. Soon now. He'd be back there soon.

CHAPTER 8

SAM INCHED HER way toward the driveway at the Department of Justice building, cursing the tourist buses that had already begun to circle the block at Fisherman's Wharf. She imagined some tour company charging fifty bucks a head to come and tour a four-block area by bus. Each bus seemed to do it a hundred times a day.

The tourists out on the street this morning wore oversized San Francisco sweatshirts in bright colors—kelly green, scarlet, royal blue. Designs of the Golden Gate Bridge and cable cars decorated the space between the San and the Francisco. There was a gold mine in the sweatshirt-making business. Tourists came from the humid summers in the East and South and believed that it would be equally warm in California. Wrong.

When she finally reached the driveway, Sam pulled her government Caprice in and pressed the white call button.

"Yes."

"Chase here."

The heavy grilled gate rose, and Sam drove down a

short ramp into the lot. The forest green of her Caprice and the absence of roof lights created the impression that it was a civilian car. But it still had all the bells and whistles—police sirens she could control with her feet, a radio hidden in the center armrest. And the trunk was full of gear—her Kevlar vest and raid gear, and rape, first aid, and evidence-collection kits.

Some of the gear had remained unused in the eight years she'd been at D.O.J. But there'd been more than one time when she was glad to have one of the things loaded into her trunk.

In technical terms, she was a special agent for the State of California Department of Justice, Division of Law Enforcement, Bureau of Investigation. The running joke was that the D.O.J had the longest names in law enforcement. Unlike Nick, whose position was with the county, Sam was employed by the state.

In many ways, the job was a lot like that of an FBI agent, except that Sam worked for California only. There were divisions within the department and she focused on the Child Abuse Unit, which maintained a central file on child abuse investigations completed by other agencies, like police, sheriff, and welfare offices. Nick liked to joke that the D.O.J. were the paper-pushers and the real action was in the sheriffs department, but Sam participated in her share of raids and made arrests. Nick was right, though. It was slower in some ways. Maybe not slower, but more manageable. On the nights when Sam did have a stakeout or a raid, she got coverage for Derek and Rob, but for the most part, she was there for them, which was where she needed to be.

She pushed eject on the tape she'd been playing and stretched her neck. She'd been listening to John Irving's *Cider House Rules* and had arrived in San Francisco in the mind of a child at St. Clouds orphanage rather than a special agent for the Department of Justice. Her mind was filled with Dr. Wilbur Larch and Homer Wells as she got out of her car, holstered her Glock, and retrieved her bag from the trunk.

She went up the cement stairs and entered the main building, then took the elevator to the third floor. Using her key card, she passed through the secured door and headed for her office. It was quiet this morning. She was in early, determined not to let the missing case file get to her. She had locked her office last night, something she'd never bothered with in the past.

Her key stuck slightly, but it turned and the door clicked open. She bent down and examined the keyhole, noting the small scratch marks around the lock. Were those new?

Pushing the door open, she flipped the light switch and studied the room carefully before going in. Dread pooled in her gut like motor oil, and she longed to turn around, get in her car, and go home. Forcing herself to enter the room, she closed the door and dropped her bag by her desk. Nothing looked out of order. Maybe the marks were old.

She settled in at her desk and picked up the stack of message slips from yesterday.

Aaron came in to drop the day's mail in her in box. "I see you found that file," he said.

Sam looked up at him as he pulled the missing

Hofstadt file from among the papers in her in box. She took it from his hand. It hadn't been there yesterday. She was sure she had checked her entire desk.

"Should I send an E-mail letting people know you've got it?"

Sam nodded. "Thanks," she murmured.

Aaron left the room and Sam exhaled, exhausted. She opened the file and was skimming through the contents when she saw the picture. Letting out a gasp, she froze. The shot was only of her face and shoulders. A snapshot, not a posed photo. A small red circle had been painted in the center of her forehead with a tiny drip that spread down her cheek like blood from a bullet wound.

She felt the same prickle of fear that she had felt as a child when she heard that certain tone in her father's voice. "Samantha Jean," he used to call out to her. Clenching her fists hard, Sam fought it off. Samantha Jean was dead.

She started to reach for the photo and stopped herself. Whoever he was, he wasn't going to get away with it. She'd have someone's goddamn job for this. She'd get the prints on it and the note from yesterday and find out who was screwing with her.

She dreaded the idea of asking Nick. It was personal, and it felt like a weakness. And she didn't like the idea of sharing it with anyone, especially not Nick.

It was a dumb thought. Nick was the closest thing she had to a friend. If she was smart, she would make something of that. No, if she was unafraid, she would make something of it. But she wasn't. She was terrified. And she had no idea even where to begin with her fear.

She pushed it aside and looked down at the picture again. Nick would do it for her. She trusted him. And she knew he would keep her confidence. In fact, he was the only one she would trust to check the prints and keep it quiet.

She pulled a tissue from the box on her desk, the box that saw use only when someone else was in her office. Sam neither cried nor got sick. Ever.

She hated photos. It was another of the things she was glad to leave behind in Mississippi. As a child, formal family photos were snapped four times a year: Easter, the Fourth of July, Thanksgiving, and Christmas. Her mother would scrub them all down, shove the girls into pink dresses and her brother, Jimmy, into khakis and a tie, and get all dolled up herself. "Smile for the camera!" The quarterly photo was supposed to be a testament to the happy family life.

The picture in her hand seemed to stare back at her. The collared shirt she was wearing was new, but it wasn't one she wore to work. He had taken pictures of her at home, with her family. "Damn you."

Using the tissue, she took the picture out of the file, slid it into a manila folder, and dropped it into her bag, wondering if they would pick up any prints. She had dusting powder in the back of her car, and she was tempted to go downstairs and dust it now.

Her phone rang. Closing her bag, she reached over the desk and answered it.

"It's Corona. You got a minute?"

Why did Corona want to see her? "Sure, but—"

"Come on down."

Before she could respond, he hung up. Grabbing a clean notebook and a pen, she told Aaron where she was going and headed to the director's office.

She knocked on the door and he waved her in without looking up. "What's up?" she asked, taking a seat in a chair in front of his desk.

Without answering, he got up and closed the door. The gesture made Sam's stomach tighten. She'd never seen Corona do that before. If something was supersensitive, they left the office to discuss it. Everything else was open door.

He was a tall, broad, Hispanic man with dark, graying hair and an almost white mustache. When she'd met him, the mustache was salt and pepper. She preferred the way it looked now. But the gentle, calm facade was a sharp contrast to the fiery temper that lurked just under the surface. Corona was known for his hearty laugh and his thunderous roar. She'd never been on the receiving end of the latter.

"Is something wrong?" she asked.

Corona met her gaze. "I was about to ask you the same thing."

She frowned. "Meaning?"

"Is there something going on?"

Sam stared at him, waiting for the punch line. It didn't come. "No, I'm fine. Why?"

"You've been acting strangely. The missing file that you swore someone had stolen from your office. I see it turned up this morning."

She gritted her teeth. She was positive that file hadn't been there yesterday. Whoever had taken her file had added the picture of her as some sort of warning. It seemed like the only answer, but how could she tell Corona that? Who would buy that story?

"It's not normal for you, Sam. And if something's going on, I want to know about it."

She shook her head. "It's nothing. A few strange things have happened over the past few days."

"Like what?"

She met his gaze. Did the photograph count as an incident? Did the note? Were they related? She hated to think it.

"What's happened?"

"A picture in the missing file. A photograph of me with blood drawn on it."

Corona let out a low laugh that was more like a growl. "Some stupid prank to rattle your nerves, no doubt."

Sam looked at him and frowned, surprised he would treat more vandalism so lightly. Maybe it was nothing, but what if it was something?

"Looks like it worked."

"It isn't funny."

Corona frowned and nodded. "I agree. It's not. But I'm pretty sure that it's just one of the guys testing your balls, Chase. You know how they are." He looked at her and added, "I think your best bet is to chalk it up to immaturity."

Maybe she was overreacting. Still, it felt like a threat to her. She straightened her back and smoothed her skirt, itching for him to tell her to get lost.

"Okay."

Sam stood.

Corona pointed to the seat. "Sit down. There's more."

Sam sank into the seat. "Something else?"

He nodded. "This one isn't so easy."

A million possibilities ran through her mind—someone was dead, or someone sent something disparaging about her to him.

He slapped his hands against the surface of his desk and scowled. His brown eyes narrowed, his mustache pinched against his nose. "I got a call from Jeremy Tomasco."

"Tomasco? About me?"

Corona lifted his shoulders in a huge shrug and then raised his hands. "That's what I said. I get calls from the district attorney about Williams all the time, but you?" He pointed. "Chase, you're my star. What the fuck is going on?" He pounded the table for emphasis, and Sam felt herself jump.

"What did he say?"

"Said there've been complaints about you."

Sam felt her face go red. "What sort of complaints?"

He raised a fist. "Shit that made me mad—missing records. I told him he had to be wrong. You're the most organized agent I've got. What the hell was he talking about? The missing file, I know, but there was more—" Corona shook his head and his gaze burned into hers. "He said you didn't have a tape ready for him?"

Tomasco was Josh Steiner's boss. Josh had obviously complained about her not having the tapes when they met. And that she'd been late to their meeting. She had already taken care of getting Josh what he needed. "I—"

Corona wiped his hand across the air and Sam

silenced. "Is something going on? Something I should know about? A medical problem or something? Are you taking some new medication?"

She shook her head. "No. I'm fine."

"I know Jeremy's a pain in the ass. I'm sure he's over-reacting. When he called, I was sure it had to do with Williams, but when he said *you*—" Corona stared at her without continuing.

She didn't respond. There was nothing to say. She had no excuse, no good reason. And the truth sounded the most far-fetched. Someone had stolen a file and then returned it and left her a strange note? This wasn't the fifth grade, and Corona wasn't the school principal, there to hold her hand and make sure no one stole her milk money. Sam would handle this on her own.

Corona stood and leaned across the desk, staring down at her. "Relationships aren't your strength, Chase. I like you, but I'll be the first to admit it—you scare some people, maybe most people. But lately, something's different. You seem less in control. Not the agent I depend on. If there's something going on, I suggest you find some way to take care of it or someone to talk to."

He didn't offer his own ears and she was thankful. She wasn't the type to spill her guts, and he knew it. She couldn't believe this mess had gone this far, but it stopped here.

Sitting back down, he asked, "Does it have anything to do with the Walters case?"

Sam shook her head. "No," she said, her voice cracking. She coughed and repeated. "No."

"The D.A. wants a quick resolution to it. The idea

that we executed an innocent man is not sitting well with the D.A.'s office."

"I know. We made an arrest yesterday, but I don't think he's our man." She'd read the report this morning that said the print on Sandi Walters did not belong to James Lugino. Now they had to figure out who the hell it did belong to.

"Then find him. And keep me updated on what you've got. I want a daily report—leave it on my voice mail. Now get out of here, you hear." He gave her a half smile that was supposed to be encouraging.

Sam left Corona's office feeling strangely out of sorts. She didn't like his reaction to the picture. He wasn't one to take trespasses of the system lightly, but the idea that he thought she was doing faulty work was more than she was willing to accept. Whoever had taken her file and put the picture in it had been determined to shake her up. And as Corona so diplomatically put it, it appeared to be working.

Not anymore.

Back in her office, she picked up her phone and dialed the main number of the Contra Costa Sheriff's Department from memory. When the officer at the desk answered, she asked for Jack Tunney, the clerk who had been researching the crime scene team.

"Officer Tunney's out," the woman at the desk responded.

Sam frowned. "This is Special Agent Sam Chase. He was working a case with me. Where's he out?"

"Wife had a baby last night. Three weeks early— a little boy. Jack junior. Kid was big, too—over seven pounds," the woman continued. "It's good thing she didn't carry it to term. Would've been an eleven-pounder easy. Both my boys were over ten and it's no fun, I tell you."

"Thank you," Sam said, although she wished she hadn't gotten quite so much detail. "Can you direct me to whoever is handling Officer Tunney's caseload?"

"That'd be Kirkwood. Hang on."

"Kirkwood," Sam repeated to herself out loud, shaking her head.

When Kirkwood answered, Sam explained why she was calling.

"I've got that right here," Kirkwood said. "Was going to call you, but Jack forgot to leave your number."

"That's fine. Tell me what you've got."

"Haber and Nakahara are still with the department here. No complaints about them. Nakahara was working that night, but Haber was off."

Sam made notes.

"Of course, Detective Sergeant Lewis is a captain now," Kirkwood continued. "Wyatt is with S.F.P.D. and Jack made a note that he put a call into their captain about that night. I haven't heard back. Monterra is up in Sacto at D.O.J. headquarters. Is that where you are, too?"

"No, I'm in San Francisco. Could you follow up on Wyatt today?"

"Sure will." Kirkwood paused, and she could hear the rustling of paper. "I also got the list of crime scene folks you faxed yesterday. None of those names are familiar, so I'm going to have to do some work on finding them."

"What about Cole, Bradley, and Sansome?" Sam asked.

"Bradley works private security now—a company called Westley. Jack has written that he works in the Bank of America building in San Francisco." He paused. "Also, he was in L.A. from Friday until Monday morning."

"What about the others?"

Kirkwood was silent.

"Hello?"

"Yeah, I don't know about them. I'll have to call Jack and ask."

Sam told him to call her later in the day with a status on the other people. Frustrated, she sank her head into her hands, remembering how she used to love solving cases. It was like a life-size jigsaw puzzle, and once you got it all together the killer was right there in the center. It wasn't always that way, though. In fact, most of the time she was scrounging for the smallest piece to try to fit in the puzzle, but at least she'd had the contacts back then to get things done.

She couldn't have gone back to homicide. The middle-of-the-night calls were bad, but mostly it was the death that had started to wear on her. In homicide, it was all death. At least in her job now, once in a while there was life. Although lately it seemed that was becoming less and less true.

As she thought about the current case again, it seemed she didn't even have enough pieces to get started, and she itched to find another link.

The fact that there was pressure from every direction on this one didn't make it any easier. Corona wanted answers, the D.A., the undersheriff—all of them waiting for her to hand them the killer. Every one of them depending on her.

Her thoughts shifted to Derek and Rob. She remembered when they were little boys and she had understood them. Now she dreaded dealing with Rob's outrageous behavior and Derek's isolation. And tonight she was having dinner with Nick—just the two of them.

If she still drank, Sam imagined she'd have a drink right now. As it was, the back of her throat felt dry and scratchy, itching for the cold, dry taste of beer. She hadn't had a drink since the day the boys came to her. And she still missed it every single day.

She longed to push the feeling away, but it couldn't be banished. Instead, she leaned back and imagined the bitter taste of beer until it was almost painful to swallow the emptiness in her throat.

CHAPTER 9

WHITNEY ALLEN SMOOTHED her pink ruffled dress and then leaned down to straighten her white socks. The dress had been almost brand-new when her mother bought it for her. "For twenty dollars, this isn't a school dress, you hear? It's for church and maybe a party, and that's it." But Whitney hardly ever went to parties where she could wear the dress, and wearing it made her feel like a princess. Whitney swore she'd be extra careful in it today. She was just going down the street to see Molly. Molly's mom had died, so Whitney wanted to look nice.

She puckered her face like her mom did when she was putting on lipstick, and then smiled into the mirror. "Perfect," she whispered, just like her mother always did.

Tiptoeing to the door, she took a deep breath and then opened it a crack and peeked out into the hall. Since her stepbrother left to visit his mother, the house had been like the library at school. Every time she said anything, her mother or stepfather said, "Shh." She didn't miss Randy. He was a twit. But it meant there was no one to order around, and Whitney was bored.

Her mother and stepfather were still in their room, and Whitney knew she needed to be quiet. Her stepfather worked at night and slept all day, so Whitney could never make noise in the house. Only Randy got to make noise. "He's a boy," her mother would say. "Plus, Randy doesn't know he's making noise." Randy was deaf. Whitney thought if he couldn't hear, he should be quieter, but Randy was the loudest kid she knew.

Whitney hurried down the hall and tore down the stairs, making as much noise as possible before skittering out the front door. The street was quiet, but Whitney knew there'd be someone around somewhere. Halfway down the block a car thundered past her, music blaring. Whitney covered her ears and cringed. She hated those loud cars. She reached down and pulled up the sock on her right foot. It had managed to fall around her ankle again. She wiped at the scuffed patent leather shoes that had belonged to someone else and wished that for once she could have something brand-new. Someday she would. She was going to marry someone very successful so she could have all brand-new dresses. Her mother said it didn't matter that their clothes were used. "It's how you wear them that matters," her mother would say.

Molly was sitting on her doorstep and without hesitating Whitney approached. "What are you doing?"

Molly squinted into the sun and shrugged. "Nothing."

Whitney twirled around. "Do you like my dress?"

Molly nodded without really looking at it.

Whitney smiled. Of course she liked it. It was beautiful. "May I sit down?" she asked, curtsying.

She shrugged again. "Sure."

Whitney frowned at the girl's response. It wasn't very polite. "Do you want me to stay?"

"I don't care."

With her hands on her hips, Whitney let out a long sigh like her mother did when she'd done something wrong. Then, pointing a finger, she said, "You should invite me to sit. It's only polite, you know."

Molly looked up at her and frowned. "Fine. Sit down."

She rolled her eyes. What could she do if Molly was rude? Her mother always told her that some people just weren't raised right. Brushing off the step, Whitney sat down, spreading her dress around her and then crossing her legs and settling her hands in her lap.

Molly pulled her knees to her chest and rested her arms on her knees.

"I heard about your mom," Whitney said, trying to raise the subject nicely.

Molly didn't answer.

"What's it like?"

Molly frowned. "What's what like?"

"Not having a mom."

She shrugged. "I dunno."

"Are you sad?"

Molly nodded, chewing on her lower lip.

"You can cry if you want to."

"I'm not going to cry."

Whitney shrugged. If her mother died, she would cry. She would cry and cry and cry. And then where would she go? She couldn't live with Randy and her stepfather. They wouldn't want her. She'd probably get shipped back to her father's house in Michigan. She scrunched her face at the thought of living with her stepmother. No, she would definitely cry if her mother died.

Whitney straightened her back and smoothed her pink skirt. A small brown stain caught her eye and she picked at it. It was chocolate—from her cousin Teddy's birthday party.

"Why are you here?"

Whitney looked over at Molly, who was watching her. "I came to see how you were doing."

The little girl narrowed her gaze. The streaks of dirt on her face made tiny cracks when she did. "Why?"

"Because I thought you might want someone to talk to." Whitney paused. "Do you?"

Molly shook her head. "No."

"We can talk about who killed your mom."

"No," Molly said again.

Every day since Molly's mom died, Whitney's mom had warned her to be very careful going outside. Whitney would look out the window at night and watch the cars go by and wonder if the killer was in each one. But once, in the middle of the night, she'd woken up and heard noises and thought the killer was in her house. It was only the wind blowing the screen door open and shut. That was scary.

Her stepbrother was outside playing when Molly's mom was last seen. He could have been a hero if he had been paying attention. But Randy never paid attention, especially when he was playing.

Whitney smoothed her skirt and turned to Molly, watching the other girl frown. Her mother always told her that her face would freeze in that position if she held it too long. Molly's looked frozen, but Whitney didn't say that. She stretched out her legs and crossed one over the other. "My mom said it was your dad what did it."

Molly sat up straight and scowled. "It was not."

Whitney ran her hand over her skirt again without responding to Molly's outburst. Molly was only a few months younger than Whitney, but Whitney had always been mature for her age. "Precoshess," her uncle always said.

"Your mom doesn't know," Molly said.

"She knows more than you do."

Molly thought about that and then shook her head. "I don't care what your mom said," Molly said. "She's stupid if she said that. My dad would never do that. He loves my mom. Your mom's a liar."

"Is not," Whitney scolded. "My mother wouldn't lie."

"Well, she did."

Whitney crossed her arms and stood up, stomping her patent leather shoe hard on the porch. "Don't you say that. My stepbrother was riding his bike when your mother came outside—he saw."

"He can't even hear," Molly snapped back.

Whitney put her hands on her hips. "He's deaf, not stupid, and he can see." It was the first time Whitney had ever stood up for dumb Randy.

"If he's so smart, how come he's older than me and still in the first grade?"

Whitney scowled. "He's not as dumb as you if you don't think your dad did it."

"Did not."

"Did too."

Molly started to cry. "Not," she said, her voice cracking as the tears made tiny red paths down her dirty cheeks.

Whitney tilted her nose in the air and gave a light shrug.

Molly stood up and stomped across the porch to the front door. "Go away," she screamed, as the door slammed shut.

Wiping off her dress, Whitney stomped off the porch. Her mother had said that Molly's dad did it, but she made up the part about Randy seeing something happen. He *was* outside, though. If she had been outside, she would have seen everything. She would be a great detective—like Nancy Drew in the stories her mom used to read to her when it was just the two of them.

Randy would be a terrible detective. Whitney had wanted to ask him a million questions before he left to see his mom, but he was too busy packing to talk to her. That was a problem with being deaf. You couldn't talk if your hands were busy doing other things. Plus, she didn't think he would be much help anyway. Her mother always said men didn't notice anything important—the same must be true of boys.

Randy was so stupid he probably saw the whole thing and totally forgot it.

CHAPTER 10

ROB WATCHED BILLY Jenkins slam the car door shut and carry the partly empty case of Old Milwaukee toward the group. They usually met here. It was a turnout behind a fire trail in the Berkeley hills and was rarely patrolled. Tall eucalyptus trees hid their cars from Grizzly Peak, out of view of nosy cops, which made it a convenient spot to hang out and drink. The times he'd been with girls had been here too, on a blanket on the ground. On warm summer nights, girls thought it was romantic to be able to look up and see the stars.

Billy sat down beside Rob and handed him a beer.

"Where'd you snag this? Your old man?"

Billy grunted. "He was too wasted to miss it."

Rob watched his face. Billy liked to talk big, but he was afraid of his father. Rob was, too. Billy's father was a real asshole.

"Fuck him," Billy muttered, pulling a can from the box and opening it with the same hand.

Rob took a long, slow drag on his beer and felt nothing. It always helped to stop feeling. He wondered why Sam didn't drink. Maybe she didn't need booze to feel nothing.

Billy dropped the can in an old pile of rusting empties and opened another.

Rob stared out at the skyline.

"Enjoying the view?" Billy asked.

Rob finished his beer and took another one from Billy. "When you going to start contributing to the flow?"

"There's nothing in my house." Rob opened the beer and took a long drag.

Billy nodded.

He wasn't so bad, Rob thought. They both went to Las Lomas High School but hadn't known each other until they got summer jobs with the stupid landscaping place. Then that dickhead Mr. Peters had busted them for drinking. Sam was already on his ass about finding another job. "You got a job yet?"

Billy shook his head and tilted his beer back. "I'm working on it."

"Yeah, me too. Your old man still on you about losing that job?" Rob asked, without looking at him.

"He's the same. He's an asshole."

Rob didn't respond.

"That crap he pulled at the station was nothing. You should see how he is at home."

Rob met his eye and took another drink from his beer.

Billy looked out.

Rob joined his gaze. From this spot he was sure he could see the lights of San Francisco.

"I'll bet Vegas is cool," Billy said.

Rob nodded.

"That's what we should do. Take off and go to Vegas."

Rob looked at him. "Yeah, right."

"I mean it. Screw school. Screw our folks. Just take off."

Rob finished his beer and tossed the can behind him. "Yeah, maybe."

"What the hell, man? What's here for us? School is bullshit. Parents are bullshit."

"I wouldn't know about parents."

Billy stared at Rob and shook his head. "Sorry, man."

Rob shrugged.

"You don't remember them at all?"

Rob shrugged again, took another can of beer and opened it. "Parts of it—my dad's slurring voice. It comes back sometimes." He shook his head, then raised the beer can and chugged the liquid until it burned his throat. He coughed and wiped his mouth with the back of his hand.

"How old were you?"

"Eight."

"That's pretty old. Don't you remember them?"

"Some of it."

"What do you remember?"

Rob thought back. None of it was good. "I don't know. Mostly I remember my mom crying and my dad screaming."

"Sounds like my house," Billy said, drinking his beer.

"My mom was really pretty, I remember that. She had long blond hair—really long. And she wore it down all the time. I used to love her hair."

"Your aunt seems cool."

Rob shrugged. "She's okay. Everything has to be just

114

right. You think your father gives you a hard time, at least you're his kid."

"You see how she handled my dad that day?"

"Yeah."

"That was cool."

Rob thought about it. Sam had always been like that. He never really thought about it as cool or not. "I guess."

"I wish my dad would die."

Rob glared at him, furious. "No, you don't. Don't say that."

"The hell I don't. Son of a bitch doesn't care about me."

Rob waved him off, then ran his hand through his hair, watching the other guys joke around. "You don't know what you're talking about. Don't wish your parents dead. Even lousy parents. At least you've got them."

Another car pulled up, and Billy lowered his beer as he looked back, checking for cop cars. The door opened and three junior girls got out. "Those chicks need to find their own hangout."

They watched Derek get out of the car. "Damn," Billy said.

Rob ignored him, reaching for another beer.

"Now I've got to give a beer to your gimp brother, too," he muttered.

Rob felt the anger rush to his cheeks. He dropped the beer and reached for Billy. "What'd you say?"

Billy pulled Rob's hand off his shirt and raised his voice. "I said, I'm probably going to have to give some beer to your gimp brother, too." He grinned at Rob. It was his don't-screw-with-me grin.

Jumping to his feet, Rob took Billy by the shirt and tossed him to the ground, then came down on top of him.

Billy fought to loosen Rob's grip but couldn't. "What the hell are you doing?"

The buzz of alcohol in his brain, Rob raised his fist and brought it down hard on Billy's face.

"Get off me," Billy yelled, twisting his hips below Rob in an effort to throw him off balance.

"You dipshit." Rob cursed in a low, angry stream as his fists connected with Billy's body.

Rob's right landed in his gut and Billy moaned. "Get him off me," he screamed, kicking and fighting.

Rob continued to pound on him. Billy took hits to his chest, arms, and shoulders. His left eye was starting to swell shut.

Derek had moved to Rob's side and was screaming. "Let him go, Rob. Let go of him!"

Two guys grabbed Rob from behind and were trying to pull him off.

With Rob's weight finally off him, Billy hurriedly got up. Derek tried to help him, but Billy shoved him away. "Don't touch me, you freak."

Derek gave him a stare and shook his head. "You didn't have to do that, Rob. It doesn't matter what he says. He's an idiot."

Rob looked at Billy and straightened his shoulders. Then he lunged at Billy.

Billy jumped back and tripped, landing on the ground again.

"Fucking loser—just like your dad," Rob said. "Let's go, Derek."

Billy got up quickly and wiped himself off. He touched the back of his hand to his lip and felt the warmth of blood.

Rob walked away.

"What'd you say to piss him off?" he heard Joe ask Billy.

"Shut the fuck up," Billy snapped.

Rob didn't look back. His arm over Derek's shoulder, they headed down the hill toward the car in silence.

CHAPTER 11

SAM PARKED ACROSS the street from the theater at Jack London Square and followed Nick's directions to Yoshi's restaurant on the next block. Though she hadn't intended to have dinner with just Nick, it sounded like fun. Carefree, adult fun.

Something people actually did. Something as foreign to her as the families she saw laughing together over pizza in a restaurant or playing a game of Softball in the park.

She couldn't remember an evening she would describe that way. Brent had never been fun, certainly not carefree. He thought he was fun, but he was too serious really. Uptight. And now, with no practice, no skills, in the middle of a crazy case and some ridiculous taunting at work, she was supposed to have an evening of adult fun.

The thought terrified her. Sushi and jazz, Nick had said, as though they were two totally normal things for adults to do. Two things, aside from fun, that Sam knew nothing about.

Somehow she had thought maybe they would end up in a sports bar or something. Now the evening was beginning to sound like a date. Her stomach made foreign flutters and she found herself tempted to turn around and retreat to safety. Already the day had been exhausting—Corona's scolding, the picture in the file.

The picture and the note were in her purse. She would ask Nick about the photo. At least she would accomplish something if the rest of the evening was miserable. And it would give them something to talk about. Something she knew enough to talk about. Evidence, crime scenes, prints—those were the things she knew.

She looked at the front of the restaurant, and a part of her longed to go home and slip under the covers. She craved the feel of her flannel sheets and wished she'd brought an extra sweater. She was perpetually cold, the last remnant of her Southern upbringing. Everything else she'd managed to rid herself of, but the constant chill reminded her of how far she'd come, both physically and mentally.

Fastening the top button of her suit coat, she straightened the sweater she had draped over the coat and moved briskly toward the restaurant entrance. Yoshi's was a wide-open room with a small area filled with people seated in traditional Japanese style, on pillows on the floor. She wanted to look at her sock choice but held herself back, hoping they were sitting at a table.

"How may I help you?" a thin Asian woman asked as Sam entered Yoshi's.

"I'm meeting someone here." Sam scanned the room for Nick.

"The name, please."

"Nick Thomas."

The woman eyed her carefully and nodded, turning her back. But before she looked away, Sam felt ice in her look. "Follow me."

Nick sat at a table for two, tucked in a corner. He stood as Sam approached. "Thank you, Ava," he said to the Asian woman and pulled Sam's chair out for her.

"You come here often?" she asked, shaking off the added chill from Ava's stare.

"I used to—back when it was on Claremont. This is only my fourth or fifth time down here."

Sam moved awkwardly into her seat. Suddenly, she wished the boys had been able to come. She felt strange being out with Nick without it being case-related. "Any word on Lugino's toxicology?"

Nick raised an eyebrow and shook his head. "You want me to celebrate my birthday by talking about Lugino?"

Flushing, she shook her head. "I just—"

Nick leaned toward her and touched her hand. "Came back today. No signs of heroin. Traces of mari-juana, as we expected. We've got him on possession. We found some pot and paraphernalia in his car. We're hold-ing him on that. It's all we can do for now." He paused. "Now, no more shoptalk, Agent Chase."

She smiled and saluted his serious tone.

He held her gaze. "You look gorgeous."

She shook her head and found herself laughing, the stress of the day draining through her toes as she started to relax. Oh, God. Laughing. It felt so good.

"That wasn't meant to be funny."

Her laugh grew heartier. Except for Nick, Sam had no friends who weren't directly related to the Department of Justice or her boys. And even he was only slightly outside that circle. Her work and her boys, they were her life. And tonight she needed a break from that life.

"I'm glad we're doing this. I could use a fun night out, and so could you."

"That's for sure." She laid her napkin across her lap. "Hellish day at the office."

Nick smiled. "Corona on your ass about the case?"

She nodded. "You too?"

"Bad. I was serious, no work talk tonight. Deal?"

"Add Derek and Rob, and I'm in."

Nick reached his hand across the table and Sam shook it. Her craving for that drink was beginning to wear off.

The waitress arrived with a teapot and two ceramic cups.

"I ordered us green tea."

Sam exhaled, remembering her last date. It was too pathetic to think about how long she'd gone without male companionship. The date had been shortly after her divorce, before the boys had come to live with her. Her neighbor had pushed Sam to meet a young friend of hers, and finally Sam had conceded. The man had ordered a bottle of wine without her knowledge and then stared at her disbelievingly when she told him she didn't drink. Nick already knew she didn't drink—and she'd never seen him drink either.

She picked up an upright menu with pictures of the sushi and read the names out loud. "Maguro, hamachi, ebi, kappa makki." She drew out each syllable and scrunched her nose.

"You've never had sushi."

She looked at him.

He laughed. "You should've seen your face. You looked like a rookie with his first corpse."

Sam blushed. "It just looks so—"

Nick smiled. "Raw?"

"Something like that."

He pried the menu out of her hands. "I'll order for us. Do you trust me?"

The silent alarms should have sounded. This was the point when they always did. But instead she just nodded. The wild thing was, she did trust him—as much as she trusted anyone.

*

Chick Corea finished his set just before ten and Nick led Sam toward the door. The sounds still surrounded her in a soothing wave of bass and drums and saxophone. She longed to go back and listen to the second set, to keep this feeling. Anything to avoid returning to the real world. She knew that wasn't like her. She shouldn't have been thinking that way, but at that moment, prolonging the escape seemed ideal.

As they stepped onto the sidewalk, an Amtrak passenger train rumbled down Embarcadero West right in front of the restaurant, and Sam savored the sound as she had Chick Corea's music and the cinnamon jazz of Nick's own voice. She was intoxicated with the relief of setting aside everything for just a few hours. She took Nick's hand and squeezed. He held on.

When the train had passed, Nick turned to her. "What did you think of the sushi?"

"It takes some getting used to, but I think I like it."

Dropping her hand, he looped his arm in hers, pulling her close. "And the jazz?"

"Same answer, detective. I take it you've listened to jazz your whole life?"

Nick stared up at the sky as he spoke. "Never got into anything else. No disco, no rock and roll. I was the only kid in college listening to Miles instead of Mick."

He laughed and looked back at her, studying her face before speaking again.

"I was the youngest of six kids. When I was twelve, my dad died. My mom's younger brother, my Uncle Ray, used to come pick me up and take me to watch his band practice. There were six of them. All of them had nicknames. Ray was called Sunnie—like Sunnie Ray—because he had the widest smile. And his teeth were so white against his dark skin. Artie played the trombone. He wouldn't let anyone call him anything but Artie. But behind his back we called him Bear-bone. Mixer played the sax."

She laughed as they walked slowly down the street. Neither rushed. "Mixer?"

"I never did find out where that nickname came from. He worked construction, so maybe it had to do with mixing cement. The other guys were Tree and Zebra. Tree was as big as his namesake, and Zebra had two white stripes through his hair on either side of his head. Then there was Runt. He was only about five-seven and he played bass. They used to call me Runt Junior."

Sam laughed, looking up at Nick. "You?"

"I didn't grow until college. I was always the shortest

kid in school." He stopped and shook his head as though living a memory. "You should've seen Runt play the bass. Man, he was good." Nick paused. "He was killed in a knife fight when I was seventeen. The guys gave me his bass. I still play, but I'm not any good."

She touched his arm. "They played jazz?"

He nodded. "All the classic stuff—Miles, Thelonius Monk, Charlie Parker, Mingus."

"Who?"

Nick looked shocked. "You've never heard of Miles Davis?"

She shrugged. "Maybe the name."

"You haven't lived until you've heard Miles Davis. He and Chick Corea used to play together. And Thelonius Monk? You don't know Thelonius Sphere Monk?"

She shook her head.

"Wow." He smiled. "You've come to the right place, then. I'll get you up to speed in no time. Sometime you can come check out my vinyl collection. I'll play you some of my favorites."

His energy radiated through Sam and she felt herself giggle. How long had it been since she'd giggled? Had she ever? Sam could feel the cool bay wind, and she pulled her coat around her neck. Nick stopped her and, turning her to face him, began to button her coat for her. She shivered.

"You're out here freezing and you've got your sweater tied around your neck," he scolded.

"It's too cold to take my coat off to put it on underneath."

Nick shook his head and touched her cheek, pulling her close.

Cars passed on the street as people filed out of the nightclub, moving in a blur of color and words. Sam didn't hear anything they said, didn't see anyone clearly.

Instead, her every neuron was focused on Nick. The way the blue lights from the window reflected off his skin, the light stubble of his beard, the golden hazel of his eyes that looked green in the cast of the lights. His chest pressed against hers and she felt his lips touch her ear. Then her cheek. She felt him coming close, nearing her mouth. She felt a wave of excitement and then apprehension. He barely touched her, his lips only brushing against hers. And then it was over and she suddenly longed for more.

"Do you want to come by my apartment hear a couple of those albums I was talking about?" he whispered.

Without speaking, she nodded. She did want to go. She just didn't trust herself to say it out loud.

"Really?"

She nodded again, forcing her feet to move alongside his. But she didn't want to move. She didn't want to leave. Unwilling to return to reality even to drive, she longed to remain in his arms, right there on that street. "Where are you parked?" she asked.

He shook his head. "I got a ride over."

"Why?"

He grinned. "I lost my car keys."

Sam laughed. "Again?"

He nodded as they headed together to her car.

"Here, then, but don't lose them," she said, handing him her keys.

He looked puzzled. "You want me to drive?"

With a quick breath, she nodded.

Nick closed his hands on the keys and narrowed his gaze. "You're sure?"

Settling her mouth around the words that she wanted to come out, she said, "Just a couple of albums, then I'll go home."

He nodded slowly. "Okay. I'd love to play a couple for you."

*

On the drive, Sam leaned back and let the music replay in her mind. Since she'd stopped drinking, nothing but reading had allowed her to escape. Night was the time when she missed alcohol most. Being able to relax enough to not worry, to get a full night's sleep without waking up hour after hour and fretting about the past and the future and the hundred other things that ran through her brain.

The photo came to mind again, and she knew she should tell Nick. But she didn't want to think about it, let alone talk about it. Not now. Not when things were so perfect. He would worry, and she didn't want that either. Tonight she just wanted to enjoy him.

Even with Brent before the divorce, she'd kept her concerns to herself. It wasn't part of their arrangement. She kept up the appearance of perfection—inside and out. And he took care of all their physical needs—house, food, cars. There weren't supposed to be emotional needs. She was a cop, for God's sake. Cops didn't have emotions.

The way Sam saw it, Brent's marrying a cop had been his way of stretching to the limit. He was sophisticated, high class, and she was in law enforcement. Look how unusual he was, how open-minded. She just wasn't the typical doctor's wife. And yet she still cleaned up well.

Marrying a beautiful cop made him seem deeper. And then there were all the great jokes with his buddies about what it was like to tame a rough one. She'd overheard that more than once. But Brent had very little sex drive—which had been fine with her. They never discussed anything emotional, never reached beyond the surface.

His definition of being a doctor was treating physical ailments. He didn't know or care what was going on in her brain. Not until he realized that she was damaged goods.

"What are you thinking about?"

Sam started. "Nothing."

"I thought you said you trusted me."

Sam turned to meet his gaze and nodded. "I do."

He raised his eyebrows.

"I was thinking about something in the past," she said, somehow unable to stop herself from speaking.

The two sides of her were at war—the one urging her to keep it all inside, the other demanding that she be truthful and not screw up her one friendship.

"Is there something about the past you want to tell me?"

She shook her head.

Nick didn't push. They pulled off at the Concord Avenue exit, into the thick of strip malls, gas stations, and video stores. Slowly the area became residential. He continued four blocks before turning left down Bonifacio Street toward Baldwin Park and then taking a right into his apartment complex.

Sam grabbed her purse and got out of the car. Nick took her hand and led her to his door. "It might be messy."

She nodded, unable to speak above the pounding of her heart. He opened the door and flipped on a light.

She wandered in a slow circle, surveying her surroundings with the same caution she used on a crime scene. The room was practically empty. A folded futon and a TV sat in one corner. Next to the TV was a stereo with a turntable and cartons of albums. "There must be three hundred here."

"Five hundred and thirty-six. Most of them were Ray's."

Sunnie Ray, she thought, smiling. "You can't get this stuff on CDs?"

"Sure you can. But do you know how much it would cost to replace this collection?"

A chair and an old bass sat across the room. She walked toward them and ran her hand over the polished wood. "Runt's?"

He nodded.

"Not much furniture," Sam commented.

"Sheila took most of it. I never got around to getting any more."

She caught his eye, but saw no feeling there. Perhaps he felt like she did about her divorce. She didn't miss Brent at all. The last name Chase was the only thing she'd kept from the relationship. And that was only because she'd sworn that she'd never be an Everett again.

She dropped her purse on the floor and turned to the one other door in the place. It was half open, and she stepped forward, glancing inside. The bedroom. She caught sight of a double bed with a plaid comforter, a chest of drawers, and a small bedside table. She backed up quickly, but Nick was standing right behind her. They collided and Nick caught her arm, righting her and quickly letting go. They laughed awkwardly. "Sorry."

"That's the bedroom."

She nodded and turned her back to it, taking a few steps away. She rubbed her hands together and looked at the blank white walls. Everything about the place felt lonely.

Nick crossed the room and knelt at the stereo, selecting an album and setting it on the turntable.

Sam walked slowly around the small room, glancing into the kitchen, where one dish sat in the sink. Nick was wrong. It wasn't messy.

When the sound of a low horn started, Sam froze, unsure whether to stand still or run away and hide. Her palms felt moist and her legs and chest shook. She was cold but hot, dizzy but clearheaded.

Nick stepped out of his shoes and reached his hand out to her.

She stared at it and then shook her head. "I can't dance," she said, breathless.

"You'll be perfect."

She felt the wings of a million butterflies in her belly.

Exhaling, she let herself put her hand in his, let him pull her close, let her body mold against his.

"I really should be going home soon—"

"We have all the time in the world. Whatever it is, Sam—whatever happened in your past, I'm willing to wait. But you have to trust me." He tapped her head lightly with two fingers. "You have to tell me what's going on in there."

She tucked her head into his chest and squeezed her eyes closed. If it were only that easy. She had spent eighteen years fighting to be independent, only to fall into the trap of what she thought was a caring man. It had almost killed her—the drinking, the desire to die. She had been that close. Only the job had pulled her through.

Then she'd gotten the boys and gone to the Department of Justice and things had become stable, even comfortable. She loved those boys. They had needed her and she took care of them. It had been simple when they were young. But now, with Rob misbehaving, it was becoming tougher.

Nick's arms tightened around her and she yielded to the comfort of his strength. She wanted to believe she could trust him.

But what if she was wrong? What if he was another Brent? She couldn't take that again. She wouldn't.

CHAPTER 12

GERRY CROUCHED IN the dark along the side of the house, waiting for the little girl to come to bed. He had a perfect view of her room. He'd first seen her with little Molly down the street, the one whose mother was dead. It made him smile. Any mother who would hurt her little girl deserved what she got. He thought about his own sister and how beautiful she was. He'd never let anyone hurt her. He would never hurt kids. He loved them—he would love them forever. He grew at the thought of getting a chance to love the little girl inside the house.

But the best part was that he'd found Sam Chase. She had come here that same day. He'd been following her for two whole days now. He'd been to her building. And he'd seen her house.

He felt like he was even getting lucky, and he knew if he found the right time, Sam would help him get back to prison. He just had to do things exactly right.

Everything was better since he'd figured out that the old lady downstairs left the keys to her car tucked above the sun visor. The car was as old as she was, but she parked it down the street from their building and almost never used it. She wouldn't miss it in the dark, and the way he figured it, the worst that could happen was they would send him back to prison. He just hoped he could get Sam Chase to do it. He wanted to go back to the same place, see Wally again.

He had wanted to follow Sam Chase yesterday afternoon, too, but the old lady had taken her car before he could get it. Probably better, too. If she'd found out it was gone, then he'd have been in big trouble.

This morning, he'd been up at four and had found money in his neighbor's laundry downstairs—eight dollars, so he'd had a good breakfast. He wasn't sleeping much, but the pills he'd found in the old lady's glove box made him feel better.

The light came on in the room, and Gerry ducked down. The Levelor blinds were bent in one corner, so he could see in perfectly.

"Get in your pajamas," someone called.

Gerry thought it was her mother.

The little girl stomped around her room, ignoring her mother's request. It made Gerry smile. She was independent. He liked her.

He'd seen her on the street earlier. There were a lot of kids on this street, but she was the best. She wore tight pink leggings and a T-shirt that was a little too short. She still had a belly. He loved that. And those pigtails.

He shifted against the building, pressing himself against the hard shingles as he watched her.

A fat, ugly woman appeared at the door, hands on her hips.

He dropped down into the corner, but he knew she wouldn't see him. He was invisible to her. He was always invisible to the parents.

Only smart people like Sam Chase would discover him.

"Whitney Anne, you get in your pajamas this minute."

Just then a little boy came running into the room, making a horrible moaning sound.

Whitney covered her ears, and so did he. But the fat woman picked up the boy and took him away, closing Whitney's door.

He watched her turn her head and stick out her tongue at the door, and he covered his mouth to keep from laughing. She was perfect.

Whitney. What a wonderful name. He couldn't wait to get the chance to talk to her.

Someone yelled something again and Whitney stomped across the room toward the dresser and began to take her clothes off.

Turn toward me, he thought. Turn and look at me.

But she didn't. He watched her bare shoulders and the way her hair cascaded across her ivory skin. She was beautiful.

Just then a door slammed and he heard someone outside talking.

He took a last look at beautiful Whitney and ducked down.

The voices got closer, and he knew they were coming to the side of the house. He thought about getting back to prison and then about Whitney again. Maybe he wasn't ready. Not quite yet. Wally would wait, but Whitney—he had to see her again.

CHAPTER 13

MOVING IN SLOW circles across the floor of his apartment, Nick held Sam as Thelonius Monk brought the song to a close. He wondered what she was thinking about, what her dreams were. So many things about her were a mystery: her bold, ruthless manner with criminals, her soft vulnerability when he held her.

She was hiding something. He wanted to shake it out of her, to command her to spill it. One thing was clear: Sam Chase wasn't used to relying on anyone. He could see that. If he wanted to be a part of her life, he knew he'd have to give her time. He just hated to think how long it might take.

He leaned back and met her eyes. Their faces only inches apart, he paused, giving her a chance to pull away. When she didn't, he leaned forward to kiss her.

He longed to pick her up and drag her into the bedroom, to tear her clothes off. Instead, he kissed her gently, holding her close. He could smell her soap, like flowers, light enough that only when he held her did he get a scent of it. He came closer, holding her mouth to his—

She stepped away.

He was suddenly confused. "What—"

She touched her lips and turned away. "It's late."

What had happened? What had he done? He had pushed too much. Damn.

"I should get home. I've got some stuff to do early, and I want to be there when the boys wake up."

He watched her brow furrow as she ran her fingers through her hair. The vulnerable, soft Sam was gone. The window he'd seen open had slammed shut, and she was self-sufficient again.

He should be happy. Sheila had been too dependent. He'd always told himself that if he fell for someone else, it would be someone strong and independent. He just wished Sam would let him in a little.

She stepped away from him and straightened her coat, looking like a girl caught by her parents in the backseat of a car.

He wanted to laugh, but he wished there was something he could do to stop her from running. Instead, he didn't move.

"There's something I need to tell you about. I didn't want to ruin the evening, but I need to show you."

He rubbed his face, trying to pull his mind back to business. "What is it?"

"It's a picture of me."

"What do you mean?"

"I'll show you."

He watched her cross the room and felt as though the temperature had just dropped twenty degrees. He tried to put his mind off the feel of her in his arms. Why the hell did everything have to be so damn complicated?

She pulled a small manila envelope from her purse and walked back, her arm outstretched. "Don't touch it."

Nick opened the envelope and looked in. He met her gaze. "What is this?"

"I found it in a file that had been missing."

He walked across the room, his mind on track again. Frustrated, he slid the picture onto the table and used the corner of the envelope to flip it right side up. It was a candid shot of her, and the first thing that struck him was how beautiful she was. Damn, he wanted to kiss her again. But in the center of her forehead, someone had made a red splash. It was meant to look like blood. He looked up at her.

Her gaze met his, her eyes narrow and unhappy. "I need you to run prints on it."

"When did this happen?"

"I found it this morning." She pulled out a standard envelope and handed it to him. "This came yesterday."

He took it and emptied it onto the desk beside the picture. It was a pink message slip with a message written in caps. *You're not invincible.* Jesus. Nick ran a hand through his hair and looked up from the threats. "Yesterday?"

She tucked in her shirt and straightened her shoulders, then nodded.

He stepped forward and took her hand. "You should have told me sooner. Are you okay?"

"Of course. I'm fine," she snapped.

He held her hand and tried to soften his tone, but he

was frustrated. "I want you to trust me. I wish you had brought this to me when it happened. Maybe we could have already stopped it."

She shook her head. "Please don't, Nick. I'm doing the best I can. It's been crazy. I am trusting you. I brought them here tonight."

"Are you telling me all of it?" The words came out in a flash, and she flinched as though he'd stung her.

She shook her head and turned toward the door. "I'm supposed to trust you, but you treat me like a child." She snatched her purse and swung it over her shoulder.

He grabbed her as she reached the door. "I'm sorry. I didn't mean it that way. I'm just worried, is all."

She faced the door. "I just need you to check it for prints. It's probably a prank. Corona didn't think it was a big deal. He thought I should just forget about it, but I don't find it amusing."

He held himself from touching her. "No. It's not funny. I'll get them to the lab first thing."

She looked up and met his gaze.

He felt his gut tighten.

"Thanks."

He kept his lips closed, wishing she would give him a sign, something that said it was okay.

She turned her back and pulled the door open.

"Thanks for the birthday dinner," he said as she moved out of the apartment.

She smiled, not meeting his gaze, and he wondered what the hell was going through her mind. "It was fun."

He watched her turn her back again and walk to her car. He should have taken her out, opened the door for her. But he couldn't move. Instead, he watched her get in, start the car, and give him a quick, friendly wave as she pulled away from the curb.

Shutting the door, he let out a string of curses and then walked into his bedroom. What had he done? Where had the mood been broken?

He pictured her high cheekbones, her wide, oval green eyes, the feel of her fingers through his shirt. He thought he was going to burst. Why in the hell couldn't he date someone normal? Hell, he'd had offers. There were normal women out there. And they would pick him. But he wanted Sam Chase. Damn, did he want her.

He crossed into the bathroom and leaned over the sink, staring into the basin, wishing he could banish her from his head, and at the same time wishing he could understand her. He turned on the tap and splashed his face with cold water. He looked into the mirror and saw her full lips. Shaking his head, he moved to the shower and turned it on.

"Damn," he said again.

*

After a crappy night's sleep, Nick spent the next morning talking to Sandi Walters' neighbors. No one had seen Lugino the night she was killed. But Wendy Mayes had sworn Sandi was picked up at the house that night. Who the hell had the gall to pick her up from her home and then take her off and kill her? It was possible that Lugino had been here and the neighbors just hadn't seen him. But his Skylark had a loose muffler, and it would be hard for everyone to miss the noise.

One neighbor said she'd heard the motorcycle that belonged to the neighbor two doors down from the Walters. "Justin Rapozo's the kid's name," she explained. "Runs that thing at all hours."

"You're sure it wasn't a car?" he asked. A cracked muffler might make Lugino's car sound a lot like a motorcycle.

She shook her head. "I saw it whiz by. Same thing every time. Likes to rev the engine right at my house. Show off to whatever chicky he's got on back," the woman had said.

The case should've been closed. They had their man. They had his semen, evidence he'd been with Sandi that night.

But Nick hadn't come up with a drop of evidence of motive for James Lugino as the killer. Sandi had no money, so it wasn't greed. She was seeing only Lugino, so it shouldn't have been a jealous rage. He had a history of drugs, but no history of violence. Why the hell would he strangle her? Nick just couldn't get it to add up.

And then there was the matter of the one thumbprint they had found on her shoulder. It wasn't Lugino's. It was possible it was the first cop's. He might have touched her to see if she was alive. It was a common rookie mistake. Nick had touched evidence he shouldn't have on more than one occasion.

Or maybe the print belonged to someone who had happened by. They were running the print against the cop's now. If it wasn't his, they might never find out whose it was.

Nick drove down A Street in Antioch and crossed the railroad tracks, turning down Railroad Avenue and up to the familiar dive. Alf's all-night diner. The chipped off-white paint had streaks of yellow from the rusted gutters that lined the dilapidated roof. The windows were clouded and streaked after years of kitchen grease layered on without washing. A faded chalkboard resting against the inside window displayed specials that never changed. The inconspicuous appearance of the diner made it a good meeting place, though Nick had never ordered anything other than coffee. Even the water seemed strangely brown. He tried not to think about that water in his coffee.

Pulling his car to the curb to park, Nick carefully avoided the biggest of the potholes. He looked down at the dash clock. He was right on time. He hoped his contact didn't no-show. Guy should've learned after last time. Civic duty and all that.

Nick took his last clean breath of air and walked inside, wishing he had a filter to breathe through. A full-bodied black woman in a short dull-yellow gingham dress pointed him toward the back of the restaurant. "Wherever you want, Sugar."

Nick scanned the room for his contact. When he didn't see him, he made his way to a back booth under a fan and carefully scanned the table's surface for residue from someone's meal before putting his elbows on it. The waitress brought coffee and left him alone. He doubted that she remembered him from the last time, but maybe there was something in his expression that said "only coffee."

Three minutes later Dougie Harris came through the door. Deep blue shadows beneath his eyes, and he was thinner than the last time Nick had seen him. He wore unhemmed cords that dragged under the heels of a pair of battered Vans. His button-down was untucked, the cuffs hanging over his thumbs. He walked stooped over, one hand dragging at his side, the other latched onto his belt buckle to hold his pants up. He was nineteen years old, but he had the posture of someone about seventy. Nick wondered if he had AIDS.

Dougie slid into the booth and nodded in his direction.

"You okay?"

Dougie nodded his head in affirmation. "Hungry," he said, the word barely a whisper.

Nick signaled to the waitress. He didn't want Dougie dying on him right here at the table. It would be difficult to explain what Nick was doing with a dealer on his day off, especially a dead dealer. "Bring him four eggs scrambled, hashbrowns, a short stack of pancakes, and a double side of bacon," he told the waitress.

Dougie made an attempt at a smile and settled back against the cushion. From the look of it, he'd lost another tooth, too.

"You been tested lately?"

Dougie closed his eyes and shook his head.

"You should, you know. You're sick."

Without opening his eyes, he said, "Fine."

Nick wanted to ask his questions and get out of there, but Dougie didn't look strong enough to answer them yet. Nick settled for watching the door and sipping his toxic coffee to save himself from boredom.

Dougie finished the food Nick had ordered and then,

in a more energetic voice, told the waitress to bring him apple pie a la mode for dessert. Nick wasn't sure where Dougie put all that food, but watching him scarf it down had given Nick indigestion.

When the waitress returned with the pie, Nick took the check and pushed his coffee aside. "Enjoy the breakfast?"

"Yeah, man. Thanks."

"I've got some questions."

Dougie nodded.

Nick pulled Lugino's picture from his pocket. "You sell to him?"

Dougie took the picture and stared at it. "I see him around."

"What's his poison?"

Dougie gave the picture back and took a bite of pie, dipping the end of it into the ice cream before shoving the whole thing in his mouth. "Crank," he said with his mouth full.

Nick got an eyeful of melted ice cream and chewed-up pie. "That it?"

"Some Mary Jane." He shrugged. "That's it."

"You deal any heroin?"

"Naw, man. That shit's bad news."

"Don't bullshit me," Nick snapped.

"I'm telling you straight, man. I don't do Horse."

"You know someone?"

Dougie looked at him and nodded. "I know someone."

Nick slid Lugino's picture back to Dougie, facedown. "I need to know if my man bought some. I need the information fast." He pointed to his cell phone number written on the back of the photocopied picture. "You call me here." Nick took the check and stood up. "You find anything out and there will be a little something for you. But I need someone I can talk to. Confirmation, you know?"

Dougie tucked the picture in his pocket and returned his attention to dessert.

Nick paid the check at the register, leaving a generous tip for the waitress. As soon as he got outside, he realized he didn't have his keys.

He ran back to the table where Dougie was still eating. The keys were nowhere in sight. Nick put his hand out. "Keys."

Dougie looked at him and then grinned, pulling the keys out from under the table. "I thought it was a gift. I could use a ride."

"Yeah, right." Nick left again, tossing his keys. There ought to be a better way to keep track of the damn things. Maybe he'd get one of those cars with the security access code. He would be able to remember a code. It was just keeping track of the damn keys that made him crazy.

Dougie should be back to him within a day or two, but probably not sooner. Nick had somehow hoped that Dougie would say he sold Lugino the heroin. It was stupid thinking on his part, but he would've liked to be able to go back to the station with something.

He headed for Mt. Diablo, intending to have another talk with the neighbors closest to the scene. He flipped on the radio and heard an old Miles Davis song. "Damn." His plan for the day had been to do anything to keep himself from thinking about Sam. It had worked up to now.

He didn't need the kind of aggravation Sam presented. She wouldn't tell him what had happened in her past, but it didn't take a Ph.D. to guess. She'd been raped or abused. He knew she'd been married once. Maybe it was that guy. It was hard to picture her letting some guy beat her up, but wasn't it always?

And marriages took a toll no matter how they ended. He knew all about that. He'd told himself he wouldn't fail Sheila. He would protect her from whatever came their way. But it turned out she'd found a better protector. He hadn't been good enough or available enough or sensitive enough or some damn thing. She wanted children and he couldn't support the kind of life she wanted. That was her last argument. He had wanted children, too. Too damn bad. She was divorcing Nick so she could marry Stephen and have his kids.

Was he doing it all over again with Sam? Trying to protect her when she didn't want his protection? He should walk away. He needed to walk away. Instead, he found himself picturing the sprinkled freckles across her nose, her full lips, the glimpse of her legs whenever she wore a skirt. All of it was torture. Plus, there were Rob and Derek.

He loved those kids. Hell, Derek was quiet, but he knew every damn Van Morrison song by heart—the album, the words, the year. And he had collected some unbelievable albums. And Rob was a great kid, too. He loved baseball almost as much as Nick did. He knew the stats, the players. Why wasn't it easier? Where was the boy likes girl, girl likes boy? Gone before puberty. And if life didn't confuse everything, Sam Chase certainly liked to add to the complication.

Now, from a hill near the crime scene, Nick watched the sky fade to scarlet and then orange and pink and finally dark. After the show was over, he started his car again and drove around, trying to clear his thoughts—on the case, on Sam. None of it had become clearer—in fact, it was more jumbled, if anything. His lights caught the reflections of families driving home together in minivans and sport utility vehicles. He should be home too. But he didn't want to go home. There was nothing for him there.

CHAPTER 14

SAM ENTERED HER office, ready to settle in. She had too many thoughts spinning around in her head and she was praying for a day of only work. She pulled her Glock from its holster, unlocked her top drawer, and set the gun inside before relocking it. Shivering, she stooped down and flipped on the space heater under her desk. A buzz cracked and a burst of electrical heat shot through her finger.

"Shit." She jumped back as sparks flew from the machine, then flames. Smoke funneled out from under her desk, and she ran for the wall where the extinguisher was kept. It was gone. "Damn it!" she yelled.

Moving quickly, she kicked the plug from the socket and turned toward the door.

Aaron was perched on his chair.

"The damn heater exploded, and my extinguisher's gone."

"I'll get the hall extinguisher." Aaron spun around and took a fire extinguisher off a wall hook outside her office. Pulling the plastic tab, he motioned Sam to stand back as he sprayed thick white foam under her desk. The fire dissipated quickly, but not before setting off the overhead alarms. Sam waited for the sprinklers to start, but they didn't.

No one on the floor headed for the exits, though. Instead, a crowd gathered in front of Sam's office door. Ignoring them, she cursed and moved to open the windows, hoping to clear the smoke.

Aaron waved his arms at the crowd. "Party's over, folks."

"The invincible Sam Chase," someone said.

Sam spun around, furious, thinking of the message slip someone had left in her office. "Who said that?"

Several people turned back, but no one took credit. Instead, the crowd moved away in a thick pack like the smoke streaming from under her desk.

She turned to Aaron. "Who said that?"

Aaron shrugged. "It's a nickname. They all call you that."

"Why?"

Aaron glanced at the empty doorway.

"Why do they call me that?"

Aaron slouched a bit. "Sam, you're a tough personality. You demand a lot from people—some would say nothing less than perfection. Not me. I love working with you. But a lot of people think you're full of yourself, that you think you're perfect."

"But invincible?"

Aaron smiled. "Among other things. Don't take it too hard. Everyone's got a nickname. You should hear what they call Williams."

Sam picked up the notes on her desk and used some tissue to wipe the thick white foam into the trash. She worked with brisk, hard strokes, trying to funnel her anger into something more useful and failing.

"Here, let me clean that up." Aaron returned with some paper towels and rags and began to clean off her desk. "Facilities is coming up with someone to clean the rug and clear away the heater. I'll order a new one."

"I don't want another one. And I don't want facilities taking this one. I want someone to look at it."

"It probably just shorted. It can happen."

She nodded, not mentioning her missing extinguisher, but she wasn't convinced.

*

At almost five-thirty, Aaron rolled into Sam's office and stopped in front of her desk.

"Hey," Sam said, forcing a smile.

"I haven't seen you this glum since Williams beat you in the annual gun tests."

Sam frowned. "Well, I'm ten times better than he is."

Aaron smiled. "You haven't said much all day. Something I can help with?"

Sam looked around the office she had once felt so confident in. She shook her head. "Just busy with this case. You should get out of here. Don't you have some training to do? You've got what, three weeks?"

"Twenty-five days and counting. I'm training six days. I swam this morning. I use a float on my feet and I do the butterfly—for about thirty minutes twice a week. Builds the arm muscles fast." He flexed.

"I'll say." She smiled and felt her chest relax. "Reminds me how great you are."

Aaron lowered his arm and turned the chair toward the door. "Thanks," he said, grinning. "If you're sure you don't need me…"

She waved him out. "Positive."

Settling back into her chair, she opened her drawer and pulled out her date book. There, in the section most people used for addresses, she had an alphabetical index of all her homicide cases. Each case had its own page, filled with her tiny block handwriting, including the location of the scene, the police and detectives working the case.

When she'd worked homicide, she'd kept a detailed journal of her cases—it was the closest she'd ever come to keeping a diary. Every day, she wrote the status of the case, her impressions of the people she'd spoken with, any detail anyone could recall that related to the case. There was nothing official about what was written and she had never told anyone what she kept there.

Sometimes, when a case wasn't moving, she would curl up in bed and read the journal as though it were a novel. The scene would draw itself in her mind, the images and characters coming alive, as in any good book. She sometimes got her best ideas that way. She wished she'd done the same with her abuse cases—but the numbers had been too high, the volume of work too overwhelming, not to mention the disruption in her life when the boys came.

Still, she hadn't scrapped the idea altogether. Now, instead of a detailed journal, she kept her date book. In it she wrote appointments and a to-do list on the left side and everything about whatever case she'd worked that day on the right. The eight years' worth of notes were in a labeled binder beside her homicide one at the back of a bookshelf in her house. The notes went far beyond the minimal reporting that was required in the job, but they'd never come close to making her feel as though she gave each case her all.

She flipped to the current week and scanned the names, dates, and clues about Sandi Walters that she had entered the day before. She flipped back to the notes on Sloan and stared at them again. Then, on a fresh sheet, she wrote the two cases down side by side. She couldn't find the common denominator. No, that wasn't true. She couldn't find the common denominator other than herself. There had to be something else she was missing. She focused on Molly Walters again, searching for something new. Her old binders from the Sloan case were at home. She would have to look through those, too.

Molly Walters had been brought to her attention after a visit from her paternal grandparents in the fall of '98. The grandparents, who lived in Oregon, had been concerned because the girl was rail-thin and bruised. It had been a difficult case to try.

None of them were easy—children rarely wanted to see their parents get in trouble. And if it weren't the irrational devotion to a parent, it was the threat of later consequences. She thought back on her own parents.

No one had ever questioned her father. She couldn't imagine what she would have told someone had they come to her. She remembered, even until the day she left, how desperately she wanted him to look at her once and say he was proud. But he couldn't.

When she got old enough to keep him away—by staying out late, sleeping in the same room as Polly, or rigging ways to lock her door—he didn't even look her in the eye. She always blamed herself—worried that he didn't look at her because he was so disgusted with her. Only now, with nearly twenty years of hindsight, did she realize that it wasn't about her at all. He was only frustrated that she had grown big enough to keep him away.

And she wished she'd been able to keep Molly Walters away from her mother. The judge had ruled in their favor, but the sentence was only a paltry eight weeks of counseling for Sandi and Molly. It was a typical run through the courts, especially for first-timers. It would have taken at least two, probably three, appearances in court before Sandi Walters would have lost custody of her child. Sam wondered how much better the grandmother, Wendy Mayes, would have been.

She continued to make notes about each of the last few days, commenting in as much detail as she could squeeze onto the compact page. Her mind drifted over the bloodstained photo. She didn't write that down. Although it seemed otherwise, she reminded herself that this case wasn't about her. It was about Sandi Walters and maybe someone who had known Charlie Sloan.

But there was no denying that someone was purposefully tying Sam to this case. The question was why. Why kill the woman she had prosecuted for abuse? Why copy the M.O. of the killer she had tracked and caught? She had no answers.

She wished she could stop her mind from returning to Nick, but her train of thought had already taken her to the other night. She'd behaved terribly. No one would blame him if he never wanted to see her again.

And as much as she would have liked to shut him out and turn away, a part of her longed to see him.

Why hadn't she just kissed him? Let him kiss her? She had wanted to. And yet, when he was close, when his lips were on hers, she'd felt her chest tighten until she couldn't breathe. She'd lost control. She couldn't lose control. For all those years, she'd been warning herself not to lose control.

Nick was the one thing in her life that had the potential to be wonderful at the moment. Her job was going okay, but not great. The boys were tough right now. And then there was this case.

Like a child after too much sugar, she'd been antsy and excited ever since their dinner, laughing over something he'd said, or listening to jazz on the car radio, wanting to ask questions about one artist or another, wondering what interesting facts Nick would offer about them. He had told her about Django, the musician who invented Gypsy jazz, who had taught himself to play all over again after being badly burned in a fire. Sam thought momentarily about Derek, wishing he'd been able to teach himself to run again.

Laying her hands flat against the desk, she pulled her chair in close until she was up against the wood surface. She spread her files out and turned her attention to work. The case, Rob's recent escapades, her involvement with Nick—all of it had thrown her work off track. She didn't need to spend more time thinking about things that wouldn't be. She needed to work.

In the quiet of the after-hours office, she returned phone calls, prepared her paperwork to be filed by Aaron the following day, cleaned off her desk, and even got through several of the reports put out by government agencies on crime statistics in the state of California. She bundled up the charred space heater to take it with her, then realized it was almost six-thirty and she hadn't heard from the boys.

They knew she was working late and she'd left a note telling them to cook a frozen pizza. Still, Derek normally called to check in. She glanced over the boys' activity schedule she kept on her computer with Aaron's help and then lifted the receiver to dial.

The line was dead. She clicked on the receiver. No dial tone.

Just then, the lights in the hall went off.

CHAPTER 15

NICK WAS TIRED. His day had passed slowly and without any progress on the case. Captain Cintrello had ordered the release of James Lugino for the homicide, and he'd probably walk on the possession charge. Cintrello also told Nick that someone was suing the state on behalf of Charlie Sloan. The D.A.'s office was fighting it on the basis that this killer was a copycat and Sloan was the real killer. Problem was, the copycat had access to inside information, and the D.A. needed to know how the information had been obtained in order to argue against the suit.

"You'd better figure out who the hell did that shit and fast, Nick," his captain had warned. "If they gather enough evidence to prove that this department executed the wrong man, we're going to get slaughtered in the press." Nick knew that in a sheriffs office, where everyone was elected, bad media attention even a year from an election could cost the whole department their jobs—from sheriff right on down.

It was five-thirty now, and he decided to drop by

Sam's house, hoping to catch her to talk. He rang the bell and Rob came racing to the door. "I'm glad you're here. Derek's sick. He's been lying on the couch, moaning. I don't know what to do."

Nick followed Rob through the kitchen into the living room.

Derek lay across one couch, a blanket pulled to his chin.

"Sick?"

Derek's eyes fluttered open and he shifted slightly.

Nick looked at Rob. "He go to school?"

Rob nodded. "He just came home and collapsed. He looks pale, doesn't he? Man, you think it's contagious?"

Nick knelt beside Derek and pressed his hand to the boy's forehead. "Derek?"

Derek's eyes opened.

"How do you feel?"

"Lousy," he whispered.

"You've got a fever. Tell me what hurts."

Derek's Adam's apple bobbed. "My throat mostly. I'm tired. Everything hurts."

Nick turned to Rob. "You have a thermometer?"

"I'm sure Aunt Sam does, but I don't know. I could check."

"Show me where she keeps the medical stuff."

Rob led Nick down a hall past the boys' rooms. It was as far as he'd ever been in the house and he suddenly felt like he was trespassing. Rob opened the door to Sam's room and went in. Nick found himself pausing at the threshold and taking stock of the room. It was white and simple.

Several Guy Buffet prints, including the famous one with the Buena Vista restaurant at the corner of Powell and Bay in San Francisco's North Beach, decorated the walls. The bed was queen-sized with a thick dark denim comforter, and he could just see the tops of navy flannel sheets. He resisted the temptation to run his fingers across them.

The room could as easily have been a man's room as a woman's. But everything about it spoke of comfort. A pile of books was stacked in perfect order on each of the bedside tables. He walked by them and glanced at the titles. *Corelli's Mandolin, Snow Falling on Cedars, Under the Tuscan Sun.*

Most were titles he'd never heard of. One had fallen to the side of the bed. He glanced down at it: *The Teenage Jungle: A Parent's Guide to Survival.* He imagined Sam in her sheets reading to try to understand her nephews. On the floor beside the bed was a thick brown folder with pockets labeled A-Z. He saw a coupon for Palmolive dish soap sticking out of the "D" pocket and smiled to himself.

"I found the medical supply kit, but there's no thermometer."

Nick followed Rob into the small bathroom off Sam's room. Rob had the medicine cabinet open and had pulled down a red plastic kit with the Red Cross emblem on it. He'd also emptied two small cosmetic bags, and the contents of all three were piled on the floor.

"No thermometer in here, and I don't know where else it would be."

Nick nodded. "I'll look up here." He stood and ran

his finger along each shelf. The contents were perfectly lined, labels front. He couldn't imagine anyone keeping a medicine cabinet so neat, but the image of Sam lining up the bottles made him smile.

There wasn't a single prescription drug, but she had every type of cold medicine from children's Dimetapp to Theraflu and Alka Seltzer. Most of the packages remained unopened. In a canister on the second shelf, he found gauze scissors and two thermometers. "Got it."

He pulled a thermometer from the hard plastic case, shaking the mercury down as he carried it and the Tylenol back to Derek in the living room.

Rob trailed behind, almost on Nick's heels. The boy's concern was evident in his wide eyes and frazzled pace.

"Derek, we're going to take your temperature," Nick said, sitting on the edge of the couch. Slipping the thermometer under Derek's tongue, he glanced at his watch.

"How long does it take?" Rob asked.

"About a minute." He motioned to Sam's room.

"Why don't you get the stuff in Sam's room put away. By the time you get back, he'll be ready to go."

Rob nodded and headed back into Sam's bedroom.

Nick ran his hand through Derek's hair, remembering being sick as a kid. His house was always so full, there was hardly ever a quiet spot to go. He shared a bedroom with two brothers until they both left home. But when someone was sick, his mother always set up quarantine in the living room. Except when someone was sick, the room was strictly for adults, its old door pulled closed to the constant mess of six children.

Nick read the mercury as 102 degrees. He passed the thermometer to Derek to let him read it.

"One-oh-two."

Derek handed it to Rob, who twisted it back and forth in the light. "Wow, that's pretty high."

Nick nodded. "Not too bad, but we should call Sam."

Rob got up and found the phone.

"Are you allergic to anything, Derek?"

He shook his head.

"Do you ever take Tylenol?"

He nodded. "Sometimes."

Nick opened the bottle and shook out two tablets.

"The *Exile on Main Street* album is great," Derek said.

Nick smiled. "I'm glad you like it. They recorded that one in France when Mick Taylor was still in the band."

Derek nodded. "Yeah, they rented some chateau because they couldn't go back to England because of tax problems."

Nick was always amazed at how much Derek knew about music. "I'll look forward to hearing it again when you're better," he said.

"She's not answering," Rob said, returning to the room with a glass of water. "I left a message. She checks them pretty often, I think. Maybe she's on her way home."

Helping Derek up, Nick gave the boy the tablets and then water to wash them down.

Derek sank back on the couch.

"You think you could eat something?"

Derek shrugged.

"I'll heat up some soup and you can just eat it when

you feel up to it. You need a lot of liquids—juice, soup, whatever you can handle."

"I'd like some juice."

"I think there's some in the freezer," Rob said. "I'll make it."

"I'll be right back, Derek," Nick said. "You call if you need us."

Derek nodded, and Nick stood up and headed into the kitchen. As he and Rob worked side by side, heating soup and making juice, Nick found himself settling into the feel of Sam's house. He watched Rob pour the frozen concentrate into a pitcher, splashing the red juice on his white T-shirt.

"Oh, man."

Nick smiled and put his arm around Rob.

"It's my favorite shirt."

"It'll come out."

Rob flipped on a radio beside the microwave, and Nick caught the familiar sound of John Coltrane.

"You always listen to jazz in here?"

"Aunt Sam's all into this station now."

Nick smiled and worked to Coltrane, listening for the sound of Sam's car as though it were the most natural thing in the world that he should be in her house, making dinner with her boys.

As he cranked open a can of soup, he felt the familiar buzz of his pager. Lifting it off his belt, he stared down at the number. His captain. He crossed behind Rob and picked up the phone, dialing the station as he put his beeper back on his belt.

"Cintrello. Thomas here," he told the clerk who answered.

"Thomas." Cintrello sounded as though he'd snapped up the phone on the first ring. "I got news."

"Another?"

"No."

"Where's the top to this thing?" Rob asked, holding the plastic pitcher with juice.

Nick turned and pulled open cupboards in search of a lid. "What's up, Captain?"

"Where the hell are you?"

"My sister's," he lied.

"Well, I'll make it short, then. I took a call about a half hour ago from a source who says one of ours is the perp."

Nick halted. He'd thought a cop could be behind the killings. Who else would have had the inside info? "You've got a line on our suspect?"

"Maybe, maybe not."

Nick frowned. "You going to tell me who this source thinks is involved?"

His captain exhaled. "Chase."

"That's bullshit," he snapped and then looked at Rob, who was staring at him wide-eyed. "Sorry," Nick mouthed. "No, that can't be right," he said to Cintrello, lowering his voice and turning away from Rob. "This guy—your source—he thinks she did it? Impossible. She's a great cop, Captain. What would be the motive?"

"Slow down, Thomas, and watch your fucking mouth. If you can't look at this thing objectively, I'll yank you."

"This is objective, Captain. I know her as well as anyone, and I'd stake my badge on it."

"That's not objective, Thomas. Jesus Christ, you're not screwing her, are you?"

"God, no," he said quickly, one part of him wishing he was lying, one part glad he wasn't. "Is there evidence?"

"Yes."

"What—"

"It's not enough to try a case on, but the undersheriff has got his panties in a knot over what happened last fall and he's not about to take chances."

Nick nodded. Last fall, the sheriff's office had ignored reports that one of their own, Officer John Patrick Yaskevich, was involved in the sale of unregistered weapons. When it turned out to be true, the sheriff got more than an earful from the governor and there was a bloodbath in the papers. "They can't possibly think this is the same thing," Nick said.

"We're not talking about it anymore, Thomas," Cintrello said. "The D.O.J. is insisting she stay on the case, but I've been told that my ass is on the line. That means your ass is on the line. Got it?"

"Got it."

"You're my insider. You keep your eyes open, and if something looks fishy, I hear about it. Are we clear?"

"I still don't—"

"Thomas, shut your trap already. We'll see what the source has. Then we'll talk. Corona is demanding that everything remain the same until then. But I'm letting you know to keep your eyes and ears open. Clear?"

"Yeah."

"If I find out you held something back, I'll feed you to IAD myself."

Nick didn't reply. The internal affairs division was a group he'd been fortunate enough never to deal with.

"Understand?"

His chest was deflated. "Yeah," he said with his last puff of air.

Nick hung up the phone and leaned against the counter.

"I found the lid," Rob announced, holding up the pitcher of juice.

"Nice work."

Rob looked at him. "Is Sam in trouble?"

Nick blinked and shook his head, pointing at the phone. "No. That was something else."

Rob nodded, but Nick wasn't sure he believed him. "I'm going to take some in to Der."

Nick put his hand on Rob's shoulder. "Thanks." As Rob left the room, Nick felt trapped. His loyalty had always been with the department, but he couldn't possibly keep this news from Sam. He didn't believe the allegations for a second, and Sam deserved to know what was being said about her. He only wondered how the hell he was going to tell her that she was a suspect in her own case.

CHAPTER 16

SAM COULD HEAR her intake of breath in the silence as she fought for a rational explanation for the sudden darkness. She'd never seen the lights off before. A guard was supposed to shut them off when he was sure the office was empty. She picked up the phone again. Still no dial tone. She put the receiver down and called out.

No one answered.

Her breath was ragged, and she inhaled through her nose to slow her pulse. Silently, she turned the key in the top drawer and opened it. She lifted her gun out, then checked the safety lock before heading out into the hallway.

"Who's there?" she repeated.

The office was dead quiet. Her department almost always cleared out by five-thirty, and without windows the darkness made it feel like the middle of the night. She took small steps and kept her back to the wall, the gun low in her right hand.

She moved slowly toward the exit, feeling her way along the wall. The only light in the room came from the tiny red LEDs on the phones and computer monitors, left on but long since in sleep mode. She knew the light switch was along the wall, but she couldn't tell how far.

Pressing forward, she felt her way past the doorjamb of Gary Williams' office. Her heel caught on a rough patch of carpet and she tripped forward, falling awkwardly. The gun fell from her hand and landed with a dull thud on the carpet. She squinted, trying to make out the shape of it in the dark, but couldn't see anything.

She ran her fingers over the floor before her. The gun was too heavy to have gone far. She moved forward, spreading her arms in a radius around her, feeling for the familiar steel of her weapon. "Shit."

In the distance she heard a phone ringing. Her pulse quickened, though the sound was as normal as her voice. "Calm down," she told herself. She made a last attempt to locate her gun but couldn't. She needed to find the lights first.

Getting to her feet, she found the wall again and groped like a blind person toward the outer office. She remembered the small flashlight in the first aid kit in her desk and wondered if she could locate it in the dark. She considered trying another phone. Maybe Aaron's would work. But she didn't want to turn around with her gun lying on the floor. Cursing herself for letting go of it, she moved forward again. Her fingers hit the outer edge of the plastic mounting for the light switch. Exhaling, she flipped the light switch. Nothing happened.

"Fuck," she muttered.

On the far side of the floor, she heard the soft brush

of shoe against carpet. She froze, the small vibrations resounding beneath her toes as the feet grew nearer.

She squatted and scanned the floor one last time for her gun, but couldn't find it. She considered hiding under a desk, but instead she straightened her shoulders and called out. "Hello."

There was no answer.

She paused, thinking perhaps the security guard was making his rounds with headphones on. It wouldn't surprise her. But surely he had noticed the lights were off.

"Who's there?" she asked again.

Again, no one answered.

The building required a pass for entry. The windows in the small, low-ceilinged lobby were bulletproof. Whoever was there had to be someone who had access. Was it the person who'd taken her file? Was it the same person who'd left the note? Her pulse drilled a frantic beat against her chest. Where the hell was her gun?

As she started to bend over, she heard the creak of something nearby. Spinning around, she snapped, "Who's there?"

No one answered.

She took a bold step forward.

The lights snapped on.

She found herself face-to-face with Gary Williams. His elflike features were drawn up in a smile. Both rows of tiny block teeth were displayed, reminding Sam of a rat baring its teeth. A mop of curly dark hair and large eyes only added to his elfish appearance. She cursed her erratic heartbeat and scanned the floor to locate her gun.

It had flown four feet across the room. She scooped

it up and spun toward Williams, clutching the weapon in a tight fist. "What the hell is wrong with you?" she screamed.

Williams had been by earlier to bother her about her notes on a case they were working on, and again she'd blown him off. Was that why he was creeping around in the dark?

Williams raised both hands in the air like it was a holdup. "Chase, put the fucking gun down. You're losing it."

Sam kept the gun pointed where it was. "Why didn't you answer me when I called out?"

"You didn't identify yourself. I thought I was walking into some trap." He motioned to the gun. "Are you going to put that down? Jesus Christ, what's up with you lately?"

"Is everything all right?" a voice called from behind her.

Sam whipped around and lowered her weapon.

The security guard stood with his flashlight, staring.

Sam glared at Williams, then answered in a tight voice, "Everything's fine. What happened to the lights?"

"Someone tripped the breaker."

Sam looked back at Williams, who shrugged and muttered, "Weird."

"What about the backup generator?" she probed.

The guard nodded. "That's where I just came from. Someone set it on five-minute delay. I can't figure why."

Sam felt an involuntary shudder ripple like icy water across her back. "I'm sure it was a mistake," she said, as much for her benefit as for anyone else's.

"Yeah, I'm sure it's nothing," Williams added. "Nice of you to check things out, though, since the little lady here gets so nervous." He gave her a wink that held no humor. "I thought she was going to shoot me."

"I'm making my rounds now," the guard said without commenting on Sam's gun. "I'll keep an eye out for anyone strange."

"Are you heading to the garage?" Sam asked, suddenly not wanting to be alone with Williams.

The security guard looked at her and nodded. "Seems like a good place to start."

She nodded, relieved. "I'll go down with you. I'm leaving anyway." She brushed past Williams without a sideways glance and packed her things in record time. Williams had always seemed somewhat envious of her. As Aaron had made clear, a lot of people didn't like her modus operandi.

Still, she couldn't understand why he'd been sneaking up on her. Lifting her chin, she tightened her coat and considered what he'd said.

What would he have done, though, if he'd reached her before the lights had come back on?

*

Sam turned her key in the lock of her front door, ready to collapse. It had been a terrible day and a worse evening. It was only eight, but it felt like the middle of the night. She pushed the door open and took one step inside to find Nick and Rob standing in the kitchen.

She turned to Rob. "What's going on?"

Rob shrugged and motioned to the living room with

an elbow, his gaze on the stain he was trying to get out of his shirt. "Derek's real sick. Nick gave him Tylenol. We made grilled cheese and soup for dinner."

"Sick?" She dropped her bag and coat at the kitchen table and hurried into the living room where Derek lay sprawled across the sofa, pale and languid. Sitting down beside him, she tucked the blanket around him.

She touched his forehead with the back of her hand and then pressed it against his cheek. Despite his pallid color, he was burning up.

She looked at Rob. "Why didn't you call me?"

"We did," Rob said, scowling at her. "No one answered and then Nick came over. It's okay, though. He's got a fever of one-oh-two. We checked," he said, giving Nick a sideways glance.

Nick gave him a smile, but Sam didn't respond. She should thank Nick for being there. But *why* was he there? She was the one who should have been home to take care of Derek. Turning her attention back to her nephew, she brushed his hair off his face and whispered to him. "How are you?"

"I'm fine," he moaned.

"You comfortable? You want something to drink?"

"I ate some soup. I feel a little better, just tired."

"Do you want me to help you to bed?" she asked.

"In a minute," he answered.

Sam kissed his cheek and stood up, facing Nick and Rob. "Thanks for taking care of your brother, Rob."

Rob shrugged and mumbled something about it being no big deal.

"We're lucky you stopped by," Sam added to Nick.

Nick shrugged too, and Sam had no idea what else to say. "I got some results from that thing you gave me," he added.

Rob frowned. "What thing?"

"Just work stuff," Sam said quickly. She felt her own pulse rise a notch with the idea of a fingerprint to go along with the torment of that photo. She waved Nick toward the back of the ranch-style house. "We can sit in the den for a few minutes." She turned to Rob. "Let me know if he needs anything."

"I can take care of him," Rob said, twisting the thermometer between his fingers. She found herself starting to warn him to be careful but stopped. She needed to stop treating them like children. They weren't. They were practically men. She put her hand on Rob's shoulder. "Okay, thanks."

She wished she was wearing something other than the stiff skirt suit from her workday, but she didn't want to wait to talk to Nick. Instead, she entered her den and flipped on the light, sat in her desk chair and kicked off her shoes. She glanced down at a run starting at her toe and quickly tucked her feet back in her shoes. "So, what did the lab say?"

Nick sat on the worn leather ottoman that matched her reading chair. "No prints on the photo. The surface was entirely clean."

Sam exhaled and dropped her head.

He shook his head. "Worse than that, there were no residuals," he added. "It looks like the photo was handled with gloves from the get-go."

"What about the note?"

"Only one set—I'm pretty sure they're yours."

She rubbed her temple. "Shit."

"It's not that bad," Nick said, moving his chair closer. "I still think there's a good possibility that it was a joke. You've got a lot of people who deal with prints all the time. They'd know to be careful. It was probably someone who was trying to get your goat and knows you well enough to know you'd have prints run."

She looked up and narrowed her gaze, inspecting his expression for signs that he wasn't telling her all of it. She found none, although his expression was guarded. She thought about the heater exploding and found herself wanting to tell him, even though it terrified her to have it out there in the open. She'd told Brent things she never should have told him.

Nick wasn't Brent. Nick was Nick. She had to start somewhere. She took a breath and forced the words out. "There were other incidents."

Nick's expression tightened. "What happened?"

"My heater exploded. It looked like a short, but it burst into flames. Then the lights went off in the whole place."

He stepped forward and she felt him reach out for her hand, but he caught himself. He scanned her face. "You're all right?"

She looked at his hand, wishing he'd touched her, then pushed the thought aside. She nodded. "I'm fine."

"What did Corona say?"

She shook her head.

"You didn't tell him?"

"I need him to trust me, Nick. I can't keep running to him for every little thing."

"Okay." He paused. "But that's some serious stuff, Sam. It sounds scary. Was anyone around when the lights went out?"

She frowned. "Only Williams."

His hand was only inches from hers. "Keep an eye on him."

"I will." She reached out and grazed his fingers, felt the warmth surging across the surface. "I appreciate you checking the other stuff out."

He nodded. "No problem." His gaze didn't waver.

She glanced at her hands and then back at him. "I want to apologize for not showing you the picture sooner. I brought it to give to you. I just didn't want to spoil the evening. And I didn't really want to discuss it, either. I'm not good at this, Nick. I'm trying, I swear I am." As soon as the words were out, she focused on her skirt, picking at the lint that had accumulated on the navy wool.

When she looked up, Nick was grinning. "What?"

"I bet that's the first apology you've given in years."

She smiled back, feeling the tension loosen. "Don't push it."

He raised his hands in jest. "I'll take it."

"Okay, maybe it has been a while. So, I said it."

He put his hand out and Sam took it in hers. "Forgiven," he whispered. "I had a good time. I'd like to do it again."

She started to speak but he interrupted.

"—sometime. I'd like to go out to dinner sometime.

Can we leave it at that? I'd rather keep my hopes up than have you crush them right here after that great apology."

She nodded, watching the way his eyes lit up when he was being playful.

He squeezed her hand. "Will you let me do that?"

"Absolutely."

He glanced down, and she caught him nodding to himself before he lifted his eyes to hers. He had something else on his mind. She could tell by the way his smile had disappeared so quickly.

"Anything new with the case?" he asked.

She thought about the two calls she'd gotten and the lights that had gone out. "Nothing. You?"

Nick looked down at his hands. "I did get one piece of news."

She frowned. "What?"

"It's not good."

She leaned forward and braced herself. "What is it?"

Nick's expression was solemn, his eyes darker than they'd been a few minutes before. "You've got to keep this between the two of us for now."

She rubbed her shoulders, suddenly cold. "Nick, of course. Tell me."

He stared at his hands again.

The silence seemed to go on forever. Her mind returned to Derek and Rob in the other room, and she suddenly had the urge to jump up and check on them. "Nick, what's going on? What is it?"

He leaned forward until his hands were almost touching hers. "It's not about the boys. I got a call from

Cintrello. Someone has it in their head that you should be considered a suspect."

Sam jumped back. "Me?"

He raised his hands. "I don't know much more than that yet. Cintrello called and said he had a source who thought you might be involved with the case. They're all a little jumpy after the John Yaskevich mess. He indicated there was some evidence, but not enough to go on. And he wouldn't tell me what. You know it's just someone smoking dope. They're pointing fingers because it's an easy out—it was your murder case and your abuse case. That's all. There's no substance to it. They're just talking out their ass."

Sam sank back in the chair, feeling the hard wooden back against each vertebra. The air seeped out of her. "Someone thinks I'm a killer?"

CHAPTER 17

WHITNEY ALLEN STOMPED through the front door in her pink tights and long sweatshirt and plopped down to take her shoes off. Dance class was so boring today. She never wanted to go back. The teacher was like Ursula, the big, mean octopus in *The Little Mermaid*. And she hated getting a ride with Katie Sherman. Katie's father always smoked in the car and Whitney hated the smell. It felt like she was choking.

But Whitney knew better than to run inside with her sneakers on. Her mom hated shoes in the house. "The new carpet," she always said when the kids walked around inside with their shoes on. Whitney couldn't understand why her mother had replaced the carpet to look exactly the same as it always had.

Even the ring of dirt on the carpet in the corner where her stepdad had put too much water in the plant was still there. But it had to be new. Otherwise, why would her mom say so? Her mother never said a word to adults about shoes. Whitney remembered when the guy from the cable company had come. She didn't tell him to take off his shoes.

Whitney started to yell that she was home when she heard low voices coming from the living room. Sneaking around the corner, she saw two policemen sitting on the couch. Barely sitting, actually. They were right at the edge of it like they were ready to leave. That's how Aunt Emily was. She sat right on the edge of the couch when she dropped off Whitney's cousin Teddy, to play with Randy, and then right away she'd say how many errands she had to do and she'd leave.

Whitney crept to the door and stared at them. The police officer on the far side of the couch was talking. Both of them were wearing their shoes, and they didn't even look clean. The one closer to the door looked straight at Whitney and winked. She burst into a fit of giggles.

"Whitney Allen, what are you doing?" her mother said. "Get in here where I can see you."

Whitney stepped into the room and looked at her feet.

"Hello, Whitney," one of the policemen said. "I'm Officer Bernadini and this is Officer Hansen."

She looked up to see both of the police officers facing her. "We'd like to ask you a couple of questions," one of them said, but she couldn't remember which one he was. She thought the one with the big nose was the one named Houdini or whatever, but she wasn't sure, so she didn't use their names.

Whitney looked at her mother, her heart racing. "Are they going to 'rrest me?"

Both officers smiled, but the one furthest from her

still looked mean. He was big, with dark hair and eyes that barely seemed to open.

"Sit down," her mother said.

Without taking her eyes off the scary policeman, Whitney made her way to the chair beside her mother and sat.

The nicer one was bouncing one leg up and down, up and down. "Do you play outside often, Whitney?" he asked.

She shook her head. "Randy does." He was probably the one they wanted, not her. He was always getting in trouble, but because he couldn't hear no one blamed him.

"We want to know if you were playing outside on a Wednesday a few weeks ago..."

"The day Molly's mom died?" Whitney interrupted.

The mean policeman raised an eyebrow and Whitney snapped her mouth shut.

Her mother shook her head. "You can't expect a child to remember a particular Wednesday over two weeks ago."

"I remember it," Whitney argued.

"Don't you fib, Whitney Anne."

Whitney scrunched her nose. She hated her middle name. "I'm not fibbing. I swear."

"She can't possibly remember one day," her mother continued.

"I do. I 'member cause it was Daddy's birthday and you let me call him. But he wasn't there, remember?"

Her mother wrinkled her face up, and Whitney knew she was trying to remember. "I'll be darned."

"Were you outside that day?" the nice policeman asked. She watched his leg bounce and wondered if he had to pee. Her mother always knew when she had to pee because of how she wiggled around. She wondered if her mother had told him where the bathroom was. Maybe he thought it was rude to ask.

She looked over at the mean one. He was staring straight at her.

"Were you outside that day?" he said again.

She looked between the two of them and shook her head. "But Randy was."

The mean policeman moved in his seat and stared at her.

"Where's Randy now?" the other one asked.

"In Ohio, with his mother. He'll be back next week." Her mother stood. "I don't think Randy will be able to help you, though. He's deaf and he lives in his own world most of the time."

"That's for sure," Whitney agreed. "One time we were getting ready to go to my aunt Emily's house—"

"Whitney," her mother said, "the officers don't have time for your babbling. Go upstairs and change out of your dance clothes."

Whitney frowned. "But—"

"Now." Her mother pushed her out the door, and Whitney took a last look at the police officers, wishing they would ask her some more questions. She didn't want to leave.

"Go. And get that room cleaned up."

Dragging her feet, Whitney went to her room. She wondered if this was how Cinderella felt. She took off her leotard and tights and put on her gray shorts and a yellow tank top and looked in the mirror. Rags, just like Cinderella.

And she had to clean her room. She flopped on the bed and stared at the ceiling, wondering what Cinderella would do in her place. She'd be figuring out a way to get to the ball, probably. But Whitney didn't even think they held balls out here. She thought about Randy and wondered what he was doing now. It was later in Ohio. Maybe he was in bed already.

Instead of cleaning her room, Whitney got her hairbrush and sat in front of her closet door. She watched her reflection in the tall mirror as she pretended to get ready for a ball.

She was still staring at herself in the mirror when her mother called her to dinner a while later.

Whitney dropped the brush and ran downstairs.

Her stepdad was already sitting at the table. "Like a herd of elephants. How can such little feet make so much noise?"

Whitney beamed, and her stepdad mussed her freshly brushed hair.

Dinner was all white and brown and Whitney imagined what Cinderella ate. Probably porridge, like Goldilocks, she figured. She pushed the potatoes around her plate and picked at the rest of it.

"Eat," her mother warned.

The phone rang before she could protest. Whitney sprang up, but her mother answered it and waved her back to her chair.

"It's Randy."

Her stepdad stood, turned on the little computer

on the desk next to the phone, and started typing with two fingers.

"Can I try?" she said, getting up behind him.

"Shh," he scolded.

"Sit down, Whitney," her mother said.

"Please, I want to ask him about that day—about being outside."

"Whitney."

"He might know something. Can you ask him, Tony? Just see what he says. Please," Whitney begged.

Her stepfather gave her mother an annoyed look. "Marge, please."

"Whitney, sit down and be quiet."

"Mom, but he might know who killed her."

Her mother grabbed her arm and pulled her back to her chair. "Talking to Ohio is very expensive, Whitney, especially like this. We're not going to waste money on any nonsense." She pressed her finger into Whitney's shoulder.

Whitney could feel the long fingernail biting through her shirt.

"Now sit and eat your meat."

Pouting, Whitney kicked at the chair. No one ever listened to her. They listened more to Randy and he couldn't even talk. "He could know something, Mom," she said half under her breath.

Her mother didn't answer her.

"Geez, Louise," she imitated her mother, "can't we just ask?"

Her mother clenched her teeth. "Not another word."

Whitney stabbed at her chicken and then dropped her fork. It fell and knocked over her milk. "Uh-oh."

Her mother snapped her out of the chair. "To your room. I don't want to see your face again. No dinner, no dessert. You go up there and think about your behavior, young lady."

Whitney felt the tears come. They rolled down her cheeks. "I was only trying—"

"Now." Her mother slapped at her bottom, and Whitney started to cry, running from the table.

Sprawled on her bed, Whitney sobbed. She hadn't meant to spill the milk. It was a mistake. She was worse off than Cinderella. She didn't even have any mouse friends to play with. Her mother wouldn't even let her have a pet hamster. She never got to do anything fun.

She buried her face in her pillow and cursed the police and her mother and most of all stupid Randy.

CHAPTER 18

HE HADN'T INTENDED to go in. He had only wanted to look in on them. But even with the flashlight he couldn't see anything from outside. All the shades were drawn. He hadn't been sleeping, and it was affecting his brain. He didn't want to go through it again. He had to check on the girl, though. Why risk going in and leaving footprints or hair? He knew all too well what they would look for.

He couldn't see her through any of the windows, and she didn't answer when he knocked. He heard her. He knew she was inside. Why hadn't she answered the damn door? He just wanted to see Becky.

He knocked on the door harder and waited, glancing over his shoulder. People in this neighborhood didn't pay attention. No one cared who was visiting a crack mom.

With his jacket shielding his hand, he jiggled the knob. The door creaked open.

"Hello?" he called, making himself polite and harmless. But she hadn't responded. Before he could stop himself, he'd stepped inside and closed the door behind him. The picture of the little girl popped like a flashbulb in his mind. Becky—just like his Becky. She needed him.

He surveyed the room, taking in the stench of soiled clothes and unwashed dishes. He swallowed his own nausea. A dreary rainbow of stains marked a ragged gray carpet. The bed had been stripped, and a stained mattress was strewn with threadbare sheets. He remembered his childhood house, his own room, the misery that had followed him there.

And yet as he looked around the dirty apartment, he realized he'd never had it this bad. Some might have even called him lucky by comparison.

The terrible stench overwhelmed him and he wanted to leave. Becky's face crossed his vision again. He halted. Turning back, he stepped over a moldy spill in the carpet and called out again. "Hello."

He could hear someone throwing things in a back room as he moved slowly through the apartment. A woman was cursing and crying. Cautiously, he followed the sounds.

When he reached the bathroom door, he looked in. The toilet was unflushed and had overflowed. Someone had shit in the bathtub and it was dry, the smell stale and old like the couch in his parents' house that stank of beer no matter what his mother did to clean it. A thin, strung-out woman was pulling medicine bottles down from a shelf. Glass crashed against the floor, the pieces crunching beneath her stockinged feet as she tore at the contents of the cabinet.

"Where is it? Where is it?" she asked, her voice high-pitched and wracked with desperation.

"What?"

At the sound of his voice, she whipped around and bumped against the toilet, nearly falling in. Her face was yellow, and deep bluish-black rings circled her eyes. Her arms were thin and bare, and he could see the tracks the needles had made, like fat blue bugs crawling up her skin.

She straightened slowly, her back slightly hunched, her teeth bared. He took a step back, but she lunged at him before he could distance himself further.

Her claws lashed out. He turned to run, but she leapt onto his back and knocked him to the hall floor. "Where is it? Give it to me," she screamed, scratching at his eyes and face. He lifted his hands to his face, protecting himself.

She caught his ear between her nails, and he howled. Throwing his right arm up, he knocked her off him. Her head landed with a thud against the doorjamb, and she crumpled to the floor. He picked himself up quickly and ran the back of his hand across his ear. It was bleeding. "Damn."

He looked back at the woman on the floor. She groaned and turned over, holding her head.

"Where's Becky?"

The woman frowned, but didn't respond.

He left her and walked into the back bedroom. It was worse than the others: the smells stronger, the foulness more penetrating. In one corner, Becky lay on the floor. Crossing the room, he started to stoop but caught himself. The grayish tint of her skin and her wide eyes stopped him.

"What happened to Becky?" he said, walking back toward the woman.

Her eyes were wide and crazed. "I don't know. She went asleep. Never woke up."

"When?" he demanded, shaking her shoulders. Her head snapped against the carpet as though it were attached by thread instead of bone.

"Don't know," she said. "Can't think. I need a fix. Please. I'll do anything," she added.

He let go of her and she rushed out from under him. He knelt next to Becky. "Dear God. Another one. Two Beckys," he whispered to himself. He had failed them both. Why hadn't he come sooner?

From his peripheral view, he could see the woman come at him again. A heavy kitchen knife was raised above her head.

He stood up. "Put that down."

She crept toward him, her eyes unblinking as she prepared to strike.

He looked for a way out, but he was trapped. "Christ." He needed to get the knife away from her.

Suddenly, she dove toward him and swung the knife. He ducked and ran into the living room. Right on his tail, she howled and he could feel the knife swish through the air next to his head. She was emaciated and weak but desperate. She caught his coat with the tip and shoved it through. He could feel the blade against the hairs on his arm. The knife was wedged in his coat—when he swung around, he took her and the knife with him. He grabbed her hand and tried to pry it off the handle.

She twisted the knife back toward him, trying to

free it from his coat. Ignoring the knife, he went for the source. He wrapped his hands around the fragile diameter of her neck and squeezed, trying to weaken her grip on the knife. Instead, she turned the handle, and he could feel the blade etch at his arm.

His grip tightened. She pressed the knife deeper. Her cheeks turned purple, her eyes bulged, but she didn't let go.

"Let go of the knife."

"You killed Becky," she choked.

"No." How could she say that? He would never hurt her. He squeezed tighter now, filled with rage, feeling a heavy throb in his forehead. His arms cramped and he felt a quick snap. The knife fell away from his arm and he loosened his grip. She was limp in his hands and he knew she was dead.

Panic buzzed through his head like a swarm of angry bees, but he waved it off. He had done what he had to do. She had tried to kill him. She had taken the girl away from him. She was the one who deserved to die.

He laid her on the floor and stood quickly, pulling the blade out of the hole in his jacket. His blood was on the blade. He looked around the room, thinking fast. He felt the slow ooze of blood on his arm but knew it wasn't a deep cut.

He had to get out. He wished he had a pair of rubber gloves. Taking a dirty T-shirt from the floor, he wrapped the knife and put it in his jacket pocket. He used another shirt to wipe down everything he'd touched. He wiped the flashlight and wrapped it in the dirty T-shirt.

He put his nose to the sleeve of his jacket and took

a quick breath before pushing on. He went outside and pulled two branches from the tree out front, careful that no one saw him. He put one behind each of her ears, double-checking that each had six leaves. Then he went back to the other room.

He knelt beside Becky and touched her cold cheek. He wanted to pick her up and hold her—to rock her against him. He would have loved her. He would have taken care of her. He wished he could take her home and watch her sleep. Even now, he wanted to make it better.

But he knew he couldn't help her any longer. They watched him too closely. He had no privacy. He thought of his own sister. Maybe the two would find each other.

With his fingertips, he closed her eyes, the skin of her eyelids cool. He leaned forward and touched his lips to her cheek. Then, wiping his wet palms on a shirt from the floor, he hurried out of the apartment.

CHAPTER 19

NICK SLEPT FITFULLY and awoke early—too early. Even after he was showered and dressed, it was only a few minutes before six. Sam's hurt voice kept echoing in his head. How could anyone think she was a killer? He'd tried to get her to open up, to talk to him, but she wouldn't.

Now he felt like crap. He should have known she would be upset. Maybe he should have kept it from her until he had something more substantial. But he didn't want to lie to her. He only wished he could get her to lean on him a little more. She needed to be alone, she'd told him. She couldn't depend on anyone. She would handle this herself. It would only hurt his career if he took her side. Damn it, he wanted to take her side. He wanted to be with her, to help her. But she'd refused.

It wasn't even such a big deal yet, but to Sam the job and her reputation meant everything. Shit like that happened all the time at the station. Lots of cops had been blamed at one time or another for becoming too involved in a case—getting in too deep, crossing the line.

But being accused of the actual crime—that was almost unheard of. Nick didn't think it would stick.

But he couldn't get angry with her. She had the right to handle it however she wanted. Worrying about their relationship shouldn't be his focus right now. He rubbed his eyes. Their relationship—there was no relationship. When was he going to figure it out? Christ, he was like a damn teenager around her, and she wanted him for running prints, playing softball with Rob, and talking music with Derek. That was it. He was a colleague, maybe a friend, but certainly nothing more. He needed to back off and get a life, find someone who wanted more. And that someone was not going to be Sam Chase.

Looking around his apartment, he realized he should've gone for a run. He could have used something to burn off steam. And right now he had enough steam for a marathon.

Instead, he got in his car and headed toward his sister's house. She lived in a town of young urban professionals. Gina and Mike had been one of the first black couples in Moraga almost thirty years before. The house was colonial style, not huge but tidy, with a deep grass yard and a brick walkway. Two large oak trees stood at opposite ends of the front yard like pillars holding up an invisible shelter above the house. The only person in his family who would be up at this hour lived with his sister. And right now he needed to see his mother.

He parked at the curb and walked to the side of the house, passing the white gate into his mother's yard. Ever since he could remember, his mother could sense when one of her children was nearby. She had a nose for it.

With Nick, she'd sniff quickly and say, "You're in trouble, aren't you?" Or "you're hungry."

He wasn't sure how that smelled, but she was always right. When he needed to talk to her, he would just stand nearby and her nose would lead her to him.

Now, he passed over the plush lawn and looked into her garden. She'd sectioned it into three parts. The largest was the vegetable garden, the middle patch directly beneath the kitchen window. She grew tomatoes, carrots, peas, eggplant, and squash. On the far side of it, she had a small rose garden. All peach and yellow roses, her favorites. And the near side had herbs and his father's geranium.

It had been a small, rather sickly red geranium that his father had given his mother a few months before he died. She had nurtured and potted and repotted that plant at every turn. Every winter she'd taken careful cuttings, rooting them in jelly glasses on the windowsill. Some of them made it and some didn't, but every spring she had new little geranium plants that had sprung from the old. Nursing had not only been her profession, it was also the way she approached life.

Early morning was her hour for gardening. Sometimes she started before it was even light enough to see well. In the summer, it was the most comfortable hour to be outside—before the temperature rose to ninety-five or higher.

"You're up early."

He looked up at his mother, coming out the back door. She wore a red gingham shirt with the sleeves turned up and big jeans, rolled at the bottom. On her head was a wide-brimmed straw hat, though the sun wasn't anywhere in sight yet. Her gardening gloves were in one hand, hot tea in the other.

"Well?"

He smiled. "Couldn't sleep."

"Last time you couldn't sleep, you and Sheila were breaking up. Your heart cracked again, eh?"

He shook his head. "My heart's fine."

"Doesn't look like it," his mother scolded. She passed him and looked over her vegetable garden as though grading its performance. "She's got you that good, she's probably worth it."

"Who are you talking about?"

She pulled her hat off and frowned, shaking her head. "Whoever you're over here to talk about. I can tell by that forlorn look in your eyes that this isn't about a case. You're never over here at this hour over a case. So I know what it's about. She's somebody, whoever she is. And special, I'm gathering. So I don't know why you're here with your old mom instead of being with her at this hour."

He turned and paced a few steps, then came back. "It's case-related too. Things have gotten complicated."

She watched him. "You're crushing my grass with that pacing. Go get my extra gloves in the shed and we'll work some of that energy off."

"I'm in clean pants, Mom."

She waved him on. "There are some kneepads in there too if you're afraid of a little dirt."

Nick saddled up in kneepads and gloves and entered his mother's garden.

"Anything looks like this," she said, waving a yellowish-green stem with clover-like leaves. "Out. And dig a little to get the bulbs underneath. Bloodsuckers, these oxalis."

Nick turned his attention to pulling weeds, and they worked in silence for a few minutes.

His mother picked at the weeds with a vengeance. "She got a name?"

"Sam. Sam Chase."

"Hard name for a lady."

"She's a hard lady."

"White?"

He nodded.

His mother stopped and smiled.

"What's so funny?"

She pushed her hat up with the back of her gloved hand. "I always thought you needed someone tougher."

He continued to pull weeds. "I'm afraid she may be too tough."

"She doesn't want anything to do with you?"

"She doesn't seem to want anything to do with anyone. But especially not me."

"How's she involved in this case?"

"The victim was her case. Some jerks are even saying she's a suspect."

"You think she's capable of killing?"

He met his mother's gaze. "No." He pulled out two more clumps of oxalis. "Someone's framing her."

"Humph," his mother said.

They were quiet for a minute while Nick tried to think about who could possibly have gathered enough evidence to make it look like Sam was guilty of anything. He would have liked to wring the prick's neck.

"You going to think out loud or do I need to start guessing?"

Nick looked at his mother. "I'm frustrated is all. No answers, and she doesn't let me in. Someone's messing with her stuff at work, leaving her strange messages. I've only seen one, but I think there have been more. She needs help, but she won't ask. Last night I told her what I'd heard about the accusations against her." He cringed at the memory of Sam's anger. "Maybe I shouldn't have told her. You know, the messenger and all that."

"No, you were right to tell her. She needed to know, even if it was painful. And if it had come out later from somewhere else, it would have been worse."

He thought about his mother's words.

His mother worked quietly and Nick knew she was considering this information, preparing her diagnosis and treatment.

"When I met your father," his mother began, "I'd been through a lot. I wasn't open to meeting a man, and especially not a white man. I thought I had enough trouble living as I was, without dealing with a mixed relationship." She smiled. "I didn't realize that every relationship between a man and a woman is mixed. Just the nature of the beast."

That was certainly true from his experience.

"I didn't know how to open up. No one ever taught me." She took her glove off and squeezed his hand. "No one until your father. I never would've asked for help—not from anyone." She pointed to the geranium. "That's what that plant reminds me of. He gave it to me after he had that first heart attack. He told me it was to remind me that love grows and ours was still growing."

Nick stared at the geranium. All these years, he'd had no idea the plant held so much significance.

"You've got to teach her."

"I don't know how—"

She waved her hand. "Shh. 'Course you do. Just give her space, but be there if she needs you. She'll come when she's ready." She blinked hard. "Now get. I got work to do."

Nick stood up and pulled the gloves and kneepads off, trying to digest what his mother had told him. How could he teach Sam Chase to ask for his help?

"You come by next week for dinner—both of you."

Nick leaned down and pulled his mother's hat off, kissing the top of her head. "You're the best, Mom."

"Good thing. I'm the only mom you've got."

Nick watched her work for a minute in silence and then headed for the gate. He wished he could bottle some of her wisdom and drink it. He knew she doled it out in exactly the right portions to provide him with whatever he needed at the moment. He thought about giving Sam her space. He needed to cool off and let her come to him. He could do that. He smiled at his mother. As he walked to his car, he thanked his dad again for finding her.

*

Maybe he could catch dinner at his sister's. He glanced at his watch, amazed to see it was half past ten. "Christ," he muttered, making a U-turn and turning his car toward home. He'd spent the day cruising past the crime scene and around the Walters' neighborhood and then to Alf's diner to try to locate Dougie.

Not a single thing in his whole day had gone right. He hadn't even eaten since the stale piece of pie he'd ordered at Alfs almost six hours earlier. He wondered what was in his fridge and realized he didn't even care.

He just wanted to go home and straddle his bass—let himself unwind. And if Mrs. Jacobs upstairs wanted to make a stink, let her call the damn cops. It would give them all something to laugh about at the station. And he could use a laugh.

He was heading off the freeway by his house at quarter to eleven when his cell phone rang.

"Thomas," he answered.

"It's Cintrello."

"What's up?"

"I need you in Martinez—at Estudillo and Marina Vista by the railroad tracks."

"I'm off."

"Yeah, well, it was my day off, too. Not any fucking more."

Nick turned his car into a driveway, then pulled out in the opposite direction. "What've you got?"

"Another one."

"Another one?" he repeated. Another Sandi Walters?

"Thought we had this all tied up with a goddamn bow with Lugino. Not anymore. Whole thing just blew apart. And the undersheriff is all over my ass."

"You want me to pick up Lugino?"

"No need. He's here. Hasn't left yet. Was supposed to be gone already, but his bail fell through on possession of

Mary Jane. I think he needed twenty-five bucks or some damn thing. Couldn't raise it. Lucky bastard. No chance this was his work."

Nick tightened his grip on the phone. "Same M.O.?"

"Pretty damn close. You'd better check it out. And while you're at it, give your friend Chase a call. She have an alibi?"

"What does that mean?"

The captain didn't answer his question. "Corona insists she be on the scene, but I don't like it. And it's my jurisdiction, so she doesn't touch anything and she doesn't go anywhere on that scene without someone watching her."

"Captain, Chase is not involved in these crimes."

"Like hell she's not. Victim's another one of her cases."

"Fine, but she's not guilty of anything."

"We'll see, but it's her victim, her M.O. Looks like the same guy. From what I hear, the fucker thinks he's clever. Go see for yourself." The captain cursed and hung up.

Another victim. And the killer wasn't Lugino. Nick hammered his open hand on the steering wheel. "Damn."

CHAPTER 20

SAM CHASE WASN'T asleep when Nick's call came. She had been sitting up in bed with three weeks' worth of coupons, cut up, sorted on her lap by product. She'd been clipping coupons since the boys had come to live with her, and every few weeks she clipped another batch and added them to a large accordion file. When the phone rang, she had just been filing a Brawny coupon under "P" for paper towels.

She'd been thinking nonstop about what Nick had told her—evidence that she was involved with Sandi Walters' murder. "Evidence." The word rang in her mind as clear and sharp as "guilty." What could they possibly have? She'd been home that night. She'd been alone for most of it. She knew the questions they would ask. Had she seen anyone? Talked to anyone?

But she hadn't. She'd heard Derek come in at curfew and that was it. The phone rarely rang for her. Sam stared at the walls of the barrier she'd built around herself, contemplating the irony of it. The same walls she'd thought would protect her left her open to their accusations. She had no alibi.

Tonight she'd been anticipating a personal call from Nick, but not this. Nick's voice was cold and tired as he gave her directions to an apartment in Antioch. She remembered the neighborhood. It was not a place she could forget. She didn't blame Nick for his tone.

She'd been the one to tell him that she would handle this alone. How could she not? How could she justify taking him down with her? It wasn't smart for either of them. But now, without his smile to look forward to, she felt very alone.

Dressed warmly, she used her roof light and sirens to move through the sparse traffic quickly. That was how she wanted this to be—quick.

Nick hadn't given her any details on the phone— no victim's name or M.O. His voice rang with the same tired frustration she felt about this case. She wanted to go back to Yoshi's, to dance in his apartment. Suddenly she wanted anything but to do the job she was supposed to do. When had it all built up? And worse, why was it crashing down so quickly?

It felt like everything had been stirred up. Sorting it out didn't even seem possible, or perhaps just not realistic. And Nick deserved more. She wanted to give him more, but how could she possibly explain what she was feeling if she didn't know? Maybe it would be better to just forget the whole thing.

She parked in front of the address Nick had given her over the phone.

The shanty-like structure could hardly be called an

apartment complex. It was a cement U-shaped building, covered with spray paintings of curses and gang markings in all colors. A few of the tags she recognized from her days in homicide. She didn't miss them.

This wasn't the first time she had been here. The memory of a little girl surfaced in her mind, and of the thin, almost decayed crack mother whom the judge had refused to see as a long-term danger to her child.

The stench rose fast against the thick, hot air of summer and the hard cement surfaces. Even the rain couldn't wash these smells away. Fire seemed the only true purifier. The corridors were quiet, people locked away behind doors. No one would have seen anything. There were no eyes in these walls. People turned their heads and expected others to do the same.

Yellow crime-scene tape marked the latest battle-ground, and Sam shoved her hands in her pockets and walked straight for it. A police officer stood at the door.

"Sam Chase," she said, showing her badge. "Depart-ment of Justice." She watched his face, waiting for his expression to judge her guilt.

Instead, he nodded her through without so much as a sideways glance. She should have felt better, but the not-knowing was making her crazy.

She shoved her personal problems aside and surveyed the surroundings. The inside of the apartment made the corridor look pristine. Sam had seen humans live in utterly foul conditions, but this was worse than she'd ever seen before, worse than the last time she'd visited this same apartment.

Lying in the center of the stained carpet was the

woman Sam remembered. Painfully thin and jaundiced, her remains were crumpled on the floor like a soiled rag. Like Sandi Walters, she had two eucalyptus branches tucked behind her ears. The tree had begun to take on the symbol of death.

Nick knelt on a tarp laid beside the body, speaking with the medical examiner. He looked up and gave her a nod. His brown eyes looked duller today, and she wondered if the death wasn't getting to all of them.

Sam walked immediately to the woman's feet and, not daring to kneel for fear of tainting the scene, crouched over to stare at the arches of her feet. Nothing stood out to her. Frowning, she circled the body, looking for something different about this one—some tag, like the gum wrapper on Sandi Walters. The wrapper had been obvious, and she suspected it had been a mistake. Even if she hadn't seen it at the time, it would have been quickly caught by the M.E. She scanned the room for something flashy and elegant that would stand out from the rubbish. She found nothing.

This dead woman, Eva Larson, like Sandi Walters, had been accused of abusing her daughter. Passed down from the attorney general's office after relatives in Utah complained of the girl's situation, the case had been delegated to Sam at D.O.J. The judge had sentenced Eva to eight weeks of rehab, during which time the girl stayed in foster care.

After that, Eva had received some job counseling and short-term childcare assistance. A service worker was supposed to check on them every few months, but it was always the same excuses: the system was overwhelmed with need, and they lacked funding and manpower to take on the massive problems. This one, another one, had simply fallen through the cracks.

"You know her?"

Sam focused on Nick, now standing beside her.

Shivering, she crossed her arms. "I knew them both." She was the only link between the cases. Sloan, Walters, now Larson.

He moved closer, so he was almost touching her, and she felt the warmth between them, thankful for the gesture.

Nick sighed. "I figured."

She was grateful he didn't say what they were both thinking, that this didn't make things look any better for her. Her alibi tonight was only slightly stronger than the last time. Derek and Rob had been in and out and had seen her. But two orphaned nephews would surely lie to protect their guardian. Any jury knew that. Sam looked around. "You find the daughter?"

Nick met her gaze with dulled eyes. "In the other room."

"How is she?" From his expression, she should have known not to ask.

Nick ran a hand across his face. "Not good." He put his hand on the small of her back and guided her toward the other room.

Sam stepped forward. The smells of urine and mold were overpowered by a stronger, more potent odor coming from the back room. She recognized it instantly and it caused a thick, syrupy rise in her gut. Halting in the doorway, Sam didn't need to go farther. She could see the blue paleness in the girl's hands and arms. Her body was way too thin and her face was sunken from neglect.

"She's been dead three, maybe four days." Nick's tone was flat.

Sam forced herself into the room. "And the mother?"

"Only a few hours."

"You think the mom killed her?"

Nick squinted in the direction of the far room. "I think she let her die. Can't tell if it was violence or just neglect. Coroner will tell us more."

Sam nodded. Had the killer been distracted from leaving his clue by the presence of the dead girl? She studied Becky's face, her closed lids. "I'd check for prints on the eyelids. Someone's closed them, and I'd bet it wasn't the mom."

Nick motioned to an officer, who wrote her suggestion down.

Sam leaned over the girl, examining her expression. Besides her closed eyes, it didn't look like she'd been disturbed in death. Her mouth was partially open, her purple tinted lips showing the signs of old bruises. She glanced at Nick, watching the muscles in his jaw tighten in concentration. "Any leads?"

He shook his head. "None."

"Lugino?" she asked.

"He's in jail. Has been since we picked him up."

"Damn," she said.

"And to add to the mess, Charlie Sloan's family is suing for wrongful death." Defeat resounded in his voice.

It didn't surprise her. "Charlie was guilty," she reminded him.

"He never confessed."

"We had half a dozen people I.D. him with four of the six victims. He was guilty, and he was working alone. The D.A.'s office will handle the petition. We've got some time."

"It's not time I'm worried about—it's answers."

Sam looked around. "This feels different." She thought about the method of Sandi Walters' death. "Lugino confessed to having sex with Walters postmortem, right?"

Nick nodded. "He didn't know she was postmortem—or so he said."

"So the signatures are identical." If they had found the presence of semen at Sandi Walters' crime scene and not at the others, it would have been easy to prove that the signature of the killer, what he did to get off on the kill, was different. If the signature was different, they had a strong case that it was a different killer. But if the semen had come from Lugino *after the fact,* the signatures were identical. It gave Sloan's family a good shot. Who the hell else could have known about the eucalyptus? *Who else*? That was the question she didn't want to ask.

"The signatures are identical—M.O.'s too," Nick commented. "We found a flashlight by the body. Maybe we'll get lucky with that."

Sam nodded. "Check the batteries. They always forget about wiping those off."

"Good thinking."

Someone from the medical examiner's office called his name.

He waved, then looked at her again. "Will you take a look around, tell me what else you see?"

"Of course."

He leaned in and lowered his voice. "We'll talk more about the other stuff. Don't worry, okay?"

She gave him a stiff smile. "Thanks, Nick."

He started to walk away.

"Sloan never used drugs with them," Sam called out to him.

"No, he strangled them," Nick agreed, motioning to the other room. "Which is what this one looks like. The transition to use of a drug could be a sign of a maturing M.O.—or someone experimenting with a new method, not necessarily a different killer."

"You have someone checking into the source of the heroin?"

He nodded.

"I've got a list of people who knew about the eucalyptus in the last case," Sam said. "It's a short list, but I'll dig deeper tomorrow." Then, scanning the apartment, she added, "I'll add what I can." The prospect of spending any more time in this depressing place made her back ache. She forced away the pity and pushed herself out of the room where a tiny girl would never have a chance for a happy ending.

*

Sam tucked deeper into the warm flannel sheets and pulled the denim comforter up under her arms. Propping her notebook on her lap, she tilted the light. It was almost two in the morning and yet she couldn't imagine sleeping, didn't feel the slightest fatigue. Instead, each time her eyes closed, she pictured the skeletal form of Eva Larson and the discarded body of her young daughter. The image was followed by one of herself before a jury. The judge was her father. "I warned you," he was saying, over and over.

A part of her longed to go pull the thick diary of her cases off the living room bookshelf. But if she did that, she knew she would never sleep. She closed her eyes and processed the scene of Eva Larson's death in her head. As she went, she opened her eyes to make notes—the location of the body, the appearance of the apartment. She drew a crude sketch of Larson's resting pose, the right hand clenched as though she'd been gripping something. A weapon maybe. But where was it? Or perhaps it was something her killer had taken from her. She couldn't imagine Eva Larson had anything worth killing for. She made a question mark on the page beside her notes and set the notebook down. She'd have to wait for the results from the sheriff's crime scene.

Tonight she had promised herself she would finish chapter six of the book she was reading, *The Teenage Jungle: A Parent's Guide to Survival.*

The peppy little pictures of parent/child relations had irritated Sam to the point that she covered them as she read. The first sentence of the chapter was "Where do feelings come from?" She made a gagging sound and forced herself to read on. There had been a quiz at the end of the last chapter. Scoring you as a parent. She'd gotten a fifty-two, the low end of the "non-nurturer." The paragraph that followed began, "There is nothing wrong with being a non-nurturer. A lot of you men out there are probably just that. And you have some real advantages over the natural nurturer." Bah. Why didn't they just come out and say, "Not fit to parent."

Sam refocused on what she was reading. The chapter was on listening to what your teenager was telling you. "Listening is different from hearing. We hear the cars on the street, but we're not listening for one with a diesel engine or squeaky brakes. This is how we have to listen to our kids. It's the best way to understand your child. Like a car, people (and especially teenagers) give all sorts of warning signals in what they do and say. This chapter is going to teach *you* how to translate this secret language."

The author's cheerful prose describing the difficulties of rebellious teenagers scraped Sam's mind like sandpaper. Older than his twin by two minutes, Rob had always been bigger and stronger, louder and more outgoing, and eminently more difficult for Sam to understand.

Sam turned the page and started the next paragraph, then heard a knock on the door. Slipping the book under the covers, she snatched a magazine off the bedside table and flipped it open. "Come in," she called.

Derek stuck his head in the door. "How come you're up?"

She shrugged and laid the magazine across her lap. "Couldn't sleep."

"Me neither." He crossed the room slowly, his left leg stiff and awkward beneath him. Despite his frequent visits to a physical therapist over the past eight years, Sam didn't notice much change in Derek's limp.

She never suggested that he stop going, and neither did he. If after all these years Derek retained the faith that he would learn to run, then she admired him for it. Hope would carry him further than any doctor. The mind was a powerful instrument, and his faith was something she refused to allow anyone to take away.

Derek sat on the edge of the bed and looked, without comment, down at the magazine Sam had been flipping through.

Sam watched him. "You want some tea?"

He shook his head.

"Warm milk?"

"Gross, Aunt Sam." He scrunched his nose and shook his head again. There was a sad look in his eyes, under it just the slightest edge of anxiety or even fear.

"Something happen?" she asked, following the advice of the book hidden under her covers to make herself available if he wanted to talk to her.

"Just stupid kid stuff." He sounded like an adult as he spoke, rubbing his hand over his bad hip and staring down at it.

"People say stupid stuff all the time," she said, guessing someone had commented on his limp. She thought of her own experience at work the day before. "They feel threatened and call people names because they're different, and they don't bother to try to understand that different doesn't mean bad."

Derek frowned and then smiled softly. "They do, don't they?"

She nodded. It was the first time either of the boys had spoken to her without being spoken to first in at least three days. She wanted to reach out and hug Derek, but she didn't dare. Instead, she put her hand on his and squeezed.

"They're such morons."

She laughed. "Mostly."

Derek stood and made his way to the door, his limp less noticeable. "Good night."

When the door closed, Sam pulled the book out and found her lost page. The book warned not to try to compare her own childhood emotions to what her child was feeling. At least *that* wasn't a problem. Nothing in her childhood was worth repeating. The doctor talked about ways to avoid pushing your own past on your child, avoiding the cyclical pattern of parent/child relations. Sinking deeper against the thick pillows and flannel sheets, Sam concentrated on every word. Maybe there was something to be said for the doctor's suggestions after all.

*

Thick smoke billowed through an open window at the far side of the room. It floated down the long length and circled the bed like a ghost. She drew up the covers and tucked herself further in, but she couldn't escape the low sound of his voice. It haunted her, stirring fears buried beneath years.

"Samantha Jean, where are you?" he called, his voice a record that played on her insecurities and mocked her successes, the Southern drawl nauseating.

She sat upright and sprang out of bed, hearing his thump, thump on the stairs. She looked around the dark basement, realizing for the first time why she slept down there when everyone else was upstairs. Her mama put her there so her daddy could come get her.

"Sammy Jean," he called again, his voice closer, his words drawn out.

Sammy froze in her tracks.

She heard him laugh, but it was a short, tired laugh. He didn't like the game. "It's not hide-and-seek, Sammy Jean. It's a different game. All the kids play games at home, Sammy. This is ours."

The sound of her father's voice sent fear skittering up her spine. It wasn't the same as with other kids. She knew it wasn't the same.

She scanned the room for a new place to hide, but she had used them all. She sprinted to the crawl space and sank her toes in the cold dirt, pushing her way to the back. Flat against the cement wall of the house, she could hear the wheezing of her own breath. Tightening her jaw, she held herself quiet and still.

Her knees pulled up to her chin, she squeezed her eyes closed and willed her father away. She blinked hard. No matter what, she wouldn't cry. Last time she went crying, her mama had said, "Worse thing you can do is cry. If you just keep your mouth shut, it'll be over in no time."

She didn't want to do it again. Why did she have to do it? The other kids in school didn't. Tammy Sue thought she was crazy when she asked. Nobody else had to touch it, to kiss it, to let them put it there.... It had hurt so much. Her lips began to quiver and she held them tight between her teeth. Don't cry, stupid.

"Sammy Jean?"

She leapt at the sound of his voice. He was practically next to her. He wasn't usually so quiet when he was drunk. Usually she could hear him coming a mile away.

"Sammy Jean, are you hiding from me?" he growled, and she could tell he was getting angry.

She willed herself not to cry. Please don't cry. Please.

Suddenly his shape filled the entrance to the crawl space and his big, hairy hand reached for her.

She screamed and kicked at him to get away.

He howled and she scrambled to the furthest corner, but it wasn't deep enough to get away. He caught her leg and pulled.

"You're hurting me!"

"You don't come here, I'll hurt you more." He yanked hard until he got her under one arm and dragged her out. Her nightie flew up and her panties showed. She tried to cover herself but he pushed her hand away.

The smell of his breath reminded her of the first time he had come into her room, late at night. He always had the same smell when he came for her.

Her daddy pulled her panties aside and touched her.

Her eyes squeezed closed, she fought not to cry, not to fight.

"How do you like that?" he asked, blowing his breath in her face.

Ignore him. She had to ignore him. She lifted her chin. At least he didn't go to Polly. She needed to keep him away from Polly. Polly was only seven. Sammy was nine. She could take care of herself.

"I said, do you like it?" He jabbed deeper.

Wincing in pain, she lashed out, throwing her hand at his face. Her palm made a loud smack as it struck his skin. She kicked hard and hit him in the chin.

He let go and she twisted fast and got up. Running for the stairs, she didn't look back.

She reached the top and pulled open the door. The smells

of the kitchen hit her as she gasped for breath. She took a step onto the yellow linoleum floor, but a giant hand yanked her back. She started to scream, but he hit her hard in the eye. She blinked hard to focus, feeling her left eye begin to swell.

"You want to fight?" he said, shaking her, her feet barely touching the floor.

She tried to pull away.

"I'll show you what men do with women who taunt and then don't put out. You can learn this lesson nice and early." He smacked her hard in the mouth and then picked her up and turned back toward the basement. She searched for a way out, but he was too big. She could already barely see out of her left eye and she knew she shouldn't fight anymore. She'd have enough explaining to do as it was.

He tossed her on the bed and tears closed her throat. She felt the hair on the back of his hand hit her belly. Sammy shut her eyes and clenched her teeth, trying not to make a sound. She could block it out. Block it out. She felt the pressure of his weight on her first, his round, hard belly pressing against her chest.

She shook her head and held back her tears. Dream about something else. Dream.

*

Sam shot up in bed, the dark sheets stained with tears and sweat, the flannel clutched in her hands. Her eyes scanned the room, her pulse like a drill in her ears. It was a dream. It was only a bad dream.

CHAPTER 21

SAM HADN'T HEARD a word on the case all morning. She'd talked to Aaron twice and learned that nothing was going on at work. With the exception of the fact that Williams had told everyone about how she'd drawn a gun on him.

"You want to talk about it?" Aaron had asked.

"No," she'd snapped before adding, "It's a load of crap."

"I figured," he told her, but she knew there were plenty of people in the office who were eating the rumors up and loving it.

And to make matters more frustrating, the space heater that had exploded on her had also disappeared from the closet in her office where she'd put it. So now there was no way to find out if someone had tampered with it. She'd had Aaron call facilities to check and see if anyone knew where it was, but they'd never seen it. Sam again wondered if Williams wasn't the obvious suspect.

She was supposed to be on the case full-time, but she wished now that she'd gone to the office even if just to pass the time. At least she could have told Williams what a shit he was. Instead, she was stuck staring at the walls, going crazy.

She'd paged Nick twice and called his house three times, only to hear the familiar sound of his answering machine. She hadn't left a message. He knew she was trying to reach him. She'd tried to sleep, but her nightmare had left her with a twisted gut and an inability to rest at all. Instead, she'd done something she had been intending to do for years. She had pulled out the small cardboard box and was sorting through the stack of Polly's letters. She dreaded the thought of coming back to these after so much time, wishing she had read them all those years ago.

But when Sam had gotten the first one, Polly was so happy at a time when Sam had felt so destitute, she'd been unable to handle her own loneliness. And now Polly was dead. She should've reached out to her sister, tried to save her. But the letter had not asked for help. Quite the opposite, in fact.

Sam untied the stack and removed the only opened letter from its envelope. With dread clawing at her, Sam read it again:

Sammy Jean,

Who knows if you'll even get this letter, but Daddy asked me to write you to see if you'd come home. He's really sick, you know. Doc Brewster says it's his heart, but I don't understand much more about it. He's supposed to stop drinking, but he doesn't. Mostly, he doesn't want to tell us. He thinks we're still kids. We're not. I'm almost twenty. My birthday's in three months, if you forgot. I finished up at NW Miss. Community College in Senatobia. I've thought about a four-year college, but I got offered a full-time job at the Wal-Mart. I've been there for about three years, so they're offering me a job as an assistant manager. Pay's real good, so I can't see turning it down for college.

Dad asks about you sometimes, when Mom's not around. Mom doesn't want anyone to mention your name since you left, but Dad does. She's real mad at you, saying you made up all that stuff about Daddy. I'm sure you had your reasons. I don't think he's mad or anything. I'm sure Mom would forgive you, too, if you just come back and tell her you're sorry.

When he asks, I tell him you're a big shot out in California and that you're real busy. He smiles. You know, I moved to the basement after you left. Funny being in your old room.

Jimmy's moved to Atlanta, chasing Tammy Smith. Mom needs me now, especially since Dad is sick. And Wayne is here. Do you remember Wayne Austin? He lived over on Church, just a couple blocks down. We've been going out for nearly a year. He's a little like Dad. Sounds strange, doesn't it? But he loves me. And I love him. I just found out I'm pregnant, so I think he's going to ask me to marry him. I haven't told Dad yet. Mom says not to tell him. She says it would be bad on his heart. I hope you have some kids by now.

I can't imagine anything more wonderful than being a mom. Take care. Maybe you can bring your family back here. I know Dad would like to see you. And Mom too, even though she wouldn't say so. Call us. Do you still have the number?

Sam read the familiar phone number and felt the tears drift down her face as she pictured their father drunk, chasing Polly down the stairs. Jimmy had left, Sam had left, but Polly had stayed. She even took care of their father. Polly put up with all of it, bought the line of bullshit her mother fed her. Her mother had never forgiven Sam for refusing to live her mother's lies.

Sam had left them and when she'd gone, she'd told her mother why. She'd told her with Polly and Jimmy in the room how screwed up she was. Sam had convinced herself she'd risen above it, and taking the moral high ground, she called her father sick and dysfunctional, called her mother weak for putting up with it. It was something only an eighteen-year-old could do. And her mother had never forgiven her, had erased Sam's existence from the family tree. Sam wondered where her mother was now. Was she dead?

She remembered the day Polly's letter had come. Sam had been through a battery of tests, and failed each one. The doctors had explained the results with grim faces. They had used words she didn't understand, identified organs she didn't know existed. "Due to previous trauma," she remembered one of them saying. It was the only time Brent had even looked at her. Through the rest of it, he had nodded without a word.

On the drive home, he was silent. He dropped her off at their house, changed his clothes, and disappeared. Polly's letter arrived in the mail that day. Divorce papers and a letter from Brent's attorney the next. It was over like that. Alone again.

She looked down at Polly's letter. *I tell him you're a big shot out in California and he smiles.* She shook her head. She was no big shot. She wasn't even sure she would have a job next week. *I hope you have some kids by now. I can't imagine anything more wonderful than being a mom.* Oh, Polly. Sam shook her head. It should've been me instead of you. You should be raising your boys.

Gripping the letter, she wished she could cry. The guilt, the anger, the physical pain, none of it would come loose. Instead, it had seeded deeper into her belly, sinking roots there. She stared at the other letters, the unopened ones. She should have been stronger. She should have been able to handle what was in them, but she couldn't. Not yet. Maybe not ever.

*

Sam sat in her car and watched Rob's team practice through the fence. She was parked opposite the outfield, and she could just barely make out Rob in the lineup. All the kids wore baseball pants that had long since stopped being white, despite the bleach and hot water that went into cleaning them.

The team was supposed to have finished up ten minutes ago, but they had a tendency to run over. A line of cars waited, mothers mostly in SUVs, talking on cell phones. Sam wondered who they were talking to—stockbrokers, friends, husbands, therapists? Sam had no one to call. She tried not to think about Polly or her family.

Nick wasn't on the field today, and she knew he was tied up with the case. She knew it was keeping him busy, but she hoped he would call her soon to give her an update. She felt certain he knew more about the accusations that were circulating around the station. She wished he hadn't told her. Not knowing what the evidence was made her feel like her job and her reputation were flying in the wind.

Seeing him last night at the crime scene, she had yearned for a chance to speak privately. It was the wrong time, but she would have been comforted by just a moment alone with him. Ridiculous, but it was how she felt. How long had it been since she'd been close to a man? Or to anyone, for that matter?

Brent had been too distant to get close to. When they were married, she didn't think she needed to share herself completely with another person. She was private. Privacy was one thing, but the complete lack of intimacy she'd had with Brent was another. Only she hadn't realized it at the time.

Even as a child, she'd blocked herself off from other children because she didn't want them to know what happened at her house. She'd never confided in them, couldn't share the little secrets that created friendships between young girls.

Sam's own secrets hadn't been so little. She had fought to protect Polly, to shelter her. She remembered the small silver ring Polly had given her before she left Mississippi. Seeing it in the box of letters from Polly had brought back a barrage of memories that Sam had kept carefully tucked away—things she still didn't feel prepared to deal with. She would probably never feel prepared to deal with them. Today, she had started to deal with what was there. She'd let it go too long.

Distracting herself from thoughts of Polly, Sam pulled out the list of the names of people who had worked the two homicide cases and went over it again. She'd put check marks next to Corona and Williams.

She knew her sense of desperation was a result of the situation at work. She needed to get answers. She would have to face Corona on Monday. He was commuting to the Sacramento office for the remainder of the week. The blackout would surely come up then. Corona would've heard Williams' version of the story at least.

She stared at Williams' name again, wondering what would have happened if the security guard hadn't shown up.

A litany of questions followed that one. Was Williams the one who had shut the electricity off? Was he responsible for the threats? Had she really made such an enemy of him? Did he really blame her for his mistakes? Had the latest fiasco with the D.A. been too much for him? Aaron had told her that people thought she was difficult. That was fine by her. But was she difficult enough for someone to want to hurt her? That subject was another one that she wanted to discuss with Corona, but it wasn't something she was willing to discuss over the phone. Since she hadn't really needed to be in the office for the past two days, she'd been doing most of her work from home. It was pretty clear that Corona supported the idea of her lying low for a while. As much as she hated it, she couldn't blame him. There was no other link between the cases but her. As hard as she searched, she couldn't find anything else to tie them together.

She glanced at the field, where Rob's team was still in full practice, and then at the clock. They were twenty minutes late. The line of cars waiting had grown, and it wouldn't be long before someone's parent got out of a car and told them it was time to quit. Sam could wait. She liked to watch the kids' enthusiasm, and the quiet gave her time to think.

Within a few minutes Rob opened the car door and got inside.

"How was practice?" Sam asked, revving the engine and starting down the street.

"Fine," Rob muttered.

Sam turned the car toward home. Something was tickling the back of her mind, but she couldn't drag it to the surface.

"I thought I was getting a ride home with Jason's mom," Rob said, breaking into her thoughts.

"I'm working from home for a few days, so I thought I'd pick you up. I hope you don't mind," she added.

"Nah. Jason's mom is a bitch anyway. Are you staying home because Der's sick?"

"No," she said. "And please don't use that word. I'm working from home because of the case I'm on with Nick out here. It doesn't make sense to go to work in the city."

Rob nodded slowly and then turned to look out the

window. "Are you and Nick dating?" he asked, his gaze locked on the passing streets.

Sam watched him for a minute before responding. He didn't turn to her. "Would that bother you?"

Rob glanced over and shrugged. "I don't know. I really like him, but I don't want to date him."

Sam smiled.

"I thought maybe you were gay," he added in a low voice.

Sam's mouth dropped open, and she couldn't help but laugh at his boldness. "You thought I was a lesbian?"

Rob shrugged. "There's nothing wrong with it."

"I agree, but no, I'm not—a lesbian, that is. How come you never asked?"

He shrugged again. Sam wondered if they had a class on shrugging at school. Her nephews shrugged better than anyone she'd ever seen.

"If you have questions, you should just ask," she said.

"You do a lot of strange stuff." Rob shrugged again. "Maybe all adults do things."

"Like what?"

"Like that folder of coupons you keep."

"A lot of people clip coupons."

"But you don't ever use them."

She didn't have a good answer to that one. It was true. She'd never brought the huge folder of coupons to the store with her, never used a single one. Instead, she clipped them, filed them, and kept them stored the way some people probably kept emergency cash on hand. Once a year or so, she'd clean out the file, throw away the expired coupons, and keep going. "True," she finally said. "Is there anything else?"

Rob shrugged, and Sam wondered if she couldn't have a harness fitted for him that would keep his shoulders from doing that. "You sleep in flannel sheets all year," he said. It was more a statement than a question.

"I guess I get cold easily."

He nodded. "It's still weird."

"As for dating," she continued, returning to the original subject, "I haven't found anyone I really like."

"But you like Nick?"

It felt like such a loaded question, but she found herself nodding. "I think so. I'm not sure. I'm not sure I'm very good at relationships."

He stared at her and nodded. "Me neither. I liked this girl Penny at school, but she didn't give me the time of day. Then, when I stopped liking her, she was all over me. Girls are weird."

Sam laughed. "That's for sure."

"What about that Brent guy?"

Sam had never discussed Brent with the boys—she had answered their rare questions, but they'd never met him, never seen pictures of him. Sam didn't even think she had any left. "Brent wasn't a very nice person," she said out loud, thinking he was actually a cold, heartless prick. She was thankful to be able to admit that the destruction of their marriage wasn't solely her fault. "Nick's a much better person. Does it make you uncomfortable since he's your coach?"

"No. But don't jerk him around."

Sam didn't mind that Rob protected Nick. Maybe he

would give Nick the same lecture about not hurting her, but she doubted it. Rob was right. She didn't want to hurt Nick. She cared about him. She wanted to get to know him, to let him know her. It was the first time she'd ever wanted someone to *know* her.

Polly's face flashed through her mind, and she squeezed her eyes shut for an instant to push it away. Even Polly hadn't known her. As she opened her eyes, she saw a flash of reddish-orange pass in front of the car—a jacket. She hit the brakes, but nothing happened.

"Shit!" She pumped harder, frantically slamming her foot to the floor. The car didn't even slow. "The brakes don't work!"

"Watch out!" Rob screamed.

Sam looked up and caught the face of a child through her windshield, his body only twenty feet from her bumper. "Oh, my God!"

Slamming her foot onto the emergency brake, she swerved the car to the right. The face got closer.

"You're going to hit him!" Rob yelled.

Jerking the steering wheel to the left, Sam swerved across the other lane and jumped the curb. She could smell burning rubber as the tires screeched on the pavement. She hit a tree and lurched forward. The airbags popped open and she felt the nylon burn against her arms.

Shaking herself, she grabbed Rob. "Are you okay?"

He moaned. "Yeah. What happened?"

Her heart racing, she shook her head. "I don't know. The brakes didn't work." She ran her hands across his face and head, looking for blood. "Are you sure you're not hurt?"

"My shoulder's stiff, but I'm okay."

"Don't move, Rob. I'm going to call an ambulance."

Sam unfastened her seatbelt and grabbed her cell phone. She dialed 911 with shaky fingers and waited until she heard an operator. "This is Sam Chase from the Department of Justice. I've had a car accident. I'm at Walker Avenue and Oak Knoll Loop in Walnut Creek. Send an ambulance."

Just then, she remembered the flash of color in front of the car. The child. She dropped the phone and pushed herself out of the car. As she ran across the street, a horn blared and she jumped back, barely missing being run down.

She found a small boy hovering beside a tree, his head down. She knelt beside him. "Are you okay?" Oh, please God, let him be okay.

The boy was shaking and didn't answer.

She pulled him back from the tree and held him in her arms so she could see his face.

Wide brown eyes stared at her, and he flinched at her touch.

"Where does it hurt, sweetie? Talk to me."

He trembled at the sound of her voice, and she scanned him for injuries. He couldn't have been older than six or seven. She thought of little Derek when he had come to live with her. So small, so fragile, he had seemed so afraid of everything. "Please talk to me."

He blinked hard and nodded.

"Are you okay?"

He nodded again.

"Did I hit you?"

He pointed to his stomach. She lifted his shirt, but she didn't see any marks on his white skin. Still, she couldn't be sure.

"Your stomach hurts?"

He nodded again, a single tear running down his cheek.

She began to rock him. "Okay, it's going to be okay." She looked down the street for the ambulance, wondering how Rob was, praying this boy wasn't hurt, cursing the ambulance for taking so long.

In the distance, she heard sirens. People had started to gather on the sidewalk, but she ignored them, waiting for the police to arrive.

"Are you all right?" one man asked.

Sam exhaled, pointing to her car. "Can you check on the boy in that car?"

The man ran across the street. When he returned, he told her, "He's got a sore shoulder is all. You call the police?"

She nodded.

"I can see the ambulance now."

"Thank God," she whispered. She ran her hand over the boy's forehead, pushing his sandy brown hair off the soft skin. He had closed his eyes, and the sight of his face made her panic. "Look at me, buddy. Hang in there."

His eyes fluttered open and he gave her a weak smile.

She smiled back, relief like a giant breath of clean air. "You feeling a little better?"

He nodded.

"I want to have a doctor look at you—just to be sure."

"I'm okay," he said in a tiny voice. "You just scared me 'cause I thought you were going to hit me."

Sam rubbed his head and nodded. "I thought maybe I was too."

The ambulance pulled up to her, and the two techs came running.

Sam motioned to the boy first. "Something happened with my brakes and I swerved to miss him. I wasn't sure if I hit him. He seems startled but not hurt. Still, I want someone to take a look."

One of the techs knelt beside her with a medical kit. "Your head okay?"

Sam frowned and touched her forehead. She felt warm, thick blood. "It's fine. It doesn't even hurt."

The tech returned his attention to the boy. "What's your name, buddy?"

The little boy looked at her, and she nodded.

"Mason."

"Okay, Mason, does anything hurt?"

He pointed at his tummy again.

The second tech brought a wooden board, and the two of them lifted Mason onto it.

"I'm okay here," the first tech said. "What've you got in the car?"

"I think it's a shoulder injury from the impact," Sam explained. "It's my nephew. He was wearing his seatbelt." She crossed the street more carefully than the first time and pulled open the passenger door.

Rob opened one eye and smiled. "I always knew men were better drivers."

The tech laughed and Sam rolled her eyes. "I'm Chad," he said.

"Rob," her nephew answered.

"I hear you've got a sore shoulder."

Sam stepped back as the tech went to work on Rob. Her pulse no longer racing, she found her cell phone and started to page Nick. She added the numbers 911 to the end of her page and her cell phone rang less than a minute later.

"What's going on?" he said when she answered.

"I've had a car accident. The front of the Caprice is pretty well smashed. I need someone to tow it to the station, and I want a mechanic to look at the brakes."

"What the hell happened?"

She felt herself start to shake and fought it off. "I don't know. One minute I had brakes and the next minute I didn't."

"Is anyone hurt?"

"No. I almost hit a kid, but I think he's fine. I think we're all okay." But we could've died, she thought. She couldn't get herself to say it out loud.

"I'll get someone to come get it. Where are you again?"

She repeated her location. "I'm going with Rob to the hospital. He's hurt his shoulder, so they're going to need to do some X-rays. Call me when someone's seen the car."

"I will. Keep me posted on the shoulder, too. That's one of my star players."

She smiled. "Right. I almost forgot." She started to hang up when she heard his voice again. "What?"

"You're sure you're okay?"

"Yeah," she said, letting her breath out. "I think we're fine. But something's wrong with the car."

"I don't care about the car."

"Thanks, Nick. We're okay."

"You be careful."

Sam rode in the back of the ambulance with Rob on one side and little Mason on the other. She'd spoken to Mason's mother and assured her that Mason was in shock but otherwise unharmed. The tech hadn't found any signs that he had been hit, but they were taking him in for routine X-rays anyway. His mother would meet them all at the hospital.

They pulled in at the emergency entrance and Sam could see Mason's mother, pacing frantically. When the ambulance doors opened, Sam called the woman over, confirmed again that everything was fine and watched as they wheeled Mason inside, his mother with him. Sam followed Rob into X-ray and tried to wait patiently while the nurses paged a doctor to assist them.

*

Two hours later, she'd given her statement to a police officer who looked vaguely familiar, and the doctors had confirmed that Rob didn't have any broken bones. Little Mason was fine, too. The doctor had put a suture on her forehead where she'd apparently hit something in the accident, although she swore it didn't hurt. They put Rob's arm in a sling.

Exhausted, Sam took Rob's good arm and the two of them walked out of the hospital.

"What happened to the brakes?" he asked when they were outside.

She shook her head. "I don't know."

"You think someone did that?"

She met his gaze. His eyes were cool and serious, and he looked older than he was. "I'm not sure, Rob."

"Mrs. Austin, you look like you've had an accident."

Sam looked up to see Derek's physical therapist coming through the hospital parking lot. She ignored the use of the boys' last name. "Hi, Patricia. Just a little fender bender," she explained awkwardly.

"Everyone's all right?"

"Fine, thanks." Sam forced a smile and looked toward the cab waiting at the curb. She just wanted to go home. "Good to see you."

"Derek's doing great, by the way."

Sam turned back. "I'm glad. Thanks."

The physical therapist said something Sam didn't catch.

Sam turned back. "I'm sorry?"

"He's doing really well," the PT said again, waving as she ran off.

Sam opened the door of the cab and let Rob climb in first. "Two thirteen Oak Tree Road," she said, leaning back in the seat, exhausted.

CHAPTER 22

GERRY STARED AT the newspaper article about Eva Larson's death. Seeing Sam Chase's name in print, he felt famous. It made him feel more alive than he had since he'd left prison. He stared at the picture of little Becky and then read the page three times before his eyes settled on the final line.

> *Funeral services for Becky Larson, age 8, will be held by her grandparents this Friday at 4 p.m. at St. Stephen's Cemetery in Concord. Donations in lieu of flowers can be sent to the National Center for the Prevention of Child Abuse.*

He tucked the newspaper into his pocket and headed for the cemetery.

*

Gerry entered the cemetery from Cloverdale Avenue and walked down the winding road toward the spot where Becky Larson was to be buried. The rolling green hills were a stark contrast to his tiny plaster-and-concrete apartment and the dirty streets where he'd been lately. He felt the fresh air hit his lungs and suddenly thought of the farmland where he'd grown up. He gazed at the single road that wound like a gray snake through the green landscape with its scattered tombstones.

He'd planned his arrival so the ceremony would already be in progress. He would just happen upon it. That way, if someone noticed him, he would say he was just taking a walk. Plus, no one had ever said he couldn't come to the cemetery.

He paused at the top of the last hill and he squatted next to a concrete angel statue, pretending to pull weeds. The angel's wings were spread, its face pointing to the sky, its hands holding a small plaque that read "Kristen L. George, March 3, 1967-June 24, 1973." Barely six years old. Six years old was almost his favorite age. He pictured little Kristen in his mind.

Standing up slowly, he looked down the hill at the small gathering at Becky's funeral. He wished he had a pair of binoculars. Then he could've sat right there and seen every detail. But he could never afford anything like binoculars. He moved twenty feet down the hill and sat down beside another tombstone.

This one was for an old guy, but if he sat right beside it, he could see Becky's funeral perfectly between it and the tombstone next to it. A group of about twenty were gathered around a tiny pine coffin. He figured it was about a hundred feet, probably a safe distance. Several adults in the front were dressed in black. There were a few children in the group, but most were hidden behind adults.

Shifting, he concealed himself behind the two tombstones. It would be hard for anyone at the funeral to spot him. Peering between the two tombstones, he spotted Sam Chase. He wanted to go and talk to her, but he knew he shouldn't. Soon, but not yet. He was starting to enjoy being out of prison and thought maybe he wasn't ready to get caught again.

Sam was looking around, so he was careful to pretend to be looking down while he watched her. She was wearing black pants and a black sweater, standing in the sun. But she didn't look hot.

He liked to watch her. He'd seen her once at her house, and he'd followed her to the office twice. He liked seeing her dressed up for work. The first time, he'd even been able to get into the building. He loved the way she looked over her shoulder, checking around like she was nervous. He wondered if she sensed him and wished he could talk to her. He saw the kid in her when she was nervous, and he liked it. Her skin had freckles like a little girl's, and he longed to touch it. Would she have soft skin like a little girl? Soft, he thought, wondering if he'd ever get to find out. She straightened her back, looking confident. Maybe he would go to her office again tomorrow.

He wiped his brow and continued to pull weeds around the tombstone, making a little pile on one side.

Sam scanned the cemetery, and for a second he thought she saw him, but then she turned her back. Gerry saw a little girl in a gray cotton dress standing at the edge of the group. She had dark hair that hung down her back in snarled clumps. He pictured her in his mind, lying still almost like she was sleeping. Poor Becky.

Then he went back to studying the little girl in the gray dress. Restless, she shifted her weight from side to side. He felt himself grow hard watching her.

With a quick look around to make sure he was alone, he continued to watch her. She didn't stop moving, swinging her arms as she danced around. She was about six, he decided. Through his pants, he rubbed his hand against himself, pretending it was her shifting against him. Vanessa, he called her. She looked like a Vanessa.

A man grabbed Vanessa's hand and pulled her to him, holding her to his leg and shushing her. Gerry wished it was him shushing her, holding her to him. He pushed himself up against one of the tombstones, rubbing his erection on the hard, cold stone and pretending it was little Vanessa. For a second he felt guilty. He stopped and looked around, but no one was there. He tried not to look at Vanessa, to keep his eyes off her, but he couldn't.

Unzipping his pants, he gripped himself in his hand. He thought about leaving DNA evidence, but he couldn't stop. Seeing her wiggle like that was too much. He kept his head down and pretended to be pulling weeds, watching Vanessa from the corner of his eye. No one seemed interested in him. He pulled and pulled, imagining it was little Vanessa's hand instead of his own. Wrong, wrong, a voice in the back of his head screamed. But he couldn't help it.

Soon, her face in his head, her little hands all over him in his mind, he released in a wave of hot pleasure. Clamping his mouth shut, he held himself back from screaming.

Then, snapping back to reality, he looked around nervously and quickly zipped himself back up.

He had the urge to get up and run, but he made himself sit and pull more weeds. He piled them on top of the spot he'd made, not allowing himself to look at Vanessa anymore. He couldn't be doing that.

Despite his self-chastising, he felt more relaxed than he had in months. It was like a vacation. He got to enjoy himself, and with the help of Sam Chase he could go home whenever he was ready.

CHAPTER 23

NICK FORCED A smile for the camera as the photographer struggled to keep the boys lined up on the infield. The sun burned their eyes and sweat pooled beneath the polyester jerseys.

"Last one, guys. Stay with me," the nervous, gangly man said.

The team ignored him.

"Hey," Nick yelled to Brooks and Jenkins, who were screwing around in the front row. "You guys keep it up and it'll be laps for both of you."

The boys groaned and settled down.

The photographer gave him a grateful smile and snapped two more photos. "That's it."

Nick relaxed his mouth and rubbed his jaw. He hated pictures. He waited for Rob to extract himself from his friends, anxious to be on his way. He hadn't seen Sam in four days, and he looked forward to having an excuse to stop by.

At the sound of his name, he turned to see Mrs. Brooks coming toward him. He waved. A divorcée, Ellen

Brooks had tried more than once to get his attention romantically. He'd done his best to spurn her advances in a friendly fashion, but the last time he'd found it nearly impossible to dissuade her and he'd stooped to lying about another relationship. He thought about Sam. Maybe it wouldn't be a lie this time.

"I saw the bit about you in the paper this afternoon," she said. "Sounds like a dangerous case."

Nick frowned. "What bit?"

She smiled and touched his shoulder, as though she was picking lint off his team shirt. "You know, the copycat case: that woman up at Mt. Diablo, and the other in Martinez. It was on the front page of the afternoon paper's Metro section."

Anger twisted his gut. The media hadn't been involved in any of the cases. The victims had been low-profile women, the locations far enough apart to keep it out of the news. How the hell…?

"I've still got the paper at my house, if you didn't see it," she offered.

Just then Rob joined them. "Hi, Mrs. Brooks."

Mrs. Brooks patted Rob on the back. "Nice playing. Where's Jay?"

Rob pointed to the field. "I think he's getting his mitt."

"Your mom see the paper today?" she asked Rob.

Rob shrugged, clearly uncomfortable with Sam being called his mom.

Ellen looked back at Nick. "She's mentioned in the article too."

Nick nodded, ready to get out of there. He didn't

have his pager on, but there was no doubt that if the case had hit the media, his captain would want to hear from him. Damn reporters.

"What article?" Rob asked.

"Just something about this case we're working on."

Rob looked confused. "What case?"

"It's nothing—"

Ellen touched Nick's chest again, and he could see Rob's eyes on her. "I wouldn't call murder nothing."

Nick backed away without comment, though he didn't miss the disappointment in her gaze. "We should get going, Rob. 'Bye, Ellen."

" 'Bye, Nick, Rob."

Rob followed him toward the car. "What's up with her?"

Nick shrugged.

"She likes you. Are you going to go out with her?"

Nick met Rob's gaze. "No. I'm not interested in Mrs. Brooks."

"Who are you interested in?"

Nick raised an eyebrow and put his arm around Rob as they started toward the car. "What makes you think I'm interested in anyone?"

"Not even Sam?"

"Has she mentioned me?"

"Not really. I asked her about it, though."

Nick pressed Rob for information. "And?"

Rob shrugged.

"You're not going to tell me what she said?"

Rob looked smug. "I think she likes you."

Nick exhaled. "How can you tell?"

Rob shook his head. "It's not easy."

Nick laughed and unlocked the car door. "I've got to stop and buy a paper. That okay?"

"Sure."

Using his car phone, Nick dialed his captain's number. Cintrello picked up on the first ring.

"It's Thomas."

"I'm glad you called. All hell's breaking loose."

"You see the article?" Nick asked.

"What article?"

"The afternoon paper—some article about the case. I haven't seen it yet. I just heard from someone here." He paused and frowned. "What hell's breaking loose?"

"Chase's fingerprints."

Nick looked at Rob from the corner of his eye. Though the boy was looking out the window, Nick knew he was listening. "Say that again?"

"The evidence I told you about—it's confirmed. Her prints were on the batteries in a flashlight found at Eva Larson's home near the body."

It didn't make sense. Sam had been the one to suggest they dust the batteries. "What about the eyelids? I heard there were prints there."

"Yeah, there were. I haven't figured that out yet."

"Have you matched them to anything else?"

"Yeah, smart-ass—the print on Walters."

"And that doesn't belong to the special agent, am I right?" he said, trying to keep Rob from knowing he was talking about Sam.

"Doesn't matter, Thomas. The light came from her

car—standard issue. She was there, and the shit's going to come down heavy on her."

"Captain—"

"Not a word to anyone, Thomas, especially Chase. I'm confiding in you because I need you on this case. But if it gets out, I know who leaked it."

"You're wrong, you know. You should be looking for whoever's print was at both scenes."

"We'll know for sure within twenty-four hours."

"What is that supposed to mean?"

"It means she's under surveillance, Thomas. For the next twenty-four hours while we run the rest of the evidence, check and double-check. If you're lucky, it'll all just go away. But I'm not holding my breath. The undersheriff doesn't want to chance another victim with no alibi for Agent Chase, so I want you on her, too. Twenty-four hours. Stay inside, make something up. Or stay outside, I don't care. But you stay on her."

"No way. You're asking me to—" He noticed Rob and shook his head again. "No."

"Watch it, Thomas. I'll yank your badge faster than you can backpedal your ass out of it. This is a direct order from the undersheriff. He gives it to me and I give it to you. Spend the night with her, if you haven't already."

Nick couldn't believe what he was hearing. It was disgusting. He also knew Cintrello was about the most stubborn son of a bitch he had ever met. He didn't respond. He didn't have anything to say that wouldn't involve insulting his superior.

"Do we understand each other, Thomas?"

Nick slammed his fist against the steering wheel.

Rob jumped, and Nick touched his shoulder and shook his head in silent apology. He thought about the evening he and Sam were supposed to have with his family tonight, trying to keep Cintrello's insinuation from tainting it. "One night?" he repeated.

"That's what I said. Our guys are around, but I want someone closer to make sure she doesn't slip. That someone's you. Maybe you'll even get a little something out of it."

Nick forced himself not to respond. Antagonizing his captain wasn't going to help anything. It was a ridiculous request, but he'd do it. He'd have dinner with her, bring her home, and then hang outside. "Fine."

"I thought you'd see it my way." With that, the captain hung up.

"I don't see it your way, asshole," Nick breathed into the dead phone. He hung up and blew out a breath. Sam Chase—killer. He shook his head. No way.

"Everything okay?"

Nick shook it off and forced a smile. "Yeah, boss is being a pain in the you-know-what, but it's fine. We just don't always agree on how to handle things."

"Is it about Aunt Sam's case?" Rob asked.

Nick nodded and then focused on the road, not wanting to think anymore about the fact that his captain had just ordered him to spy on the woman he wanted to be dating.

He stopped at a corner store and bought the paper. As soon as he was back in his car, he pulled out the Metro section and found the article.

It was worse than he'd thought. Somehow the media

had gotten hold of nearly every detail of the case and put it in print. The M.O.'s were there, including cause of death. The eucalyptus behind the ears, the gum wrapper they'd found on Walters' foot, even the presence of seminal fluid. The same was true for Eva Larson. Only the part about the number of leaves on each eucalyptus branch was missing.

The article mentioned that Eva's daughter's body had also been found in the apartment, though it appeared to authorities that she'd been dead for some time. It was like someone on the force had written it. Only the recent news of Sam Chase's apparent guilt went unmentioned.

Slapping the paper down, he put the car back in gear and drove toward Sam's. Rob picked it up and read in silence. Nick didn't stop him. The boys would inevitably hear about it in school, since both his name and Sam's were included in the text.

He parked in front of Sam's house, and Rob folded the newspaper and handed it to him. He wondered if Sam had seen it yet. Better to hear the news from Nick than from Corona. She'd be getting bad enough news from Corona. He paused before getting out of the car, preparing himself to hold back what he knew. He thought about what would happen if the situation were reversed. Would Sam tell him? He clenched his fists and banished the thought from his head. This was his job. He would do everything he could to protect Sam, but he couldn't lose his job. He could do both. He and Sam had plans to be together tonight anyway. He would watch her. Probably he wouldn't be able to keep his eyes off her and then he could prove to Cintrello that he was dead wrong.

Rob opened the door and stepped inside, calling out to Sam. When no one answered, he shrugged.

Nick frowned. Her car was in front. "Maybe she went for a run?"

Just then, he heard Derek's voice, screaming. "You bitch! How could you do that to my mother?"

Nick stiffened. "Stay here," he told Rob, motioning to the kitchen. Nick moved toward the noise. He heard a low level of conversation, but he didn't recognize the other voice.

Pushing open the door to Sam's bedroom, he saw her hunched over on the floor. Derek was standing over her, glaring as he waved a fistful of papers at her.

A cardboard box on the floor was empty and turned on its side.

"What's going on?" he asked.

Sam looked up, and Nick saw the agony on her tear-streaked face. "Please, don't."

"Tell him what's going on, Sam," Derek hissed. "Tell him what you did."

Sam swiped at her face and pulled herself to her feet, erasing the image of any weakness as quickly as possible. Lifting her chin, she spoke in a firm voice. "Stop it, Derek. This doesn't involve Nick."

"Maybe it should," Derek snapped.

Sam walked to the bed, sank down and rubbed her eyes.

Nick stepped forward. He'd never seen Derek act out like this. Rob was the one who tended to fly off the handle. Nick wondered what had set Derek off.

"Please don't," she said again, looking back at Nick. "Please go."

"No, he deserves to know," Derek yelled. "You're involved with him. He should know what kind of a person you are."

"Derek, don't talk to your aunt that way," Nick said. Closing the distance between them, he touched Sam's shoulder. "Tell me what's going on."

She looked up at him and then at Derek and shook her head.

"Fine, she won't tell you, then I will." Derek handed the papers he was holding to Nick, who glanced down at the large, cursive writing, still baffled.

"What—"

"Those are letters from my mother," Derek said. He motioned between himself and Rob, who was still lurking at the edge of the room, looking confused. "Our mother."

Nick frowned. So what?

Derek pointed back at Sam. "Unopened letters. She's had some of them for sixteen years and she never read them. I came in here to ask for money for the movies and I found one open on her bed. There was a whole box of them—a whole box of unopened letters. They're all about us—me and Rob and our dad. My mom asked Sam to come home. Begged her to come back and help her," he spat.

"Help her with what?"

"With us," Derek said. "We were poor and our dad was—" He stopped and stared at Rob.

Rob's eyes widened, but he didn't speak.

"He was drunk. He didn't work. Mom asked Sam to

come back and help her move, to get a new start. All of us but Dad. And our wonderful Aunt Sam didn't even open the damn letters. She didn't even care enough about us to read the letters."

Sam's shoulders drooped and Nick could see she was crying. He touched her, but she flinched. He didn't let up. "Sam, talk to us. What happened?"

She didn't respond.

"Then she got stuck with us," Derek continued, his face red, the veins in his neck bright blue and bulging. "That must've really sucked for you, huh, Sam? Did you try to get out of it? Did you tell them you didn't want us? Why didn't you send us somewhere else?"

"No," Sam whispered. "That's not true."

"It's crap, all of it."

"You don't know what was happening with her, Derek," Nick said. But he couldn't figure out why on earth she wouldn't have read letters from her sister. And why, if she hadn't read them, had she bothered to keep them?

"Why doesn't she tell us, then?" Derek said, his anger still at the boiling point.

Nick waited, trying to think of a reason.

Sam didn't speak.

Derek jumped on the silence. "See, she doesn't have a reason."

"You don't know that," Rob countered. "She had to have a reason. Sam?"

Shaking, Sam looked up. "I was going through my divorce."

The boys were silent, but Nick felt like he'd been hit in the gut. His own divorce had been terrible, but it had never driven him away from his family. He didn't know the circumstances for Sam, he told himself. He didn't know anything about it. But he found himself jumping to conclusions anyway. And then he wondered if it was even his place to speak. He didn't belong there. Did she want him to leave? He watched her, the tight line of her lips, the pain in her eyes. He couldn't help himself. "Maybe your mom and Sam had a big falling-out before she left Mississippi."

"Mom always talked about how great Aunt Sam was," Rob said from the doorway. His frame slouched, he seemed smaller suddenly. Sinking to the floor, he put his head in his hands.

"Sam, were there problems between you and your sister?" Nick asked.

She shook her head.

"She hates us. She never wanted us here," Derek said, his voice cracking.

"That's not true," Sam said, moving to him.

Derek pushed her away.

She stood and straightened her back, though Nick could see the weight of the situation in her slumped shoulders. "Sure, I was surprised when I got the call about you boys. But I love you guys. You're like my own children." She tried to touch Derek again, but he turned his back. Then she turned to Rob, but he wouldn't look at her either. In the end she sat down on the bed again. "I didn't realize that Polly needed my help. She always seemed so self-sufficient. I had no idea."

"Why didn't you read the letters, then?" Rob asked, his voice quiet, almost hollow.

Her gaze met Nick's, but he couldn't find it in himself to comfort her. He didn't understand how she could turn her back on her sister.

"The divorce was terrible," she whispered to Nick.

He nodded. "I've been divorced, remember?"

Her eyes sparked with anger. "Don't you dare judge me based on what you think I went through. You have no idea."

Nick found himself angry too, and he fought to suppress his reaction. "Then explain it."

She looked at the boys. "It was just terrible."

"Why?" Nick pressed. "What was so terrible?"

Sam sat in silence, her hands gripped together as though she was gathering her strength to speak. "Brent was a doctor," she said finally.

The boys looked at her. No one spoke.

"We got married when I was so young. He was eight years older—twenty-nine to my twenty-one. He thought I was a perfect Southern girl. I didn't date in college. There wasn't time." She paused. "And I wasn't interested. We'd met through his younger sister. She was my roommate.

"After we were married a year, he wanted to have kids, so we started trying." She shook her head, and Nick watched a tear fall down her cheek. "We couldn't get pregnant." She looked at Derek and then Rob. "He couldn't understand why not. He insisted we have all sorts of tests—both of us." She pressed her hand to her belly. "I thought I knew. I wasn't sure, so I went through with the tests."

She looked at Nick, tears streaming down her face. "I couldn't have kids. It was me." She brushed a hand across her cheek. "I tried to talk to him, to explain, but he refused to listen. As soon as he found out, he called me all sorts of terrible things. He didn't come home that night.

"The next day when I got home from work, he was gone—no note, nothing. He had cleared out the accounts, the furniture, everything. I had a week to find a new place to live. When I finally reached him and asked how I was supposed to live, he told me, 'A dirty whore could go back to the streets.' The day after that, I got papers—divorce papers and a letter drafted by his attorney. He had itemized what things I could have from the apartment my clothes, pictures, almost nothing else. He refused alimony or any support and warned me not to touch the bank accounts. He said if I tried legal grounds, he'd have me proved a slut in court. And he said I should keep away from all of our friends. If I didn't do as he said, he'd tell everyone why I couldn't have kids."

She looked up and sucked in a deep breath. "I got the first letter from Polly that same day. I had a hundred and twelve dollars in cash and that was it. No car—it had been in Brent's name—no savings, nowhere to stay. In that letter, Polly was so happy, I couldn't..." She stopped and dropped her hands. "I couldn't take it. I'd never felt so alone."

Rob moved toward her and Derek sat down on the floor.

Nick felt a terrible pit in his stomach.

"I started to drink too much, I almost lost my job, and by the time I got her second letter, I was ready to kill myself." She pulled in another raspy breath. "I couldn't handle hearing how good things were for her, hearing about her babies." She motioned to the boys. "I was so jealous of what I thought she had." She took Rob's hand and knelt in front of Derek. "I thought things were great for her. I had no idea." She reached for Derek's hand. "I should've read those other letters, but after hearing how happy she was in the first one, the thought of her happiness was just too painful. I'm sorry. It was selfish."

Derek nodded.

Sam sat down and pulled Derek to her chest.

Rob moved closer, too.

Nick ached to join them, but he didn't move.

"Why couldn't you have kids?" Rob asked.

Nick looked down and met Sam's pleading gaze. He knew. It made sense. Her guardedness, her inability to express herself, it was all fear. He moved to the floor with them, grasped her knee, and nodded. "Tell them."

She squeezed his hand and then turned back to the boys, still holding his fingers. With a deep breath, the tears still falling down her cheeks, she said, "I was abused." The sentence shot from her lips. Slowing down, she said it again. "I was abused." She looked at Rob and then at Derek. "My father abused me."

"How?" Derek said, his mouth open, his voice a hoarse whisper.

She held tight to Nick's hand but didn't falter. "Sexually," she whispered. "He abused me sexually. From the time I was about three, I think."

She looked at Nick. "That night you were here and I got that call—"

He nodded without speaking, worried that any sound might stop her.

"It was my brother. He called to let me know that my father was dead. Despite all he had done to me, I was still shaken. Still miserable that I'd never gotten to say good-bye to him."

With the words finally out, she turned to Nick and began to sob. He pulled Rob and Derek close as Sam's head dropped onto his chest. He held her, rubbed her back, and rocked her tenderly. Let it all out, he thought. She had needed this for so long. Rob put his arms around her too. Derek started to cry.

She had felt she would never have a family, Nick thought, but there they were, loving her. He only wished he could keep them there, comfort her.

He held her tight and prayed for them all.

CHAPTER 24

WHITNEY SAT CROUCHED beside the house with the mirror and lipstick she had taken from her mother's drawer. Holding her hand steady, she drew her lips red just like her mother did. Her hand slipped and the red slid down her chin. She frowned and looked around for something to wipe it off with. She tried using one of the branches from the big bush in front, but it was prickly and scratched her skin. She looked down at her pink T-shirt. It wasn't as dark as the lipstick, but they sort of matched. Plus, she had Jell-O stains on this one already. She pulled up the corner of the shirt and wiped the lipstick on it. When she was done, though, the shirt had a big mark. Whitney picked at it with her finger, but it was still there.

"Whitney," her mother called. Whitney jumped and dropped the shirt, staring down at the lipstick and mirror she'd taken. She thought about her mouth. She couldn't go in now.

"Whitney, it's time to take a bath," her mother called

again, and Whitney could tell she was in the back. She'd be coming out front next.

Whitney shoved the lipstick and mirror into the prickly bush and ran down to the street. She turned the corner, toward school, and ran smack into a leg.

"Oh, my, someone's in a hurry."

Whitney backpedaled and looked over her shoulder, but she didn't see her mom. She looked up at the man, who was watching her curiously, and frowned.

"Oh, sorry," the man whispered. "Are you hiding?"

Whitney looked over her shoulder again and then stared at him without answering.

"Are you hiding?" he repeated, still whispering.

Whitney tossed her head back and pushed her lips out like her mom did when she was talking to some men. "I'm not supposed to talk to strangers," she said.

"Very smart," he said.

"Whitney," her mother called.

Whitney jumped behind the man.

"Whitney Anne," her mother called again, louder.

Whitney ran as fast as she could to the neighbor's hedge and ducked behind it.

She could see the man watching her, but then he turned his back and she saw her mom.

"I'm sorry. I was just looking for my daughter."

The man smiled and looked down the street in her direction.

Whitney gasped and covered her mouth, but then the man shook his head. "I haven't seen any little girls, I'm afraid. I'm just looking for my cocker spaniel, Murphy."

He smiled. "I'll keep an eye out for your daughter if you'll do the same for my Murphy."

Whitney's mom smiled at him and pushed her hair up on one side with her hand like she did with the man at the grocery store. Whitney pushed her hair up, too, wondering if that was what men liked. It just looked goofy to her.

When her mother had gone, Whitney fell over in a fit of silent giggles. When she looked up, the man was smiling down at her.

"Why did you tell my mom you hadn't seen me?"

He shrugged. "Because I thought you were hiding from her."

"I was, but you're a dult."

"A dult?" he repeated.

"Yeah, like a grown-up."

"So, I'm supposed to tell her where you are?"

Whitney shrugged. "I guess so."

"Because dults aren't fun."

She shook her head. "No."

He frowned. "That's too bad. I'm fun."

She put her hands on her hips. "You can't be."

"Because I'm a grown-up?"

"Yep."

"Well, I guess I thought you were grown-up, too."

"How come?"

"Because you look so grown-up in that lipstick."

Whitney remembered the lipstick and kissed the back of her hand. She had to figure out a way to get rid of it before she saw her mom.

Just then, the man handed her a hankie. "You can wipe it on that."

She looked at the white hankie and thought about how mad her mom would be if she got red lipstick on something that white. She looked up at him, but he just nodded.

She wiped her mouth on the hankie and then looked at it. It was bright red, all right. She tried to hide that part when she handed it back to him.

"That's okay. I can wash it."

Whitney didn't want to tell him that she thought lipstick stained. That's what her mom told her last time she got some on something.

"See, I'm not like most grown-ups."

"How come?"

" 'Cause I like kid stuff more," he said.

Whitney frowned. If he could stay a kid, maybe she could too. "What kind of kid stuff?"

The man looked both ways and then pulled a plastic bag from his pocket. "How about this?"

Whitney peered at the little plastic bag. "What's that?"

"Candy."

She looked a little closer.

"What kind?"

He smiled. "Cherry."

"All cherry?"

He nodded.

"How come?"

"Cause cherry's my favorite."

Whitney licked her lips. She wasn't allowed to have candy. Only at Halloween and Easter, and sometimes when she found the candy her mom hid. She didn't know that Whitney knew about it.

"Do you like cherry, too?"

She nodded.

He handed her the bag. "Why don't you take it?"

She started to reach out and stopped herself. "All of it?"

He put it in her hand. "Sure. I've got lots more."

Whitney pulled the sack toward her. There had to be like a hundred pieces of candy. She even saw some jellybeans.

"Do you have a favorite kind of candy?"

She nodded.

"What is it?"

"Jellybeans and taffy," she said quickly.

"I think there's some jellybeans in there, but I'll bring taffy next time."

She nodded.

"Whitney," her mother called again.

"You'd better go inside."

She nodded and turned away. Then she remembered her manners. "Thank you for the candy, mister."

"You're welcome, Whitney."

She started to leave, then said, "What's your name, anyway?"

He gave her a big smile and reached for her hand.

Whitney gave it to him, but instead of shaking it, he lifted it to his lips and kissed it just like a prince. She giggled, even though she knew that wasn't what she was supposed to do.

"My name is Gerry," he said. "I hope to see you again soon, Princess Cherry."

"Princess Cherry?" she asked.

He nodded, smiling. " 'Cause you get all the cherry candy." He paused. "If you want it."

She nodded.

"Very nice to meet you," he said.

"You too."

"Now, you'd better get inside before your mom catches you."

She pulled the candy to her chest and turned around.

"And hide that candy. That's our secret, okay?"

"Okay, Mr. Gerry." Whitney waved and ran up the stairs toward the house. Stopping along the path, she tucked the candy under the small bush with the mirror and the lipstick, then ran around and up the back steps.

Mr. Gerry was the neatest dult she'd ever met. She hoped he came back with more candy soon.

CHAPTER 25

SAM DROVE TO Martinez and followed the directions to the auto shop where her car was being worked on. It was just after four and the mechanic was almost off duty, so she did her best to hurry. Traffic on 680 was packed, and Sam wondered how people lived this far out and commuted to the city. Martinez was flat and industrial, and she was glad that she didn't need to visit often. The police station and Hall of Justice were the city's proudest buildings—the only ones with a solid chance of surviving against the city's vandals.

Sam found the street, took a right, and turned into the driveway where she saw three black-and-whites parked. Good business, fixing cop cars. Contra Costa County had spent three million dollars on new cops and cars just last year, and at least they were keeping the cars in good shape. She glanced up at the name on the mechanic's sign: Epifani Brothers Auto Body. The Epifani brothers were doing well. It probably helped to have some friends in law enforcement.

Sam stepped out of the car in the parking lot and met

a man with a thick mustache and hair that was graying at the temples.

"Agent Chase?"

She nodded. "Ken?"

"That's me. I was hoping it'd be you. I was getting ready to close up." He waved her in. "The Caprice is out back."

"Have you had a chance to look at it yet?"

"Oh, yeah. The front's all banged out and the lights are replaced. I'm waiting for the right color paint to finish it. I can have it done by tomorrow. I've got a pickup in Walnut Creek, if you want my guy to drop it at your house."

She shook her head. "I've got someone to drive it back to the city for me." She wasn't eager to drive the car again. It could sit in the garage at the D.O.J. for a few weeks. "You look at the brakes?"

Ken whistled long and low and nodded. "That's some fancy handiwork."

Sam ignored the tight sensation in her throat and said, "So someone cut the brakes?"

"It's not nearly that easy in these new cars. But some-one definitely got to 'em. Come back here and I'll show you how it works."

Understand it. Working through a problem had always been Sam's response to fear. But these days it crept up her neck and gripped her back and shoulders despite her attempts to shake it off. Someone wanted her dead.

Pushing the thought aside, she followed Ken into the garage and to the back, where the Caprice was parked. He lifted the hood and locked it open. Then he walked away.

Less than thirty seconds later, he came back carrying two flat wood crates with wheels. He sat on one and pushed the other toward her. "You want to get under and look at it or are you afraid to get dirty?"

"No fear here," she answered easily. She sat down and leaned back on the crate, feeling the wood rough against her shoulder blades as she adjusted her position.

Ken rolled under the car so she could see only his feet.

She followed, thankful she wasn't a mechanic. She wasn't great with small spaces.

Ken turned on a flashlight, and Sam stared up at the underside of her car. He reached up and pointed to a black hose that ran from the frame of the car to the front left wheel. "This is the brake line. You've got one on each side." He turned his light to shine directly on it. "You see the small punctures?"

"Yeah. Someone did that?" Seeing the evidence of his handiwork made the fingers of dread tighter around her neck. Who hated her this much?

"Yep. On both sides. Basically, the brakes work okay for a day or two, depending on how much you use them. Each time you brake, some of the fluid leaks out and the hose weakens. Eventually, the brake fluid's gone. That's what happened to you."

Ken moved over and showed her the punctures in the brake line on the right side.

"That's someone who knew what they were doing."

"How long would they have needed access to the car to do this?" she asked.

"Five minutes at least, with good light. You got to think about who had that kind of access to your car."

Sam pictured the front of her house. It would have been tough for someone to work out there without being seen, but late enough at night anything was possible.

"How long would it have lasted, working like that?"

"As I said, about a day or two, depending on how you use the brakes. Freeway miles, you could go a while, but one hard brake and you'd be done."

Sam thanked Ken for his help and slid out from under the car, thankful to be on her feet again. As she headed home, she considered who had had access to her car a day or two before she'd had the accident. She'd driven in Nick's car for most of the week. In a hurry to get to Eva Larson's scene, she'd taken her Blazer because the Caprice was in the garage. She frowned. The Caprice hadn't been parked in front of the house. It had been in her garage at home that whole week. How the hell had someone gotten to it?

The only other possibility was when she'd been at work. She thought about Williams, the blackout, and the missing file. He had certainly had access to the car at work. But wanting her dead seemed so extreme. Was it even possible?

Or was there someone else out there who hated her enough to want to kill her?

CHAPTER 26

NICK PULLED TO the curb at his sister's house and shut off the engine. The sour taste of apprehension filled his gut. He hadn't brought a woman to meet his family since Sheila.

Sam sat beside him, her white-knuckled hands clutching a bright bouquet of flowers. He could only imagine how nervous she was. It had been a rough day for her—Derek's outburst, finding out about the damage to her brakes, and spending the morning at funeral services for Becky Larson. Sam had identified a man from one of her old cases there, a pedophile named Gerry Hecht, and the police were busy trying to track him down now.

Nick just hoped he and Sam could enjoy the evening without thinking about the case, but he knew it would be tough. This was one of the most consuming he'd ever worked. And every time he looked at Sam, he thought about his conversation with Cintrello.

Nick had no choice but to keep his trap shut. It wasn't going to do Sam any good if he was kicked off the force. But damn, he hated the fact that she didn't know what was going on. Keeping tabs on her while they checked her out. How ridiculous was that? He just hoped they cleared her fast.

The flashlight was no problem. Someone had taken it from her car and planted it in Eva Larson's home.

But who? And how? And why, for God's sake? The more time passed, the more anxious he felt about how and when they would tell her about the evidence, until he just wished they'd do it so he wouldn't have to suffer. Selfish bastard, he thought to himself, patting his hands over his hair to make sure it wasn't going crazy. He exhaled, feeling his chest deflate.

"You got someone to take the car back to the garage?" Sam asked out of the blue.

He looked at her and grinned. "I already told you I did. Are you stalling?"

She looked at the house and back at him. "I'm a little nervous."

"Maybe this was a bad idea."

She shook her head. "No, I'm looking forward to meeting them."

"You grip those flowers any tighter and you're going to kill them before we get to the front door."

Her face broke into a smile and he felt some of her tension slip away with it. She slapped the flowers against his shoulder. "Just no work talk, okay?"

Nick couldn't meet her eye, unwilling to see the trust she'd placed in him, knowing how he'd let her down. The whole thing could blow over and she might never know. He prayed that would be the case.

"Okay?" she prompted, touching his arm.

He nodded. "Okay."

"We don't have to think about Rob or Derek. It'll just be a mellow evening." She paused. "With your entire family."

Nick looked over at her and the two of them burst out laughing. "Oh, God. You make it sound like torture. Let's go before you change your mind." He stepped out of the car and caught the motion of the front curtains. Their arrival had already been announced, no doubt.

She was stepping out of the car when he got to her side. Beneath her breath, she was mumbling.

"What did you say?"

"I'm trying to remember all the names. This is your oldest sister Gina's house and her husband is Mike. They've got two kids, Tracy and Kevin. Kevin lives back east with his wife, but Tracy will be here. Tracy's husband is Brian and they've got two boys, Allen and Will, and one on the way—a girl. Then, your brother Phil and his wife, Alison. And your mother." Her eyes snapped open. "What should I call your mother?"

"No, no, you've got it all wrong. Gina's married to—" He paused and watched her face drop. Laughing, he put his arm around her. "You're so cute when you're concentrating."

She pushed him away. "I can't believe you did that. You scared me to death."

He laughed, pulling her close again. He wished more than anything he could skip right over dinner with his family and take her home. Since she'd told the boys about her past, the thick wall around her had dissolved. Or perhaps he'd just gained entrance.

"What about your mother?" she whispered after he rang the doorbell.

"Ella. Just call her Ella."

His sister answered the door. Her graying hair was pulled up and she wore a blue cotton blouse and black slacks. "You look nice," Nick said, kissing her on the cheek and then introducing Sam. The two women shook hands and Sam offered the flowers.

Gina thanked Sam and said to him, "I see *you* didn't bring me anything."

"I brought you me. What else could you want?"

Gina laughed. "Can you believe him?" she said to Sam. "Just like a man."

Nick took Sam's coat and hung it with his on the old wooden rack that had been by the door in their house growing up.

"Everyone's out back," Gina said, leading the way. Nick let Sam go ahead of him as they made their way to the back of the house. Gina's house centered around the kitchen. It was the biggest room in the house and also the nicest.

In the years after Kevin and Tracy went off to college, Mike and Gina had spent their weekends and evenings redoing it. It had high ceilings and bright white cupboards with six-pane glass doors. A large bay window took up one side, where a casual dining table was always set for at least one extra. Tonight, dinner would be in the dining room on an old pine table that had served Nick as a kid when dinner had been only rice and beans with a side helping of chaos. Now the group was huddled around the island where Mike was chopping chives and telling stories, grandkids running around his feet.

Nick watched Sam suck in a quick breath as they entered the room and she took in the size of the group. Gina made introductions.

"Uncle Nick!" his great-nephew screamed. Nick picked Allen up and turned him upside down, holding him by his feet and making monster noises. Allen shrieked with joy.

"Me next!" Will shouted, tugging on his pant leg.

Nick repeated the exercise with Will, watching Sam out of the corner of his eye.

"Me again," Allen said as soon as Will was back on the floor.

He picked them both up, one under each arm, and carried them to where Sam was being introduced to his mother. Setting the boys down, he kissed his mother's cheek.

"Me," Will screamed.

"No, me," Allen insisted.

Will pulled on Sam's pant leg. "What's your name?"

Smiling, Sam bent down. "I'm Sam. You must be Will."

Will's mouth formed a giant O as he looked at her.

"I've heard a lot about you guys," she said. She reached out and shook his hand. "But Nick didn't tell me how handsome you were."

Will stared at the ground, swinging his body left and right while his arms flopped against his sides.

"What do you say?" Nick prompted.

Will furrowed his brow. "Can you play airplane with us?"

"Wrong answer. You say thank you."

Will shrugged. "Thank you."

"Now will you play airplane?" Allen asked.

"Hold on, guys," Nick said.

Sam laughed.

"Uncle Nick," Allen begged, "come play. Please."

"Will, Allen," Tracy called to them. "Go watch TV while the grown-ups visit."

"But Uncle Nick was playing airplane," Allen protested.

Tracy swatted Allen's butt playfully. "He'll play later. Now git."

Allen started to say something else, but Tracy turned him around and gave him a gentle shove toward the door. He stomped two steps, and then when Will raced past him he took off after his brother.

Nick said hello to his niece, noting she was starting to look uncomfortably pregnant. "How are you feeling?" he asked.

"Ready to be done," Tracy said, patting her swollen belly. "Five weeks and counting."

"Everyone to the table," his mother announced, tapping her spoon against a glass.

They settled into their chairs as his mother directed them, making sure no one sat next to their own spouse or anyone of the same sex. She took the head of the table, as she always did. A purple satin cloth ran down the center, on it two large wrought-iron candelabras with bright purple candles. The napkins were purple with blue-and-purple ribbon tied around them. When Gina looked over at him, he winked to let her know how nice everything looked.

Mike's cooking was wonderful. He served salmon steak with melted chive butter, steamed asparagus, and new potatoes. Gina had made strawberry shortcake for dessert.

Nick listened to Tracy talk about the baby's room while Gina gave stray pieces of advice to her daughter. Turning his attention, he listened to Tracy's husband, Brian, who was a stockbroker, talk about the downfall of the new-economy stocks.

"I know a lot of brokers who just refuse to trade them," Brian was saying. "These companies were returning a hundred percent in a day or two. You look at their market cap and P/E; it's not rational. Now they're tanking and people are upset."

"You probably own every one of those irrational stocks," Tracy said.

Brian shrugged, then smiled. "Well, of course. No guts, no glory."

"I'm sure that's what they said in 1929, too," his mother added, scolding her son-in-law.

"You would know. You were there. Right, Mom?" Nick said with a wink.

"You stop it right there!" his mother said, smacking him on the arm.

They laughed.

"You want me to get into stories, Nicky boy," his mother started. "Have you told Sam about your first B&E?"

"Oh, no," Nick groaned.

Tracy clapped over her swollen belly. "Tell it, Grandma. Tell that story."

"No, Sam doesn't want to hear that," Nick countered.

Sam waved her hand at him. "Of course I do."

His mother tossed her head back and laughed. Nick loved the musical sound of her laugh, like a deep, low saxophone all drawn out. It was one of his favorite sounds. Settling back in his chair, he waited for his mother to tell her story.

"Nick was my youngest, of course. And by a lot." She looked at Sam, who leaned forward to listen. "He was born when the next oldest, Alexander, was already nine. Everybody was busy with their own thing, including me. So, some days he'd come home from school and let himself in." She looked at her son and shook her head.

He grinned.

Sam laughed and he winked at her.

"I'm telling a story here. Do you mind?"

Sam blushed and Nick hung his head in mock shame.

"So, when he did that he was supposed to start on his homework. I was very clear about what he was supposed to do. No TV, no friends over, no playing until that homework was done. So I'm at the school with one of the older kids and I get this call from the principal, asking for me. I go down there and he tells me the police are on the line."

Sam grinned and Nick watched her watching his mother.

"The police!" his mother exclaimed, her palm to her chest. She said "po-lice," like it was two different words.

"You know what that does to a mother's heart? So, I run to the phone, cursing up and down. I'm thinking about what I'm going to do with whichever one of the kids is in trouble. The officer tells me that they caught someone breaking into my house." She paused for a dramatic breath and let her mouth drop open. "Someone in my house!" she exclaimed, her voice rising.

Everyone was mesmerized by her voice, leaning forward to catch every word. His mother could capture an audience like no one he'd ever seen. And here she was, telling a story most of them had heard a hundred times. He smiled and watched her, glad that he had brought Sam to meet her.

"Dear Lord! My first thought was my baby Nicky was at home in that house. Before I could utter a word, that police officer—he told me the thief said he was my child."

She paused and shook her head, looking up at the ceiling and pretending to talk to God. "My child," she whispered, still shaking her head. "My child. My child was robbing my house? The police officer tells me that they caught this child breaking a window to get into my house. And then this child claimed he lived there."

She shook her head some more and looked around the table. "So I said, 'Officer, what is this child's name?' And the officer said—"

"Nick," Tracy and Kevin and Gina all spit out together. Then the whole table dissolved into laughter.

"Nick," his mother repeated. "They said that my six-year-old son had broken into his own house. I said to that police officer, 'Why?'" She grinned, focusing on Nick from across the table. "But I already knew why. See, my baby Nick can't ever keep track of his keys."

Sam burst out laughing.

"She knows you already," his mother said.

Nick put his hands flat on the table and leaned toward Sam. "I've never lost my keys with you," he shouted playfully. "How come you're laughing?"

Sam looked up, her eyes bright with laughter. "Rob says they've had Triple A at two practices already this year. You're always losing your keys on the field."

The room lit up and Nick shook his head.

He shrugged. "You got me there."

"That's not nearly as bad as his first case," Gina piped up.

Nick threw her a threatening look, but she didn't even blink.

"What about his first case?" Sam asked, looking back and forth between them.

"Nothing," he said, smiling.

Sam looked back at Gina. "Tell me."

"Well, here's Nick, this rookie, right? It's his first crime scene. He's there with his partner and it's a burglary. So, they look through the house, and at some point Nick puts the keys to the squad car down—in the middle of this crime scene.

"They take a statement and call it in. Turns out the detective lives nearby, and he gets there before Nick and his partner can leave. As they're heading out, Nick realizes he doesn't have his keys." She grinned.

Sam laughed.

"So they go back into the house, but by this time the

detective has already found the keys and put them in an evidence bag—because the lady said they didn't belong to her."

"Oh, no," Sam groaned.

"Nick tries to get them back, but the detective says no. Wants to teach this rookie cop a lesson." She paused for effect, just as her mother had done. "So the detective impounds the car and sends it to the lab to be printed. Nick and his partner have to check out another car and deal with their captain about where theirs is. Finally, after three days, the detective releases the car."

"It took me a full weekend of cleaning that damn car to get the printing dust out of the seats."

Sam laughed and shook her head.

"But I never did that again," Nick said.

"Yeah, now he leaves his keys *in* the car," Gina added.

Everyone laughed.

The room settled into normal conversation, and Sam looked over at Nick and smiled. He could tell she was genuinely enjoying herself, and he loved seeing her with her guard down. Wide-eyed, she watched his family interact as though she couldn't imagine a family having such a good time together.

When they were finished, Sam offered to help with the dishes while Nick listened to his brother Phil update him on his boys. Phil's oldest, Tyler, was only six years younger than Nick. It had always struck others as odd that Nick's nephew was so close to his own age. Growing up, Tyler had followed Nick around like a little brother.

Nick had always been responsible for whatever mess Tyler got into. He remembered the time Tyler had thought to dig for gold in the backyard. He had come back into the house covered in mud. Of course, Nick got in trouble for not watching out for him. Tyler was now happily married, the father of two. Nick was the one who still had to get things together.

Excusing himself, Nick headed for the kitchen in search of Sam. Gina and Phil's wife, Alison, were huddled in conversation over the counter, looking out the window, their voices low.

"Uh-oh."

Gina turned around first.

Alison shook her head. "I remember when your mother pulled me outside. Scared the hell out of me."

Nick's mother was head honcho, no matter how old everyone got. No one new was allowed in without passing her inspection first, and Sam was no exception. "How long have they been at it?" he asked.

"About five minutes," Alison said.

Nick peered out the window. He could see the backs of the two women, his mother gesturing to her garden while Sam's head nodded agreement. She wasn't wearing her jacket, and Nick knew she had to be freezing out there.

"She'll be fine, Nick. She's a very strong woman."

"I'm not worried about Mom." Nick continued to stare out the window.

Gina laughed. "You know, you can hear them from the porch off the den," she said in a hushed voice.

Nick raised an eyebrow and then hurried through the kitchen to the den. At the window, he looked through the shades. His mother and Sam were still facing the garden, though neither of them appeared to be interested in the plants now. His pulse dancing as though he was actually on surveillance, he tested the lock and then unlatched the sliding door quietly. He watched his mother and Sam, but neither looked back to the house. He eased the door open and let the shades fall back.

Their voices were low across the yard. Nick stepped onto the porch and pressed his back to the wall. Sinking to the ground, he listened.

"I grew up in a rough family," his mother said.

Sam was silent, and Nick longed to hear the sound of her voice.

"I'd had boyfriends before Franklin, but no one like him. Where I grew up, it was fight or be killed."

Nick watched Sam look at his mother.

"That's where I got this," his mother said, pointing to the scar that ran along the side of her neck. Nick concentrated on his mother's words. All the kids had asked her about it at one time or another, but she'd told them it was from a cat when she was little.

"From a man?" Sam asked.

His mother nodded. "He didn't like it when I told him I'd find my own way home. He did this with a key."

Sam shuddered, and so did Nick. He pictured the ragged tear and wished he could get his hands on the son of a bitch who had done that to his mother.

"Then I met Franklin. He didn't seem to care." His mother laughed. "I mean he didn't care what it looked like. It didn't bother him at all. 'Course, he wanted to kill the guy that done it. That's just men."

They fell silent for a minute.

"I suppose what I'm saying," his mother continued, "is that we all have scars of one sort or another. For a while after we get them, we hide them and don't let anyone see. Then, later, maybe we hide behind them, use 'em to try to scare people off from caring. That's all fine for a while. Eventually, you have to let them be part of who you are, instead of what you are. You've got to give life another chance."

"I think I know what you're saying," Sam said. "But how—"

"I just figured you would understand." His mother bent down and picked a leaf from a plant. "My son's pretty smitten."

Nick rolled his eyes and silently banged his head against the outside of the house.

He could hear the light ringing of Sam's laugh. "Your son is a wonderful man, Ella."

His mother handed Sam the leaf.

"I'm glad you think so. That's a mint leaf. My mama always said the smell of mint drove men mad."

Sam took it and pressed the leaf to her nose.

"You test it out for me, you hear?" Then his mother put her arm through Sam's and led her back toward the house.

Nick stood up quickly and slipped back inside through the den door, sliding it closed and clicking the lock into place. He got back to the kitchen just in time to see them come through the back door.

Sam smiled at him, and he was relieved to see she didn't look furious or miserable or both.

"Coffee for anyone?" Gina asked.

"Please," Nick agreed.

Sam took some, too, and they headed back into the living room.

Before he could catch up with Sam, his mother caught his arm and pulled him back.

Nick steadied his cup to keep the coffee from sloshing over the edge. "You were about as obvious as a fox in a chicken coop out there," she scolded.

Nick grinned. "What are you talking about?"

"All that fuss with the window shades, you could have waked the dead." His mother slapped his shoulder. "She's a good woman, Nick. You treat her right. Now get in there before she thinks you're ignoring her."

Nick kissed his mother's cheek and walked into the living room with a distinct bounce to his step.

CHAPTER 27

DEPUTY DIRECTOR OF the Department of Justice Andy Corona dialed the number on his pager and frowned. He'd like to know what jackass thought he could interrupt his evening. He was trying to have a quiet night with his wife to celebrate their anniversary. They'd just come home from a late dinner and dancing, which was Elaine's idea. He'd almost passed out on the dance floor. But now they were home, and he just wanted to go to bed. It was after two in the morning. The house was quiet, the kids were all sleeping at friends' houses, he and his wife had all morning to sleep in, and then his damn pager starts buzzing. Shit.

"Cintrello."

Corona raised an eyebrow. "It's Corona here, Bob. How are you?"

"Doing well, Andy. And you?"

"Good." He rolled his hand in the air as he played along with the bullshit routine.

"How are the kids?"

Corona answered with fake enthusiasm. "Driving me crazy, as usual."

Cintrello laughed. "I can relate, let me tell you."

"I'm surprised to hear from you on the weekend. Where are you?"

"I'm at the station, actually."

"Work? Hell, I'm sorry to hear that. What've you got going on?"

"Same thing as you, I'm afraid. I heard we just got another vic on the eucalyptus case."

Corona hated the word "vic" for victim. What was the sense in cutting out three little letters? How much time did it really save?

"Came in about ten minutes ago."

"Where?"

"Martinez. Vic is a male Caucasian, early forties, multiple gunshot wounds."

Corona rubbed his fingers on his brow. "Your guys are on the scene?"

"Yep." Cintrello paused, as if he was gearing up to say something really important.

Corona did his best not to fall asleep before he got it out.

"Three of them out there now, but I want to hold off taking Chase and Thomas to the scene."

"Why's that?"

"Well, Andy, I think we need to get Sam Chase checked out before she goes to any more scenes."

Corona frowned. Politics told him to at least hear the jackass out before telling him where to go. "I'm listening."

"The lab's been working on the batteries, and they've got almost a full set of good prints."

"And the outside was wiped clean? It's too obvious. You think she wouldn't have known to wipe batteries?" Corona said, trying to make Cintrello realize what a jerk he sounded like.

"Her cases, ones she failed to lock up."

"There's no way my agent is capable of murder," Corona said.

"You willing to stake your career on it?"

He hesitated. Hell, yes, he thought quickly, and then he thought again. He couldn't screw it up, not this close to retirement.

"That's what I thought."

Corona bit his tongue.

"It's just to clear her, but the undersheriff wants it done and I'm not going to argue."

"Just to clear her," Corona repeated, wishing he could swallow that load of bullshit.

"To rule her out, of course."

"You're wrong."

"I'm not hanging my ass out on this one. Not after the shit that went down with Yaskevich. The undersheriff's going to draw blood if we're wrong."

Damn John Yaskevich and his guns.

"And we've got the psychological profile on her. Our guy thinks it could be a fit."

Corona shook his head. The profile had been part of her application to the department. As far as Corona was concerned, any profile could be twisted into something negative. The fact that Sam Chase had expressed her views on abusers was unfortunate. But she'd never said anything about committing a crime. She'd talked circles around killing abusers, making them finally pay for the shattered lives they left behind. Some of it was extreme, but Corona thought it made her all the more dedicated to her job.

The flashlight was circumstantial. He'd been concerned at first. But, after hearing about her failed brakes, on top of that business with the photo and the exploding heater, he was leaning toward a setup. People touched batteries all the time—no crime in that. Planting them at a scene would've been easy too. But he had to admit it still looked suspicious, especially to someone as gun-shy as the undersheriff. "I still don't think you have any evidence that she committed a crime."

"Of course I'm with you, Andy, but I think you ought to consider some CYA here."

Corona only half listened. Chase was Corona's employee, so if she was a killer, it would come back to haunt him, Cintrello was saying. He'd be smart not to get caught in the crossfire. Corona wondered if this call had anything to do with the fact that Chase was seeing Nick Thomas, one of Cintrello's detectives. His wife came into the room, and he put up his index finger, praying that Cintrello would get to his point in the next minute.

"She's not capable, Bob. It's a setup."

"No one wants to believe that more than me, Andy. She's your best agent, but I think it's a liability to have her on the team right now. I think the undersheriff would agree."

"Are you asking me to pull her off this case?" Corona tensed his jaw. First, they'd asked for Chase to be on the case. Now they wanted her off. Fucking sheriff's department.

"Yes, I am. And we're checking her out."

"Checking her out?"

"A judge is signing the warrant tonight."

"A warrant? For her home?"

"As a precaution."

Corona paced his office and thought about his ruined evening. "Oh, Jesus, Bob. This is ridiculous. It's the middle of the damn night."

"But we've got another vic. If it's her, I want to know now. And she's not at home now. It's the perfect time."

"You're going to serve a warrant at midnight to another cop? I think it's crazy. At least wait until morning."

"Normal procedure is to call Thomas and Chase to the case now," Cintrello argued. "If we think she's involved, we can't do that. Not even Thomas alone. We need to know if she's hiding something first. It's all about covering ourselves, Andy. I don't want to find out she's guilty later and not have checked it out." He paused. "The undersheriff agrees with me."

Corona shook his head and thought about his pension. Some days he would have loved to just tell the department to shove it. If the undersheriff agreed, they had the jurisdiction to go ahead without him. Damn it all. Chase deserved better, and yet his hands were tied. He blew out his breath. "Fine, but keep it off the wire. I don't want this to be a fucking news event, Bob."

"We'll be discreet."

Corona thought that was about the funniest thing he'd heard all day. His best agent was about to be dragged through the wringer, and there wasn't a goddamn thing he could do about it but sit back and hope he could pick up the pieces tomorrow.

"World's fucked up," he muttered, sinking into his chair and leaning back. "Happy fucking anniversary, Elaine. Happy fucking anniversary."

CHAPTER 28

THEY HAD DRIVEN back to Nick's apartment in near silence. Both of them knew where they were headed, but Sam knew he'd had to be sure. He'd started to ask. She'd simply touched his leg and nodded.

He stopped the car and gripped the steering wheel with whitened knuckles.

"It's okay, Nick," she whispered. "It's what I want."

"What about the boys?" he asked.

"Derek's feeling better. The neighbor is staying the night," she said.

He turned to her and ran his knuckles across her cheek.

She closed her eyes, concentrating on the feel of his touch and the smell of his soap.

"Sam," he whispered, drawing her back. "Maybe we should wait—"

Her eyes open again, she saw the worry in his. "I want to go in, Nick," she said, hearing her own voice crack as she spoke. She did want this. The unevenness in her tone was not insecurity—it was raw excitement and nervousness. Nothing more. "I want to be with you."

He took her hand. "I want you to be sure, Sam."

She nodded.

"I want this—" He motioned between them. "I want us to last."

She smiled. "I do, too."

He rubbed his thumb across her cheekbone. "But the case and everything—it's so crazy right now." He paused. "The accusations about you…"

"You believe them?"

He gripped her hand. "God, no. No, Sam. I don't believe a word of it. But if something happens, if they think you were involved—" He stopped.

She pulled her hand loose. What was he talking about? "Is it your career? Are you worried that being with me will ruin your chances for promotion?"

Nick laughed out loud and pulled her to him, kissing her cheek. "Would you let me finish? I'm just worried that you'll push me away if things get complicated. I don't want that to happen. I don't want to move too fast." His lips were almost touching hers. "I don't want to scare you."

She put her hands on his face. His chin was rough against her fingertips, like worn sandpaper. She ran her fingers down his neck. She could taste his breath, feel it on her lips, on her skin. "Kiss me, Nick. Please don't talk. Just kiss me."

Nick let out a soft sigh, his fingers shaking ever so slightly as he placed them on her cheeks and pulled her to him. Then his lips touched hers, soft and warm against her. His touch was exhilarating and sexy but strangely comfortable.

"Inside," she whispered. Pulling away, she stepped out of the car and walked to his front door, feeling him behind her.

A week ago, she would have sworn it would have taken longer for her to feel this way. A month ago, she would have wondered if it would ever be possible. Tonight, having watched him interact with his family, feeling welcome there, his mother's words, all of it made her realize what she had somehow missed before. Nick had gotten under her skin.

Now, in his living room, Nick wrapped his arms around her and pulled her close, the sound of Miles Davis drifting around them. The distant hum of the old record player sang along with the tune of Miles' horn, and Sam could picture Nick playing with the old band. She pictured his arms around his bass, wondering if he could possibly offer the bass more passion than she felt right then.

In his arms, feeling him pressed against her, she was dizzy in a wonderfully giddy way. She hadn't had a sip of alcohol to warp her thoughts. Instead, it was another drug, wholly internal, that was affecting her brain. One she hadn't enjoyed since Brent. And even Brent had been entirely different. Less intense, she thought. No, Nick was as close to perfect as she had ever known. Not that she had much experience.

Dancing, they moved to their own slow rhythm despite the quickening beat of the music around them. He kissed her again, and she held on to him.

Her tongue melded with his, her hands gripped his shoulders, her body pressed to his. When she pulled away, it was as though the air had been sucked from the room. Stepping back, she pushed one hand through her hair, keeping hold of him with her other. She smiled at his wary expression. Feeling her own pulse leap, she took a step backward. Then, slowly, she pulled him toward the bedroom.

He exhaled, and she saw the thrill in his eyes, felt it in her own chest. Without a word, she opened his bedroom door. She crossed the room and sat on the edge of the bed, slipping her shoes off. Her hands shook, and she longed to be through this initial awkwardness, to lie beside him, to feel him naked with her. She ran her hand across the top of the bed, inviting him to join her, playing the game of seductress and yet feeling like a young girl ready for her first time. A young girl offering her virginity—something Sam had never had the choice to give. But none of that mattered now.

Nick sat down beside her. She kissed his lips softly and then stood straight, her body between his legs. She watched him, feeling his excitement and her own, heating the room, flushing her skin. Without looking down, her fingers found her top button and she worked it out of its buttonhole. Followed by the next and the next. Nick didn't move. When she was done, she pushed her shoulders back and let the shirt slide off her creamy, freckled flesh. She was shaking, and she closed her eyes to fight off the fear.

Forcing herself not to think, she reached behind her back and unfastened her bra. She dropped her hands and it fell to the floor. Feeling naked and cold, she shivered. Just then, she felt his strong arms draw her close.

"Sam," he whispered, the sound of his voice uttering her name as wonderful as any sound she'd ever heard. "Look at me."

She opened her eyes and he smiled.

"Are you okay?"

"Nervous."

He laughed. "Me, too. We can wait. I'll wait for you."

She shook her head. "I don't want to wait anymore."

Nick held her chin. "You're sure?"

She nodded. Then, reaching down, she worked at the buttons on his shirt as he kissed her shoulder and then her neck. She spread her palms over the smooth skin of his chest and ran them along his sides.

She pushed his shirt off his shoulders and leaned forward to kiss his chest, then made her way up to his neck. She kissed his shoulder and felt uneven skin beneath her lips. She ran her hand over an old scar. "What's it from?" she whispered.

"Breaking up a bar fight."

She smiled.

He drew her close and kissed her neck. "What?"

She thought of her own wounds. "I've got one, too."

He ran his hands over her shoulders and down her arms. "Where?"

Watching him, she stood and slowly unfastened her belt buckle and the buttons of her pants. She pushed them over her hips and let them drop to the floor. She felt the cool air against her skin.

He made a hoarse sound as his eyes explored the shape of her.

She put her hand under his chin and lifted his gaze. "Here," she whispered, pointing to an inch-long scar halfway between her belly button and the rounded bone of her hip.

"How?"

"Guy pulled a knife before I could get out of his way," she whispered, kissing his ear and pressing herself against him.

Taking her by the hips, he turned her around and sat her on the edge of the bed, lowering himself to kiss the scar and then her belly button and then lower. Sam fell back on the bed and pushed her panties over her hips and down her legs. As she lay naked on his bed, he stood above her, studying every inch like a man who had discovered a lost treasure. She smiled and tried to roll over, but he held her down.

"You're beautiful, Sam Chase. The most beautiful woman I've ever seen."

"Come here," she whispered, reaching out to him.

He shed the rest of his own clothes and lay beside her.

*

She awoke to the incessant beeping of a distant car alarm.

Nick was sitting up in bed, rubbing his eyes.

Running her fingers across his back, she yawned. "What is that?"

"I think it's a pager."

She sat up. "Damn, it sounds like mine."

"I'll get it."

"It's in my purse."

Nick came back, carrying her bag. He set it on the bed.

Trying to wake herself up, she found the black machine and pushed the green button to read the message. It was her home number. She looked at the time on the screen and then at the digital clock on Nick's bedside table. It was three-fifteen in the morning. What the hell was going on? The idea that someone was hurt flashed across her mind.

Nick handed her the phone and she dialed.

"Hello," Derek answered, his voice strained. She heard noise in the background.

"It's Sam. What's going on? Where's Mrs. Dennis? Is everyone okay?"

"There are a bunch of police here. They were asking for you. They want to look around. They say they've got a warrant."

"A warrant?" Sam felt her throat catch. She glanced at Nick, but he was rubbing his eyes. "Put one of them on the phone."

There was a pause and she heard voices in the background, easily five or six people. She pictured them tearing apart her house and felt like spitting.

"Sergeant Henry Harding."

"This is Sam Chase. What the hell's going on over there?"

"We've got a warrant to search the premises, Agent Chase."

"A warrant? What the fuck are you looking for?"

Nick sat up and put his hand on her back, but she shook him off.

"I want to know what the hell you think you're doing there at three-fifteen in the goddamn morning, warrant or not. Who's in charge?"

"We're instructed to search for items relating to the murders of Sandi Walters and Eva Larson. Orders come from Captain Cintrello of the sheriff's department, ma'am."

"Don't you touch a damn thing until I get there." She slammed the phone down and started grabbing for her clothes.

"Sam, what's going on?"

"They're at my house right now, looking for evidence. A warrant at three-fifteen in the fucking morning." She stopped and stared at him, her entire body shaking. "You tell me what they're doing there, Detective Thomas. The order's from Cintrello. You going to tell me that you didn't know anything about it?"

"I didn't know," he said quickly. "Not about the warrant. Not that they'd do it like this. Cintrello told me to stay close to you tonight. I thought I could protect you, create an alibi in case something happened."

She clenched her teeth and pulled her clothes to her chest. "You were providing me with an alibi." The words spat out of her mouth. "Won't Cintrello be proud. You certainly did a good job with that, Nick. Heck, getting me into bed was just about the best alibi possible."

"That's not what I meant. I didn't plan that—"

"Right. I made that part easy for you. That whole sob story outside about how the case was so crazy, how you didn't want me to push you away if something happened—you knew about the whole damn thing." She pulled her shirt on and fumbled with the buttons, cursing herself for being so stupid.

"Sam, listen. I had no idea they would do it like this. I'll go over there with you. We'll figure it all out."

Sam wasn't listening. His words spurred her anger. "Was this some sort of trap? Get me out of the way so that they could search my house without me knowing—maybe plant some evidence while they're there?" She pulled her pants on and stuffed her feet into her shoes. "You did a hell of a job, Nick. You ought to get that promotion for sure now."

"That's not fair."

"Not fair, my ass." She picked up her purse and her jacket. "I'm being investigated for murder and I'm not being fair. Fuck you, Nick Thomas. Fuck you." She started to walk away, then spun back. "Sorry—I guess I already did."

CHAPTER 29

NICK CLOSED SAM'S den door and dialed his captain at home. It was four-thirty A.M., but he couldn't wait a second longer. He'd spent the last hour trying to calm Sam down and comfort Rob and Derek. None of it did any good. Sam's house was swarming with cops on the inside and reporters on the outside. The cops treated Sam like a common criminal. Only when Nick intervened did they even bother to try to straighten as they searched. And a cop's idea of straightening was to avoid pulling the stuffing out of everything.

The media were even worse. At least there weren't so many at this hour, but the few who lingered were vicious. Nick had sent a cop out to get rid of them, but the story was too sensational. The best he'd been able to do was to keep the front door shut so they couldn't get any more pictures.

"Cintrello," his captain answered, and Nick knew he was awake. It should have been a relief, but instead it meant things were worse than Nick had imagined. "It's Thomas."

"I'm going to venture a guess that the man I just saw walking with Chase outside her house on Channel 5 was you. You're lucky they didn't catch your face. And from what I saw, you looked like shit."

"Thanks." Nick was angry, but he tried his damnedest not to let it take over. "You want to tell me what the hell's going on? You never said anything about a warrant, Captain."

"I don't owe you explanations, Thomas. If anything, you owe me some."

"My private life is not police business."

"It is when you were supposed to keep your girlfriend in line tonight."

"Jesus Christ, Captain. Doesn't this seem farfetched?"

"Maybe to you, Thomas. But you're wearing your dick for glasses."

Nick didn't say a word—he didn't trust himself. Instead, he paced and gripped the phone so hard he thought he might crush it in his fist.

"When you're done sulking, they could use you at Haven Street in Martinez."

"What the hell's there?"

"The next victim."

He halted and let his breath out in a slow, steady stream. "When?"

"Last night, about midnight, I guess. Wife came home from her sister's and found him. I made them preserve the scene—they're waiting for you."

"Sam was with me at midnight."

"I know that, Thomas. Figure out if it's the same

killer first, and the exact time of death, then we can talk about Chase's alibi."

"Why serve a warrant on her in the middle of the night, then?"

"Because we had to move fast, find out if she was involved. I'm trying to solve this thing before any more evidence points her way. If you were smart, you'd do the same thing. Now that there's a third vic, you'd better keep your distance from her for a while—especially if you want to work this case. As it is, I ought to pull you."

Nick clenched his jaw. "You can't pull me off this now—we're in the middle of a murder investigation."

"I'll think about it. Just keep a low profile and stay off the damn TV, okay? And get over to that scene as soon as you can. I want this thing solved."

Nick heard the click of the phone before he said good-bye. He hung up and went back into the living room. Sam paced the room, trying to straighten up where the police had made a mess. They hadn't found anything. Just as he'd known they wouldn't. But that wouldn't stop their idiotic theories. He needed to find the real killer before Sam could be taken off the proverbial hook. "Can I talk to you?"

She didn't even look at him. "There's nothing to talk about."

"We've got another murder. I've got to go."

She stopped fussing, but she still refused to look at him. "What's the M.O.?"

"Multiple gunshots to the head, but the victim's got eucalyptus behind each ear."

She frowned but didn't speak.

"Sound familiar?"

"Sounds like the Son of Sam," she said, referring to the infamous serial killer in New York who shot his victims. "Who's the victim?"

"Martin Herman."

Sam flinched. "It's mine."

"I figured." His beeper buzzed again, but he just shut it off. He knew what it was. He'd be there soon enough.

"Abuser?"

She nodded. "His wife and kids. Very physical. I got her to press charges once, but it didn't last. She pulled them two days later."

He watched Sam move, wishing he could get inside her head. He'd brought her back to the house, stayed beside her while they searched. All the while, she wouldn't look at him, wouldn't talk to him. She deserved to be angry, but what could he do? She'd have made it a mess if he'd told her about the flashlight. How did he know that they were going to serve a goddamn warrant. He'd have lost his job. Plus, they wouldn't have had tonight. Maybe he was just a selfish son of a bitch.

"It doesn't fit," she said after a period of silence.

"What do you mean?"

"I mean, Martin Herman doesn't fit. It's not right."

"Why not?"

She shook her head and pulled her legs into her lap, effectively tucking herself up into a closed ball.

He tried to keep from reading anything into the gesture, but he still found himself thinking that she hated his guts.

"He's male, more than one child. Has a boy and a girl."

Nick thought about it a moment and shrugged. "So, maybe the killer ran out of single moms."

Sam looked up at him. "Maybe, but I don't think it fits." With that, she stood up and left the room.

Derek had locked himself in his room and refused to answer any requests to talk to him. There was nothing Nick could say to Sam to alleviate the pain. The whole thing was a nightmare.

Nick found Rob in his room, lying on his back, tossing his ball up into the air and catching it in his glove. Obviously, his arm was feeling better. "You going to be okay?"

He continued to throw the ball. "Are they going to arrest Aunt Sam?"

Nick snatched the ball out of the air and ran his thumb across the red stitching. "No. It's just a big mess up right now, bud. They'll figure it out. I've got to run." He tossed the ball back and then pulled a card from his wallet and wrote his cell phone number on it. "Call me if you need me, okay? And tell Derek, too."

Rob nodded and went back to throwing the ball.

*

The city of Martinez was amazingly busy at four-fifty in the morning. Women stood beneath lampposts in short skirts and high boots in pink and red, or tight black pants and platform sandals. Cars slowed as they drove past or rocked from side to side when stopped at stoplights. Some cars were easily twenty years old, with purple lights shining from the undersides and gold crowns in the back window. Others were painted bright yellow with fins, as though the ornamentation would cause the onlooker to overlook the original price of the auto the way some thought the cut of a suit could make up for cheap fabric.

Nick glanced at the empty seat beside him. He just wished that things were still the way they'd been eight hours earlier. How could the department be so stupid? He slapped his hand on the steering wheel.

Nick concentrated on what he knew about the new case. The victim was found by his wife, Betty Herman. Mrs. Herman had been out, visiting her sister with their two kids. Someone had already called and checked her alibi with the sister. The sister, Dolores, confirmed that Betty left at one-fifteen. The call came in at one-forty. Dolores lived in San Ramon, about a twenty-five-minute drive. It all fit together so far.

He wondered why Betty was at her sister's house so late with two young kids, but apparently Dolores' husband had passed away recently, so Betty had been staying there a lot to comfort her. Tonight was the two-month anniversary of her brother-in-law's death, and it had been a particularly rough day for Dolores.

So why not just stay the night? Martin was coming home from business in Sacramento tonight, but if Dolores was having such a hard time, it would've been easier just to stay. He'd have to pursue that angle.

According to Betty, she arrived at home with both kids asleep in the back of the car. Instead of waking them right away, she carried in her purse and a duffel bag. That was when she found him. She called 911 and went back to the car until the guys arrived. Last Nick heard, the kids were still asleep in the car.

Had Betty called home to tell Martin she was running late? Had she stopped anywhere on the drive home? Things like phone records and sightings by convenience store clerks could be checked. The kids were young, both under five. Too young to provide good testimony about what had happened.

His mind kept coming back to the notion of a male victim. The serial killers he'd tracked had all chosen female victims. It didn't mean it didn't happen—there was Manson, of course, and Son of Sam, although his first intended victim was always the woman. It just wasn't common. Though Martin Herman did fit the bill in terms of abuse. He was a known offender—one Sam had prosecuted. And like the others, he'd never been convicted.

When Nick arrived at the scene, he found one officer standing beside Betty Herman's car. Through the windshield, he could just make out the shape of the two sleeping children. The smaller of the two officers, a Hispanic man with a thin mustache, stepped forward. Nick recognized him from the station—Lorenzo. "Dispatch called the coroner. Their guy's on his way."

"Crime scene team?"

The officer looked at his watch. "Should be here."

Nick nodded. "Send them in when they show." He headed into the house.

Nick recognized the female officer sitting beside a woman at a small yellow Formica kitchen table. Nick assumed she was Betty Herman. She had a tiny frame, frizzy bleached-blond hair, and the dark, splotchy skin that identified lifelong sun-worshiping smokers. She wore a turtleneck, the top pulled almost over her chin.

Unlike Sam, who dressed in turtlenecks to stay warm, Betty, he was sure, was wearing it to cover war wounds. As she turned to look up at him, Nick could see the purplish shadow of a bruise under her left ear.

"Who are *you?*" she asked in a raspy smoker's voice.

Nick noticed another officer, a wiry man with round glasses, leaning against the kitchen wall. His name badge said R. Auger. Nick stepped forward and sat down at the table. "Mrs. Herman, I'm Detective Thomas. I am going to look around, and then I'm going to need to ask you some questions. Okay?"

Betty nodded.

Nick spoke in low tones to the officer at the table about the location of the victim. Officer Karen Mann pointed to the next room, and Nick made his way toward the body.

Martin Herman was sprawled out on the living room floor. Unlike the other victims, he'd been shot. The tie around his neck was loose, and he still wore his coat. Over each ear was a small twig of eucalyptus.

An inexpensive suitcase was on its side next to the body. Blood had soaked into the cheap yellow carpet. Without a medical examination of what was left of his crooked teeth and heavy jowls, it would be impossible for someone who had known him in life to recognize what was left. He'd caught a bullet right between the eyes, and his face was destroyed. Nick diverted his gaze and noted the way the body had landed.

From the line of the body, it looked like the shooter was already in the house when Mr. Herman got home.

"Mann," Nick called to the kitchen. The officer poked her head in the room. "Take Lorenzo and go ask the neighbors if and when they heard gunfire."

"Sure thing," she said.

"And track down the damn crime scene team," Nick called after her.

Nick stepped closer to the twigs and let his breath out. He would've loved to connect this murder to the two before it. Sam had an alibi for this one.

But someone other than their perp had killed Martin Herman. Nick knew because the twigs, although euca-lyptus, were much too big to match the others—ten to twelve leaves, at least, not six. That was the one detail the media hadn't gotten hold of, not even in the Sloan case. Nick dropped his head in his hands and muttered a low curse.

CHAPTER 30

GERRY HAD NOTICED the new cars coming down his street lately and he was getting nervous. He hadn't seen Sam Chase in the cars yet. He had hoped she would be the one to come, but they were all men. Sitting in the bathtub, he thought about Whitney. He hadn't seen her in almost two days. He'd tried, but the old lady downstairs had taken her car and hadn't been back. The more he thought about prison, the less sure he was that he wanted to go back there. He was starting to like it out here. He at least needed to see Whitney again before he went.

Tonight, he needed to go get some groceries, but all the cars on the street made him nervous and he wanted to wait until it was dark. He found himself replaying the scene at the funeral the other day. He had been very bad, he told himself. But he hadn't done any harm. He was there to protect the children, right? He was like Sam Chase. He would keep them from harm, from the terrible mothers who hurt them.

He just needed someone to talk to. He had a parole officer who was supposed to come by, but he hadn't seen her since the picketers started. Maybe she couldn't get through. Or maybe she got busy with other parolees. He thought about Wally in prison, and that made him smile. But then he wished he were still there.

If he went back to prison, Wally would be disappointed in him. Wally had told him to straighten up and survive on the outside, but he needed a job. And he needed to control himself better than he had at the cemetery. He could do that, couldn't he? He thought about little Whitney and he grew hard again. Angry at his own reaction, he jabbed himself in the nuts and doubled over in pain. Stay in control.

When the pain stopped, he concentrated on what he needed from the store. Since the refrigerator didn't work anymore, he had to buy things that didn't spoil, but he longed for some milk. He longed for a lot of things—like a ham-and-cheese sandwich with American cheese and mustard and mayonnaise. But he didn't have the money for that.

Seven dollars and twelve cents was it. It would last another week, if he stretched it. He hadn't found any more money. He reminded himself to look through the old lady's car next time. Or maybe he'd be able to get into her house and get to her purse.

Pulling himself up from the bathtub, he ran his hand across his scratchy beard and smoothed his hair down. He gave himself a quick glance in the mirror, thinking he'd never looked so bad. Who would want an employee who looked like him?

At least he'd be safe in jail. He wouldn't do any more bad things there. How desperately he wanted to be in the library filing books with Wally. When he was feeling down, Wally would pull a book off the shelf and hand it to him. "You should read this one." Then he'd add, "It'll pick up your spirits." Without another word, Wally would push his book cart on down the aisle and be on his way.

The last book Wally gave him was Hemingway's *A Farewell to Arms*. When that Catherine Barkley died, Gerry went back to the beginning and read it again.

"She died," he'd said to Wally the next day. "How come she died?"

"Didn't matter she was dead," Wally said, pressing his hand against the book. "True love is everlasting. She would live through Lieutenant Henry forever. Read it again."

So he did. He read it three times. He didn't understand it like Wally did. Still, he had cried each time he read about Catherine in the hospital, dying. And the weird thing was, Wally was right. The book did make him feel better.

Thinking about Wally, he wished he had a good book. He looked around the dark room. No books there. He thought about how expensive books were to buy. He could go to a library. Didn't cost to join, either. His chin lifted a bit as he thought about it. Long as the library wasn't at a school, of course. And he'd have to stay clear of the children's sections. But that was okay. He could do that as long as he kept his eyes on the floor.

Tomorrow he'd go to the library during the day. Then, at night, he'd go see Whitney, his Cherry Princess, again. That old lady better bring that car back soon.

He looked around the room. He would have to pick up another candle at the grocery store tonight, so he could read. His was almost burned to the end.

He bundled up and headed out, surprised that the outdoors was almost warmer than the inside had been. He had his seven dollars tucked carefully in his shirt pocket beneath his sweater and coat as he started down the street toward the convenience store.

It was quiet and he breathed deeply, sucking in the clear night air. Night air was something he'd never experienced in prison and he enjoyed the sounds and smells of nighttime.

Turning the corner, he saw the old lady's car. With a quick look around, he ran toward it and tested the door. It was unlocked. He opened the door and found the keys. He felt more excited than he had in days.

He started the car and drove toward Sam Chase's house. It was too late to see Whitney, but maybe Sam was home. He loved to drive, and he stayed in the slow lane and followed the rules carefully. The longer he was out, the more he remembered all the things he couldn't do in prison.

He drove past Sam's house, but it looked dark. He looked at his watch. Maybe she was still at work. He checked the gas gauge—it was full. But he still had to pay two dollars for the bridge toll. He only had seven, so two seemed like an awful lot.

He turned down the next street and made a U-turn. He saw something slide across the floor and reached for it. It was thin and dark against the dark floor, and only when he had it in his hand did he realize it was a wallet.

Checking for anyone watching him, Gerry made sure the coast was clear before tearing the wallet open and looking inside. He gasped at what he saw. He pulled the bills out and thought he'd gone to heaven. He counted twice, but got different numbers. Still, the wallet had more than eighty dollars plus two credit cards. He could definitely afford to go to Sam's office now.

Putting the car in gear, he headed for the city.

*

It was quiet when he reached her building. He found a place to park and took the cash from the lady's wallet, then tucked the wallet, with the credit cards in it, deep under the seat. He wished he could call up to Sam's office and see if she was there, but he knew that was a bad idea. It took almost a half hour before someone came out of the parking garage. As the gate was closing, Gerry snuck under it like he had before.

He was beginning to really like Sam's office. He walked slowly around the garage until he saw the right license plate. He moved closer to the car, then halted. Someone was inside.

Gerry ducked down, his heart pounding. That wasn't Sam. He hid behind a big cement pillar and tried to watch, but there was another car in the way. From what he could see, the man appeared to be looking for something. Maybe he was cleaning out the car. Gerry wondered where Sam was.

He sat down behind the pillar and waited for what felt like at least ten minutes. He didn't have a watch, so all he could do was guess. The garage had gotten very quiet, and suddenly he was tired and very hungry. Maybe he didn't need to see Sam tonight.

He stood up and peered around the pillar, but he didn't see the man anymore. He decided to come back another day. He checked again for any sign of anyone in the garage and then headed up the short ramp for the side door.

He hadn't gotten more than ten steps when he heard a man call out. Gerry didn't look back and he didn't stop. He reached the exit and pushed it open from the inside, running to the street.

He had almost gotten to the corner when he felt a hand grab the back of his shirt. He tried to twist free, but the man was stronger and pulled him down.

"Who the hell are you?"

Gerry struggled but didn't answer.

The man yanked him up and pulled him down the street toward a dark alley. "No," Gerry cried.

The man threw him to the ground.

Gerry rolled over and got to his knees, but the man kicked him in his gut. He moaned and fought to catch his breath.

Tossed onto his back, he rolled again and felt another kick to the ribs. Then there was another, and another.

"Fucking pervert," the man hissed, and he felt a kick to his head. "I saw you at the funeral, whacking off on the fucking tombstones. You sick son of a bitch. I'm going to kill you."

"The police will find you," Gerry yelled at his attacker, trying to throw him off guard. He could hear his own voice shaking.

The next kick was harder. "Bullshit, asshole. You can't get closer to the police than I am. You call them, I'll probably answer the goddamn phone."

He tried to get a look at his attacker, but the blows were coming too hard and he did his best just to protect his face. "Sam Chase will find you. She'll catch you."

"Sam Chase isn't going to be able to save your sorry ass," the man said, landing another kick to his chest.

Gerry didn't have an answer to that. Attacked by a police officer. He remembered the man who had come when the picketers were hurling rocks through his window. That man had looked at Gerry like he wanted to kill him himself. Gerry curled up and held his head in his hands, trying to cushion himself against the blows. He could feel the warmth of blood on his forehead and hands. The hits grew faster, harder, the names and curses more angry. A quick snap sounded in his chest and he felt a wave of red nausea in his belly. He kept himself from touching the broken ribs, knowing from experience that it would drive the guy to kick that spot harder.

Suddenly his attacker was pulling on him, dragging him to his feet. "Stand up, faggot."

He played dead, too afraid to face the guy's anger. Go away, he thought. Go away. He let out a long, slow breath and prayed the man didn't see it.

The guy dropped him back to the ground and gave him another kick. Gerry knew the man was going to kill him. Panicked, he squeezed his eyes shut, praying for it to be quick, wishing he'd never gotten out of prison.

Just then, a bright light shone on them and for a second he thought he was dying.

"Shit." His attacker froze.

Gerry looked up, though only one eye opened.

He saw the silhouette of the man's face and remembered where he'd seen him before.

Then the sound of his attacker's feet grew distant, and Gerry let out a little sigh of relief despite the pain. But he worried he might still die.

He wondered if this was what death would feel like. Lifting his head, he tried to open his eyes again. The pain in his head made the movement excruciating. He let his chin fall to the ground and threw up, tasting the metallic flavor of blood.

Lying with his eyes closed, he heard the click of a car door and the crunch of loose gravel as someone came toward him.

"You okay?"

He couldn't open his eyes. He needed his brother, Bobby. He couldn't take it anymore. He felt like throwing up again, but it was too painful.

The voice disappeared, and he felt like he was on a rocking ship. He tried to keep his eyes on one spot, but the ground was swaying. His thoughts were foggy and sounds swirled around him like angry waves.

He heard a siren and more doors open. He cringed, waiting.

Someone opened his eyes and shone a bright light into each one of them.

"I need to call Bobby," he said. "Bobby."

"Who's Bobby?" the man asked.

He moaned.

"Don't know. He's been saying that since I got here," someone else answered.

He was lifted off the ground. Fighting to open his eyes, he felt his body tense so hard it hurt, and then everything went black.

CHAPTER 31

THERE WAS A knock at the door to the den and Sam pulled her gaze away from the paper. She'd read the hateful article a dozen—no, two dozen—times and she still couldn't believe it. The ramifications, the implication of the words were impossible to digest. But the idea that one person was fabricating all of it—providing the victims and framing Sam for their deaths—made perfect sense. Whoever he was, he was doing a damn good job.

She'd talked to her attorney, been advised to just sit tight and not say anything to the press. Easy for him to say, but all she could do was think about it.

Someone had accessed her old cases somehow. Had whoever it was been in her office? Gotten into her car and taken her flashlight? She cupped her hands, feeling the urge for a drink, almost tasting the liquor burning her throat.

She heard another knock.

"Sam. Open up," Rob called.

"I'm not taking any phone calls. Just let the machine pick up." She'd been listening to the messages as they came in. Aaron saying he was worried and asking what he could do. Nick speaking in a somber tone about the different size of the twigs on the latest victim. He didn't need to tell her what that meant—she knew. The one murder she'd had an airtight alibi for hadn't been committed by the same killer.

Or if it was the same killer, it was meant to look different. Did the killer know she'd been with Nick last night? Was that why the eucalyptus was different? Was he following her, watching her all the time? She picked up her pen and jotted down "first officers at new scene." Was it possible that the killer could have found out about her alibi and changed the twigs?

"This isn't a phone call, Aunt Sam," Rob said through the heavy wood. "It's me. Can you unlock the door?"

Sam exhaled, wishing everyone would just leave her alone. She'd drawn the shades, but she could still hear the banter of the press outside her windows. Dragging herself out of her chair, she went to the door and pulled it open. "I'm not much company right now."

Rob brought in a sandwich and a glass of juice and set them on her desk. Then, scrunching up his nose, he flipped on the lights. "It's like a dungeon in here."

"I like the dark."

"Aaron's called a bunch of times, and Nick too. Don't you want to talk to them? They're worried about you."

She shook her head. She'd already left Nick a message telling him she wanted to know who had been confirming the information about her old cases to the media. Cops and agents lost their jobs for leaking the kind of information she'd read about herself, but that didn't stop them from doing it. And whoever had been talking had intimate knowledge of the case. As far as Sam was concerned, that person was the prime suspect.

"You can't stay in here forever," Rob said.

"I might just try."

Rob plunked onto the loveseat and crossed his arms. "It's just a stupid article."

"It's a stupid article that says I killed two people—maybe more. Plus, they ransacked my house—" She waved her arms around.

"So what? What did they take? Some gum."

Sam dropped her head into her hands, remembering the gum wrapper she'd found on Sandi Walters' foot. Extra brand, her favorite kind. The kind she bought at Costco in twelve-pack boxes. And now the police had taken her gum to see if they could trace the wrapper from Walters' foot to a pack she had in the house. It was a method that the evidence labs used on duct tape, too. They would check the evidence against another piece of tape from the suspected roll. They could determine how close together the two pieces were manufactured, and, therefore, what the probability was that they came from the same roll, or in her case, pack. She'd always thought it was cool until now.

"And you're just going to let them say that you're guilty?"

Rob's blue eyes were wide. She saw Polly in those eyes and looked away. "I don't know what I'm going to do, Rob."

"Don't they have any idea who the real killer is?"

She shook her head and rubbed her eyes. "No idea. We don't have a damn clue."

"Then you should find him."

"Or her."

Rob shrugged his shoulders. "You should find him or her. Then they won't blame you."

Sam stared at the expression on his face. He believed it was that easy. Just go look and she could find the real killer and she'd be free. The article, the murders, all of it would be gone. She nodded. "Okay."

Rob sat up. "You're going to do it? You're going to find him?"

She smiled. "Sure. I'll find him. And then I'll be free. Now, I need to do some thinking. Are you okay?"

He nodded.

"Where's your brother?"

"He went out."

She didn't say anything to that. If she weren't being accused of murder in the press, she'd want to get out too. As innocent and simplistic as Rob's advice was, it was true. She knew she wasn't guilty, which meant someone else was. She took a sip of the juice and wished it was something stronger. But alcohol wasn't going to help her right now.

Rob was right. The best way out of the noose she was in was to find the right neck to put it around.

CHAPTER 32

NICK SAT DOWN in the interrogation room across from Betty Herman. The woman's small brown eyes watched his every move, and Nick did his best to be nonchalant. He'd been sent in to talk to Betty—heart to heart. But Betty didn't act like she wanted to talk.

Her official statement had already been taken. So far, none of the neighbors could even say that they'd heard gunshots. The weapon was yet to be found. Martin Herman had a twenty-two-gauge shotgun, but the bullet that killed him had come from a .44 Magnum. The police were still checking to see if either Betty or her sister, Dolores, had a registered weapon.

"Coffee?"

Betty nodded.

"Black, right?"

Her gaze narrowed.

"I remembered from your house," Nick explained.

Betty crossed her arms and waited.

Nick stood up and left the room, purposely leaving the door wide open. It was a psychological thing. It meant that Betty was free to go. She wasn't being held. The police were just asking for her cooperation on some questions. They had also called in Dolores, who was being interviewed by another detective.

Nick fetched two cups of black coffee and brought them back, placing one in front of Betty. He wanted to be done with this—he needed to be working on the other case, finding whoever was trying to frame Sam. Instead, he sipped his coffee with the casual air of someone who had all the time in the world.

When Betty had taken her first sip, Nick spoke. "I need to ask you some questions about Martin."

Betty didn't look up but shrugged to acknowledge the question.

"When was the last time he hit you?"

Betty tucked her head down against her turtleneck.

"I can see the bruise on your neck." It looked fresh.

Betty's head snapped up. "He did that three days ago, 'fore he left for the trip."

Nick held on to his cup and kept talking. "I know this is hard for you." He didn't know shit. "Did he hit the kids too?"

"Not this time."

"But?" he prodded.

She stared at the table and then nodded. "But yeah, he hit 'em. He hit us all. Little Jamie's had two broken arms, an' she's only four."

Nick nodded. "I'm sorry."

"People always said, 'Why don't you leave him?' It ain't that easy."

Nick felt the slight change in the mood. He was

getting somewhere. "Was your sister helping you leave him?"

"She wanted me to. She offered to help. I was figuring to leave next time he was out of town. But he'd know where to find me. He always said he'd come find me and he'd kill me if I left."

"He's not going to kill you now."

Betty lifted her chin and set her mouth in a thin line. "No. No, he ain't. And I can't say I ain't glad. I am. I'm glad someone shot him. But it weren't me."

Nick finished his coffee and tossed the cup in the trash. "Is there anything else you want to tell me?"

Betty didn't hesitate. She shook her head. "I want to see my kids."

"Of course." Nick thought she seemed a lot stronger than other abuse victims he'd seen. From what he'd heard Martin used to do to his wife and kids, Nick wasn't sorry Martin Herman was dead. Unfortunately, he still had to lock up his killer. And he hoped it wasn't Betty, but his gut was telling him otherwise.

Nick left Betty and wandered back to the conference room that had been turned into the headquarters for their case. He stared at the victims' pictures, waiting for something to hit him, anything. Nothing did.

Sometime later, the door opened and a red-haired police officer stepped in. Nick didn't even know what Curly Matthews' real name was. He'd been Curly ever since he'd come in from the academy. It was a soft name for the man, who was easily six-five, with broad shoulders, a thick neck, and a barrel chest. "They found it, Detective. A forty-four Mag registered to William Holmes."

"Dolores Holmes' deceased husband."

"Yes, sir."

Betty Herman's sister had a .44 Magnum.

"They're speaking to her in the interrogation room at the end of the hall."

Nick followed the officer out the door. It didn't look good for Betty now, and that meant it wasn't good for Sam either, because last night's alibi was no longer going to help her.

Out the corner of his eye, Nick watched the D.A.'s expression as they listened to Betty Herman tell the story of killing her husband. Alice Carlson was doing an imperfect job of masking her disgust for Martin Herman's abuse.

Nick couldn't help but think of how Betty's children would grow up without a father and with their mother in prison. Betty had waived the right to have an attorney present, but he wished at least Sam had been there. She probably wouldn't regret what Betty had done. He knew that in Sam's mind anything was better than growing up with an abusive father.

His own anger stirred in reaction to Sam's abuse, and he realized his mother was right: he'd fallen hard for Sam Chase. And now she wasn't speaking to him.

Betty Herman pulled down the collar on her turtleneck and raised her face, showing the blackish blue and purple bruising on her neck. "He did this to me tonight. I hadn't even unloaded the kids from the car and he grabbed me by the neck. Why wasn't I home earlier? he asked me." The word "asked" sounded like "axed."

Nick nodded at Betty, trying to encourage her to

get the story out. He watched the tape recorder spin and waited for her to continue. He wanted to go home.

"He grabbed me by the neck and started shaking."

Alice leaned forward and put her hand on the table, careful not to touch Betty. "What happened then, Betty?"

"He finally let me go. I fell to the ground. I swear, I couldn't feel my legs or nothing." She made a fist. "He pulled me up and threw me toward the bathroom. I hit my head too. He told me to run a bath. So I went and got the gun," Betty said, her voice almost a whisper.

"Please speak up," Nick said.

Both women frowned at him.

"Tell us exactly what you did, Betty," Alice said.

"I got up from the floor and went into the bathroom. I started the water and then went into the bedroom. Dolores gave me the gun a few months ago, right before Willy died. She was worried Martin would kill me. I had it hidden in a shoebox, so I ran and got it out. My hands were shaking so bad. I didn't even check to see if it was loaded. I just went back into the living room." She was holding up an imaginary gun as she spoke. "He didn't even look at me. 'Get me a beer and something to eat,' he said. 'I'm hungry.'"

She shook her head. "I said, 'No.' He jumped out of his chair before he saw I had the gun. I just started pulling the trigger. I had my eyes closed. I just pulled and pulled and pulled. I don't know how many times. He wasn't but ten feet away, but I didn't even think I'd hit him. Finally, the gun just stopped firing. I opened my eyes and there he was, laying there." She lifted a shaky hand to her face. "His face was all—" She stopped.

Nick nodded. He could picture the face.

Betty's eyes widened. "It was gone. His face was gone."

"What did you do then?" Nick asked.

Betty looked at Alice, who nodded. "I put the gun back and called you."

"Did you wipe the gun off? Try to erase your finger-prints?" he asked.

Betty shook her head adamantly. "No. I just put it away. I didn't want the kids to see it."

Nick wondered if it had occurred to her to prevent her kids from seeing their father missing his face.

Betty grabbed Alice's hand. Alice started, but didn't pull away. "He was going to kill me. Maybe not tonight, but one day. He was going to kill me. Right?"

"It's going to be all right," Alice said.

"So I was right to shoot him? Don't you think so? He would've killed me. I had to kill him first. I put those twigs on him. I was hoping it might look like one of those other killings I heard about. But mainly I just had to do it before he killed me."

Alice nodded and so did Nick. Unless the battered-woman defense came through for her, Betty Herman would be put away for a long time. She might not see justice, but maybe Martin Herman finally had.

CHAPTER 33

DUMB RANDY WAS back and Whitney had been trying to get a chance to ask him if he'd seen anybody strange talking to Molly's mom. Randy was out on the street all the time. Her mom didn't say so, but Whitney was pretty sure it was because he was so loud. He loved anything with a motor and he made really loud engine sounds and inside you could hear him everywhere. He was in a special school that only met part of the day, and the rest of the time he was outside.

Especially when her mom's soap pop was on. That's what her mother called it. Her soap. That wasn't the name of it, and Whitney didn't understand why it was called soap because she'd never seen anyone with any soap on it, but her mom told her to never mind.

The soap had a long twisty, turny name that Whitney could never remember. She'd watched parts of it some-times when her mother wasn't paying attention and didn't see her. But mostly she wasn't allowed. It must have been sad, though, because even in the parts where people were laughing and kissing, her mom still cried. And they kissed a lot. That's mostly why Whitney liked to watch it—for the kissing.

The soap was very important, her mother said. She even talked about it with her friends on the phone while she made dinner. Whitney always heard her talk about tons of people she'd never met like they were her mom's friends and stuff.

Whitney hoped maybe the people on TV were her long-lost cousins. She hoped so, because they were all so pretty, and right now all she had was dumb Randy. The ladies on the TV were blond and tall and had really pretty clothes.

Once, Whitney had hidden under the coffee table and watched, and she'd seen them all go to a fancy party. They were in the most beautiful dresses. Whitney almost said something to her mom, but her mom was crying again because some man was saying something about finding a little boy.

The woman on the soap had this blue dress with a million tiny beads, and Whitney decided that was the one she wanted. Maybe she'd get married in it. Her mom said people got married in white the first time, but after that they could wear whatever they wanted, so Whitney would wear that.

Whitney walked down the outside steps, and around the corner, looking for Randy. Usually, she could find him a hundred miles away. But he was awfully quiet now. She saw him sitting on a tire down by Justin Rapozo's house. Whitney thought Justin was cute. He always flirted with her and made her blush. He said she was cute when she blushed. Justin was a mechanical genius. At least, that's what he said he was.

Whitney wasn't sure what that was, but he spent a lot of time working on cars and bikes. Right now, he was under the hood of the old blue car. He had three old cars in his driveway—a blue one, a silver one, and a red one. They were always there and he was always working on them. Maybe the genius part meant that he could work on them for a really really long time.

He and his brother lived in the house with their dad. Justin was really friendly, but his brother, Drew, was kind of mean. They both rode motorcycles, and Justin had promised to let her ride with him when she was older. But if Whitney was standing too close to the edge of the street, Drew would zoom by her and make the engine real loud right beside her, so she jumped. He laughed when she jumped.

Her mom said boys did lots of stuff just to be jerks, and she said Whitney would just have to get used to it. She said there was no good way to tell the jerks from the other guys, but Whitney didn't think that was true. She knew who the jerks were at school. There were a lot of jerky boys at school.

That mean Tommy Reicher stabbed her in the arm with his pencil. That really hurt. She had tried not to cry, but it hurt too much, and then they laughed at her.

She sat down next to Randy and tried to think of something clever to say to Justin. Nothing came out.

Randy started making shrieking noises, and Justin signed him to be quiet. Justin had learned some sign in order to talk to Randy. One of the first things you had to learn with Randy was how to say be quiet or you're too loud. She'd learned shut up, too, but her mom got real mad when she used that one. And Randy always told. Sometimes he told even when she didn't say it.

Whitney watched Justin work, but he barely did anything. Once, he lifted his head and slammed it against the hood, and that made her giggle. He gave her a dirty look and said, "Thanks."

But then he went back to working again.

And Randy was busy using a rusty metal box like a car and driving it along the edge of where Justin was working.

Whitney needed someone new to play with. She wished Mr. Gerry would come back again. He'd brought her more candy since the first time, but he hadn't been back in a few days. He said he was going to teach her some fun games when he had time, but he was always in a hurry when he came.

She thought he must have a very important job that kept him running around. But he called her his Cherry Princess. He said he had a daughter a lot like her, but she lived far away now. Whitney wondered if his daughter knew how much he missed her. Maybe her dad missed her that much, too. Maybe she didn't need a husband. Maybe her dad would come and fly her away like Peter Pan. Or maybe Mr. Gerry would take her home and she could be his daughter.

She thought about that for a minute. She might miss her mom some, but she wouldn't miss dumb Randy.

Randy came over and ran the metal box over her shoe. It left a dark track on her foot.

She got up and pushed him back. "Look what you did to my shoe, stupid," she yelled.

Randy looked at her and smiled. "Line," he signed.

"Yeah, you made a line. That was bad."

"Line like the motorcycle," he signed.

She frowned.

"What's he saying?" Justin asked.

"Line like what motorcycle?" she asked back, saying it out loud as well as signing.

Randy pointed to the end of the street.

Whitney shook her head. "He's not making any sense. Something about a line the motorcycle made."

Justin shrugged. "Probably just Drew burning rubber."

Randy went back to driving his metal box.

Justin started pounding on something under the hood.

Whitney covered her ears, but he didn't stop.

Randy didn't mind, of course, but the noise was driving Whitney crazy, so she got up and walked away, looking for something interesting to do.

CHAPTER 34

SAM WANDERED THE house, thankful it was almost restored to normal. A day had passed, and things had finally quieted down—or so she hoped. It was early still, just past eight, and the boys were asleep, finally getting a full night's rest. She'd tried to sleep too, but to no avail. Instead, she got up and opened the shades, thankful to see the press had gotten bored and gone home. She'd avoided the newspapers. She didn't see any reason to put herself through more grief.

Her concentration had to be on the case. And since she wasn't working it, she needed to struggle harder for every bit of information. Nick said he would help her—if she let him. But she couldn't get past the sick feeling that he'd tricked her. She'd opened herself up to him, and he'd used that for his job. She'd fallen for another jerk. When would she learn?

She made her way outside and watered the plants. She was still dressed in her running clothes, and the sweat, now cooled against her back, felt refreshing in the morning breeze.

She heard a car pull up and started to head toward the house when she heard the familiar voice. When she turned, she saw Aaron lowering himself on a small mechanical platform from the side of his van.

Aaron lived in the city. "What are you doing way out here?"

He rolled his chair up her path, and she watched as he pushed himself up the one step and continued on. He had incredible arm strength, and she always admired how he negotiated obstacles. Nothing ever seemed to stop him.

"You wouldn't come to me, so I came to you."

Sam sat down on the step. "It's been a bad couple days."

"So I heard. I read that article. What an idiot."

She didn't respond. She didn't want to think about it anymore. It was time to move forward. "What's going on at work?"

Aaron handed her a stack of papers, but held back one manila envelope. "I brought you the important stuff. There's not much going on."

"Have they been through the office?"

Aaron looked at her and nodded. "Yesterday morning. There was nothing there." He paused. "Except gum. They took the gum."

She nodded. The news that they hadn't found more should have been a relief, but she couldn't get past the image of her colleagues watching as a group of uniforms tore apart her desk.

Aaron looked down the street in both directions, making a slow circle with his head.

Sam thought to do the same, but held back. "Aaron, who are you looking for?" she finally asked.

Aaron snapped his gaze back to her and exhaled in one quick spurt. "Work's been creepy lately."

"Creepy how?"

"It's going to sound ridiculous…"

"Spit it out."

"It's like the papers on my desk seem… neater," he blurted out.

Sam had to smile. "Neater?"

"You know how I keep things in my own piles by case. Just court filings and stuff, nothing sensitive. But I've come in a couple mornings this week and the piles seem different—more exact."

"More exact?"

"I know. I told you it sounds ridiculous, but that's the best way to explain it. Last night about six, I came by and found Williams looking through my papers."

Sam raised an eyebrow.

"So, of course, I immediately thought it was him, too. But when I asked him what he needed, he said the court information for the Mahoney case. I looked at my desk and it was a mess. Whenever he paws through my files, he makes a mess."

"That's pretty typical Williams," she said, but her mind drifted to the night the lights had gone out and she wasn't so sure.

"I agree. Williams always messes my piles. He doesn't try to hide that he's been there. He doesn't even apologize when I call him on it." Aaron shifted slightly in his chair before angling it closer to her. When he looked back at her, he shook his head. "This is different. The only way I can really explain it is that it's neater."

"What about my office?" she asked.

"I used the keys you gave me for your office, and before the police came yesterday I poked around in there. It doesn't look like anyone's been in there."

She exhaled.

"But then I was filing some old statistics in the cabinet in the cube next to mine, and I noticed that those files looked disturbed too. It's like someone straightened them. Then I found this in the trash." He handed her the manila envelope he'd been holding in his lap.

Sam opened it and peered inside at a single plastic glove. "One of the agents could've had it in a pocket and thrown it away."

He nodded and began to fiddle with the wheel-lock mechanism on his chair.

"But you don't think so."

He shook his head. "I called Corona's office first, but he was—"

"Out of the office all week," she finished for him. "He's at home, though. I could call him."

"Yeah, Nancy said I could leave a message for him, but what would I say? 'The place looks cleaner and I found a rubber glove. We've got a nosy maid on our hands.'"

Sam smiled. "You did the right thing." She knew from her experience with Corona that he wasn't taking things as seriously as she thought he should have been. "There's nothing more you can do except keep an eye out for what changes—and keep the sensitive stuff locked up."

Aaron nodded.

"That heater ever turn up?" she asked.

Aaron shook his head.

She frowned. "Of course."

"I'm sorry," Aaron said.

"It's not your fault." She thought about her car brakes. No headway there either. She looked up at Aaron and saw the misery in his expression. "Don't worry about it, Aaron. I'll get this guy." She waved her hand to change the subject. "Now, tell me what's going on with you—not work stuff. How's the training going?"

Their conversation turned to his race, and Sam listened as he talked about the rigorous training schedule and the people he'd met through training. The race was three weeks from today and Sam loved hearing his enthusiasm. One of these days she needed to get Derek to sit down with Aaron. Maybe Aaron's go-get-'em attitude would rub off.

As Aaron spoke, Sam tried to think of a good present to get him for the accomplishment. Something cool for his new chair, she decided.

"I should get going," he said when they'd caught up on the race and his plans. "You going to be okay?"

"Perfect."

"Will you call me later in the week?"

"I promise," she said as she heard her phone ring.

Aaron waved her into the house.

Sam headed for the kitchen and the portable phone.

"You've got a package out front," she heard Aaron yell.

"I'll get it."

"Okay, I'm off. Have a good day."

"Sure," she muttered.

"Well, try at least," Aaron called back.

She smiled and picked up the phone. "Hello."

"Did you get the present I sent you, Sammy Jean?"

Sam felt her knees buckle beneath her and she gripped the counter. Her number wasn't listed. And no one called her by that name. She shook her head. She couldn't let him get to her. She stiffened her weak leg muscles and clenched her jaw. "You son of a bitch. I'm after you."

"Take it easy now, Sammy. You'd better go get it before either of you gets too hot. Wouldn't want you to explode."

The line went dead.

Explode, she thought. "Jesus Christ!" Sam dropped the phone and ran to the front door. There, leaned up against the house, beside the doorstep, was a box. She could see only one word, handwritten across the side in black ink: BOOM. A bomb!

The street was empty. Aaron had gone. The boys! She had to get the boys out and then call for help. Pushing the door closed, Sam bolted to the back of the house, waiting for the explosion to hit.

She pushed Rob's door open and screamed at him to get up. "We've got to get out of the house! Now, Rob, now!"

Rob sat up and blinked hard.

"Come on," she urged him. "Hurry up."

She ran past his door to Derek's and opened it. The bed was empty. The room was empty. Where was Derek?

"Derek!" she screamed. "Derek!"

Rob stumbled into the hall behind her. "He's in the shower. Don't you hear it?"

Sam looked at Rob and blinked, hearing the water for the first time. "We've got to get him out of there." She rushed to the back of the house and tried the knob on the bathroom door. It was locked. "Derek!" she screamed, pounding on the door.

"You know how weird he is in the shower. He always locks the door. He'll be out in a minute."

They didn't have a minute.

She turned to Rob. "Work on getting him out of there. Then go out the back door, through the Dennises' yard onto the other street. Stay away from the front of the house. Okay?"

Rob blinked. "Why?"

She didn't want to panic him, but she knew he was old enough to handle the truth. "There might be a bomb in the front yard. I need to get you and Derek out of here."

"A bomb," he repeated, his mouth falling open.

"We have to hurry," she pressed. "We have to get Derek out of there."

Rob turned to the bathroom door and started to pound on it. "Derek! Derek, there's a bomb."

Sam pounded with him. "We need to get out of the house!" Her mind raced. How quickly would it detonate, how much or how little time did she have to get it away from the house? She didn't want to touch it. She didn't know what would set it off. She had to do something. The car brakes, the heater—Jesus, he *was* trying to kill her.

He wouldn't have called if it was going to be activated by motion. She would never pick it up now. So she had to assume he'd put a timer in it. She thought about calling for the bomb squad, but she didn't have the time. "Come on, Derek."

She knew nothing about bombs, had never even seen a live one. She'd heard once that a bomb had been deactivated by rain. With that thought in mind, she rushed out the front door and picked up the water hose. With the faucet on all the way, she pointed the hose at the box and sprayed toward the street. The box nudged into the path. She cringed but it didn't explode.

She held the lever at full spray, watching as the box skipped down the front path to the sidewalk. It surprised her to see it move so quickly, and she wondered what kind of device was so light.

"He can't hear us," Rob said, running out to the yard.

"Keep trying! I'm going to get it away from the house. Stay back there until you can get him out and then go out the back door."

She squeezed the spray gun harder. It was still too close to the house. "Come on," she whispered.

Almost there, she thought, looking at the empty street. She stopped the water and pumped it on again, giving the box a last push to the street. It fell over the curb and she dropped the hose, turning back to the house. She had to call the police. As she reached for the doorknob, she heard a honk and turned back.

Nick's car was pulling toward the curb.

"No!" she screamed, waving her arms to stop him.

He stopped inches from the box.

As he opened his door, she yelled to warn him. "Run! It's a bomb! He sent a bomb!"

Nick left his door open and came around his car, keeping distance between himself and the curb.

"Come on! Hurry up," she urged, feeling sweat trickle down her back.

Nick looked down at the package and then at Sam. "This isn't a bomb, Sam."

She watched him lean over and pick it up. The word "boom" was gone now. The outer packaging had dissolved, and inside she could see a familiar white box. She shuddered as he pulled the loose, wet cardboard the rest of the way off.

"I think it's chocolate, Sam, not a bomb. It looks like See's Candies." He frowned and took his cell phone off his belt. He dialed and Sam could hear him talking in hushed tones to someone on the other end. After a minute, he nodded and replaced the phone on his belt. "Someone's going to come check out the box. You want to tell me what the hell happened?"

Sam sank down onto the wet grass and covered her face with her hands. She was shaking. She fought to pull herself together, remembering that the caller had said not to let them get too hot. He'd led her to believe that the package was a bomb. Was he watching her now? She looked up and down the street and saw no one.

Nick leaned over her, his hand extended. "Come on. You did the right thing."

She ignored his hand and stood up, feeling the muscles in her legs quake beneath her.

The front door opened and Derek and Rob rushed out. Derek's hair was still dripping wet and his flannel shirt was pulled on inside out. "What happened? Is everything okay? Where's the bomb?"

"Fine," Nick said. "Everything's fine."

Sam couldn't speak. Instead, she leaned over, pressed her palms flat to her knees, and tried to catch her breath. It was the same guy—the missing file, the photo, the exploding heater, the cut brakes, and now this. He knew she'd think the threat was real. The others had all been real. Maybe he was expecting her to call the police and get a bomb squad out there. Nothing would damage her credibility at this point more than something so humiliating.

"It wasn't a bomb. I was wrong." She looked at Rob and shook her head. "I'm sorry."

The boys mumbled something between themselves, and Sam stood up and paced in front of the house. She could feel Nick right behind her. She shook her head without turning back.

"He called me, Nick. He told me it would explode. I thought after the heater at work and the car brakes that it was a bomb. I was sure it was a bomb."

Nick turned her around and pulled her against him.

She pushed herself away. "I can't, Nick. I don't think I'll ever be able to again." It took all the fight she had left.

"Sam, you're going to have to trust me. I didn't know about the warrant. I thought I was protecting you." He shook his head. "I should've known. Cintrello's been out to hang someone for this thing from the start. You were just the easiest target." He took her shoulders. "Please give it a chance."

"I don't know, Nick. It's too much right now. I can't

think that way." She looked out at the water-soaked box and felt weak and tired.

"I'll be here when you're ready," Nick whispered. "In the meantime, we're going to catch this S.O.B. We're going to catch him and make him pay."

Hearing him talk made her want to cry. He believed in her. He might be the only one who did. "Is he trying to kill me or just make me look like an ass?" she asked. "This feels like something different from the murders. Is that even possible?"

"I don't know, but we're not going to let him do anything else. We're going to fight back, you hear me? Fight back."

"How about the boys? I don't want them subjected to this. What if he pulled a stunt like this when I wasn't here? They could get hurt."

"We'll work it out. Between the two of us, we'll make sure someone's here for them. It's going to be okay."

She nodded, drinking his words like water, refusing to think about what would happen if he was wrong.

CHAPTER 35

NICK FLIPPED ON the little shower radio to the jazz station and caught the end of the John Coltrane rendition of "My Favorite Things." Damn if jazz didn't always make him feel better. Even though he hadn't had more than two hours' sleep any of the past three nights.

He studied the case as the water massaged his skin, thinking about the latest stunt this guy had pulled. He had really gotten under Sam's skin, and Nick was glad it was he who had arrived and not someone else. He didn't blame her for thinking the box was a bomb, but reacting like that wouldn't have gone over without some raised eyebrows at the station. He'd had the contents checked out, and it was nothing but chocolate.

Out of the shower, he made coffee and scrambled eggs loaded with salsa. It was supposed to be his day off, but as soon as he slept for an hour or two, he was going back to work on the case. With the stereo on, he kicked back on the futon as he ate and flipped through the paper. Halfway through his breakfast, his cell phone rang. He frowned. It was only nine in the morning and no one he wanted to talk to would call him on the cell phone. He thought about Sam. Maybe one someone.

"Thomas," he answered.

"Yo, Nick. It's Dougie D."

Nick laughed. "Dougie D?"

"Yeah, man. You know. Dougie Harris."

"Right, I know. What's up with the D?"

"Ah, man, everyone's going that way, you know. Down here, we got Leroy M and Bobby T. I figure I try it out."

Nick took a long drink of his coffee. "What are you doing up so early, Dougie D?"

"When you say that shit, sounds all fucked up, you know?"

"Okay, Dougie. Why are you calling?"

"I been out last night, talking, you know. I heard some shit. Thought you'd want to hear."

"I'm listening."

"Nah, man. I can't tell you over the phone. We got to meet, you know."

"You saying you hungry?"

"Now you talking. I'm hungry, all right."

Nick leaned back on the futon. "If you're jerking me around, Dougie, I'm going to show you a world of hurt. You understand me?"

"Hey, I ain't busting your chops. I got real stuff for you. It's good. About the horses you talked about last time."

"Okay. I'll meet you at the diner. I can be there in twenty minutes."

"That's too soon, man. I got some business now. How about later—four o'clock okay?"

"Four's fine. See you then, Dougie D."

"Yeah, I'll see you. And don't be making fun of the name, man."

"No fun. Later." Nick flipped the phone shut and put it on the table. Dougie's sickly, drug-fiend figure flashed through his mind. His eggs were cold now, and he'd lost his appetite. He was tired and should've slept, but now sleep seemed like a waste of time. They had solved Martin Herman's murder, but he was still no closer to the killer he wanted.

Nick pulled a little black notebook out of his coat pocket and slumped back down onto the futon couch. He opened the notebook and found his notation of Sandi Walters' death. July 12.

Eva Larson had been killed the night of July 21. The twelfth and the twenty-first. Was there some connection between the dates? He found a clean page and made two columns with the women's names—Walters first, then Larson. Under Walters, he wrote "12th, abuser, eucalyptus, naked, Mt. Diablo, heroin, semen."

Next he turned to Larson, filling in the same data: "21st, abuser, eucalyptus, clothes, home, no heroin, no semen." Beside the dates, he wrote "opposites?" and then thought about the two women. There were some similarities—both of them single mothers, both accused of abusing their daughters, who were only children and were in early grade school. The mothers had both been known to use, if not abuse, drugs.

But besides the abuse, there wasn't that much more

in common. They lived in different neighborhoods, had different lifestyles. Eva Larson's life had been spent from fix to fix. Sandi Walters had worked somewhat steady jobs and had had boyfriends. According to her mother, she'd even remained friends with her daughter's father. He put a star by "abuse" in both columns and moved on. The fact that they were Sam's cases still seemed to be the best link between them.

He moved down the list. Was there a reason the killer had used heroin with Sandi but not with Eva? Or had Sandi done that herself? Had the killer been angry enough to subdue Eva Larson without drugs because of the dead girl? Or perhaps because Eva Larson was so physically wasted? What did that say about him? The killer wasn't very big? And while he'd have needed help subduing Sandi Walters, he could handle Eva Larson on his own? Nick wrote down his questions and moved to the next item on the list.

Had the killer gone to Eva's home because he'd been unsuccessful in luring her out? Or had he simply become more brazen? He wrote again, smaller this time, barely fitting all the information on the page. There didn't seem to be any answers—only more questions.

Laying the book beside him, he retrieved the phone and dialed the lab. He was still waiting to hear the results of some of the tests.

"Zimmerman," his favorite lab tech answered. Linda Zimmerman radiated good cheer. In their line of work, it was as rare as innocence. She'd been with the department only two and a half years, and for a while many had suspected she wouldn't last. No one so happy would really want to do police work.

But she was still there. She worked odd hours and occasionally brought in her seven-month-old son, Ben. Ben had inherited his mother's disposition and a set of green eyes that would make most women jealous. He took to everyone, and Nick couldn't help picking the little guy up when he was around.

"It's Nick. Ben in there with you today?"

"Hey, Nick. Nope. He's running errands with Daddy today."

"What's going on over there?"

"We're working the holdup at West Sun Bank downtown. You hear about it?"

"I think I caught some of it on the radio. Catch the son of a bitch?"

"They ought to. He left his prints everywhere and smiled right into one of the outside surveillance cameras after dumping his ski mask."

"That's good news. Anything more on our eucalyptus guy?"

"I tell you about the blond hair that matches one taken from the Walters scene?"

"No. You done up a profile with the DNA yet?" Nick was waiting for the day when they could feed a piece of hair into a machine that would spit out a picture of their perp. Blond hair brought thoughts of Sam, and he hoped this wasn't more evidence linking the case to her. The police had collected hair samples when they came to her house. He didn't want to think about it.

Linda laughed. "Soon, I hope. For now, you're going to have to bring me a live suspect."

"Damn."

"Sorry I don't have more."

"Hey, no problem. Good luck with the robbery," Nick said, keeping the disappointment out of his voice. He knew how these cases went. If it wasn't solved in the first forty-eight hours, the chances for solving it decreased exponentially.

He set the phone on the couch and pulled himself to his feet. His mind was back where it should be—on the case. But the case wasn't going anywhere. He dialed the station and got put through to one of the clerks.

"Anything on tracking who sent the package to Special Agent Sam Chase yet?" he asked.

"Hang on," she said, smacking gum in his ear. "We heard anything on a package to a Sam Chase?" she screamed across the room.

Nick waited while people talked in the background.

"Nothing yet," she said, popping the gum as she hung up.

Nick slapped the phone against one palm, trying to make sense of everything that had happened to Sam. Was it possible that someone in her office hated her enough to target her? He had to agree with Sam—somehow the trouble there felt different than the murders, more personal. Less violent.

The Sloan case felt all wrong, though. Sloan's lawyers had stalled on the wrongful death suit and Nick knew it was just a game they were playing. Sloan had been as guilty as Nick was male. No, this was something different.

He had a hunch it couldn't be traced back to Sloan at all. He shook his head. But besides one lousy hunch, he couldn't make any sense of what was going on.

Nick picked up his plate and set it in the sink with three dirty glasses. He turned the water on and let it fill the dish. He didn't bother to do the dishes—he still had another glass and a few plates before he ran out.

His eyes drooped and he padded toward the bedroom. Stopping by the stereo, he turned the music up and lay down on his bed, exhausted. He closed his eyes and pressed his face into a pillow, promising to sleep for only an hour and then get up and stir up some ideas on the case.

This bastard wasn't going to get away.

*

Nick pulled into Alf's diner at five to four and dragged himself out of the car. He was too old to be staying up all night and sleeping all day. His bedroom had western exposure, and the afternoon sun had streamed through his shades. It was too hot to sleep comfortably. Instead, he'd tossed off his blankets and gotten his ass to the shower. The only things keeping him moving were that Dougie had some news for him and that he would see Sam in three hours, if only briefly. He was picking Rob up for practice tonight, and he hoped she would be at home.

Nick met Dougie coming in the door and they made their way to a back booth without speaking. Nick was relieved to see that Dougie looked healthier this time and hoped whatever he'd been on last time was in his past.

As was their tradition, they ordered before talking

business. Dougie ordered the works, as always, and Nick ordered a Coke instead of coffee. He figured it would be a stretch for them to make that worse than the coffee.

Dougie slumped against the red vinyl of the booth and let his head drop back as though it had taken all his energy just to order. Nick waited.

The waitress returned with their drinks and Nick took a sip. Too much syrup and not enough fizz. He put the drink down and reminded himself to stick with coffee next time.

Propping his elbows on the table, Dougie took a long drink of his own Coke. Nick kept his head angled at Dougie, but checked out the diner with his peripheral vision.

Dougie pulled the picture of Lugino from his shirt pocket and slid it back across the table, face down. "I talked to my boys on the street about that horse."

Nick took another sip of the awful Coke to give him something to do.

"None of 'em sold to your guy in the photo."

Nick didn't tell Dougie that he was nearly two weeks late with that info. "Who'd they sell to?"

Dougie looked around and then leaned forward. "Heat's on with the smack out here, you know."

Nick narrowed his gaze. "What do you mean?"

"I mean, rumor is you get caught selling heroin, you go down harder than some other shit, you know?"

Nick nodded. He could believe it. "So what are you saying?"

"I'm saying no one's selling it now."

"Someone's selling it," Nick countered.

"Yeah, man, sure. But no one's admitting that they are. It's bad news. So I talked around, but people are—" He zipped his lip. "You know what I'm saying?"

"So you didn't find out who bought the shit?"

"People ain't talking about it. That's why I didn't get back with you sooner. Last night, I was down by the tracks with some guys. Real fucked up, you know, bitching about some lady he'd been selling to—real strung out."

"What did the lady look like?"

Dougie shrugged. "Just some lady."

Nick wondered if Sandi Walters had gotten her own heroin. "Can you get a description of her?"

"Uh, white."

Nick leaned forward. "I need more than that."

"Blond."

"That could be a thousand people. I need more."

"All I know is she was a blond bitch and some asshole on a motorcycle was following her."

"What kind of motorcycle? What was the guy like?"

Dougie shook his head fast and hard. "No way, man. That's all I know and I can't ask for more. They're not talking. I'm telling you, they're spooked. I raise it again and they'll figure me for a snitch."

Nick didn't remind him that he *was* a snitch. He pulled a picture of Sandi Walters out and slid it across the table. "Bring this around. Let me know what you find out."

"I'll do what I can."

"Do it, Dougie, or the free meals are over."

"Yeah, man. I'll try. I promise."

Nick took out his wallet and pulled out a ten and

a five to cover the food. He was frustrated that Dougie hadn't offered him anything more specific. "Tell them not to sell that stuff anymore, Dougie. I mean it. It's bad shit and they'll fall hard."

Dougie raised his hands in defense. "I don't sell it, man. I swear."

"Pass the word on, then."

"Yeah, man, sure. I just told you they don't. The heat's on, man. The heat is on."

Nick heard a tune in the back of his head and pushed it away. He passed the waitress carrying Dougie's platter of food, and, handing her the cash, murmured thanks. Heading home, he felt as deflated as the fizzless Coke.

CHAPTER 36

GERRY WOKE UP in heaven. It was warm and bright and a dark-haired angel looked over him. She wore white, although it was not the angelic white he had seen in the movies. No, her top was slightly more yellow than he would have expected. But she was a child. Even God had a sense of humor about children. They could never keep anything white.

Her round face was familiar. Wide brown eyes gazed down at him, and it looked as though she was floating several feet off the ground. He saw that she was gripping the handle of a stepstool and smiled. She was so life-like, so real, not even floating but standing on a stepstool beside his bed.

He felt instantly as though she was meant for him. Her familiar face, her childlike qualities—God had chosen this angel especially for him. She rubbed her nose with the back of her hand and continued to stare. It made him smile, and although his eyelids were heavy he fought to keep them open. He wanted to memorize her face.

His eyes won the battle and he closed them, feeling

more at peace than he could ever remember. In God's eyes, he wasn't a sick pervert. God had sent this child, this angel, to prove it. His faith restored, Gerry was prepared to die.

He pressed his hands against the soft, warm sheets and opened his palms to the sky. At any moment he expected to see bright light, feel incredible warmth or even pain. He waited for the sign that the next stage was starting, but nothing came.

He opened his eyes and looked back at the angel. She didn't speak and he wasn't sure what to do. He waited. He watched her. He blinked. She blinked. They repeated the dance several times, and he got the impression she was mimicking him.

A minute later she squinted at him, turning her head as she did.

He blinked again.

She blinked. "You awake?" she asked.

He nodded, feeling nervous at the sound of her child-like voice.

The angel opened her mouth to speak but stopped. Her head cocked toward the door and she listened.

He did too. He heard a click and then the slam of a screen door.

The angel's eyes widened, and she jumped off the stool and spun to the door. He wanted to stop her, to tell her to wait, but he couldn't. He knew instinctively that he would have to wait through whatever was coming— whatever journey would lead to the other side.

Thump, thump, thump. The floor seemed to shake beneath him. He felt his breath catch like dry cotton in his throat. He tried to avoid cowering but found himself shaking.

He closed his eyes and took a deep breath as the sound came closer. He could hear the strained breathing of the other creature. He imagined the evil monster, a giant, lumbering beast trying to pull him to hell. How could that little angel fight such a monster? How could he?

He squeezed his eyes shut harder and prayed. Come back, little angel. Don't leave.

He heard a low whistling, and his body settled. With a deep breath, he opened his eyes.

What he saw stole the breath right back. Bobby's wife, Martha, was standing over his bed.

"Finally awake, are you?"

He looked around the room. He wasn't dying. He was at his brother's house, out in the room off the barn, healing from the attack. The realization was empty of any relief. He wished he could go back to the dream. He knew why the little girl had looked familiar. She was his brother's daughter, his niece, Jane. He wished he could be with his sister instead. But he knew he couldn't. She couldn't have helped him. Her husband wouldn't have allowed it, and she wasn't strong enough to fight him.

Martha got in his face and blew hot, raw-fish breath on him. "I'm not happy 'bout you being here, you hear me?" She was close enough that he could see the roll of skin under her chin and the thick, bristly whiskers that stuck out from its surface.

He nodded.

"I'm taking care of you because you're family. While you're here, you'll obey my rules, you hear?"

He nodded again, pressing his head back against the pillow and fighting to escape the disgusting smell of her breath. But the harder he pushed, the closer she got.

"You so much as look at my daughter and I'll cut you into pieces."

He blinked hard, feeling the tears fill his eyes. He was pathetic. God didn't forgive him. He hadn't sent an angel to take him away to heaven. Gerry wished he'd died in the hospital.

"I brought you soup." She put the soup on the table with a resolute clank and turned and lumbered out of the room. As soon as she was gone, Gerry rolled onto his side, pulled his legs to his chest, and began to cry.

That evening he made his way out to the oak tree at the far side of his brother's property. No one would find him there and he felt safe beneath the thick, crooked branches. From one of the higher ones, a white rope dangled and Gerry wondered if anyone had ever killed himself out here. Hanging from a lone oak tree. He thought he'd heard a song about that when he was a kid, and it was nice to know someone related to how he felt. At least the injuries were healing. He still had some stiffness in his back and neck, but it was much better.

He had dug the paper out of the recycling bin in the back of the house and brought it here to read start to finish. He knew that his brother had books in his house, but Gerry was afraid to ask to borrow them. Martha had never liked him, so he didn't want to push things by asking for anything else. All day long his little niece, Jane, had followed him around like a puppy. Gerry knew what would happen when Martha caught him with her. He wasn't safe in his room in the barn. Jane came in and sat beside his bed or hid in a closet. She scared him to death the way she kept showing up. He always expected Martha to come in with a shotgun at any second.

He leaned his head back against the tree and felt the wind on his cheeks. It was nice out here, the way some days had been in the prison yard. If only he could keep Jane away, he might actually be okay to stay.

Gerry opened the front section of the paper and read an article about the conflict with China. The paper was a few days old, but it didn't much matter to him if he was a few days behind. There were really important things going on in the world, he reminded himself—more important than himself or Martha or even little Jane. He rarely understood all the news, but he caught bits and pieces when he could.

Gerry focused on his paper and read on. When he got bored with the front page, he took a break and read the funnies and then went back to the front section again. Sundays were his favorite because of all the comics and also because of the ads. He loved to look at the pictures of the kids in clothes and with toys and stuff. He ran his hand across his forehead, wishing he had something cool to drink.

Turning the page, he stopped on an article headlined DEPARTMENT OF JUSTICE AGENT PRIME SUS-PECT IN TWO MURDERS. He folded the paper into a neat square and lay down on his belly to read it. It was about Sam Chase.

Veteran Contra Costa County Homicide Detective and Department of Justice Special Agent Samantha Chase watched the tables turn on her last night when police detectives appeared at her home just after 3:00 a.m. with a search warrant. According to a source within the sheriff's department, evidence in the murders of two women, both accused child abusers unsuccessfully prosecuted by Agent Chase, points to her involvement in the deaths.

Although not at liberty to discuss details of the case at this time, the source did say that the evidence against Chase includes fingerprints discovered at the scenes.

Agent Chase declined comment on the allegations against her.

Oh, no. He didn't want them to think she did it. He shook his head. Gerry thought about the man who had attacked him. He'd been in Sam's car. If that car hadn't come by in the alley, Gerry was sure he would be dead. He pictured the man's face. Gerry knew who he was. Maybe he could help Sam. He smiled at the thought. It would be great to help her. Then she would definitely try to help him.

He put the paper down and sat up, holding his hands together. What should he do? What if the man came after him? He wanted him put away, but he remembered that guy's warning. "If you call the police, I'll probably answer the goddamn phone," he'd said.

Gerry thought about that man. He couldn't find

Gerry here. It was too far away. Gerry would just call Sam at home and tell her what he knew without leaving his name. That would be safe. If that guy answered, Gerry would recognize his voice and hang up. He could do that.

Gerry looked at the picture of Agent Samantha Chase in the paper. "Don't worry. I'm going to help you." Smiling, he gathered the paper and headed for the house. He mattered now. He was helping with the case. Gerry Hecht would do anything to help his friend Sam Chase.

CHAPTER 37

SAM CUDDLED INTO bed at barely nine o'clock. Nick had called twice, but she'd been out for the first call and in the shower for the second. She'd gotten the message that he had heard from his contact on the street, who had confirmed that Sandi Walters had bought her own heroin. According to Nick's contact, there had been a guy on a bike following her. But it was nothing they could track. Another dead end.

She'd also missed Nick when he came to get Rob. She hadn't talked to him since the chocolate bomb incident. The past few days had been so charged, she was hoping it would die down. She couldn't sort her feelings about Nick from her feelings about the case. It was too much to think about. And with her own involvement in question now, she was letting Nick handle the case on his own. She needed to stay close to home, to be here for the boys.

Opening her book, she laid it against her bent knees and tried to focus on the words. She read the same paragraph twice and then closed her eyes, rubbing her fists against their achy redness. She shut the light off and curled down in the bed, too tired even to close the book.

*

Her eyes flashed open. She scanned the empty room and saw her book sprawled on the floor. Her heart pounded, her muscles stiff from fighting invisible sandbags. She glanced at the clock. It was midnight.

Click. Scrape. Sounds came from the living room. Sam shot upright in the silence, listening. Her ears honed, she could almost hear the air as it escaped her lungs. Then, click, scrape, thud. Someone was in the house. Derek and Rob were spending the night at a friend's. Had they come home unexpectedly? She didn't think so. They would have come to say good night.

Without turning the light on, Sam opened the drawer in the bedside table and felt for her gun. Her hands shaking, her fingers tight, she lifted the Glock and pulled a magazine from a small wooden box, checking the bullets before clicking it into place.

Rising from the bed, she opened the door inch by inch until she could slip through. She peered into the darkness, waiting as the forms developed like photographs exposed to chemicals. She saw the two couches in the living room, the table and chairs in the attached eating area. There was no motion.

She eased herself onward into the hall, crouched, back to the wall, gun drawn. One, two, three. Move. She took three steps, counted and moved again.

She paused with the kitchen in view and waited for a sound. As she started to move again, a shadow crossed the kitchen, heavy feet thudding against the wood floor. Derek or Rob, she thought. But why would they leave the lights off? No, it was not her boys. A stranger was in the house.

Fear tightened her throat, but she continued to count, forcing herself to move forward. One, two, three. Move. One, two, three. Move.

At the entrance to the kitchen, she reached around and found the light switch with her left hand, aimed her gun with her right.

One, two, three. Move. She flipped the switch. "Freeze."

A face turned. A glass dropped. She heard the crash as it hit, the crackle of the pieces scattering across the hard floor.

Sam dropped her gun to her side and felt her knees go weak. "Jesus Christ! Jesus Christ, I almost shot you! Why are you home?"

Derek shrugged. "I was bored." He picked up a towel off the counter and began to mop up the mess as though nothing had happened.

She removed the magazine from the gun and made sure the chamber was empty. Then, setting the gun on the counter and holding on to the magazine, she wrapped her arms around Derek. "You scared the devil out of me here in the dark."

"Sorry, Aunt Sam. I was trying to be quiet."

She nodded, stroking his back. "I'm just so glad you didn't get hurt."

Derek wrapped his arms around her, and she felt him lean on her. It was so infrequent that the boys did that.

"Are you okay?"

She felt him nod his head against her shoulder. She gripped him tighter.

He pulled himself away, and she crossed the kitchen to get some wet paper towels.

"Being a teenager is hard, eh?"

He looked up at her and nodded.

"I wouldn't go back, either. Is there anything I can do to help?"

He looked at her for a minute as though deciding, and then shook his head. "I think I'm just going to go to bed."

She nodded, wishing she'd been able to break through whatever was holding him back. "You let me know if you need to talk."

"Okay. Good night."

Sam had finished cleaning up the glass and started back to bed when the phone rang. It had to be Nick. "Hello."

"Is this Sam Chase?"

She drew in a raspy breath. But it wasn't the same voice. "Yes. Who is this?"

"This is Gerry Hecht."

Gerry Hecht? From the cemetery? Was he behind all this? But the voice sounded wrong. How had he gotten her home number? It was only listed under the boys' names.

"Do you remember me?"

She didn't answer him. "Why are you calling me?"

"Uh, I, I—I wanted to tell you about a bad man…"

"Call the police," she snapped and started to hang up.

"Wait!" he cried in a shrill voice.

She brought the phone back to her ear and waited.

"Are you there?" he asked.

"For about another ten seconds."

"There's a man who's trying to hurt you. I saw him."

She paused and considered hanging up. "Where did you see him?"

"At your office. He was inside your car."

Sam felt the muscles in her stomach tighten. "Start talking, Gerry."

CHAPTER 38

HE WALKED THROUGH the lobby and waved at the posted security guard. By now, his routine was perfectly established in everyone's mind. He was never late for work. He had a perfect attendance record. His record was clean. And he was the best special agent. Sam Chase had the tits, but he was the senior. And he was going to make everyone see how fragile Sam Chase was.

She had tried to smash his career. She'd insulted him in front of their boss, insisted on the best cases, but he wasn't going to take it. No one made a fool of Gary Williams.

The elevators on the fourth floor opened slowly, displaying the dim hall lit only by the occasional exit sign and the blue hue of computer screens left on over the weekend. Morons. Passing the main desk, abandoned at this hour, he quickly surveyed the area. He flipped on the two lights in the main hall and moved slowly through the halls just as he always did. Only he knew that his purpose was not what it seemed.

Since she'd started, Sam Chase had been clawing her

way to his level. He'd been there twenty years, and no woman was going to get between him and the next level. He deserved the best cases, not her. And he deserved the director job when it came open. But she'd always been willing to do whatever they asked, such a kiss-up. Now, slowly but surely, he was getting to her. He could see it in the way she glanced sideways when she walked through the hall, the fear in her eyes when the lights had been out. The unflappable Samantha Chase was flapping. He covered his mouth and made a coughing sound that was actually a laugh. You never knew who was in the office.

And people would agree that Sam was starting to lose it. He heard them whispering about her, about how she was falling apart. They read about her in the paper, wondered what was going on in her personal life. They couldn't imagine he was setting her up. It would never cross their simple minds.

As he moved, he cast a furtive glance over his shoulder to confirm that he was alone. Then, ducking around the side of a cubicle, he withdrew the plastic gloves from his coat pocket. He pulled them on quickly, enjoying the snap as they settled against the hair on the back of his hands.

As he had expected, no one was in the office at this hour. Government employees were not known for their long hours. He was an exception. He took pride in his job. And what had he gotten for it? No respect. But not for long.

Samantha Chase was not popular. People wanted to see her suffer, they wanted her to fail. And he was making it happen. Already he'd heard through the grapevine that she was out of the office for mental health reasons. That wasn't the official word, but he'd heard it more than once. He was making her crazy. Sooner or later he would push her right over the edge. He turned the corner at her office and paused.

He wondered how many people knew the truth about her. It had taken him these few months of watching her to realize. Samantha had brushed him off. That had been his first clue. Now he realized it was because she didn't like men—she liked women. Even her name reeked of false masculinity. Sam. He should have known. Women didn't belong in law enforcement as it was. Now they had dykes. It was too much.

He was the one who belonged in this job, not her. He returned his attention to his work. Her office was dark, but as he had suspected, locked. He pulled out the key and slid it into the lock. The security desk had a huge ring of keys for the building. Every single door was on it. He'd gotten hold of Samantha's early on and had it copied. He'd made the small gouges in the lock to scare her, but all along he had been getting in with a key. The thought made him smile.

He let himself in and, after a quick look around, closed the door behind him. He stood in the dark with his back pressed to the door and inhaled deeply. She wore no perfume, but the room was filled with her essence.

He flipped the light switch and moved quickly around the office. Starting with the files on her desk, he searched through everything, hunting for the perfect next move. As always, he was cautious to move one thing at a time, replacing it meticulously before moving on. He ran his glove over the small black print of her handwriting. He'd been through the files over and over and had already worked with the interesting items. The rest of it seemed dull. Still, he couldn't stop now.

He moved deftly, like an expert. And really he was. He'd been doing this long enough to know Samantha's habits. Once, he'd even seen her date book with the carefully recorded notes here in the office. He'd thought it too bulky to take at the time, but in hindsight, he wished he'd kept it. He could imagine the things he would have learned. He'd looked for it in her car, but he hadn't found it. He spotted an important file on her desk and took a few of the pages from the back to plant somewhere. He tucked them into his jacket and moved on.

He reached down to pull open her drawer and heard a click behind him. He spun around and caught the door opening.

Samantha's assistant, Aaron, pushed the door open and rolled himself inside. "What are you doing, Gary?"

He remained straight-faced, though he knew this was a bad situation. No one should've been here now. He felt angry that he'd been interrupted. "I'm looking for a file Sam took from my office."

"What file?"

"Hofstadt," he said.

The gimp's eyes narrowed, and he wheeled further into the room. Without another word, Aaron scanned his gloved hands and then started to slowly move backward.

He could sense the kid didn't buy it. He tried to remain calm, but his blood began to boil.

"What the hell are you up to?"

He slipped the gloves off and tucked them into a pocket, smiling. "I told you, I'm just getting a file."

"You're the one," Aaron said. "The car, her files, you've been breaking in here."

Williams shook his head and started to walk past Aaron. "That's ridiculous. I just came for one file, but I guess I'll get it later."

"Don't even think about it. You're not going anywhere until I call Sam."

Williams didn't stop, but he started to panic and tried to find a good place to dispose of the gloves and papers as he moved down the hall.

Aaron came chasing after him. "Stop," Aaron shouted, and Williams could feel him closing in from behind.

Williams turned and ran for the stairs. It was his word against Aaron's. He'd just dump the stuff and get out of there.

Aaron followed him.

There was a security call button in the stairwell that Williams didn't want Aaron to get hold of, but he couldn't think of where else to go.

Aaron was right behind him when he pulled open the stairwell door.

Williams tried to shut it behind him, but Aaron was too close.

He followed Williams into the landing and smacked the alarm button. Williams heard the siren sound just as he started down the stairs.

Aaron caught his arm. "Let go of me!" Williams yelled, but Aaron had a strong grip.

He struggled to free himself. Desperate, he reached for Aaron's throat with his other hand.

The chair held firm, but Williams fought to pull it off balance so Aaron would let go. He didn't.

The alarms screamed and Williams knew he was out of time. He had to get away.

Dropping to his knees, he reached for Aaron's brake and flipped it down.

The wheelchair moved.

Williams grabbed the banister and pulled himself away. Suddenly he was knocked sideways as Aaron and his chair went tumbling down the cement stairs.

Just then, the door smashed open, and Sam Chase and two security guards burst in.

CHAPTER 39

"GET HIM!" SAM shouted, pointing the security guards to Williams. She saw Aaron at the base of the stairs and ran toward him. "Call an ambulance."

"He was attacking me!" Williams screamed, fighting one of the guards. The other had gone for help.

"Don't let him go until the police get here." She knelt beside Aaron, her breath ragged. His forehead was bleeding, and his left arm was trapped under his chair. "Cuff him to the banister and get down here. I need help."

She heard Williams yelling at the security guard.

"Shut up! If he's hurt, Williams, I'm going to have your ass in jail."

"You don't know what you're talking about," Williams hissed. He looked back at the guard. "I'll have your job."

The guard hesitated.

"He's not going to have anyone's job," Sam responded. "Now get down here and help me."

The guard scrambled down the stairs, wearing a panicked expression.

"Help me get him out of this chair," Sam directed,

trying to remember everything she knew about emergency medicine. She prayed it was just a concussion. "Keep his neck and spine straight," she ordered, not knowing what the injuries were. What the hell was Aaron doing at the office at this time of night?

Williams was clattering the handcuffs and complaining, but Sam ignored him.

She laid her arm along Aaron's neck and upper back as they lifted him off the chair and onto the floor. His left arm was definitely broken. She opened his eyes and looked at them. There was no pupil activity. "Come on, Aaron!" Where were the damn paramedics?

"Let him die. He's just a damn cripple."

Sam ran up the short flight to Williams, who was looking down at her.

"Turn your back," she ordered the guard.

She raised her left knee and drove it hard into Williams' groin.

He doubled over and started to gag. "You bitch! That's police brutality."

Sam gritted her teeth and glared at him. "You say another word, and I'll give you my fist. It's a hell of a lot stronger."

Williams shut up and Sam returned to Aaron. She touched his neck and felt the thready pulse. "Hang in there, buddy. You're going to be okay."

Within two minutes, the door opened and the second security guard came in, followed by two E.M.T.s with a stretcher.

They paused at Williams, who was still doubled over, but Sam waved them down the stairs.

"The police are on their way," the second guard said.

"Stay here until they arrive." Sam knelt with the paramedics as they worked on Aaron. She took his hand and squeezed, clenching her free hand against her chest and praying like she hadn't since she was a little girl.

*

Sam paced through the halls of San Francisco General, pressing her hands into tight fists. Everything about the hospital made her sick to her stomach—the smells, the people who milled about and waited for death, even those waiting with hopes of life. It all gave her an eerie chill. Announcements over the loudspeakers were crackling calls of panic and desperation. People stood with their heads bowed, the low sound of crying like the constant surf of a distant sea.

Not to mention the fact that this particular hospital was where Brent practiced. He wouldn't be here. He wouldn't. She repeated the mantra to herself without slowing her pace.

She studied the last door she'd seen Aaron disappear through as though the door itself might disappear at any minute. She'd been waiting for three hours. It was two o'clock in the morning, and every time she asked someone what was happening in there, they told her to sit down. She couldn't sit. If she'd thought seriously about Williams as a suspect sooner, she could have saved Aaron. If he wasn't okay, she didn't know what she was going to do. A million thoughts, all jumbled, spun around in her brain.

She continued to walk the halls, wearing off the

caffeine from her third cup of coffee. She'd had a granola bar, too, something to keep the coffee from burning a hole in her stomach, but she was tired and hungry.

The door opened, and a nurse in scrubs came through. Sam stopped her. "Aaron Ferguson?"

The woman smiled. "Special Agent Chase, you're in luck. He's out of the ER, and they're about to move him to Room 916." She pointed. "It's the third room from the end."

Sam leapt forward.

The nurse caught her arm. "But you can't go in there without his doctor's permission. The doctor's on his way out to talk to you."

Sam halted, exhaling deeply, and the nurse let go. "How long?"

"Agent Chase."

Sam turned to see a trim Japanese man with streaks of gray and a cool demeanor approaching her. His slow movements and calm expression suggested anything but an ER doctor. He put out his hand. "I'm Dr. John Okamoto."

She shook his hand. "I'm here about Aaron Ferguson."

The doctor nodded and motioned her to come along with him toward Aaron's room. He walked at a slow, even pace and spoke the same way, in a voice that was steady and rhythmic. "Aaron is stabilized, although he's still in and out because of the medications. I'm told you're a special agent with the Department of Justice."

"That's correct."

"He won't be in any position to answer questions

about the incident—perhaps not for several days, maybe more."

"But he will be okay?"

The doctor nodded, his hands clasped together. "His vital signs are strong. He's got considerable damage to one leg and he's suffered a concussion, so we've got him connected to an I.V. for nutrients. There may need to be some surgery to the leg, but there's no way to say how much until he's up and about. Also, we've set the arm. It was a compound fracture, so that might slow him down a bit."

The doors opened and two nurses brought Aaron through on a gurney and wheeled him down the hall.

Sam stared at him. His body was so still. Only the faint color in his cheeks and the slow, steady drip of the I.V. suggested he was still alive.

The doctor paused at the door, and Sam watched the nurses attach Aaron to the machines inside the room. "You can go in and see him, but I'd like to limit the visit. I'll send a nurse down in about ten minutes."

She thanked Dr. Okamoto and took a deep breath as she entered Aaron's room.

He lay flat on his back, a breathing tube in his nose and cords connected to both arms. She heard the beep of the machine watching his pulse and saw the drip of the I.V., keeping him fed. Her chest tightened.

She stopped at the edge of the bed and looked down at him. She realized she'd never seen him stretched out. He was significantly taller than she would've imagined. His blond hair was curled over his forehead, his eyes closed. She brushed the hair off his face and spoke to him.

"Aaron, I'm so sorry. This is all my fault." She looked around the room again, both unused to and uncomfortable with the idea of talking to herself. She prayed Aaron could hear her.

"Williams. I never imagined it was him. I should've figured it out sooner. I'm so sorry." She sat beside his bed and covered his hand with hers. His hands, too, were big and manly, and she wondered if someone loved Aaron like she was starting to love Nick. She wondered if he had brothers and sisters. Were his parents alive? There were so many things she'd never bothered to find out. She needed to reach his parents and let them know what had happened. She would call first thing in the morning. Since Aaron was stable, there was no sense in waking them up.

She took his hand. "The good news is that they've got him. They're interrogating the bastard right now," she said. Strangely, she felt no relief. Her fear for Aaron surpassed her anger and outrage at Williams' crimes.

She squeezed Aaron's hand again and looked around the sterile room, reminding herself to send something over for him when he woke up.

When the door opened, she expected the nurse and was surprised to see Corona's face. "Andy."

"I heard I might find you here." He motioned to the hallway. "Come out when you're ready."

He left and Sam looked back at Aaron, pushing a stray curl off his face. "Get better, you hear?"

With that, she left the room and found Corona leaning against the wall several doors down.

"I thought we might grab a cup of coffee." He started

down the hall and she went along. "Doctor says he's going to be okay."

She nodded.

"That's good news."

"What's going on with Williams?" she asked.

"He's squealing like a pig on the breaking and entering and leaking the stuff to the media. Your brakes, too."

"What about the murders?"

He gave her a hesitant look out of the corner of his eye. "Nothing yet."

She exhaled, disappointed. "But he had access to my flashlight and the gum wrapper. He's a good suspect."

Corona nodded. "Now that we've got him, we'll work to match hair, fibers, that sort of thing. Anyway, don't sweat it. You should be celebrating."

"I'd feel a hell of a lot better if my assistant weren't down the hall being fed by a tube."

"Of course. We're all worried about Ferguson. He's going to be okay. I contacted his parents."

"Thank you."

"They're coming down from Washington tomorrow." They reached the cafeteria and Corona pulled the door open. He bought the coffee while Sam waited at a two-top in the back of the room, away from the crowd of tired-looking visitors. What a depressing place.

Corona set the coffees in front of them and sat down. He paused and then wrapped his hands around his coffee and looked up at her. "I owe you an apology."

She nodded. She thought he did, too, but Corona apologizing was something she'd never seen before.

He was usually right. She knew this would not be easy for him.

"I should have taken the threats more seriously to start with." He shook his head. "And I should've seen that Williams was losing it. Jesus, I knew he was competitive with you, but I had no idea." He looked out the window, his eyes narrowed and sunken. He looked tired. "I should've seen it."

She didn't respond. She should have seen it, too. They all should have.

"But that's not what I'm really sorry about."

She frowned.

"I'm really sorry that I didn't put up a bigger fight about letting Cintrello's guys serve that search warrant."

Sam closed her eyes and tried to block out the image of the police in her home. "It was pretty shitty."

"I know."

"And I'm still not off the hook," she added. "Not if Williams isn't singing on the murder charges."

"That's why I'm here. I know you're not a killer."

She nodded without saying anything. Those words were no longer enough. She needed proof now.

"But to get you off the hook entirely, we've got to get the right guy on the hook."

"You don't think Williams is that guy?"

"I don't know. Maybe. But if he is, we need some evidence."

"How do you propose to get that?"

He shook his head. "Shit, Chase. I don't have the slightest clue, but I'm hoping we can put our heads together and come up with someplace to start."

"I'm still off the case, right?"

"Officially, yes." He took his eyes off her and stared down at her coffee. "But I think you should take some time off—paid, of course." He glanced up at her and rolled his hand like she'd seen in Mafia movies when they were telling someone to lie about something. "Take some time to get things back together. Do what you need to do." He returned his hand to his coffee cup. "You know what I'm saying."

She met his gaze and nodded. "I do."

Then, before she could say thank you, Corona got up and told her they'd talk sometime later in the week. "I've got some ball-busting of my own to do," he said as he walked away.

CHAPTER 40

SAM WOKE UP at seven the next morning, thinking about Aaron. She called the hospital and confirmed that he was in stable condition. The doctor wasn't available, so she left a message to have him call her at home. A minute later the phone rang.

"Chase."

"It's Nick."

She half smiled when he didn't say Thomas. "I heard you got your man."

"That's what they're telling me. Did Corona tell you that we verified Gerry Hecht's story?"

"No."

"Records show he was attacked in San Francisco, just like he said."

"Why was he close to my office?"

"Been following you, I guess."

"Where is he now?"

"Been living in Martinez. Then early last week he was attacked in the alley right outside your office. Broken ribs, fingers, bruised kidney, lacerations—you know the drill."

"Williams."

"Yep. I guess a car interrupted the attack and Williams made a run for it. Hecht called the police department after he called you. He said he thought the guy who killed the others and framed you had tried to kill him."

"How would Gerry know it was the same guy?"

"Something the attacker said. And when he talked to the police, he told them he'd caught Williams in your car. We think Williams went back and replaced whatever he took or got out whatever he'd put there. We haven't found anything incriminating yet."

"That's how he could have gotten the gum and the flashlight. Although the timing is wrong. He'd have had to do that sooner."

"I know," Nick agreed. "We're working him for the murders, but we need to get our hands on Hecht again."

Sam felt her blood start to rush. This was good news. "Where's Gerry now?"

"That's the unfortunate part. We sent a couple of cars up to his place this morning. Gerry's gone. His stuff's still in the apartment, but no one's seen him since he was released from the hospital. We're trying to see if there's any contact information with the doctor, but it's not looking good."

Sam rubbed her eyes. "Damn. There's no way to track his call to the house?"

"No. I wonder why he called you there. And how the hell did he get that number?"

She shook her head. "It's listed under the boys' names. Maybe he somehow got that."

"Right. 'Austin' is on the mailbox."

"Jesus, you think he was out here?"

Nick didn't answer. "We've got guys checking through his things, looking into his background—see if he left us any clues."

"Williams still won't confess to the murders?"

Nick sighed. "Not a peep. We found snapshots of you in his desk, and he's starting to squirm on the brakes, but nothing on the killings."

"You think it's possible he didn't do them?" she asked.

"Shit, I don't know. Be a lot to swallow, you know?"

She didn't know what to say.

"You doing okay?" he asked.

"Not great."

There was an odd silence.

"I want us to talk, Sam, about everything. Can I come by tonight?"

"I don't know, Nick. I'm not really ready to think about that now."

"But we need to talk. I want you to understand why I did what I did."

Her mind went back to the other night, to his body, the scars. His touch. She shook her head, trying to shake the thoughts free.

"Sam. Please."

"I've got another call coming," she lied. "I'll call you later."

She hung up quickly. How could she trust him again? He was good with Derek and Rob, and she believed he cared about them. And probably about her, too, but was she willing to risk that? She pushed it aside and shifted her thoughts back to Williams.

She shuffled the pieces around, trying to get them to fit. He'd almost killed Aaron. He was certainly capable of murder. Was he simply holding off the inevitable by denying his involvement?

She pulled herself out of bed and dressed for her run, then started the coffeemaker. The boys were still asleep, and she tiptoed through their rooms, gathering laundry. Rob's room, as always, was a mess. Most of his clothes were already on the floor, and it was impossible to tell what was clean and what was dirty. She did her best guess-work, even finding some dirty-looking sweatpants and a couple of T-shirts tucked in the back corner of his closet. She took the load to the laundry room and dropped it on the floor to be sorted.

One of her first lessons as a parent had been to check pockets. When the boys had first arrived, she'd loaded their clothes in the washer on hot without real-izing that one pair of pants had a pocket full of chewing gum. Everything in the wash, including some of her own clothes, had been ruined.

She started her own load first and then went to the living room and pulled down the first of two binders of case notes she kept on the top shelf. She was surprised the police hadn't confiscated them when they searched her house, but maybe they had missed them. Settled into a chair, she opened the binder and turned it right side up, wondering how she'd managed to put it back upside down when she'd last used it. She flipped to the begin-ning of the binder and paged slowly through her early days in homicide. Before she'd kept her daily journal, her most detailed notes had been taken on lined notepads and three-hole-punched into the binder. She had fit five years of notes into one three-inch binder. It had been, and still was in many ways, her bible.

She'd meant to go through the notes earlier, but things had gotten away from her. Paging ahead, she looked for the section on Charlie Sloan's murder of Karen Jacobs, but didn't find it. She frowned. Had Williams somehow gotten hold of her notes on the Karen Jacobs case? Would this prove he was involved? She stood up and had started for the phone to call Nick when something on the bookshelf caught her eye. Standing on a chair, she pulled out a book on victimology from her coursework and flipped it open. Tucked inside the book were folded pages. She opened them up and found her notes on Karen Jacobs.

How had her notes ended up in another book? Had Williams been inside her house? It wasn't possible, was it? Putting the book back, she unfolded the notes on Jacobs. She sat down on the couch and stared at the bookshelf, thinking. But she couldn't come up with an explanation for why her notes were out of the binder and in another book.

Turning her attention to the notes, she reviewed what she had on the Jacobs case. Her first notes included the site and layout of the victim's body. Karen had been Sloan's first. The detailed study of her victimology— her background, how she'd been lured to the site of the attack, what clues were found at the scene, the six-leaved branches. Flipping onward, she read about Karen.

The next five victims followed within seven months. Each one had an extensive description like Karen's. None of them had stood out as Karen had. Somehow that first victim of any serial murder case, like Sandi Walters now, always remained the freshest in her mind. None of the other pages appeared to have been disturbed.

She thought about the woman who cleaned the house twice a month. Perhaps the binder had fallen while she was dusting and the pages had come loose. Maybe the cleaning lady had tucked them in the other book because she didn't know where they went. Or one of the boys could have knocked it down or even looked through it. It wasn't as though she kept it locked up. The buzzer sounded on the washer, and she went to forward the wash into the dryer.

The wet clothes hung heavy in her arms as she lifted them toward the dryer. The smell of detergent filled her nose, and she thought how nice it would be to take a hot shower after her run was over—maybe even a bath. She loaded the dryer, added two softener sheets, and set the timer for an hour. Then, turning to Rob's pile, she began the process of sorting through his pockets.

She tossed the whites in one corner to be washed with Derek's and pulled the darks into the washer as she emptied the pockets. She found seventeen cents in one pocket, two bottle tops in another—one for a beer. She frowned and set them on top of the dryer. In a shirt pocket, she found a felt-tip pen without a top. Thankfully, the shirt was dark denim. She set the shirt aside to soak before washing so it didn't stain the rest of the clothes with black ink. In one pair of jeans she found an unused condom.

"Jesus." She wished she knew what to do with Rob. If the alcohol wasn't enough… She stopped herself.

At least he was being safe. He was sixteen. A lot of kids probably carried condoms. It didn't mean he was using them—or so she told herself.

She felt around in his sweatpants and pulled out something small and sharp. Catching it in her fist, she shook it and then opened her palm. In her palm was a broken piece of metal from a mechanical pencil or something and a couple of leaves. She wondered how on earth the boys collected things in their pants like that. She pulled it all out and dropped it on top of the dryer. As she pushed her bangs off her face, she caught a subtle smell on her hand. It made her flinch.

Eucalyptus. She wondered how long it would be before that smell stopped representing this case. She knew she would never forget it. It was always that way. She turned back to Rob's laundry and lifted a flannel shirt off the pile. As she did, she caught sight of something on the sleeve. She pulled it closer and saw that the sleeve was ripped. But there was something else. On the rim of the tear, she saw a dark spot. She rubbed it between her fingers and the red stained her skin. Blood. She looked back at the eucalyptus leaves and then down at the blood.

"Holy shit."

She ran for the phone.

CHAPTER 41

THINGS HAD SEEMED better for Gerry over the past few days after talking to Sam. He'd called the police and spoken to a woman officer, so he'd known the officer wasn't the guy who attacked him. She'd pressed him for his name, but he'd refused. He wasn't that dumb. She'd told him the information he was offering was very valuable, and she'd made him feel very good.

Gerry could feel Jane behind him almost all the time now. He looked forward to the fall when she went back to school. When he spotted her, she'd shriek and run off like it was all a big game. But she would never be gone for long. He'd shooed her away for days, but he longed to talk to her, to talk to anyone, for that matter. Bobby was too busy, and Martha only grunted and growled at him. He knew if he talked to Jane, though, he might as well have died in that alley.

He'd finally gathered the nerve to ask Bobby for some books. Bobby had brought him a whole stack, but most were Martha's romance novels, and he read through them in no time. He hated to ask for more, so instead he read them again until he could remember each of the seven stories inside and out. He wasn't sleeping much, despite the warm bed. He still missed Wally and the prison.

He found a stack of playing cards in the pantry and laid them out for a game of solitaire in his room in the barn. He'd been playing for two hours straight when he heard the squeak of the door. He looked up, saw nothing, and returned to his game. A minute later he heard it again. Dropping the cards on the table, he walked to the door and pulled it open. Jane looked up at him wide-eyed, then backed away from the door.

He stepped into the barn and waved her off like a stray dog. "Get on out of here."

She moved back a few steps and stopped. "Are you a monster?"

The sound of her small voice touched him, and he longed to say no. He pressed the heel of his hand into his chest and nodded. "Yes."

She shook her head. "You don't look like a monster."

"Well, I am."

"Maybe you're like the Beast," she said, rolling on the balls of her feet with her hands tucked behind her back.

She looked so sweet, he had to look away. "I am. I'm like the beast. You should leave." He felt so pathetic, looking into her wide eyes and telling her to go.

"You're like the Beast in *Beauty and the Beast.*" She looked around and then started again. "See, he's really a prince, but he got turned into a Beast by a wicked queen. All he needs is someone to love him and then he turns back into a prince. Maybe you're like that."

He shook his head, but the idea that she thought he

might be a prince in disguise brought tears to his eyes. He shook his head again and covered his face. "No. I'm not a prince."

He felt her hand on his arm. "It's okay, mister. You don't gotta cry."

Her voice made him cry harder and before he knew it, he was wracked with sobs and sinking to the barn floor. She didn't even know he was her uncle. His own brother was so ashamed, he was hiding the truth from his little girl. He covered his face and sobbed.

She patted his back and rubbed in little circles, and he thought he might die right there. He wished he could will her away, but he couldn't. "It's okay," she whispered, her breath like a feather at his ear.

She wrapped her arms around him and squeezed.

He didn't move, feeling himself stir and wishing he were stronger. He just cried. God, please help him.

"Shh. It's okay." She rocked slightly as she hugged him.

He felt himself melt. Instead of pulling away, he tucked his head against her chest and she continued to hold him, innocent as to the terrible thoughts that were brewing inside him.

She lifted her head and dropped her hands, turning her ear toward the door.

He pulled back. If Martha found them, he was dead. He put his hand over his crotch to hide the bulge. This was his niece. What was he thinking? He wasn't strong enough to live. He couldn't be strong around her. "What is it?" he whispered.

"Dunno." She headed for the door and peered outside. "Wow!"

"What? What do you see?"

"Two police cars."

Gerry panicked. They knew. He'd barely touched her, and already they knew. He ran out the back door of the barn and through the field and kept running and running. He wondered if they would take him back to Wally. He shook his head. No. They'd take him somewhere new. He couldn't handle being new again. The lies. The huge men who wanted him. The threats. Without Wally, he'd never survive.

He ran and ran until he came to his oak tree. He sat down beside it to catch his breath and wondered how soon they would find him. He couldn't be found now. He couldn't face Bobby when he found out. Couldn't handle seeing Martha. Couldn't hurt little Jane with the truth. He thought of her angelic face and started to climb the tree toward the rope, hanging high above. When he reached it, he lay on his back on the branch and tied the rope tight around his neck. He closed it with a knot and wondered if it would stay. He'd never been a Boy Scout, so he wasn't good with ropes.

He suddenly wished he owned a gun. It would be so much faster with a gun. He could hear voices in the pasture, and his name carried toward him on the wind. He wondered if they would be able to save him. Or if they would even try. He thought about his mother. She was the only person who still loved him, and even she couldn't stand the sight of him.

Rolling off the limb of the tree, he prayed. The rope tightened around his neck with a wrenching pull, and he felt the back of his head slam against the tree. Then he saw his angel's face.

CHAPTER 42

NICK HEADED DOWN the hall toward his office. The lab was processing Gerry Hecht's prints, but so far they hadn't matched anything from either of the crime scenes. Nick hadn't expected Hecht to be involved, but it was worth a shot. Sam had picked Hecht out from more than one hundred feet away at the funeral. He shook his head. She was good.

"Thomas."

Nick wiped the smile from his face so he didn't look like an idiot.

Paul McCafferty ran to catch up with him. "I've been looking all over for you. You heading to your office?"

Nick nodded. "I was."

"I wanted to, uh, warn you."

"Warn me what?"

"There's someone waiting in there."

"In my office?"

He nodded.

"Who?"

"Name's Marge Allen. She lives down the street

from Sandi Walters. Hansen and Bernadini talked to her during the neighborhood sweep. They got nothing back then. She came in today claiming her stepson, who's back from the Midwest somewhere, knows something about the Walters case. Said he saw a guy who was hanging around on a motorcycle the day she was killed."

"A motorcycle." He looked back toward his office. "And?"

"We went through the pictures with the kid, but he didn't recognize the perp."

"What about Williams?"

"First picture I showed him."

Nick scratched his face. "Damn." Who the hell had been on that bike if it wasn't Williams? "Set the kid up with a police artist."

"I suggested that. The kid's deaf."

Nick shrugged. "So what? Have the mother translate. Or get Michelle Halloran to do it. She signs."

McCafferty nodded but didn't speak.

"What?"

"She's in your office."

"Why?"

"Said she wanted to talk to whoever's in charge directly. Made a stink."

"Damn." Nick rubbed his face. "What's her name again?"

"Mrs. Allen. The kid's Randy—Randy Allen."

"Thanks." Nick marched toward his office.

From the hall, he could see a woman with red hair too bright to be natural. The curls were pulled into a tidy ponytail with two loose ringlets on either side of her head that gave the look of bright red springs attached to her ears. She wore a button-down striped shirt in teal and pink and cotton stretch pants in a matching aqua. Her feet were in white house sneakers that looked too large for her. Her hands were crossed over her purse in her lap, and she stared blankly across the room. Next to her a little girl mimicked her gestures. The boy sat on the floor, making loud noises that were off pitch. The mother didn't seem to notice him.

Nick entered the room, stopped beside the woman, and extended his hand. "I'm Detective Nick Thomas. You must be Mrs. Allen. I understand your son has some information for us."

The woman nodded but didn't speak.

Nick sat on the edge of the desk and waited.

"Isn't there someone who needs to interview him?" she finally asked. "You haven't solved the murder yet, have you? My son is a witness."

"Actually, we haven't solved the murder, and we do appreciate your son's help," Nick answered, gritting his teeth. "What we do is have him look through some books of faces, see if he recognizes anyone. I believe he did that already, did he not?"

The boy was now driving an imaginary car up Nick's wall, and the buzzing sound had increased tenfold.

The woman merely spoke louder. "Yes, but Randy didn't see the man in those pictures."

Nick nodded and had started to speak when Randy threw his car into high gear. He glanced at the child and then at Mrs. Allen, but she remained silent. "The next step would be for Randy to work with a police artist. Do you think he could describe the man he saw?"

Mrs. Allen looked at Randy for a minute and then nodded. "Of course."

Randy quieted the car and began to drive behind Nick's desk and up his chair.

"Great. Let me make a call and we'll set up a room for him. We certainly appreciate you coming forward with this information."

Mrs. Allen nodded primly. "Randy is very excited. When we told him he would be identifying a murderer, he could hardly wait to get down here. He really loves the police."

The little girl nodded, too.

Nick picked up his phone and dialed McCafferty's desk, trying not to think about what a waste of time this probably was. "We're set for an artist now," he said when Paul picked up.

"Got it."

He put the phone down and turned back to Randy's mother. "Does Randy need an interpreter?" He knew some parents of deaf children didn't know sign language.

"I can do it," she said.

He nodded. "Someone should be down in a few minutes." As he started to explain the process, Randy let out a piercing scream.

Even Mrs. Allen flinched and stood up.

Nick saw that Randy was holding a picture frame that he had picked up off Nick's desk. Nick reached for the boy's hand, sure that he'd cut himself.

Randy's eyes widened and he dropped the picture.

Nick let the plastic frame fall to the ground and kept his hands on Randy's. He pulled open the tight fist the boy had clenched and looked for blood. There was none. "What's wrong with him?"

Mrs. Allen didn't respond. Instead, she knelt down to Randy's level and started to speak with her hands.

Nick's phone rang, but he ignored it, watching instead as Randy picked up the picture again and pointed to something, then set it down in order to explain to his mother. The picture was the one Nick had just gotten of the baseball team he coached. He couldn't figure out what had interested Randy. Maybe he wanted to learn to play baseball.

Mrs. Allen shook her head and moved her hands again.

Randy nodded and spoke back. His mouth moved, and he made harsh sounds when he signed, as though he was trying to make the words come out of his mouth.

Nick looked over at the little girl, unsure whether to excuse himself. She sat in her chair watching them, and for a moment he wondered if she was mute. He turned his attention to the mother and son again.

Finally Mrs. Allen picked up the picture and waved a finger in the air.

Randy pointed to a face.

Mrs. Allen looked up at Nick.

"What is it?"

"He sees the man."

Nick frowned. "What man?"

"The one on the bike."

"Someone who looks like him?" Nick asked.

She shook her head.

Randy was looking back and forth from one of them to the other. When Nick looked at him, he pointed again.

"No, he sees *the* man."

Nick turned the picture so he could see it. "Which one?"

She nodded to Randy, and he pointed to a kid in the back row.

Nick leaned in and studied the face at the end of the little boy's finger. It was Rob Chase. He felt a strange sucking sensation in his throat as he tried to speak. "He has to mean the man looks like him."

Mrs. Allen spoke again to Randy.

"He's sure," the little girl said, and Nick started at the sound of her voice. "He says it's *that* kid. The blond kid," the girl repeated.

Nick opened his mouth but found he couldn't think of a thing to say.

Just then, McCafferty appeared at his door. "Sam Chase is here. She says it's urgent."

"I'm in the midd—" Nick started to say.

"It's about Rob Chase," McCafferty added.

Nick felt as though he'd been kicked in the head. The gum wrapper, Sam's flashlight, now the I.D. He saw the pieces fall into place, and yet it was all wrong. It couldn't be Rob. Sam's whole life was riding on this, and suddenly he felt he was right there with her. If Rob was guilty... He shook his head. He couldn't even fathom it.

CHAPTER 43

WHITNEY ALLEN KICKED her feet against the tall
wooden chair while her mother watched the people come
into the courtroom. Randy was sitting on the other side of
her mother, making low groaning noises like he did when
he was bothered. Whitney wished her mother would tell
him to shut up. She herself was too far away to punch
him or sign for him to stop. Instead, she settled into the
rhythmic *clack clack* of her scuffed patent leather shoes
against the legs of the chair. From their third-row seats,
Whitney studied the people in the room. Most of them
were old and wore dark colors. She thought the people
in court on TV never looked like that. Maybe this was a
special court for killers and so everyone wore black. She
looked down at her frilly pink dress and smoothed it over
her knees. She stood out like a candy cane. She wished
she got to be the one who got to talk to the lawyer. Randy
always got to do all the fun stuff.

Whitney saw a blond woman come in. That was
another thing there weren't a lot of—girls. Except for that
lady, Whitney, and her mom, there were only about two

or three others that she saw. One of them was a woman sitting at the back of the room with a notepad in her hands. The woman sat with her back perfectly straight. Her hair was pulled up so tight, Whitney wondered if it hurt. Sitting herself up straighter, Whitney put her hands in her lap, wishing she had a notepad.

"Sit forward," her mother snapped.

Whitney looked at the blond lady again. She sat down in the front row and started talking to a black man next to her. She looked sad. Whitney wondered if maybe she was one of the dead person's friends.

She had freckles like Whitney's but lighter, and Whitney thought how pretty she was. She wished she had blond hair like that. The lady was dressed in a black jacket and pants and a gray sweater. Whitney thought she looked sort of like a movie star. She couldn't remember the movie star's name, but she played in a funny movie—something about not sleeping in a city. Whitney had seen part of it over at Jodie's house. Jodie had cable. But her mom had caught them and changed the channel. Whitney didn't know what the big deal was. She'd seen one kiss and that was it. It wasn't even as good as the ones she'd seen watching Jodie's older brother with his girlfriend.

Anyway, this lady looked like that one. Only, she wasn't wearing any makeup. When grown-ups were sad, sometimes they didn't wear makeup. She remembered that from when her mom and dad split up. Her mom had been too sad to wear makeup. She said every time she put it on, she ended up crying it all off. Thankfully, her mom didn't cry anymore. Now she could wear her makeup just fine.

A man in a black robe came into the courtroom and everybody stood up. Whitney was going to stay seated, but her mother grabbed her by the arm and yanked her up. She put her hand on her heart and waited for them to start saying the national anthem or the pledge of 'legience. She saw the flag in the corner, but no one spoke for a minute. Then, the guy in the robe banged his hammer on his desk and everyone sat. Whitney was surprised no one got mad. When she hit things on her desk at school, the teacher made her sit in the corner. They hadn't said the anthem, either.

She thought that guy had a good job and wondered if the black robe came in other colors. It would be fun if it was pink.

People started talking and Whitney got bored. She looked around the room again, but no one was moving. Everyone was listening to the robe man talking. Whitney tossed her head back and stared at the ceiling. It was white and plain and very boring. She tugged at her hair, sitting back against the chair and feeling it pull as she lowered her head. When it was loose around her shoulders, she did it again. She'd heard if you pulled on it, it would grow faster.

Her mother grabbed her arm and started to stand. "I'm going up there with Randy. Don't move."

Whitney faced forward, her hands at her sides. Her mother moved out of the row, pushing Randy in front of her. When she reached the end of it, she looked back and pointed at Whitney. Whitney still didn't move, but she noticed people staring at her. When her mother turned her back, Whitney put her hands under her legs and smiled shyly. She heard someone laugh.

Then it was really quiet and everyone was watching Randy. It got really boring while Randy was explaining. There was a man sitting up by the judge and translating for him, but she could barely see him. And she couldn't see Randy or the translator from where she was sitting. And she couldn't move. The only part she understood was when Randy pointed to the man sitting behind the table up front. He was the killer. Whitney stood and crept to the aisle to get a good look at him. She was about to go even closer when she caught sight of her mother. She had those big lines between her eyes, which meant she was real mad, and she was pointing at the chair. Whitney went back to her chair and sat down.

The guy at the table wasn't even really a man. He looked like her cousin, Alex. Alex was eighteen. She thought that was old, but her stepdad said it was real young. He also said you don't know your head from your zipper at eighteen. She didn't know what that meant because she already knew her head from her zipper. Her stepdad sometimes said weird stuff like that.

When Randy was done, an old man sat in his chair. Before the old man said anything, a man gave him a book and he put one hand on the book and the other in the air and said something. Whitney wondered if Randy had gotten to touch the book too. She hadn't seen him do it. Boy, she wished she'd been the one to see the killer. Ever since Randy got home, everyone was talking about what a hero he was. But it was Whitney that told them what Randy saw. She sighed deeply. A man in front of her turned around and gave her a stare and she snapped her mouth shut and looked back at the man who was talking. He kept talking about the 'ceased. Whitney didn't know what that meant, but she knew the 'ceased wasn't there, because they kept showing her picture.

The man in the special chair said he saw the boy Randy saw too, but he saw him by a lady named Eva's house, and then he ran down the street. Whitney didn't think that sounded bad, but the man in the robe looked like it was. Then the man in the gray suit asked questions, and the old man pointed to the guy Randy had seen.

Whitney thought the man in the robe should have been asking the questions, but maybe he decided to let someone else do it. From what she could figure out, he was sort of like Santa Claus, only you didn't sit on his lap. Instead, you sat in a chair next to him and told him your story. Then, if you did it right, he let you go. The man in the robe had dark hair that was almost all gone on the top of his head, and he didn't look at all like Santa Claus.

Whitney's mother whispered to her from the aisle, and Whitney shook her head. She wanted to stay and listen. But her mother came over and yanked her off her chair. It hurt but she didn't yell. People were looking at her again, but she stared at her shoes as she and her mother and Randy left the room. As soon as they were in the hall, her mother turned to Randy and started telling him how great he was. Whitney stood behind her and rolled her eyes. When he looked at her, she made a gagging face. She wished she'd never opened her mouth about her dumb brother being outside that day.

She spun around in her dress while her mother talked

to Randy. She pictured a whole group of people watching her dance and applauding. Then she would be the famous one.

"Whitney."

Whitney saw her mother and Randy down the hall.

"Come on," her mother ordered.

Whitney ran to catch up, her patent-leather shoes slapping against the fancy floor.

CHAPTER 44

THE BACKSEAT WAS cold, and he shivered in his T-shirt, trying to stay warm. His father had his window rolled down, and the cold air blasted against him. He pulled his arms inside the shirt and held them against his chest. Next to him, the baby slept. And next to her, his brother. Neither of them looked cold. Maybe only he was cold.

His father was grumbling to himself, but the wind and the metal ticking sound of the car made it impossible to understand the words. He pulled his knees up to his chest and dropped his head to his lap. They would be home within an hour. He could survive another hour. It wasn't that cold. Shivering again, he raised his head and looked around the backseat for something to cover himself with, but the baby's blanket was the only thing back there except his dad's cooler.

His father reached back, his hand feeling for the top of the cooler and lifting it to reach for another beer. He brought it forward, dripping, and handed it to his mom to open. She crossed her arms and shook her head.

"Open it," he snapped.

She looked at him and started to shake her head again when something stopped her. From the backseat, he couldn't see his father's face, but he could visualize the stare. Eyes narrowed, thick nose flared. It was a look that warned everyone in the house not to screw with him.

He shivered again, harder this time. It was probably already too late. His dad had already had too much to drink. Nine beers since they got on the road. Once his dad got that look, he was already wound up and mean.

When they got home, they were in for a beating. Mom first because she had started it. Then him next. Once or twice, he'd been last. By then, his dad was always tired and too drunk to hit as hard. That was if he was lucky. But his dad never missed anyone. Luck didn't last that long in his house.

Usually he was first. His brother was smaller. And the baby was only little. She wasn't really a baby anymore, but that's what everyone called her. Not that it mattered to his dad. He'd been beating them up since he was four. His dad even hit his sister from time to time when she cried too much. She barely cried at all, but even that was too much to his dad.

When it was over and his father had passed out, he always took care of his mother. He got the rubbing alcohol from the bathroom and cleaned the wounds and put bandages on. He wrapped her wrist the time it got broken. And when his father had taken her hand and punched it through the window, he had picked out the slivers of glass with a pair of tweezers.

His brother mostly hid. He'd even gotten out of a few

beatings that way. But it meant his dad got him and his mother even worse. His mother looked at his brother in a weird way he didn't understand. Like she was real sad or something.

His father's head bobbed slightly, and he could see his mother grip her seat. She didn't say anything. He tucked his head back in his shirt and squeezed his eyes closed.

"You cold, honey?" she turned around to ask him.

He glanced at the back of his father's head, shook his head quickly, and tucked his head back down.

"Shut your window," she told his father. "The kids are cold."

His father mumbled something that he didn't hear. He wasn't watching, but he heard a quick smack and the sound of his mother gasping. He shut his eyes tight, trying to block it out.

"We'll be home soon," his mother whispered. He didn't need to see her to know she had tears in her eyes. He wanted to cry too.

He wished they could speak some secret language. If they could, he would tell her not to worry. He would tell her it was going to be okay. His mom started to sing, low and soft. Even his dad loved his mother's singing. She had the voice of an angel, he'd heard his dad say once.

She did sound like an angel. He loved her voice. He closed his eyes and listened to her, letting all the bad thoughts out.

His father growled something.

His mother kept singing.

He looked up and watched her. He wanted to tell her

not to fight with him. But he knew she was trying to be strong, trying to stand up to him.

Just then, his father's hand shot out. He grabbed his mother by the neck and banged her head against the window.

"No," he screamed, jumping forward. He pounded on his dad's shoulders, fists flying.

His dad slapped back at him, and he fell against the door. His head smacked hard against the handle of the door, but he didn't make a sound. He tasted blood on his lip.

"I'll deal with you when we get home," his dad said. "Don't you make me have to pull this car over."

His mother was crying softly in the front seat, holding her head.

"Shut your yapping," his father said.

His mother stopped.

He looked over at his brother. You okay? his brother asked him without speaking. He nodded and tucked his sore head back into his shirt, blowing hot air to keep himself warm.

The car grew silent. He could hear the clink of his dad's beer can as he tapped a rhythm against the steering wheel.

He curled up in a ball, resting his head against the baby's seat and trying to sleep. No one else moved. Even the baby knew enough to pretend nothing was happening.

He wished it was just the kids and his mom. He wished his dad would die. He wished his dad would get drunk and drive himself into a tree like old Mr. Potter did last winter. Or maybe fall in a pool and drown. Or go hunting with Sam and Lowell and get shot. How come his dad drank so much and always ended up okay?

He'd heard his father and Sam and Lowell talking about hunting accidents when they were sitting on the porch drinking. His room was right there, and he could hear everything. Some guy had aimed at a buck and took the head off another hunter. How come nobody did that to his dad?

He had to think of something. He had to get them away. The car swerved and his father snorted. His mother gasped but kept her silence. Just then, he got an idea.

He caught his brother's eye. He tugged on his seatbelt and pointed to his brother. He nodded and pulled the belt away from his chest to show it was on. He pointed to his mom. His brother peered between her seat and the door and then looked back, nodding. He checked the baby's seatbelt. Everyone was belted in but his dad. He had learned about seatbelts in school. They'd watched a video with two dummies. One had worn a seatbelt and one had not. The one without the seatbelt was all messed up, springs coming loose and his head almost falling off. But the one who wore the seatbelt was fine. The seatbelt would keep everyone safe. And then they could live happily, without his dad. He smiled at his idea.

His brother looked at him and frowned, but he shook his head. He couldn't explain or his dad would wonder what was going on. Pretending to sleep, he rested his head against the baby's seat and closed his eyes.

He counted to twenty-five and then opened one eye. His father's head bobbed once and then twice and then popped back up. He reached his foot forward, resting it on the emergency brake just out of his dad's sight. He waited, the muscle in his leg tense, until he saw his father's head bob again. Then he kicked as hard as he could, pushing his father's hand into the gearshift.

His father cursed and the car careened to the left. His father jerked it back, and he felt his head slam against the window.

Through the windshield he looked for the road, but it was out of focus. Grabbing hold of the baby's seat, he heard his mother scream as the car hit the guardrail and broke through.

*

Rob woke in a sweat and wiped his face with his jacket. He stood up and tried to shake the images out of his mind. He couldn't make them go away. He rubbed his head. He hated the dreams the most. Waking, he always felt like he was right there. He wanted to cry.

He paced the little room like a caged animal. Sweat poured down his back and pooled at the elastic waistband of his shorts. He'd long since shed his sweatshirt. Everything had gone crazy since Nick had awakened him that morning. Without any explanation—at least none that made sense to him—they brought him here and people started pointing at him like a killer. They'd taken his photo and his fingerprints, made him fill out forms.

Then they'd been in a courtroom and two people had I.D.'d him. Him. They'd said he was the killer. He put his hands in his hair and pulled. Tears caught in his throat, and he couldn't hold them back. Please, God. What was going on? How could these people have seen him do something he didn't do?

He was being punished. God was punishing him for what he'd done all those years ago. Jesus. He tugged at his hair, the spiky pain making tears run down his cheeks. He hadn't meant it. He felt his knees shake at the memory of that day. Poor Becky. He'd never meant to hurt her. She was just a baby.

He leaned up against one wall and sank to the floor, crying. "I'm so sorry, Becky. I'm so so sorry." He dropped his head onto his folded arms and let the quake of tears loose. The salty river was cathartic, draining his fear from him.

When the tears subsided, he was left with exhaustion, pure and simple. He swept his dirty shirtsleeve across his face and waited—waited for whatever was next. He had hoped the release would ease his anxiety, but every minute that passed built it back up until it threatened to overflow again. He stood and began pacing, trying not to think about anything. Just move, he told himself. But every time he paused, the word "killer" flashed through his head and brought with it the sharp, cold stab of terror.

By the time the door opened and Nick came in, Rob nearly sprang on him. "Oh, thank God, man! Thank God you're here! What the hell's going on? What were those people saying? I didn't do this, Nick. I didn't do anything. I swear. It's some mistake."

Nick nodded and put his hand on Rob's shoulder. "Calm down, buddy. Calm down."

He pulled a chair out and motioned for Rob to sit.

"I can't. You don't know what it's like in here. I feel

like I'm in prison." His mouth fell open. "That's what it's going to be like, isn't it? Oh, God. Prison."

Nick took him by the shoulders and pushed him into the chair. Then he pulled another chair up and sat in it. "I'm as shocked about this as you are, believe me. You're not going to prison. I'm sorry you had to wait in here, but I had to talk to some people. I'll get you out as soon as I can. But you've got to help me answer some questions. Can you help me do that?"

"Yeah. I'll do anything. Where's Aunt Sam?"

"She had to go to the courthouse and talk to the judge to make sure you can go home tonight, and then she had to find your brother. She told me to tell you she loves you and everything's going to be fine. She'll be here soon."

Unable to control himself, Rob started to cry again. Sob was more like it. His shoulders shook, tears tracked down his face, and he could taste their sweaty flavor when they hit his lips. He'd thought they were all gone, but a new batch had stored up that quickly.

Nick put his hands on Rob's shoulders. "I swear, Rob. It's going to work just like that." He leaned forward. "Everything is going to be okay."

Rob swiped clumsily at his tears and nodded. "Sorry," he sniffled, trying to gather his composure.

"No problem. In the meantime, you and I need to work to answer some questions, okay?"

Rob nodded. "I didn't do it. I swear, I didn't kill those ladies," he said.

Nick narrowed his eyes and watched him, nodding slowly. "I know."

"What do we do now?"

"It's like I said, Rob," Nick said, meeting his eyes squarely. "We just need to answer some questions."

"What kind of questions?"

"You've heard of a polygraph test?"

Rob shrugged. Every time he tried to clear his brain, a rush of panic blew clouds over it again. He couldn't think of what anything meant.

"It's a lie detector test," Nick explained. "They want you to take one of those for them."

He bolted from his chair. "A lie detector test? No way. I've seen them fake those things on TV. Hook me up to some wires and then make it look like I did something I didn't do."

Nick stood in front of him, their eyes almost exactly level. "Sit down," he said, pulling on Rob's arm. "It's not going to be like that. No one's tricking you into anything. A lie detector test is going to prove you didn't do it." Nick's eyes met Rob's as he made his point, and then he looked away.

"You think I did it," Rob charged. "My God! You think I could have killed someone."

"Of course not. But imagine how they're seeing it for a second. These people—not just one but two of them—came forward and identified you. The deaf kid from that street, the man who said he saw you by Eva Larson's house. How could that be?"

Rob's breath came in fast, wheezy waves. "I don't know. I have no idea." But he did.

He thought about the other person in this world who looked just like him. Derek wouldn't do this to him. He wouldn't let Rob hang. He wouldn't kill. Why would he have killed those women?

But an image kept coming back to him. Rob remembered the way Derek had responded to their father, the fear in his face whenever their father got close. Rob bit his tongue. It couldn't be Derek. He shut the door on those thoughts and studied the hope in Nick's eyes. "I'll take the test, if that's what they want."

Nick nodded and stepped away from him, sitting on the edge of the table. He was silent for a minute. "Rob, what about Derek?" he asked, finally.

Rob stared at the floor. "What about him?"

"Could he ride your motorcycle?"

"No way," Rob said, suddenly angry. "Leave Derek out of this. He can hardly walk. He's been through enough." Rob knew what Nick was thinking. The man who said he had seen Rob run down the street. Run. Rob could run. He was a good runner. But Derek wasn't. Derek could hardly walk without a limp. How could he possibly have run down the street or ridden his motorcycle? Rob didn't want to think about it. Derek couldn't walk. He rubbed his face. He would know if his brother could walk.

"Rob, what are you thinking?"

Rob looked up at him. "Nothing. I don't know."

"You're sure about Derek?"

Rob's heartbeat started to pound in his ears.

"Rob?"

"I'm—" But was he sure? Not really. He forced himself to nod. "I'm sure. Now when can I take the test?" he asked.

*

Rob watched the man set up the lie test. Polaski was his name. He was ugly with badly pockmarked skin, a huge scar, and a mean glare. Nick sat in a chair beside Rob and talked to him while the man worked.

"All you've got to do is tell the truth," Nick explained. "The machine reads your heart rate, then prints it out on paper." He pulled a test from someone else out of the trash and showed Rob. It was a continuous piece of long paper like the kind in the printer at the school library. On each page was a line that squiggled up and down like Rob had seen from the machines on TV that measured people's brain waves or something.

"When people lie," Nick continued, "their heart rate increases and the paper shows these peaks." He pointed to one.

"Unless they're sociopaths," Polaski cut in. "Sociopaths can lie without the least reaction at all." His eyes rested on Rob. "And I've seen 'em younger than you," he added.

Rob's mouth dropped open, fear preventing him from saying anything. He thought if the machine was hooked up to him now the red line would be off the top of the paper.

"I've heard assholes test similarly," Nick said. "How about you, Polaski? You a sociopath or just an asshole?"

Polaski frowned. "No need to be nasty, Thomas."

"One more comment like that, and your ass is out of here," Nick told him. "This is a minor, not one of your usual suspects."

Flushed, Polaski turned back to the machine and began working intently on something.

Nick turned to Rob and smiled. "Forget about that," he said, as though the ugly cop had left the room. "Like I said, all you have to do is tell the truth. This isn't a trial and it's not going to be used for anything except helping the police figure out who did this. So you've got nothing to lose. Understand?"

Rob nodded, thankful Nick was there.

"Fucking prep the witness," Polaski muttered, barely low enough to be considered under his breath.

Nick patted Rob's shoulder and spoke without turning around. "Polaski, I'll be asking the questions. Once you've got it set up, you can leave us alone."

Polaski looked up from the machine, his gaze a hot laser in the back of Nick's head.

Nick smiled and winked, even though he hadn't seen the ugly cop's expression.

Rob almost smiled, but he was still too scared.

Once the machine was set up, Polaski hooked some weird wires to Rob's left arm, like the doctor did when he took Rob's blood pressure. "Test it," he said to Nick.

"What's your full name?" Nick said to Rob.

"Robert James Austin."

Nick looked back at Polaski, who nodded and then left, muttering something. Nick pulled his chair closer to Rob.

"So, like I said, just answer the questions honestly, okay?"

Rob nodded.

"You ready?"

Rob nodded again, unable to bring himself to speak while the machine was recording unless absolutely necessary.

"First, can you tell us where you were on the night of Tuesday, July twelfth?"

Rob licked his lips. "I went to the lookout with a bunch of kids."

"Where's the lookout?"

"Off Grizzly Peak in Berkeley."

"What did you do up there?"

"We usually just hang out."

"Just hang out?" Nick asked.

Rob looked at the floor and then up at him. "And drink."

Nick just nodded.

He exhaled.

"What time did you get home?" Nick continued.

"About twelve-thirty or one."

"When is your curfew?"

Rob felt the sweat start up again. "Uh—"

"Just answer honestly," Nick said again.

"Twelve."

Nick wrote something down. "Have you ever met Sandi Walters?"

He shook his head. "No."

"Did you kill Sandi Walters?"

"No."

"Did you ride your bike to Mt. Diablo?"

"No."

"How about Eva Larson? Have you ever met her?"

"No."

The questions continued about the women who had been killed. Nick asked about certain streets, about Mt. Diablo, and about his bike.

"I think that's about it," Nick finally said.

Rob could feel the sweat on his back begin to cool.

"Have you ever killed anyone, Rob?" Nick asked.

Rob felt his heart lurch, knocking like a pinball against his insides. He thought he might be sick. He gripped the arms of the chair and tried to focus. Images of Becky and his mother came rushing at him.

"Rob?"

He heard Nick's voice, but he was unable to focus on his face or to make his mouth open even just to say he was okay.

"Rob? You need to answer the question."

His head spun and his stomach clenched tight and hard against his ribs. He sucked in a deep breath with a heavy wheezing sound. "Oh, God," he finally said. His eyes found Nick's and he shook his head.

Nick stared, his expression shocked.

"Oh, God," Rob repeated, searching for the words to say something else, to try to explain.

Nick glanced at the machine beside them and frowned.

Rob imagined what the machine was registering as he fought to compose himself.

"Who did you kill?" Nick finally asked, his voice low.

Rob met his stare, tears streaming down his face. "No one," he lied. The machine's alarm was silent, but Rob felt it, heard the lines registering off the page at his lies. Liar, liar, it screamed. Tight bands gripped his chest, the machine compressing his ribs with every lie. He waited for Nick to say something—anything.

Nick stared at him, but didn't speak again. Instead, he just shook his head. "Slow down, Rob, and tell me everything right from the beginning."

Rob looked at Nick and took a breath. Then, nodding, he started his story.

CHAPTER 45

SAM RAN INTO the empty house. "Derek," she cried.

She needed to find Derek and get back to the station house. Derek knew some of what was going on, but they needed to be together now. A family. And she needed to get back to Rob. He needed her now more than anyone. Nick would take care of him, but she needed to be there.

"Derek," she cried again, running to the back of the house.

By the time she'd spoken to the judge and Corona and gotten back to the station, Nick had already started the test, and encouraged her to go find Derek so that he wouldn't be alone or hear the news from someone else. She hadn't wanted to leave Rob, but she agreed that Derek needed someone with him. And she trusted Nick.

That Rob could be guilty seemed impossible. Why would he do it? The same Rob who had come into the den and encouraged her to find the real killer? She couldn't get the pieces to fit.

The phone rang as she reached Rob's room and glanced in at the hurricane the police had created in their search. She ran back into the kitchen and picked up the extension, praying it was Derek. "Hello."

"Sam, it's Aaron. You sound winded. Are you okay?" His voice was hoarse and he sounded tired, but she knew from the doctors that he was going to be all right.

"I'm just looking for Derek. He's gone off without telling anyone," she said. "How are you feeling?"

"Better. Still sore in the leg and arm."

"The doctors sound positive, though," she said, looking around for a sign as to where Derek might be.

"Yeah, I'll be fine. With a little physical therapy, doctors can fix almost anything."

Neither of them mentioned the fact that he was still in his wheelchair.

"I wanted to thank you for the pack."

Sam was thinking about the lie detector test. Was it over? Why hadn't Nick called? And how would Derek be after this? She didn't blame him for running off. How had she expected him to react? His identical twin had been accused of murder.

Where was Derek?

"Sam?"

"I'm here. Sorry." Bringing her concentration back to Aaron, she thought about the pack she'd sent. "I guess you're going to miss the marathon."

"Yeah." His voice rang with disappointment. "But there will be others."

"I'm really sorry, Aaron. I had no idea that Williams was a threat." She stopped. "I should've known."

"Hey, don't blame yourself. You couldn't know. I'm just glad you showed up when you did."

But he was wrong. There was no excuse for not knowing. The same was true about Rob, she realized.

Who else besides Aaron was in jeopardy because of her?

"Sam!"

She stared at the phone and blinked hard.

"What's going on?"

"Aaron, I'm sorry. I've got a lot on my mind. Are you home from the hospital?"

"Yeah, I'm home. But what's going on over there?"

"I can't explain right now. Can I call you back tomorrow?"

"Sure. I've got physical therapy in the morning, but I'll be back home around eleven."

Sam picked up a pen and wrote "call Aaron at 11 a.m."

"I'll call you then."

"You sure there's nothing I can do to help?"

"I wish there was. Just work hard at your physical therapy."

"Talk to you in the morning."

Sam held the phone to her ear until she heard the click of Aaron hanging up. Now he was going to worry about her for no reason. She should have explained herself. But what could she tell him? My nephew's been arrested for the very murders I've been working to solve? The ones I was suspected of until they found someone else close to me to blame?

She straightened the phone and put the notepad back next to it, tearing off the sheet and placing it on her pile of things to do. She saw the calendar and noticed that Derek had physical therapy in the morning.

Unable to move herself to do anything constructive, Sam scanned the kitchen, thinking maybe Derek had left a note. She could use the company, and she hated the thought that he was out, dealing with this alone. She thought about the night less than a week before when she'd actually drawn her gun on him.

In the kitchen with the lights out, Derek had moved across the room so quickly. She could have sworn it was an intruder. The image of that figure flashed across her vision. Then she saw the man take the stand and swear that he had seen Rob run down the street in Walters' neighborhood. Rob had looked so genuinely shocked, it was impossible to believe he was guilty. "Not guilty," she whispered. A wave of nausea rushed over her, and she clapped her hand onto the countertop. It wasn't Rob. But the alternative was no better. She had to be wrong. He couldn't have faked a limp all this time.

She turned and looked at the calendar with Derek's physical therapist appointment and felt a steely numbness wash over her skin like ice water. God, not Derek. But the image of his smooth motion snapped in front of her again and she knew something was desperately wrong. Scrambling for the phone, she dialed the physical therapist's number.

"Walnut Creek Sports Therapy," a receptionist answered.

"Patricia Lark, please. This is Sam Chase."

"I'm afraid Patricia is gone for the day."

"This is an emergency," Sam said, her own heart

racing at the impending doom of her discovery. "I need to reach her."

"I can try her on her car phone."

"Give me that number."

"I'm afraid I can't—"

"This is a matter of police business. Give me the number." She knew that it wasn't anger but fear that created the harshness in her voice.

The woman recited the number and Sam scribbled it down. Before the receptionist could speak again, Sam hung up and, hands shaking, dialed the number.

Ring. Ring. "Come on, damn it!"

"Hello." The hum of traffic buzzed behind the far-off voice.

"This is Sam Chase, Derek Austin's aunt."

"Hi. How did you get this number?"

"It's not important. I need to know Derek's status."

"His status?" The voice crackled over the line.

"How he's doing. How the therapy is coming along."

"It's coming along great."

"Great, how?"

"Great. I don't know. Can we talk about this tomorrow? I could call—"

"No," Sam's voice cracked. "I need to know now."

"What do you need to know?"

Somehow, despite the urgency she felt, Sam couldn't get herself to say the word.

"Mrs. Austin?"

"Does he—"

"Hello?" she repeated.

"Does he run?"

"Run?"

"Yes," she croaked.

"Oh, yeah. He's up to about three miles with me. He said he runs with you, too. Don't you run together?"

Sam's legs could no longer support her weight. Setting the phone down, she splayed her palms on the counter and exhaled. "Oh, God." She didn't know how long she sat there before she heard the faint moan of the floor beneath her, shifting under someone's weight.

She spun around and saw Derek in the doorway to the living room. She held back a gasp and stared at the front door. "You didn't come in the front door."

Derek didn't answer.

When she forced her eyes back to him, his expression was dark. She took a step toward him before she noticed the black steel piece in his hand.

Her Glock was tight in his grip and aimed just above his right ear.

CHAPTER 46

LIGHTS FLASHING, SIRENS blaring, Nick drove the car with the pedal flat to the floor. He pointed at Rob. "Put your seatbelt on," he directed as he steered the car onto Highway 24 toward Walnut Creek and Sam's house.

"I don't need it," Rob answered.

"Put it on—now," Nick demanded.

Rob pulled the strap across his chest and locked it into the metal fastener.

Nick thought about Rob's performance on the lie detector test. There was no way anyone could interpret the results otherwise. Rob had simply not been involved in the murders of Sandi Walters or Eva Larson. The test was clean, even with Polaski's badgering.

But if two eyewitnesses had identified Rob and it wasn't Rob, that left only Derek.

After Nick had pressed Rob again on the subject of Derek, Rob confessed that he was starting to have doubts of his own. It had seemed impossible that Rob could be involved, but at least Nick had seen Rob's anger. He'd seen Rob overheat—seen the potential of deep anger in him.

Derek was the opposite. Nick had never seen him angry. He seemed so mild-mannered, timid almost. How could he be a killer? Still, when Nick hadn't been able to reach Sam by phone, he'd had to get to her to be sure she was all right. It had taken a few minutes to get his captain to agree to let him take Rob along, but he had lied and said that he was taking the boy to one of the crime scenes to scare him into a confession.

Nick took his foot off the gas, then pressed it down harder as though it might give him a new boost of power. It just wasn't fast enough.

If only he had known, Nick would have been on his way to Sam's an hour ago. If Derek was behind these murders, would he take that same anger out on Sam?

Nick swerved the car off the exit ramp and around a car that had failed to yield to the sirens and lights. "Moron," he snapped, thinking something even less kind.

As they sped toward Sam's house, neither spoke. Nick gripped the wheel and studied the road as if he were taking an entrance exam for the Indy 500. Damn. If anything happened to her…

Only one night. There had to be more. He needed more. He deserved more. He pounded his hand against the wheel and blasted the horn at a driver in his lane.

At the corner of Sam's street, he switched his siren and lights off. If Derek was in there with Sam and something was going down, he at least wanted to retain the element of surprise. He parked in front of the house across the street and jumped out of the car. He pushed the door shut until metal touched metal, but he didn't latch it. He didn't want Derek to hear it.

Rob was right behind him as he crossed the street.

"Wait in the car."

"No."

Nick continued toward the house. There wasn't time to argue. He had to get to Sam. He reached the front door and heard a low murmur of voices, but was unable to make out the words.

"What's going on?" Rob asked.

Nick pressed his finger to his lips and moved around the side of the house. At the first window he stopped and crouched low, looking through the corner of it.

He could see the kitchen. Sam stood at one side, her back to him. Derek was in front of her. They appeared to be talking. He exhaled.

Just as he was about to move back to the door, he caught sight of something in Derek's hand. Ducking back, he squinted into the window and saw that Derek was holding Sam's Glock, the barrel trained on his own head.

Nick dropped, his knees cracking. "Shit."

Rob leaned toward the window, and Nick grabbed him and dragged him down. His expression was wide-eyed and startled, and Nick remembered that this wasn't just another hostage situation for Rob. This wasn't his job—this was his life. "It's going to be okay," Nick lied.

"What's going on?"

"I need you to go back to the car and call for backup. Just pick up the radio and press the lever on the side. Tell them you're with me. Give them the address and have them send someone immediately." Nick gave him the code for an armed suspect holding a hostage rather than telling Rob what he'd seen through the window. He was better off not knowing. And Nick didn't need any panicking on his hands.

Rob grabbed Nick's shirt. "Why don't we go in?"

"We can't."

Rob looked up at the window and then back at Nick. Narrowing his gaze, he dropped his voice. "Why? What did you see?"

Nick let out his breath. "He's got a gun. I need you to go back to the car and call for backup." He pushed Rob toward the car. "Now."

Rob measured his gaze and then nodded. Ducking down below the level of the windows, he ran back toward the street.

Nick eased himself up to the window again. Derek was still clutching the gun. Nick moved slowly toward the back of the house, searching for an open window, mapping out a plan to stop Derek from doing something drastic. He found a window and pressed his hands against the sill, willing it to open. It was locked. "Damn." The next one he found was locked, too.

"They're on their way," Rob said when he returned several minutes later.

"You should wait in the car until they get here."

Rob shook his head, the muscles in his jaw working. "No way."

Nick cursed under his breath, concentrating on his next move. He closed his eyes and focused on the layout of the house. It was all one level, but he didn't remember a back door. "Is there another way in?"

"Through Sam's room. A door."

"Show me."

Rob stood up and Nick pulled him back down, pointing to the windows. "Stay below the level of the windows."

Rob bent over and ran the length of the house. Nick followed right behind.

At the back of the house Rob stopped and pointed to a door.

Nick grabbed the knob and turned. "It's locked."

Rob nodded and reached down to a large metal hook and faucet that were meant to hold a garden hose. Off the back of the hook, he pulled a little tin box and slid the top open.

Nick slapped his shoulder and took the key from the box, unlocking the door and pushing it open as quietly as he could. Drawing his gun, he motioned Rob back, knowing he would follow anyway. In his situation, Nick would have done the same thing. He kept himself in front and hoped the sight of Rob would calm Derek.

The door led them into Sam's bedroom, and he smelled her in the air. Silently, his gun in front of him, he said a prayer and headed toward the front of the house.

At Sam's door, he clutched the knob, turning it slowly until he heard the light click of the lock releasing, and pulled it open a half inch at a time. The purposeful motions contradicted the erratic thumping of his pulse.

As the door reached the halfway point, he looked out. He couldn't see either Sam or Derek from where he was, but their voices were a low murmur. It was a good sign. No screaming, no yelling. Perhaps there wouldn't be any violence. This family had been through enough. All of them.

He turned the corner and saw Sam begin to cross the room toward Derek.

"Don't get close. I'll do it. I swear," Derek shouted at her.

Sam glanced at Nick and then looked immediately back to Derek. Nick watched her lay five fingers against her right thigh. Then there were four, then three. Nick nodded, ready to run.

When there was only one finger, she launched forward and Nick ran for Derek.

Derek stepped backward and started to drop the arm with the gun to his side.

Sam ran toward him, the gun aimed in her direction.

Nick saw it and dove for it. He felt his fingertips touch it, pushed it away from Sam. But he was too late.

He heard the pop of the gunfire and saw Sam fall forward.

CHAPTER 47

THE FIRST THING Sam felt was heat and a wave of nausea.

Derek screamed.

Rob reached for his brother, but Nick held him back.

Rob struggled, only Nick was stronger, and Sam saw him push Rob to the ground, out of the way.

Sam sat sprawled out on the floor gripping her left arm. Derek had shot her. Dear Lord. She watched the blood soak through her fingers and drip on the white linoleum floor. A million thoughts swarmed her mind. She focused on staying calm.

Derek leaned against the kitchen cabinets, the gun aimed at the air in front of him.

Nobody moved. No one spoke.

"Oh, God," Derek finally sobbed, the gun trembling in his hands. "You shouldn't have gotten close. I just want it to be over. I just need to end it."

His words made Sam feel as if her heart were breaking but she stayed silent, trying to save her strength. She had no idea what to say to that, what to say to this child she realized she hardly knew.

Rob started to cry. "No, not like this. Please, don't."

"Let's put the gun down, Derek," Nick said, trying to ease himself closer.

Derek shifted the gun. "Stay back. Please, Nick. Please don't get closer." He was crying and his breath was ragged.

Nick backed off. "Okay. I'll stay back, but you've got to help me, Derek. Put the gun down, okay?"

He shook his head.

Rob cried harder.

Derek got on his knees and crossed to Sam. He wrapped an arm around her shoulder, still holding the gun. "I didn't mean to hurt you, Sam. I swear I didn't."

"I'll be okay, Derek," Sam said, her voice gravelly to her own ears. She wondered if she'd ever be okay again, if any of them would. God help them all. "I need to go see a doctor, but I'll be okay. We're all going to be okay, but you need to listen to Nick and put the gun down."

"No. I need it to be over. I need to see Mom and Becky." He stroked her shoulder, tears streaming down his face. "I didn't mean to hurt you. You weren't one of them."

"Why, Derek? Help me understand," Sam said, searching his face. A rush of images of him growing up flashed by her. At that moment, he looked like a little boy again. Where were the signs? Where had she gone so wrong?

"I started reading your old cases," Derek said. "Not all of them. Just the first ones. There was all sorts of stuff

420

in there —unfinished stuff, like single moms who hurt their daughters. Hurting boys was bad enough. But girls. Look what it did to Becky… and Mom."

"I'm so sorry about your mom. It's all my fault," Sam said. "I should have done something." She had known about Becky, of course, from the accident, but the boys had never wanted to talk about her and Sam had finally given up, leaving it in the past.

Derek didn't seem to hear her. "All I could think about was how our mom was dead and those moms were hurting their girls," he said, turning to face his brother. "I thought about Becky, Rob. I don't know why, but I went to see those girls. I even met one—her name was Becky, too. I wasn't going to talk to her, but she had big green eyes. And she looked so lonely."

He flinched as if it was painful. "Then I watched their mothers. I wanted to know what those terrible women were like. And I saw what they did." He looked over Rob's head at Nick. "I followed Sandi Walters. She did drugs. She went and bought heroin and got high. She even danced around naked. And she was so happy." He rubbed his hands together and Sam could see his anger, an anger he had kept hidden from her. How had she not seen it? "She hurt Molly and then she went and got high." He paused. "I just snapped."

Derek shut his eyes and swiped at his tears with the back of the gun hand. "It doesn't matter now. I didn't do anything wrong," he said. "They had it coming." He waved the gun toward Nick and Rob.

"You killed them?" Rob whispered.

"Sandi Walters didn't deserve to live. I went up there

to the woods to watch her. I went to talk to her, to tell her not to hurt Molly again. And she told me that she could do whatever she wanted. She was like Dad. She said Molly was her kid and she had every right to hurt her."

Sam tried to touch Derek, tried to pull him closer, but he pulled away, sobbing.

"She made me so mad. I was so mad. I couldn't stop. She finally looked scared, and I thought, Now she understands how Molly feels. And then she was dead." The gun continued to shake in his hand. "I just wanted to make her understand."

Sam prayed the gun didn't go off again. Don't let him kill again. "Derek, it's okay. We're going to get you help," Sam said. "It's going to be okay." Moving slowly, she started to get up but the pain was too much.

He shook his head. "I was so scared. I didn't mean to kill her, so I got the twigs like that Sloan guy did."

He looked up, his eyes wide, and Sam wanted to hold him, to make it better. But in her heart, she knew it would never be better.

"You didn't mean to hurt Eva Larson either, did you, Derek?" Nick asked. Sam knew he was trying to keep Derek talking until he could make a move for the gun. It was all so surreal. How could this be her own nephew?

"I didn't mean to do it again. I went to check on little Becky." He choked out a sob. "She was already dead. Her mother had let her die. She tried to say I had done it. That made me so mad. She killed Becky. She killed our little Becky."

Rob stood and pushed past Nick. He was crying and his voice cracked as he spoke. He dropped to his knees in front of Derek. "It's my fault, Der. I killed Mom and Becky. I killed them." He choked on a sob and pushed on. "I thought they'd be okay. They were wearing seatbelts. I thought everyone would be okay except Dad.

"I only meant to kill Dad. The way he used to hit us. Even Becky, remember?" Rob reached out to his brother. "And Becky was only a baby. It's my fault that Sam has to take care of us. It's because of me. I tried to get rid of Dad and I killed them all."

Sam felt her own shock and saw Derek's. Rob blamed himself for his mother and sister's deaths. Sam caught Nick's gaze. He had heard the story already, she was sure.

"It's not your fault, Rob," Sam whispered.

Nick nodded. "You were just a kid."

Rob stared at Derek. "I didn't mean to, but I did. Remember in the car that night? I told you to put your seatbelt on. Remember? Dad wasn't wearing his. I thought if everyone else was, we'd all be safe. And he'd be gone." Rob moved forward. "Then he couldn't hurt you anymore. I know how he hurt you, Der."

Derek shook his head. He stood up. "No."

"I know now what you went through. I didn't then." Rob stopped and his shoulders sagged. "Or maybe I did and I just couldn't think about it. He was a terrible person, Der. But we don't have to be like that. We can be whoever we want." Tears were rolling down Rob's face.

"We've all done bad things," Sam said softly. "And had people hurt us. But that's no reason to call it quits. We have to stay together." She tried again to pull herself up.

Derek took her hand and helped her. "I can't, Sam. I can't do it." He moved away from her.

Sam swayed and reached a hand out to steady herself, leaving a thick bloody print on the counter.

Derek saw it and flinched.

Sam looked over at Nick. He was trying to appear reassuring, but nothing could undo what had been done. They just had to get the gun from Derek. Get it away and keep him safe. That's all she'd ever wanted for her boys.

"Come on, Derek," Rob said. "We need to get some help for Aunt Sam. She's all we have. We're a family."

"I can't be here now. I killed them. That makes me as bad as they are. And it wouldn't have stopped. I know it wouldn't. It felt too good."

"We'll get help for you," Sam said. She watched Nick. He was getting ready to go for the gun. Sam tried to hold Derek's attention. "You didn't mean to hurt them. We can work through this, Derek."

"But it felt so good when they were dead," Derek whispered. "It was like I was killing Dad. I wish I had killed him. I thought about it so many times."

"It's okay, Derek. It's all over now," Sam said, reaching her bloodied hand toward him.

Derek shook his head. "I'll never get over what he did to me."

Sam moved in to hold Derek. "Yes, you will, Derek. My father raped me. He raped me just like yours raped you. He raped me a thousand times and I thought I'd never be better." Sam choked on the tears that spilled down her cheeks. "I hated him a million times. I dreamed of tearing his eyes out and of stabbing him over and over."

She paused and let her sobs loose, shaking. "He's dead and I have to let go of how much I hate him."

Derek cried beside her.

Nick reached in to try to take the gun and Sam heard the sound of sirens in the background. The backup had arrived.

Derek heard it too, lifting his gun again. It shook in his hand. "I can't go to prison. I can't."

"You're not going to have to, Derek," Sam said, though Derek had moved away from her. "I'm going to help you. We'll keep you safe. You're still under eighteen. We can keep you out of prison." She thought about the promise she was making. They tried children as adults for crimes much less severe than Derek's.

"Please, Der. It'll be okay," Rob added, taking a step forward.

"Don't," Derek snapped, tears still streaming down his face. "Leave me." He started to back out of the kitchen toward the front door.

"Come on, Derek," Sam said, following him. "Put the gun down."

"I can't, Sam. I have to go. I can't stay—not after what I've done. I'm sorry. I'm so sorry." Derek turned and ran, pulling the front door open as Sam and Rob and Nick all rushed after him.

Nick reached the door first and screamed to the backup, "Don't shoot! Don't shoot!"

Sam reached the door in time to watch Derek lift the gun and aim it at one of the squad cars.

"No," she shouted. "Don't—"

The pop of gunshots cut her off and she watched as

Derek was knocked to the ground by the bullets. She closed her eyes and felt herself fall backward. "Oh, God."

"No!" Rob screamed, trying to push past them.

Nick grabbed him and held him in the doorway, shielding his face from the sight of his dead brother.

Sam couldn't move, couldn't look away. "No. Not Derek. No," she whispered.

Rob sobbed and Nick held him as Sam slowly sank to the floor. She reached up and took Rob's hand, pulling him toward her. She didn't care about the pain in her arm. She held him there as tight as she could, as though somehow by holding him, she could protect him from everything that had just happened.

They only had each other now and that would have to be enough.

EPILOGUE

Eight Months Later

SAM CLASPED ROB'S hand in hers as they walked out of the therapist's office. They each felt a bit stronger every month. Some days were bad, others were better. It amazed her what things Dr. Hessel could get Rob to talk about. They often cried and occasionally laughed in their sessions. Mostly, they worked through a lifetime of built-up hurt. She hoped Derek could see them from wherever he was. And she hoped he was finally in a place away from the pain.

As they neared the street, Sam could see Nick leaning against his Honda. She and Nick were doing better than she'd ever thought they would. He had transferred to work under a different captain after managing to come up with enough on Cintrello to get him reprimanded. Sam appreciated the effort. It turned out that Gary Williams was partly responsible for Cintrello's poor opinion of Sam. Williams and Cintrello had worked on a handful of cases together in their younger days, and Williams had done a pretty good job of making Sam sound like the devil to Cintrello. But

Sam didn't feel bad for the captain. A good captain would have checked his sources more carefully.

Williams was in jail, awaiting trial on six felony charges, including attempted murder. But Sam wouldn't be happy until he was behind bars for life. Aaron, on the other hand, was enjoying the celebrity status he'd gotten in the papers. And he'd met a woman reporter who was going to train for the next marathon with him. Sam was working on a handful of cases on a consulting basis. She wasn't ready to be back in the thick of it yet. She wasn't sure she ever would be. She and Rob would deal with that as time passed.

"I thought I'd take my two favorite people to Chevy's," Nick said as they approached.

Rob looked at Sam and she nodded.

"Yeah," Rob said. The tears had left tiny streaks on his cheeks. She was sure her own were no better, but neither she nor Nick mentioned them. Instead, Nick patted Rob's back and handed him the keys to the Honda. "You want to drive?"

"Sure."

"I'm sitting in the back," Sam said, teasing.

"I was going to call backseat," Nick countered.

"Very funny," Rob said, tossing the keys into the air and catching them again.

Sam got into the backseat and buckled her seatbelt as Rob started the car and pulled out into the street. The boys' talk turned to baseball, and Sam leaned back and watched the streets pass. The trees had lost their leaves, and now the days brought more rain than sun. Christmas had gone by in a blur of dark days, and the three of them had gone to the mountains for a week to be away from the hoopla of the season. They'd celebrated by exchanging letters about the things they were thankful for. And then Sam broke down and got Rob a new computer and Nick bought him two games to play on it. She had to admit Rob looked very excited to see a real present on Christmas morning, and the games had provided good fun for them when they needed a distraction. And fun was a hard-won luxury.

They thought a lot about what to do on the anniversary of Derek's death, but so far they hadn't come up with anything appropriate. And they hadn't tackled Derek's room yet. Sam and Rob often met in there to talk about what had happened and what made Derek do the things he'd done. She still smoothed his bed covers and straightened his books as though he might be coming home any day. Rob had said he would help her clean it out when they were ready. She knew the time would feel right eventually.

It seemed to help Rob that Nick was with them as much as he could be. It helped Sam too. Since Derek's death, Nick had spent all but half a dozen nights at their house. First on the couch, but more recently, he'd started to share Sam's bed. They hadn't been intimate again, but she knew they would be.

"You guys want to go see the Raiders this weekend?" Nick asked.

"The Raiders? I hear their fans are insane," Sam said, not interested.

She could see Rob's eyebrows rise in the rearview mirror. "Insane, like what?"

Nick shrugged. "They're pretty crazy."

"Cool," Rob said.

Sam shook her head.

"Come on, Sam. It'll be fun," Nick pleaded, smirking.

"You guys know how much I hate football."

"But you love us," Rob countered.

She met Rob's eyes in the rearview mirror. "I do love you," she whispered.

Nick's head spun and he looked at her.

She nodded. "And you."

Rob and Nick exchanged a look and laughed. "She said she loves us," Rob teased. "She'll definitely go to the game now."

"Yeah. She must be insane to tell us that." Nick looked back at Sam. "Are you okay?"

She crossed her arms and shook her head at their antics. "Fine."

He looked at Rob, who shrugged and said, "Maybe she's having a brain stroke or something."

Sam laughed and shook her head. "No strokes back here. Just following the doctor's advice and sharing my feelings."

"Wish we had a recorder," Nick said, winking.

"Yeah," Rob agreed. "At least you've got a witness in case she ever denies it."

"There's no denying it," Sam said. "I love you both."

"Definitely a brain stroke," Nick said.

"Definitely," Rob agreed, grinning as he pulled into Chevy's parking lot.

AUTHOR'S NOTE

The first person I would like to thank is you—the reader. Thank you for reading *Chasing Darkness*. While we're at it, thank you for every book you've ever read. It is the greatest gift you can give an author like me. Without you, there would be no books, and what a terrible world that would be.

If you have enjoyed this book, please consider taking a moment to leave a review on Amazon or elsewhere. Reviews and recommendations are vital to authors. Every good review and every recommendation for one of my books helps me stay hunkered and warm in my basement, doing what I love best—writing dark, chilling stories.

To claim your free short story, to learn more about me or my writing, please visit me at www.daniellegirard.com.

Now, please turn the page for a preview of Danielle's thriller, *Savage Art*.

ACKNOWLEDGMENTS

I WANT TO first thank Department of Justice special agent Karen Norwood for spending time to show me what she does. Everything she told me was accurate and honest; if I got it wrong, it's entirely my fault. I also want to thank the talented authors who took time away from their own projects to offer their honest criticism of mine: Joanne Barnes, Taylor Chase, Diana Dempsey, Lisa Hughey, Malia Martin, Monica McLean, and Sonia Rossney. And thank you for the extraordinary love and support: Chris, Claire, Nicole, Tom, Steve, Blake, Bob, Donna, Sue, and Marcie. And to Helen Breitwieser and Genny Ostertag for your insight on and passion for these books. You make them real.

PREVIEW FROM RUTHLESS GAME

PROLOGUE

March 17, 1971

THE WET FABRIC started to slip and she held her bound hands to her face and tried not to watch. It was too terrible, too terrible. She just wanted her mommy. Where was her mommy? Where were all their mommies?

"Fourteen is just too many," he growled as he lifted the body of Jimmy Rodriguez and set it next to the others.

There were eleven. She had counted. Eleven times she'd heard them scream, eleven times she'd heard them stop. She was last in line, but he was getting closer. Only Billy and Marcus were before her. He'd be to her soon. She shifted against the cold cement floor, the puddle she'd made like wet ice cream against her skin.

She heard Billy sobbing and she started again, too. She couldn't help it. She kept waiting for someone to come and save them, but no one did. He had killed Mrs. Cooney and Mr. Choy. He walked onto the school bus and shot them. And then he forced each of them to drink a cup of punch. He put something in it. She saw him.

And she shook her head when he told her to drink it. But he hit her hard and she knew she had to or he'd shoot her like he did Mrs. Cooney.

He looked at her now and licked his lips. She started to cry harder, pushing herself away from him. "No," she whispered. "No, no, no."

"Can't I save some for later?" he called.

She stopped crying and looked around, peering out of the small gap in her blindfold. Why was he asking them that?

She nodded. Save some for later.

"Tomorrow, I'd be fresh and ready again."

She nodded. "Tomorrow," she whispered. "Tomorrow."

It was quiet for a moment and she moved her head to look out of the corner of her blindfold. She heard feet moving toward her. Was it him? Looking down, she saw white sneakers like Brittany's.

"What do you think you're doing?" he screamed.

She jumped, feeling someone behind her. But his voice was far away. Someone touched her hands and she could feel the rope on her wrists loosening. "Billy?" she whispered, but no one answered.

Then, her hands were free. She rubbed them together. She wanted to pull at her blindfold but she was afraid he would see her so she didn't move.

"I said what do you think you're doing?" he repeated.

She held her hands together as though they were still tied. He was yelling at her. But he wasn't getting closer. Just stay still, she told herself.

"You can't shoot me, for God's sake," he screamed.

Suddenly, someone was behind her again. She heard a

loud clacking sound and then it was silent. She whipped her head around but couldn't see. She started to shake.

There was something hard and cold in her hands. It was heavy. She remained silent, feeling her hands shake as she held the heavy thing. She looked out of the corner of her blindfold and saw all white. White with wings, she thought. Wings.

She didn't feel scared, though.

Someone moved her finger and she heard a loud pop. Then another. She dropped the heavy thing and pressed her hands to her ears.

And then it was over.

CHAPTER 1

Twenty-nine years later

THE HARSH BLARE of a car horn pulled Alex Kincaid from sleep, an uncomfortable ache burning in her lower back. Shifting positions, she felt the rough edge of a chair. She must have fallen asleep in the den. It had been years since she'd done that, awakened with an empty bowl of popcorn in her lap and an old rerun of *Taxi* on TV. Her mind meandered through the evening before, but she didn't recall if she had been reading or watching television before bed. She settled back in to sleep a few more minutes.

A car rushed by and she shifted again, wondering when her street had become so noisy. Usually no more than one car passed every twenty minutes, but this morning it sounded like there were a parade going by. No wonder she never slept in the den.

No, that wasn't right. The den was in the back of the house. The cars couldn't be heard from there.

Forcing her eyes open, she stared out her windshield.

Her windshield? Confused, she looked at the car around her. Sitting upright, she clutched the steering wheel. What the hell was going on? Above her, the yellow leaves of the fall oak trees sheltered the morning sun, creating patterns of light across her dash.

A cover of dew beaded across her windows. The cool California morning made her shiver. A row of Victorian and Tudor homes stared down at her from the hillside like thick-necked soldiers preparing for attack. What was she doing in her car?

She glanced down at the familiar navy sweat pants and gray Cal T-shirt, trying to remember going to bed the night before.

She'd taken something one of a handful of doctors had given her to help her sleep—Restoril. The endless insomnia had finally driven her to be so exhausted, so totally beat, that she'd regressed to trying the meds again. She'd slept. She'd actually slept. But when had she gotten up? And left her house and driven to—she looked around at the houses—big houses, larger than anything in her neighborhood, all built high off the street, their large windowed fronts staring down at her questioningly.

And where the hell was she?

Leaning forward, she ran her hand over her lopsided ponytail and looked around. There has to be a good explanation for this. Her eyes closed, she rubbed at the pain in her temples. Someone must have called her. Her brain kicked into gear as she tried to picture her phone, tried to remember it ringing. Her mind sputtered and stalled like a dying car. She didn't remember talking to anyone.

Hoping one of the houses would nudge into her

memory, she stared back at the imposing facades. The block didn't look remotely familiar.

Cars raced down the street, their drivers dressed in ties and suits. Work! Her fingers searched her wrist for her watch. It wasn't there. But she always wore her watch. Turning the key in the ignition, she glanced at the clock on the dashboard. It was nearly seven a.m. "Damn it." She was going to be late for work.

She started the car and glanced at a street sign. Yolo Avenue. She'd never heard of that street.

She'd been sleepwalking; that had to be it. She'd never done that before. It had been so long since she'd even slept through the night. And this was worse than sleepwalking— she had sleep-dressed then sleep-driven and who knew what else.

Fighting off the battling anger at not remembering, she steered the car down Yolo until she saw a familiar street sign. Henry. She was in Berkeley, actually only a half dozen blocks from the station. Yolo was on her beat, but she had never come across it before. Ingrained in her subconscious, somewhere, was this street. That was why she'd ended up there. She shook her head and sped across Shattuck to Ashby. That was the last time she was going to take sleeping pills.

Wishing she had a siren, she blared her horn at the slowpoke drivers around her and sped for home. She parked the car in front of the small home on Pine Lane that had once belonged to her mother. The front grass needed cutting. The hedges had grown up and begun to block the front windows, giving them the appearance of shaded limousine windows, only in green. The Spanish-style house needed painting, too. Its pinkish salmon color always looked as if it had been bought on sale. She wanted the house to be white. But until now, she hadn't realized how much she'd let the house go—suddenly, the house was a disaster.

As she locked the car door, she felt both strangely rested and also unnerved. Neither was a sensation with which she was familiar. She brushed the nervousness off. She didn't have patience for catastrophe now. Rushing up the steps, she shivered, her T-shirt much too thin for the cool morning air.

As she moved, she reminded herself of the positives. At least she had awakened in her own car. What if she had found herself in a stranger's house? What if she had done something crazy—like driven into a pole or a dog or a child? What if she had robbed a bank?

What if nothing. Nothing had happened. She opened the door to her house and looked around. Everything was normal here.

The drug had a strange effect on her sleep patterns or something. Alex's sleep patterns, or lack of them, had been a popular subject in her household growing up. Maybe she would have a chance to stop by James's office and ask if he remembered anything like that.

She was a very logical person—calm, cool, collected. She didn't drink heavily, exercised religiously and kept her distance from suspicious people. She walked in the crosswalk and flossed her teeth, for God's sake. Things like waking up on a strange street did *not* happen to her.

A man's face suddenly popped into her mind. He had been in the bagel store yesterday. He had approached her as she was getting bagels and coffee for herself and her partner. He'd used her name and then Greg had come in and she'd turned away. When she looked back, he was gone. She'd never seen him before or since. And why was she thinking about him now?

Pushing it aside, she just hoped she still had time to shower and dress to be at the station before eight. The patrol captain had little tolerance for tardy officers.

Rushing around, she cursed herself for not programming the coffeemaker the night before. The thought of going without a caffeine fix was torture, but there wasn't time. She glanced at her wrist for the third time in ten minutes. Where the hell was her watch?

Thankfully her job didn't require much primping, and she preferred it that way. She had never worn much makeup. The last thing she wanted to do was look more dainty and feminine. At only five foot three, it was difficult enough to be taken seriously. As she passed the mirror on her way out the door, she caught her reflection.

She cringed at the way her normally curly auburn hair hung limply on her shoulders. Dark circles stood out beneath her eyes, which were so bloodshot it was impossible to tell they were green.

Back in the car, she considered trying to remedy her appearance but decided against it. The one day she had actually put on lip gloss, her partner had teased her that she looked more like she belonged in front of a group of kindergartners than in a police uniform. And while she knew Greg had probably been joking, she was sure there were others who would readily agree with him without so much as a hint of humor. She didn't want to be singled out, just left alone. She was proving herself as a rookie—top of her class, best record so far. No sense screwing it up by reminding them that she was a girl. She could swear that every once in a while, when things were going really well, they forgot. And in those moments, she loved being on the force more than anything.

At ten to eight, she pulled into the parking lot next to the familiar gray building that housed the police department. The yellowed windows on the lower level still bore the bars installed after the station had been bombed back in the sixties. Though she had been on the force only a short time, she'd learned to enjoy the history and idiosyncrasies of the building. It would be strange when the new building was finished.

Alex straightened her back and got out of the car, thinking about what tests today would bring. As one of the few females on the force, Alex was at the receiving end of more than her share of jokes. She was used to it. Facing the teasing of the other officers was fine most days. Bra and panty jokes, she could suffer through.

Issues of her strength, her tolerance, her endurance for the job, those she wouldn't. She'd been a physical trainer for eight years before the rundown with a mugger made her realize she wanted more.

And she'd been tired of women whose idea of getting in shape was leg lifts while having their bikini line waxed. Alex was faster than all of the women and some of the men on the force. She'd proven it at the academy and she'd do it again if anyone questioned it. But mental strength and stability were not so easily measured and she refused to let anyone question hers.

And if anyone found out about last night, that would be the first thing to come into question.

She just prayed no one ever found out.

CHAPTER 2

ALEX LOCKED HER car and ran in the front door and up the closest of the two half-circle staircases on either side of the lobby. The stairways always reminded her of an elegant hotel lobby from some old black-and-white movie, and they seemed out of place in the middle of the dilapidated station entrance.

At the top of the stairs, she ran into one of the consulting psychologists, carrying a tall stack of files. As they bumped, the files dropped to the floor.

"Sorry," Alex said, leaning down to scoop them up.

"Don't worry." Dr. Richards straightened the files in her arms. "It's a zoo in there today."

Alex nodded, handing her a stack of papers. "Always is." That was what she loved about police work. Every day was a new adventure.

Alex edged her way through the crowd of people waiting at the desk.

"I'm telling you, he said he wanted to buy the cycle," one man yelled. A black leather jacket covered his white dress shirt and the jacket of a gray suit, a helmet tucked under his arm. "Brand-new BMW bike. Fuck," he muttered under his breath.

Alex moved past another man who rolled up his sleeve and showed his tattoo to the administrative officer. "Does that look like an eagle to you? It's a goddamn Tweety Bird. I paid a hundred bucks for an eagle and the asshole won't give me my money back."

Alex looked at the tattoo. It was definitely not an eagle. She thought even Tweety looked tougher than the wimpy bird on his shoulder. Rotten luck.

"That's really not a police issue. You should contact the consumer bureau to file a report," the officer behind the counter explained.

"A report? I ain't going to file no damn report. I want my fucking money back."

Alex wished she had time to stay and watch the man get himself thrown in jail for assaulting an officer. Through a large solid oak door, she entered the administrative division where they housed the fingerprint and mug-shot files. The department planned to scan them all so they would be accessible by computer at any station in California and eventually the nation. Great intentions but the process was unbelievably slow. She'd had to "thumb" through the records more than a few times in her months on the force, and it wasn't an enviable job.

"Morning, Alex," Detective Sam Portreo called. A brown tie curved over his round belly as though it had been starched against a bowling ball. This particular tie was his favorite because it hid the coffee stains.

"Hey, Sam. How's it going?"

His coffee cup raised, he gave a half smile. "I could complain, but what good would it do?"

"Exactly. Nice tie, by the way."

"Never been cleaned," he said proudly.

"I'm impressed."

"Knew you would be."

On the way down the hall, she leaned into her brother's office.

"Hey," James called, waving her over.

She leaned over his desk and pointed to her empty wrist. "I'm late, but I wanted to ask: Do you remember if any of us walked in our sleep as kids?"

James raised an eyebrow. "Sleepwalking now?"

She shook her head, realizing the question sounded strange coming from someone already late for work, especially to James. James was Internal Affairs and his intense stares made an average cop's suspicious nature seem like child's play. "I just thought I remembered something from when we were kids."

"Not that I know of." Then, turning back to his work, he added, "You'd better get to work. And no sleepwalking walking on the job."

Feeling better, she almost smiled at the remark. It was the closest James would come to humor on the job. He took his work very seriously. It was something she respected about her brother despite the fact that it occasionally made him difficult to be around.

In the locker room, she dressed as quickly as she could. It was normally a ten-minute process with the lace-up ankle boots, the twenty-five-pound equipment belt, and a bulletproof vest. This morning, she finished in five. The first few steps with all the extra weight always made her feel as though she were walking through water. Today, rushing around, it felt more like she was running through water.

As she reached the second-floor squad room—a square, windowless area—she scanned for her partner. They were due in the briefing in three minutes.

Four patrol officers, one with a ball tucked under his arm, headed in after their morning two-on-two basketball game.

"You should join us some time, Alex."

She smiled and waved off the comment. "I'd hate to embarrass you guys."

"I think they need bigger help than you can offer," another joked.

"And I thought guys always swore size doesn't matter," she sparred back.

The first one laughed and the two exchanged high fives. One of the others mumbled something about kicking their butts tomorrow. Alex turned back to search for Greg.

Other officers waved from tables, but Greg was nowhere in sight.

"I wondered when you'd show up. Late date last night?"

Alex turned to see Brenda behind her, her long, lean frame easily six inches taller than Alex's.

Alex covered her mouth, remembering. "I was supposed to pick you up this morning! I'm so sorry."

Brenda laughed, her flawless black skin creasing into tiny lines around her eyes as she smiled. "No biggie." She waved her finger at Alex. "I did call your house, though.

No answer. Who's the latest? Because when you cut him loose, I've got someone to set you up with."

Some people seemed to find it weird that Alex was thirty-five and happily unmarried. Alex had relationships—some short, some longer. But none had worked out. In the end, it was always for the best. Some people were good at relationships, some weren't. Alex put herself in the "suck" category. If she met someone special, she'd worry about it. For now, it was one less thing to concern herself with.

Brenda's huge almond-shaped hazel eyes widened as she waited for an answer. "So, is it still Tom?"

Alex smiled. "Not last night."

Since going through Los Medanos Police Academy in Contra Costa County with Brenda, Alex had found herself sharing more with her than with anyone else. But confiding wasn't something she did much of. Her former fiancé and her best friend in L.A., both cops, had often said she kept more secrets from them than they did from each other. Nobody knew her better than those two.

And they knew each other very well, too, she realized when she found them in bed together two months before the wedding. Still together, from what Alex heard from friends in L.A.

Strangely, after a brief pissed-off period, the whole incident had rolled off her like water off wax. She was further from being concerned about marriage than ever.

"I totally overslept," she lied, thinking it wasn't so far from the truth.

Brenda frowned. "Overslept? You all right?"

"I know, the one time I can actually fall sleep, I can't wake up."

"You don't look rested. You sure you slept at home?"

Alex looked up at Brenda, catching the jest in her gaze. "Positive."

Someone yelled Alex's name and she turned to face her partner, Greg Roback. Thankful for the distraction from Brenda's questions, she took a step toward him. Greg was easily six foot five and so skinny he looked like he might break in two like a pencil under pressure. Only slightly meatier, Alex knew why they were often called the bean team.

"Are we late?"

He shook his head. "But we're about to be."

The shift briefing meeting was held in a cramped windowless room in the center of the building. The walls were littered with everything from wanted posters and APBs to furniture sales and baby announcements.

People milled about as Alex sank into a hard plastic seat and the captain started the meeting. He was in a sour mood, so the normal repertoire of jokes was kept to a minimum. He went over a couple of internal memos and let them know they had an armed robber on the loose driving a white Honda Civic.

"Great. That'll be easy to spot," Officer Nancy Yim joked from up front.

There was a round of laughter and the captain cracked a crooked smile.

He read off the car assignments and tossed his clipboard on the table. "That's it. Get out there."

Alex stood and headed for the door. "What's up with the captain?" she asked when they were out of earshot.

Greg shrugged. "Political bullshit, probably."

She followed Greg out the door toward their squad car, stifling a yawn. She almost always drove the first shift, preferring to drive in the morning when she was most awake and alert. Usually that meant right after the first cup of coffee of the day. Today, without her caffeine and a good night's sleep, Alex thought she'd fall asleep before they were out of the station's parking lot.

"You know what Al Capone's business card said?" Greg asked, throwing out the first trivia of the day.

"Used furniture dealer."

"Damn. How'd you know that?"

"Saw *The Godfather* six times," she said.

Greg shook his head. "You're the weirdest chick I know."

"Thanks. What's up with Lori?"

"Over," he answered flatly.

"Why?"

"She threw a fit when I wanted to watch the game." He shrugged then looked over. "I missed breakfast. Want to run by Noah's?"

"I'm dying for a cup of coffee," she agreed.

His seat belt clicked into place as she started the car. "Miss your morning fix?"

She nodded.

"Coffee machine broken?"

"Something like that."

"I heard you missed a pickup, too."

"I overslept, Roback. Drop it, okay?"

"Sure. You overslept. From the woman who never sleeps. I'll buy it."

Alex didn't answer him, but she was thinking he was

right. She'd never even slept through the garbage pickup. How had she slept through driving somewhere in her car?

Greg pulled something off the seat. "Alex, this is gross."

She looked over at one of her chewed-up pens and snatched it from his hand. "Deal with it. At least it doesn't stink up the car like that monstrosity you eat for breakfast."

"It's getting worse. Everywhere I look, I find some slobbery pen. You know, there are easier ways to get out that aggression. Joe in Narc's always looking at you. I bet he'd go for some one-on-one."

"No way." She backed the car out of their spot and pulled through the parking lot.

"This must be the no cops rule. You ever going to explain that to me? What did a cop ever do to you? I mean, besides that jackass fiancé. Is that what this is about?"

"I get enough of cops at work, thank you."

"Speaking of which, when are we going to do that report for the captain?"

More at ease, she gave him a smug look. "Finished it yesterday after you went home."

"You didn't."

She grinned.

"I knew there was a reason I loved having you as a partner."

"We both know there are a thousand reasons. But don't think I'm giving you any credit for this one, Roback."

He grinned. "You wouldn't leave me out."

"I'm actually looking forward to it," she said.

"Yeah, right."

She winked. "What about this one: AH the clocks in *Pulp Fiction* were set on one time."

Greg smiled. "Four-twenty."

"You've heard that one before."

"It's one to one." He looked over at her. "See the game last night?"

"Knicks won?"

"You missed the game?"

She shrugged. "I was busy."

"Busy last night, overslept this morning. You going to tell me about him? He's got to be something if he's getting you to fall asleep. He wear you out, or what?"

"Quit probing," she teased. "What are you—jealous?"

"You're dreaming," he snapped back. After an awkward beat, he said, "Did you know the giant squid has the largest eyes in the world?"

Alex laughed. "Did you know an ostrich's eye is bigger than its brain?"

"They use Murphy's Oil Soap to clean elephants."

She looked over. "What the hell's Murphy's Oil Soap?"

Greg smiled. "How the hell would I know? I'm a bachelor, for Christ's sake."

She laughed again. "Did you know cats have over one hundred vocal sounds and dogs only have about ten?"

"Dogs are still cooler," Greg responded.

"Definitely."

They drove the rest of the way to Noah's in silence. Another police car sat at the curb in front. Alex smiled at the way Noah's bagel shop had replaced Dunkin' Donuts as a cop hangout. At least it was healthier.

For them, stopping at Noah's had become a ritual, always ordering the same thing. For him, it was an onion bagel with garlic cream cheese. The smell in the car got so bad even the people who had to ride in the back complained about it.

"Hey, I'm addicted," he would say with an exaggerated shrug of his shoulders. She had taken to keeping a pack of breath mints for him in the glove compartment.

"The usual?" her partner asked.

Nodding, she leaned back against the interior of the front seat and closed her eyes. She heard him close his door and walk around the car.

"Maybe I should get you a decaf."

Prying her eyes open, she looked at Greg, his long, skinny frame bent down in the door. She smiled and closed her eyes again. "You trying to kill me?"

He laughed. "That obvious, eh?"

Squinting against the sun's morning glare, she opened her eyes. "If I don't have coffee in my stomach in three minutes, I'm going to get violent."

Greg raised his arms in surrender. "Sheesh, I can take a hint."

She blinked hard, taking in the familiar sights of downtown Berkeley. Across the street was Barnes & Noble. It was where she came on her days off—her favorite brewpub, Jupiter, was two blocks in the opposite direction. In the last decade, this area of Berkeley had really cleaned up. That change made it very easy to patrol and she was thrilled that it was part of her beat.

Of course, bagels and coffee on the way to work in the morning didn't hurt, either. And nothing made her happier than a cup or three of black coffee first thing.

Motion caught her eye and she glanced down the side street, her internal alarms sounding. An older female lay on the sidewalk, and she spied a young Caucasian male running up the street.

Alex glanced toward the bagel shop, but Greg was nowhere in sight. The woman started to get up, so Alex revved the engine and sped after the suspect. Sirens screeching, she lunged through traffic. A car leapt in front of her. She swerved to miss it. "Shit!"

The running man made no move to stop.

Almost on his tail, she halted. The bumper of the squad car came within feet of the perp. Moving quickly, he ducked down a narrow alley. Her hand was on the door before the car was completely stopped. The emergency brake on, she threw open the door and bolted after him.

Alex drove her feet against the pavement, determined to catch him even if it meant a marathon around the damn city. She pressed her shoulder radio. "Officer Kincaid here." Her eyes nailed to her suspect, she sucked in a quick breath.

"Go ahead," came the voice of dispatch.

"Female down on Dwight at Shattuck. Suspect proceeding down alley at Shattuck and Channing," she panted. "I'm on foot pursuit. White male juvenile, seventeen or eighteen years, six foot, plus or minus. Dress is jeans, red T-shirt, black baseball cap."

"We read," came the response.

Alex knew backup would be on its way immediately, but there was no time to waste. If she stopped, she was guaranteed to lose him.

The suspect shot a quick glance over his shoulder.

"Stop, police," she yelled.

The kid leapt onto the fence at the end of the alley

and climbed like a monkey scaling a tree. She had no doubt he had done this before. But so had she. On the other side, he jumped to the ground and continued running. He had a good head start.

"You can't outrun me," she muttered. She pulled herself up the fence. The sharp wire cut her hands, but she didn't ease up. She swung her legs over the top and dropped to the ground on the other side. Concrete jolted her ankles as she landed.

The perp disappeared and she forced her legs faster, keeping her breath at an even pace. She hoped the suspect wasn't a damned marathoner.

At the other end of the alley, she bolted onto the street, glancing in both directions. He was gone. "Damn."

Spinning around, she caught a glimpse of the suspect just as he came down on top of her. She hit the ground with a thud, her head knocked sideways against the hard pavement. The perp was above her, holding her arms.

Trapped, her breath came faster. She struggled against his strength, fighting off the wave of nausea that always came with being confined.

His grip tightened.

Focused, she contained her breathing until she felt a slight loosening of his tension. Then, in a lash of anger, she freed one leg and rammed her shin into his groin.

With a groan, he rolled off her onto his back. She was on him before he could recover.

Shaking off the pain in her head, she pulled her cuffs from her belt. His right hand in her grasp, she bent it back and rolled him over with a forceful tug. Her heel digging into his back, she cuffed his right hand. "Didn't your mother teach you any manners?"

"Fuck off."

She wrenched his left arm behind him and cuffed it. "I don't think so."

With a hard yank, she dragged him to his feet and shoved him toward the street.

Just then, Greg pulled around the corner and jumped out of the car. "Saw the car down the street and knew something had happened. You okay?"

She nodded, pushing the perp toward the car and letting Greg handle him. As Greg put the suspect in the back, she touched the area just above her ear and felt a warm spot of blood. She moaned.

In the car, she leaned back as Greg drove toward Shattuck. "Arbor's bringing the woman down to the station to identify him," Greg said. He motioned to the perp. "We just have to drop him off. Arbor should meet us out front. He'll do the paperwork."

"Yeah, yeah, fine, but where's my coffee?"

"I didn't have time to get it. We've got to run back after we drop the thug off."

A moan fell from her lips as she closed her eyes.

In front of the station, Greg stopped and pulled the suspect out of the car, handing him over to Arbor.

Alex waved to Arbor as Greg drove off again.

"Let's get some coffee before you attack your next victim," Greg joked.

"I'm serious. I don't think I could do it again without some caffeine."

He parked in front of Noah's. "This one's on me, Wonder Woman."

She smiled. "It's the least you could do, Robin."

"I don't even get to be Batman?"

"Not the way you drive."

In less than a minute, he was back. When he opened the door to hand her the coffee, he touched her head.

Wincing, she pulled away.

"Jesus Christ, Kincaid. You're bleeding."

"No shit, Sherlock."

"You need a doctor."

"It's barely a scrape. Come on."

As Alex took a long sip of French roast and started to relax, a call came through.

"Adam Nine, code four-fifty-nine at the corner of Henry and Yolo. Please report."

Alex nearly choked at the address. *Yolo Avenue.*

ABOUT THE AUTHOR

Danielle Girard is the *USA Today* bestselling author of *Chasing Darkness*, The Rookie Club series, and the Dr. Schwartzman Series—*Exhume, Excise, Expose*, and *Expire,* featuring San Francisco medical examiner Dr. Annabelle Schwartzman. Danielle's books have won the Barry Award and the RT Reviewers' Choice Award, and two of her titles have been optioned for movies.

A graduate of Cornell University, Danielle received her MFA at Queens University in Charlotte, North Carolina. She, her husband, and their two children split their time between San Francisco and the Northern Rockies. Visit her at www.daniellegirard.com.

Made in the USA
Las Vegas, NV
13 March 2022